THE SIXTH EXTINCTION

AND

THE FIRST THREE WEEKS

(OMNIBUS EDITION BOOKS 1–8)

OUTBREAK

RUIN

INFESTED

THE ARK

and

NOAH'S STORY

RED'S STORY

BETTY AND LENNIE'S STORY

DOCTOR LAZARO'S STORY

GLEN JOHNSON

www.sinuousmindbooks.com

Published by Sinuous Mind Books

www.sinuousmindbooks.com

The Sixth Extinction is also available as an ebook download from Amazon.

Cover image: Shutterstock

Cover design by www.sinuousminddesigns.com

Typeset: Caecilia LT Std/Italic.

Also by Glen Johnson from Sinuous Mind Books
(Available in ebook or paperback from Amazon)

Horror

Lamb Chops and Chainsaws: Nine Disturbing Short Stories About the Darker Side of Human Nature.

Lobsters and Landmines: Another Nine Disturbing Short Stories About the Darker Side of Human Nature.

The Devils Harvest: The End of All Flesh.

Occult/Supernatural

War of the Gods: Part One – The Devils Tarots.

Dark Fantasy

The Gateway: (with Gary Johnson) Close the World Enter the Next. World One of the Seven Worlds.

The Spell of Binding: Part One.

Children/Young Adult

Parkingdom: You Can Be Small and Still Make a Big Difference.

For –

Everyone who has found me, and befriended me on my Facebook page, and who has 'Liked' my publishers page.

Acknowledgments

I would like to thank my older brother, Gary Johnson who went over the raw manuscript with many read-throughs, editorial help, and suggestions, and for his continuous help with my writing career (who has also joined me in a seven book series – check out The Gateway).

Also to Matthew Chilcott, Kate Pike, Anthony Pike, Victoria Tamkin, Sarah Shapter, Rachel Shapter, and Pete and Jo Butchers. All of whom didn't contribute to this book in anyway, but they like to see their names in here nonetheless.

The locations in this book are a fusion of real and imagined, but the events and characters are merely a fabrication of my overactive imagination.

Any mistakes are of my own making.

Furthermore, please be aware that I am not a biomedical expert, or have had any training whatsoever in any of the fields described throughout this book. I have researched and studied the topics to the best of my ability, and have tried to make it sound as genuine as possible, while trying to keep the story within the realms of scientific probability.

Any mistakes are of my own making.

"There are plenty of problems in the world, many of them interconnected. But there is no problem which compares with this central, universal problem of saving the human race from extinction."

John Foster Dulles

"The more we exploit nature, the more our options are reduced, until we have only one: to fight for survival."

Mo Udall

"The cell, over the billions of years of her life, has covered the earth many times with her substance, found ways to control herself and her environment, and insure her survival."

Albert Claude

Please note that I am an English author, so I use English spelling throughout. You will see doubled letters (cancelled), ou's (colour), 're' (centre) ce's (licence), ise's (realise), yse's (paralyse) as well as a few other slight variations from American spelling.

In addition, here are a few slang words used in England to describe people.

Chav: a young lower-class person typified by brash and loutish behaviour and the wearing of (real or imitation) designer clothes.

Yob: a rude, noisy, and aggressive youth.

Lad: the British version of guy.

Geeza: a slang word used to describe a male.

Tea: as well as a cup of tea, it refers to the late evening meal. In England, the midday meal is called dinner and their evening meal tea.

Authors Note

When I first started the four-part Sixth Extinction Series, I never imagined it would become a bestseller on Amazon UK Horror Short Stories (and a regular in the American top twenty).

The four books are based over a twenty-four-hour period.

From the feedback I received on my Facebook page, I realised the readers wanted more.

The original four book series is set three weeks after the virus outbreak started, and it picks up after the five main characters have already survived three weeks of upheaval and chaos.

So I decided to write a short book on each character(s), describing the tribulations they went through over the first three weeks. Some of their actions are already described in the first four books, and some information is repeated. However, the four new books go much deeper into the first three weeks, building on the characters.

So, I decided to put these eight books together in the same sequence that I wrote them.

Glen Johnson

Prologue

The Sixth Extinction is also referred to as the Holocene Extinction – the Holocene epoch is a period of time from present to around 10,000 BCE – where a large number of extinctions span numerous plants and animals, including birds, amphibians, arthropods, and mammals.

Four hundred biologists were interviewed in 1998 by New York's American Museum of Natural History. Seventy percent believe that the world is in the grip of a human-caused mass extinction. They believe that if left unchecked twenty percent of all living things could become extinct by 2028. One famous biologist, E. O Wilson believes that if humans continue to destroy the biosphere, then half of all species on the planet will be extinct within one hundred years.

Almost nine hundred extinctions have been recorded by the International Union for Conservation of Nature and Natural Resources since the 1500s. However, that is just a drop in the ocean, according to the scientific species-area theory; it estimates that one hundred and forty thousand species are becoming extinct every year.

The main reason for the hundreds of thousands of extinctions, which is speeding the sixth extinction along, is due to one mammal – the homosapien. Without intervention, the human race will cause the next mass extinction.

However, it would seem that Mother Nature has a way of making sure that one species does not overpopulate and dominate her planet at the expense of everything else. Viruses and plagues are her way of culling and controlling.

PART ONE: OUTBREAK

1

Third Week of the Infection

Noah Edward Morgan
Newton Abbot, South Devon, England
Flat 17b, Union Street
Friday 5th January 2013
7:08 AM GMT

Noah Edward Morgan's sleep was fitful. He awoke several times covered in sweat.

"The same dream again," he mumbled. Even though he knew it was the same he had no recollection of its content, only of the colour red, for some reason.

Blood maybe?

However, the dream did not leave him with the feeling it was violent, rather; it seemed to put him in a peaceful state. He couldn't explain it, he felt like something was missing. All he needed was one-piece of a puzzle, and the dream would become obvious.

"Pissing TV," he whispered into his hot pillow, diverting his mind from the strange feeling he gets just after waking up from the dream.

The television could be heard in the background, a monotonous monologue of one man's voice. The whole country was watching the TV. He had no idea about what was transpiring in other countries.

What he did know, before the news channels had stopped broadcasting live feeds, was it started three weeks ago near Marolambo, Madagascar, when a logging company had to airlift nine sick workers out for medical treatment, after they became severely ill while logging in an uncharted section of the jungle. Within a week, more cases were registered in Cape Town, South Africa. Mexico City, Mexico. Wien, Austria. Perth, Australia. Moscow, Russia, and Virginia, America. Then after two weeks, there were reported cases in almost every major city on every continent.

After nine days cases appeared in the English cities of London and Manchester. Within eight hours, the British government grounded all flights and docked all boats. Great Britain was declared quarantined, and locked its borders. The government then started to control the news feeds. The outside world was cut off.

After fourteen days, the World Health Organization had reclassed it as a pandemic.

Noah rolled over onto his side. He looked up at his dull white ceiling. His small maisonette was located in Newton Abbot's town center, on Union Street, above a fish and chip shop.

The smell from the chips cooking in the evening made him feel either hungry, or nauseous, depending on his mood. However, the business was closed for the last week, just like every other business in the town and whole country. Everyone locked away at home, hiding, trying to stay safe. Praying.

Noah had no job to go to, because Asda's where he worked closed a week ago. Lorries had stopped transporting goods, and what with all the frenzied buying, there was nothing left to stay open for; there was no food on the shelves. Gangs of yobs, who broke shop windows and set light to what they could not eat or carry, had taken the meager supplies that were left.

There was nothing to get up for. No family to sit with and wait for the end of the world. No girlfriend to comfort and protect. There wasn't even a single plant in the flat that depended on him. He was completely alone. Just the way he liked it.

Noah kicked back the duvet and stretched his tired muscles. His five foot six skinny body twitched as he stretched and yawned. He rubbed his hands down his stubbled face. Even at twenty-one, his stubble was patchy.

I cannot even grow a beard properly, he thought. *Story of my life.*

Noah rolled over to look across his small maisonette to the television, which rested on a wobbly cabinet this side of the small kitchen. The word kitchenette probably described it better, just one short piece of work surface, with a small round sink, and a microwave-oven combo with two rings on top, with a few cupboards above and below.

Normally, the sink would be full of unwashed dishes, but today it was spotless. He could not open the windows to let out the smell of the rancid plates, and congealed coffee cups, and he had to keep busy, to take his mind of the world-changing situation. He didn't realize a metal sink could shine so brightly.

The television channel showed old news, from a week ago, a riot in some city, possibly London or Manchester. People were hungry, desperate, and scared. They could only hide indoors for so long. People need food and water, and even though the power and water were on for now, the utilities would not last forever.

The government kept running short calming reports every thirty minutes, trying to calm the population. News and reports were now controlled. There was no more freedom of information; everything was restricted, for the populations benefit, trying to keep mass hysteria at bay, everything had to be passed by the government before it was aired.

Even though a new virus was ravishing the world, few videos had yet to be leaked. Even *You Tube* was locked down under the new governmental laws. The internet – when it worked – was being regulated.

Great Britain was slowly becoming less great.

The power flickered and went off. It had been doing that more often of late. It normally came back on within the hour, but Noah knew that at some point it would not.

The power flicked straight back on. He could hear his old fridge-freezer gurgle and rattle as it kicked in.

He swung his legs off the bed, while reaching for the remote to switch the television on from standby. He sat in his boxer shorts, just staring at another calming government report.

He had tried to sleep in his clothes, in case he had to get out quick, but it was just so uncomfortable. His clothes were in a rumpled pile next to the bed, where he had taken them off piece-by-piece during his fitful sleep.

A thin man in his fifties, with grey patches at his temples, and decked in a military uniform, stood in front of an important-looking podium – with some government logo on – was droning on about how the situation was under control.

"Do not leave your home. Do not try to leave the cities and towns. Stay put. Keep calm. The government is doing all it can to sort the situation out. Keep your families together and seal all windows and doors. Do not go outside! Do not approach anyone who looks infected!"

Noah grunted a laugh. "Yeah right, as you all sit in your reinforced bunkers deep underground, waiting for us to all die off.

"And how are we supposed to know what the infected look like?" No news channel had released any image or video of an infected person.

"Wankers!"

The Mayans did say the end of the world was in December 2012, on the 21st. It was now January 5th 2013. *Maybe it started then, and the repercussions are hitting us now. A gradual death.*

Noah pulled on some camouflage trousers and a green tee shirt, then his socks and steel toe capped brown hiking boots, from the pile next to his bed; in case today was the day he had to make a run for it.

Always be prepared.

Noah stood slowly and cracked his back like a stack of dominos. *Too many years wasted sat at an uncomfy chair in front of the computer;* he thought.

He navigated around the supplies piled up against the walls, and on every surface. Food he stole from shops, looting along with everyone else. All bank accounts were frozen. Not that it mattered; every shop was shut, with the shop owners hiding along with their families.

The looting had started at the end of the second week, after all the panicked buying had taken everything of use. However, while the gangs of yobs and chavs ran off with plasma TVs and Blue-ray players, x-boxes and play-stations, Noah had concentrated on collecting as much food as he could find. He had even looted the chip shop below, after a gang of wandering adolescents had kicked in the front door.

He had struggled upstairs with the large tote bins that they kept their cut chips in. After washing the bins out, he stored water in them, preparing for when the water was cut off.

For the first week, he had lived almost exclusively on fish, sausages, and chips that he had stolen from the freezers downstairs. He could not open the windows, and even now – two weeks later – the smell of greasy, dirty oil saturated the whole flat.

Resting against the two-seater couch was his bug-out bag. It had everything in it that he needed to survive for thirty-six hours, if he had to bail out of his flat – food, water, clothing, sleeping bag, and cooking utensils, as well as fire starting equipment, until he could find more supplies.

Hopefully not for a while yet.

The doorway to his flat was in a back alley. The shop rented him the dingy flat, and they shared a back door.

When all the looting and fighting had started, Noah climbed down the fire escape and nailed his door shut, and then pulled a large cabinet in front of his entrance. To make sure no one checked behind, he had emptied the contents of the wheelie bins over the cabinet, and then tossed some raw fish in as well, from what was left in their freezers – that had spoilt – so after a few days the stench was gut wrenching. No one had tried to move the cabinet yet, even though a couple of times he had heard people rooting around downstairs in the shop, possibly looking for food. His home was safe for now.

He had even ransacked the chip shop, throwing anything combustible out into the street, so no pyromaniac, with twitchy fingers, would try to set light to the place. There had been a lot of arsonist coming out of the woodwork. Every morning, when he looked out his windows, over the flats opposite, he could see another thin line of dense smoke rising to heaven. Cleansing by fire.

In addition, when he returned upstairs – using the fire escape – he had pulled the metal ladder up, out of reach. His flat was cutoff from the floor below.

Noah changed the water in his water bottle, attached to his bug-out bag. He changed it every morning, just to make sure if today was the day he had to leave, that he had fresh water on him.

He boiled the kettle for a cup of coffee. For breakfast, he had toast and jam. He was trying to use up all the fresh bread he had scavenged before it went too stale. Before he dropped the two slices into the toaster, he picked mold off one edge.

While he listened to a new sanctioned news report about an outbreak in the city of Bristol, Noah moved over to the drawn curtains.

His flat was classed as a maisonette in his contract, because it was on two floors. The top floor was an open planned, twenty-seven foot by thirteen-foot kitchen, front room, and bedroom all in one. The freezing cold bathroom was downstairs next to his front door.

Noah slowly moved the curtain aside with two fingers, while munching on his toast; crumbs cascaded down his green tee shirt. Silver duck-tape plastered the rickety window frame, covering all the gaps.

One of the only details the government had released was the infection was airborne, like the bird and swine flu. However, unlike them, where only a handful had perished, this strain was deadly – if you caught it, there was no chest infection or runny nose, this one carried only death.

Noah stared down into the road two stories below. The street looked like a war zone. Smashed out shop windows, with useless objects either dropped or thrown around. Burnt-out car shells were dotted along the street. No one was about. It was like a ghost town. Across the way, a building had grey smoke rising from its ruins. Dogs barked off in the distance. Paper and garbage danced down the street as the January winds picked up. He could also hear a bass drum, and feel a slight vibration through the soles of his boots. Someone close was enjoying the end of the world, their dance music cranked right up.

Seagulls screeched and cawed as they ripped into the trash, looking for anything edible. His hometown was only twenty minutes drive from the coast, right next to the English Riviera. Seagulls – the rats of the sky.

If it ever came down to it, there would always be seagulls and pigeons to hunt.

Noah noticed a curtain twitching opposite – obviously someone else who opted to sit tight rather than run.

In the first week of the outbreak, most people seemed to fill their cars with everything they loathed to leave behind, and then jam their family into the space that was left, and simply drive away. Noah had no idea where they were heading; possibly, somewhere they thought they would be safe.

How quickly it all changes, how fast it all turns to shit! he mused as he watched a Tesco carrier bag float up past his window, before it whisked away. He pushed the last bite of toast into his mouth. He made sure the curtain was back in place.

Noah had a small handful of work-related friends, but none had tried to get in contact with him. He knew they were simply friendly because they worked together. They never met outside of work for drinks or socializing, he was too much of an introvert for that, he had always preferred his own company. He found it awkward and difficult to try to mingle in with a crowd, unless it was faceless, disembodied voices on Call of Duty MW3, which he used to play online with 'friends' from around the world on his x-box, before the world turned crazy.

Noah crossed to the small kitchenette; on the work surface, charging, was his Samsung Note. The 02 mobile network worked spasmodically.

It probably will not be long before it fails altogether.

He had no messages.

There was no family to check he was all right, because he had none. A drunk driver had mounted the pavement and slammed into his mother while she pushed his pram. On his birth certificate, it stated father unknown. He was eight months old when he became an orphan and entered the system.

Noah had spent the first six years being passed from family to family, before they got bored with his antics and sent him back – he was not blood, no kinship pulled on their heartstrings. Six was the magic number, once you were over six the likelihood of adoption plummeted, due to becoming institutionalized. From the age of seven, he was transferred from one children's home to another. He knew how a dog felt in the pound, with people walking past, deciding whether to give him a chance, and then realizing it was too much responsibility.

Noah walked across the room to the other window; he slowly pulled the curtains apart. He could see up the long main street from his location. There were smashed windows, with bent and twisted metal shutters lying deformed from mod riots. Objects littered the streets. Burnt-out bins scattered like melted bodies. Benches torn from the ground and used as battering rams. An information kiosk smashed and ransacked, then set alight. One part of a building had even collapsed into the Vodafone shop below, from a fire. It was a mirror image of the view from his other window; it was just this one was on a grander scale.

He noticed a group of yobs rummaging through Iceland. Noah knew there was nothing of use in the shop, because he had ransacked through it himself a week ago.

He could hear their muffled shouts as they smashed up shelving and freezer units. A cashier's chair sailed through a broken window, bouncing off a twisted metal shutter, just missing a teenager wearing a bright-red hoody. The adolescent screamed abuse while the others laughed at his expense.

Propped up next to the window was Noah's prized possession, a XS78 CO2 .22 air rifle, with a 3-9x50 mildot telescopic sight. He used umarex AirForce 5.5 mm pointed lead Pellets. The 12-gram double-charge C02 cartridge, along with the telescopic sight, could propel a pointed lead pellet accurately for about three hundred meters. He knew this because he had been practicing on a series of objects that ran off down the street into the distance.

Noah had found the rifle, along with four tins of pointed pellets, and a pack of ten unopened C02 cartridges, when he had looted Millets. While everyone else was interested in stealing electrical goods, he had made a beeline direct to the camping store.

The place was ransacked, but most of the equipment was still there, he just had to sort through it on the floor. Noah had collected a seventy-litre, dark green backpack, along with a three-season sleeping bag and self-inflating mat, and filled the bag with a windup torch and radio, a compass, hiking boots and socks, and cooking equipment, and everything else he would need to survive.

The rifle had been in an office upstairs, in a cupboard, along with two knives that looked illegal, both being over three inches in length, not that it mattered anymore. He took both knives as well.

Noah could see the youths heading down the main street; they all had weapons; a baseball bat, a curtain pole, a cricket bat, and one even had what looked like a samurai sword. There wasn't open fighting in the streets yet, but it wasn't far off. The food and water would only last so long, and when people realized no one was coming to help them, they would take matters into their own hands.

The yobs disappeared up a side street.

Good riddance, Noah thought. He pulled the curtain back into place.

The worse part of the situation was waiting. Things were only going to get worse, and he had to hold up for as long as possible. His supplies of food and water were here. If he moved, he would only be able to carry so much on his back.

Luckily, just before the shit hit the fan, and the world turned upside-down, he had been watching a TV show from America, called Doomsday Preppers. It showcased American families, or individuals, who believed the end of the world was coming, by either war, disease, solar flares, social or economic collapse, or a long list of other global catastrophes. There had been eleven episodes, and while the internet was still working, he had downloaded them all, and had watched them repeatedly. He was by no means an expert, but he certainly had a better idea about surviving in the wild if he needed to.

Noah moved over to his laptop. The internet was intermittent, his service provider, Virgin, was still working, but he did not know how long it would last. And when it was up and running, quite a few sites had been disabled by new government mandates, as if they were trying to keep information away from the general population.

Next to his laptop is a thick spool of lottery scratch cards. He took them from under a heap of metal shutters at Asda's tobacco counter when he was searching for anything edible. He spent some time scratching off a dozen at once, to see if he would have been a millionaire in the old world.

Noah pushed the tickets to one side and tried *You Tube* again. Nothing. A notice on a white page stated the site was down.

What are they trying to hide? Is it worse than they are making out?

On the Google home page, he typed in pandemic. Thousands of hits returned. On the main page, many of the sites were faded out, and as he tried to click on them, they stated the site was down, or it gave the 404-error notice. The only sites available were sites that had nothing to do with the pandemic that was sweeping the globe.

Noah turned back to the television. The same clip was playing again. He flicked through the channels on his Virgin Media TiVo box. He only had the basic package, but even so, only about twenty channels were working, and most were simply playing reruns.

He tried CNN and Fox, both were down, with the same calming broadcast cutting into the static every thirty minutes to play the two-minute government clip.

Noah turned back to the laptop. He entered the video feeds, and a list popped up. Once again, over half was faded, showing broken links. One caught his attention: *The Real Truth,* posted just eight minutes ago. Just as his mouse hovered over the link, the power flicked off.

"Jesus," Noah muttered.

Due to the closed curtains, the room was dark, with a little light glowing around the edges.

Noah sipped his coffee.

The power could flick back on within minutes, or hours. Noah realized when the power cuts had first started how dependent people had become to constant electricity. It is not something you ever think about when it is always there, but as soon as its not, you realize most of the things you own are reliant on it; most things become just a chunk of useless metal and plastic.

Noah shakes his head from side to side, and rubs his hands down his face. He thinks he has the start of cabin fever; he has not left the flat for almost a week.

Maybe it is time to go on another scavenger hunt, see what I can find.

His hand moved to his most prized possession, a British gasmask. He found it in the army surplus store at the end of Newton Abbot's main street. While most of the equipment in the army surplus store was outdated, and just not up to modern equivalents from Millets, the gasmask was a great find. It even came with a small wad of spare filters.

The power flicked back on. He rebooted his laptop. Each time he restarted it – after it had been turned off by a power cut – he expected the blue screen of death, but so far, he had been lucky.

He reentered his last search. The same words appeared *The Real Truth*. He downed the last dregs of his coffee while the computer loaded the site. He clicked on the video link before the government found it and deleted it.

2

Doctor Melanie Ann Lazaro BSc PhD
Exeter University, Exeter, Devon, England
The Biosciences Department
Friday 5th January 2013
7:46 AM GMT

Doctor Melanie Ann Lazaro BSc PhD was tired – beyond tired. She had been working twenty-hour shifts for a week, with no letup in sight. A week ago, two military personnel had turned up at her house and collected her. She was told she had twenty minutes to pack what she would need. She was ordered to live at the university in the student block; she was not allowed to go home and hide along with the rest of the city.

Dr. Lazaro was twenty-three and single and still lived at home with her parents. She didn't have time for boyfriends. It had taken a total of six and a half years at university before she completed her qualifications to become a scientist. Three years for her BSc degree in Biomedical Science, and three and a half years for her PhD.

Her parents were told she was working on something of national importance. They were not allowed to talk to her via any form of telecommunications. All calls in and out of the university was strictly monitored and controlled, because the British army had commandeered the campus. The whole complex was setup like a military compound, and was completely barricaded in. No one was allowed to enter or leave.

Dr. Lazaro was told that eighteen universities across the country were in the same situation; all were working on the pandemic situation under military supervision.

Dr. Lazaro was the youngest of the twenty-nine doctors working in the Biosciences Department. Twenty-five were brought in from outside the university. Where they had come from, she did not know. Everything was departmentalized, on a need to know basis, and they had obviously decided she did not need to know.

She was one of the three original doctors who worked at Exeter Universities Biomedical Sciences Department before the outbreak; she knew the equipment and buildings like the back of her hand. At present, her job, forced on her by the military, was to identify the virus and map its genetic DNA profile.

It was early, but she had been up all night finishing her report. Dr. Lazaro had analyzed hundreds of Petri dish samples of the virus. She had completed her finding's late last night, what she had found out had made sleep impossible. She was ordered to give a debriefing of her findings to the commanding officer.

Two young army personnel, decked in camo uniforms, and carrying Browning pistols at their sides and each holding a SA80 rifle pointed at the floor, escorted Dr. Lazaro to the Brigadier General's office.

Dr. Lazaro gripped the magnolia file, as she was guided through the corridors. This section of the university was turned into the brigade's barracks.

She had never heard of the term brigade before, but she had learned that it was a major military tactical formation of soldiers made up of between three and six battalions. Stationed at Exeter University was only one divided, combined arms brigade, of infantry and armoured, as well as support staff. A typical NATO brigade would comprise of between three and five thousand troops, but because of the situation, and stretched resources, there were only four hundred stationed at the university.

The university's gym was turned into the army's disease control center for the South West of England.

As Dr. Lazaro was escorted into the large gym, she could see four large bio-contained pods set up in one-half of the hall, behind a thick series of containment barriers. This side of the gym, behind the large metal and thick glass compartments were table's chockfull of monitors and analytical equipment, with technicians in white lab coats stood in front of almost every machine. The room was awash in white noise from the machines and conversations, with strange animalistic sounds coming from the pods. However, because of the thick barrier and a labyrinth of apparatus, it was hard to see what was making the noise.

"Dr. Lazaro, how nice to finally meet you. I have heard great things." The voice belonged to a man stood ramrod straight, in military uniform, who was extending his hand. He had stripes and bars on his arm, but that meant nothing to Dr. Lazaro.

"Hello," she said as she shook the outstretched hand. His grip was firm; he was a man used to being in control.

She could not be sure but he looked to be around forty, with short dark military trimmed hair, and a clean-shaven face. His body suggested rigorous training. Under his uniform his arms and chest looked like they were about to burst the seams.

"I am Brigadier General William Hay," he stated as he released her hand.

She noticed his piercing green eyes.

"Please, call me Melanie," she said.

"You're dismissed," the general said without breaking eye contact with the doctor.

Melanie watched as the two soldiers saluted, turned, and left without a word.

"Please follow me, Dr. Laz– I mean, Melanie," the General said, as he turned and headed to a set of double doors.

She followed close behind. As the double doors swung back into place, the sounds from the gym were replaced with the sound of the general's boots clicking on the tiled floor.

"Here we are," he stated. "After you doctor." General Hay held the door open for her.

The office once belonged to professor Keen. It was now the general's private quarters and office. The desk was pushed to one end, up against a full wall bookcase filled with academic books. An army cot with a large green canvas holdall next to it filled the other end.

"Please take a seat." The general dropped down wearily into the plush, studded green leather wing back chair.

Melanie took the ordinary, standard office chair on the other side of the desk.

"Sorry about the cot." The general waved a hand at his bed, as if Melanie hadn't noticed it already. "It's a little cramped, and even I have to make do with any space available."

Melanie did not say anything. She simply placed the magnolia folder on the desk.

There was a knock at the door, which was slightly ajar.

"Yes!" The general simply said. A private entered.

"The latest report from the Husky, general," the private stated as he passed the folder over. The general took the report and placed it in a tray.

"Thank you, that will be all, Private Collins. Please close the door on the way out."

"Yes sir," the private said while saluting, then turning, and leaving. The door clicked shut.

"A Husky?" Melanie asked, curiosity getting the better of her.

"Yes, a Husky. It is an armoured support vehicle. I have one continually driving a grid pattern over the city." He offered no more information.

His eyes are so piercing; she thought.

"I believe, Melanie, that you have some news for me?"

In other words, *focus on the problem at hand*, it felt like he was saying.

"Yes." She reached for the folder, and flipped it open. "There has been a break-through, I have isolated the gene."

The general sat forward. "Please explain."

"I have finally located the locus position of the genotype of the virus on the DNA double helix, and have mapped the individual gene.

"The cell cycle has four stages: the first stage is during prophase." She pointed to a graph on the second page of the report.

"The prophase is the longest stage of mitosis and meiosis, when the virus is first contracted. The chromatin condenses when the mitotic spindle begins to form, and the nucleolus starts to disappear, leaving the nucleus intact. Then the virus goes onto its second stage: metaphase, where the duplicated chromosomes line up along the equatorial plate of the spindle." Her finger moved down the report to a second graph.

"The third stage, which technically isn't third stage, but for argument's sake, I shall refer to it as the third stage, is the telophase, which is the final stage of mitosis and of meiosis I and II, in which the chromosomes reach the spindle poles, and nuclear envelopes form around each set of daughter chromosomes, and the nucleoli reappear. This would form a different set of characteristic traits in the host's body." She pointed to the third graph.

"And lastly, the fourth stage: anaphase, which even though I call it the fourth stage it's technically the third phase of mitosis and of meiosis I and II, in which the sister chromatids separate and move toward the poles of the spindle." This was emphasized by pointing to the fourth graph.

"Then a completely different cellular process begins, where the cell is divided into two. This stage is called cytokinesis. The divided cell then divides again and again at an exponential rate. The subject can literally triple or quadruple in size within an hour." The last graph was pointed out.

"Then the crossing-over is complete; the DNA polymerase phrase has been reached, by adding a new addition of nucleotides to the existing DNA chain, and the subject has a completely new form of DNA.

"The genome it creates has the complete instructions for making an organism; all the genetic material chromosomes. So when it is breathed in by another host, the process can start all over again during the replication period." She flicked the page to the end of the report.

"And I also conclude it is not technically a virus; it doesn't follow typical viral laws of reproduction. The only thing I can find that comes close to its genetic makeup is a particular genera of flora."

The general listened intently to the doctor speak. He leant forward and picked up the folder; he started to flick through the twenty-page report.

"Could you break everything you just said down into a few sentences, in layman's terms, please doctor. Do not take this the wrong way, but I am a soldier; I did not spend five or so years at university. Half of what you just said went completely over my head." He leaned back, fixing her with his green gaze.

Melanie blushed. She hadn't considered the fact that all the scientific terminology would shoot right over his head.

"Sorry, of course." She coughed to clear her throat. "Basically, we are talking about a new, undiscovered species of carnivorous plant that uses a human host to carry, and distribute the fungi spores.

"There are four stages. All I can tell you from my findings are the four stages change the carrier, but I cannot say how. However, you will be able to notice the four stages physically, because the DNA is altered so drastically. I do know that the last stage bloats the carrier to the point of popping, or exploding the host, so the spores can be disbursed over a large area."

The general closed the report and dropped it back onto the table.

"So we are simply talking about a kind of parasitic plant life that latches onto a human host and uses it as food and transport?"

"Basically, yes." Melanie nodded.

"So now you can pinpoint its genetic markers on the DNA strand; you can create an antidote to reverse the effects?"

Melanie sat back.

“No.” She pointed at the report. “It’s not as easy as making a tablet or antidote.”

“I don’t understand. If you can pinpoint the problem, why can’t it be fixed?”

“There is nothing to fix. Once the host is infected, the DNA is adjusted on a molecular level. The host is no longer classed as human, but a new species. It would be like trying to create a drug to turn a butterfly back into a caterpillar – it’s impossible to reverse.”

The general leaned back and rubbed his hands over his face, and gave a long sigh.

“Can something be created to stop people from becoming infected?” He almost had a pleading in his eyes.

“Yes I believe so,” she stated. “It is not a virus that can replicate only inside the living cells of an organism, which can be removed or killed off. The host becomes infected by physically inhaling the spores into the lungs, which then attach and start the process of changing the host’s DNA. Therefore, a drug cannot be produced to reverse the effects, but maybe one can be created to stop the genotype latching onto the particular section of the DNAs double helix. In the pharmaceutical trade it is called a blocker.”

"We feared it couldn't be reversed," he stated. "But a blocker that could stop the spread of the infection would be invaluable."

"We?" Melanie asked.

It was almost as if he knew the outcome of the conversation before it started.

"I have a direct line to the Secretary of State for Health, and the Secretary of State for the Environment. As do all the eighteen groups across the country who is working on the situation." He sat back and rubbed his face.

"This was our worse fears, that it was some kind of virus or infection that could not be reversed. But at least it can be stopped before it is too late, before too many are infected." He looked at her with his piercing eyes.

"How long would it take you to create the blocker?"

"With the right equipment and supporting staff, maybe a few days to a week. However, it would need multiple testing and readjusting." She shrugged her shoulders. "But the university doesn't have half the apparatus I require."

The general was already reaching for the phone. "There is a military laboratory close by that is state of the art, and has forty doctors and scientist on site. I will have your findings sent over, and a helicopter will take you there to help them make the blocker a reality." He picked up the phone and dialed an extension.

"Private Drake, arrange a helicopter dispatch for pickup. It is to have top priority. The cargo will be doctor Lazaro and a file, to be transported to our science department on Dartmoor." He listened for a moment. "Okay. Make the arrangements." He then hung up.

"I will have all your data sent electronically to the Dartmoor lab, as well as the hardcopy you will be taking with you.

"The chopper is en route. It will arrive in forty minutes. I have just enough time to show you one more thing before you depart. Something you need to see to fully understand how much we need your theory to work."

3

Noah
Newton Abbot
His flat, Union Street
7:53 AM GMT

A grainy video filled Noah's laptop screen. A person's breathing could be heard, loud and fast, as if the individual had just been running. The screen had yesterdays date in the corner, and a time stamp of 6:29 PM.

"Can you hear me Ginger? Over." The disembodied voice asked.

"Affirmative. Reading you five, loud and clear Frankie. Over." Another voice stated.

Noah got the impression that two people were in different locations, and they were talking via headsets, while one was watching the other on a live feed.

"I'm just entering the warehouse now. Over." It was impossible to tell if it was a video camera or a mobile phone taking the video. The image was jumping around wildly.

"I can hear something? Over." The voice lowered slightly, and had an edge to it, possibly from fear.

"Roger that. Be careful Ginger. Over."

"Wilco. Copy that Frankie. Over."

Noah found their overuse of radio jargon annoying, as if they had watched too many police or war movies.

The warehouse was dark, and the only illumination was from the recording device's light, creating a tunnel of vision in the otherwise dark confines of the warehouse. Dust motes danced in the strong beam.

The voice was so low now it was difficult to catch the man's words. "Come in. I think I am close. Over."

The other person did not reply, as if he was also engrossed in the video footage.

A sound was picked up by the recording device; it sounded like an animal of some kind.

The man continued to slowly make his way through the building. He turned a corner. Small windowpanes were on his left-hand side, a whole wall of them. The moons grainy light was picked up by grease and grime on some of the panes of glass that were not smashed. To the right was a long dirty concrete wall, with rusty pipe's spider webbing over its surface, in no discernible order.

The sound was getting louder – grunts and snarling.

The camera panned the corner and illuminated the scene in its harsh light, cutting a bright wedge through the dark warehouse.

Noah physically jumped in his seat at the image on the laptop's screen.

The camera operator was frozen in place by fear. The image only slightly shook from the operators shaking hand. His radio jargon now forgotten.

"Oh, fuck!" A voice said quietly. Noah couldn't tell if it was the camera operator, or the other man on the headset speaking.

Some kind of animal was spread out on the ground; it looked like a dog, but it was hard to tell because it had been ripped apart. Blood and intestines littered the concrete. However, that wasn't what was holding the filmmaker's attention, the naked middle-aged male on his hands and knees, with his face buried in the animal's stomach, was. The man then sat back on his haunches, with his hands coming up to his face to pull at the long, wet intestinal track that was hanging from his mouth. The man was filthy, covered in blood and grime.

The person with the camera was whimpering softly, with the camera starting to shake more violently. The man then started to slowly take steps backwards. A wet pattering sound could be heard. It could have been from the man pissing himself from fear.

Realization dawned with the naked feasting male, when he realized a light was being pointed at him. His blood covered face slowly turned to look toward the glaring light. To Noah his face looked distorted, but because of the grainy image, it was difficult to tell why.

Within a split second – looking far too fast for a human – the man sprang forward.

To his credit, the camera operator did not drop the device; rather, he turned and ran. His footsteps slapped the concrete floor, as he was sped on by the animalistic sounds echoing behind him.

Noah sat forward in his seat.

Is this real?

The camera's light flashed off dirty walls and piping as he ran down some narrow hallways. Doors flashed by on either side.

"Run Ginger, run!" The other person was shouting, as if Ginger needed the encouragement.

The hallway led into another large open area. Piles of chairs and tables littered the concrete floor to one side, illuminated by large skylights. The grainy moonlight bounced off the floor and heaped up rubbish. The running man was whimpering and crying loudly, as he ran for his life. He tripped and fell forward, crashing onto the gritty floor. The camera flew from his hand. However, the camera continued to film.

"Ginger! Ginger! Are you okay man? Ginger!" The other voice screamed.

The camera wedged up against something, giving a view of Ginger for the first time. He was a slightly overweight ginger teenager, with a pale face covered in red freckles and streaked tears.

"Ginger get up! Get up buddy!" The voice pleaded.

Ginger was gulping in air, as if the fall had knocked the wind from him.

The teenager got to his unsteady feet, while reaching for the camera. The screen blurred as he spun around, possibly checking the blood-soaked man was not about to attack. The camera showed no screaming attacker. Instead, it showed piles of something all over the floor, possibly one of the object's Ginger had tripped over.

"What the fuck?" The voice faded.

On the floor, dotted around the broken piles of chairs and tables, there were possibly twenty huge bloated objects, which could have once been humans. They were bloated almost beyond recognition. The skin was almost translucent from being stretched so far, with veins mapped out over the thin, vile brown and black stained surface.

Ginger was slowly backing away from them, when he bumped into something behind. He swung around, making anyone watching queasy. He had just bumped into another bloated body. It gave off a groan.

Shit, they are still alive! Noah thought.

"They're still alive!" Frankie stated, echoing Noah's thoughts. "Get out of there Ginger, we have what we need."

However, before he could move something started to happen to the groaning, bloated person in front of him. The body started to vibrate. Then with a loud wet popping sound, the body in front of the camera exploded; blood, organs, and bones flew through the air.

Ginger gave off an ear-piercing scream, sounding savage and raw. The camera flew from his hand again. This time the screen only showed Ginger's feet. The screaming continued, bordering on psychotic. Then Noah understood why, when Ginger tried to sit up; half his face was missing from the mouth up, as well as his left arm. Blood sprayed in an arc to the rhythm of his heartbeat – an arterial red fountain. Blood also dribbled from some type of bone that was protruding from his chest. Noah couldn't tell if it was a compound fracture or a bone from the exploding body. Then the screams turned to coughing. The air around him, reflecting in the camera's light, was awash with floating black spores, like raining ash.

"GINGER!" Frankie screamed.

Even in his state, the survival instinct had kicked in and Ginger was trying to get to his feet, trying to get to safety. Until a blur knocked him back to the ground, as something sprung at him from the side.

The camera tipped forward. No picture was showing, but you could hear Ginger screaming again, as it sounded like some ferocious animal was ripping him apart.

The video stopped, and Noah leant back in his chair. Instinctively, he opened up a program to download the video onto his laptop, in case he wanted to go over it again, or before the government realized it was there and removed it.

The images played over in his mind.

"Jesus, what's happening out there?"

4

Doctor Lazaro
Exeter University
The Gym
8:17 AM GMT

Dr. Lazaro followed General Hay back into the gym.

"Please put these on," the general asked, as they reached the large, thick dividing wall, with the pods on the other side. Hanging from hooks were type II hazmat suits, which would protect against liquid and gaseous chemicals. They both suited up with help from two soldiers.

"Ready?" The general asked via a small radio headset, positioned inside the SCBA – self-contained breathing apparatus.

So far, Melanie had not asked any questions, but just followed the general's instructions.

There was an armed soldier stood to either side of the double, sliding door. They both saluted. One then turned and with a key pass, opened the door. With a hiss, it slid open. They both made their way into a small eight-foot by eight-foot area, which looked as solidly built as a bank vault. The door slid shut behind them. A beeping could be heard, and within seconds, a spray of white mist engulfed the small chamber. Just as quickly, it was sucked through the ceiling by powerful extractor fans. Another beep announced the fumigable transfer hatch was ready to exit.

Through the hatch were four large, twenty-foot-by-twenty-foot pods. Each pod stood thirty-foot apart, and between them were tables full of monitors and equipment. However, what caught Melanie's attention were the autopsy tables inside smaller biocontainment laboratories that were designed to prevent the escape of microorganisms. In these chambers were high containment isolator units that had humans inside, which were being dissected and studied by scientist in type I hazmat suits, with their arms in thick rubber sleeves going into the sealed units.

She turned to say something.

"Please, leave your questions until I have shown you everything." The general said through the small SCBA speaker. He led her to the first pod.

Melanie noticed the large bio-pods had tunnels leading out through holes that had been punched through the gyms wall, leading out into a car park behind.

Scientists, donned in the same hazmat suits as them, moved to one side to allow them both a view of what was inside the first large bio-pod.

Melanie could not believe what she was seeing.

5

Noah
Newton Abbot
His flat, Union Street
8:24 AM GMT

Noah felt nauseous.

Was the video real? Was that what was happening in the outside world? Is that my fate?

His head was spinning. His hand held the mouse arrow hovering over the download bar; it was almost downloaded.

I need some fresh air! He walked over to the curtains and pulled them apart.

The only thing his mind could associate the image that was playing over and over in his mind with, was a stereo typical zombie.

That shit can't be real. Can it?

The room felt claustrophobic. He rested his head against the cold windowpane. Even feeling as bad as he did, he would not risk opening the window. Even more so now.

What was that black mist? It looked like burnt pollen.

Jesus, no wonder the government is blocking and censoring everything. Just imagine the panic that would ensue if everyone knew what was happening outside their locked doors.

That is when he noticed the smoke.

Shit, now what?

Dark thick smoke was wafting over, past his window. He craned his neck, but he couldn't see if it was from next door, or from a building at the end of the street.

Goddammit, just what I need.

Just then the four youths from earlier ran out onto the street from the hairdressers next door. The yob with the red hoody was holding a burning clump of rolled up paper. He tossed it back in through the broken window, as he ran off laughing along with the others.

The smoke passing his window became thicker. He could hear cracking sounds, almost like gunshots, from the furniture and wooden beams in the shop, cracking under the immense heat.

The idiots! Noah could not believe his bad luck. *Of all the places they could have set alight. Jesus!*

He shut his laptop, pulled out the plug, and forced it into the protective sleeve. He rolled up the adapter and put it in the bug-out bags side pocket. The laptop went in as well.

Noah knew this day would eventually come. However, it was still a shock to realize he had to leave almost everything he owned behind. Most of the important stuff was already in the bag. He pocketed his mobile. The charger went in with the laptops plug.

He scanned the room. Everything was too heavy, or too big to lug around, and most of it was useless in the outside world. He grabbed another smaller rucksack, and knelt in front of the fridge, filling the bag, as well as taking as many tins as he could fit in.

Smoke started to seep through the floor-boards over by the adjoining wall.

Shit! All my stuff! He looked around at the television, the Virgin media box, DVD player, the couch, his bed, the fridge. All shitty cheap junk, but it was his shitty cheap junk. He now understood the actions of people on the news, when you saw them running back into burning buildings to grab one more item. When you watched it, it did not make sense. *Why risk your life for inanimate objects?* Looking around his room, he now understood.

Noah rubbed tears from his face. He had never had much, but now even that was being taken away from him, because some chavy teenagers felt like setting light to something.

Bastards!

He put on a dark green jumper then a thin waterproof, dark green coat, and then pulled the gasmask over his face. It smelt like rubber. It was almost overpowering. He remembered the black spores floating through the air in the video. *I will have to learn to like it*, he reasoned.

Smoke was wafting along the ceiling. There was a loud cracking sound, and the floor buckled at the other end of the room. Flames danced along the carpet, spitting as it engulfed the cheap underlay.

Noah strapped a nine and a half inch survival-hunting knife to his right leg. The other knife he had found was in the backpack. He then hefted the large pack onto his back, while arching his shoulders to position it better. He then hitched the smaller pack on his front, putting it on backwards. He grabbed the .22 air rifle from next to the window.

Flames were climbing up the far wall, arching along the ceiling. Smoke poured into the room, filling the top three feet, and slowly getting thicker, and moving down. A couple of posters disappeared in a flash of flames. The light bulb at the end of the room popped. The edge of the other curtains caught alight. Noah was amazed at how fast the curtains went up in flames. What was left of them floated onto the couch, setting it alight.

Time to leave.

Noah pulled up the sash window. The instant he did the flames behind intensified; now they had more oxygen to consume.

Noah jumped onto the fire escape, and twisted to the side, just as a ball of flames licked out the window. He could hear the ceiling collapse.

He had no time to think about all his worldly possessions going up in smoke; he had to get away from the burning building.

With a hard boot, the fire escape's ladder rolled down into the alley with a grinding, grating screech. He hooked the rifle over his shoulders, wedging it against the pack. With difficulty, he swung around and started to climb down. The weight from the two bags was astonishing; he was already sweating.

The weight will soon go when I start eating the food. Then I will be wishing it was still as heavy.

Noah jogged to the end of the alley, away from the burning building. Fire spewed out the back of the hairdressers, igniting the piles of rubbish.

Now what? Where to now? Should I head towards Bakers Park woods and set up camp there, or find an empty house to hold up in, while there is still electricity I can use, and maybe food the homeowner has left behind?

As he rounded the corner onto the main street, the choice was taken out of his hands.

6

Doctor Lazaro
Exeter University
The Gym, Bio-pod Area
8:38 AM GMT

Inside the first pod, a middle-aged woman sat on a metal bench that was secured to the gym's floor. Next to her was an old man in his sixties and a child of about nine. They were all dressed in white medical one-piece garments, with attached boots, just leaving the hands and face free.

Dr. Lazaro knew there had to be a reason why the three civilians were locked away in a containment pod. Her first instincts were to spin around and demand an answer from the general, until the scientific part of her mind kicked in.

What is wrong with their eyes, why are they all blinking so much?

All three were blinking repeatedly, almost nonstop, and they had red rings around their orbits, with what looked like small veins over their puffy eyelids and cheeks.

Realization dawned.

"It is stage one, isn't it?" she asked, while not taking her eyes off them.

The woman sat crying while blinking, as she rocked back and forth. The man sat rigid, and apart from his eyes, only his hands showed any movement as he clicked his nails together. The boy was now walking back and forth like a caged animal, while constantly rubbing his eyes and mumbling something to himself.

"Yes," the general stated. "It is stage one, just like you described." He did not turn his head to talk to Melanie, but kept staring into the pod.

She ignored the sounds coming from the third pod, and concentrated on the first. She would get to see what sounded so animalistic in a moment.

"The first stage lasts about five days to a week. It starts with the newly infected blinking uncontrollably. There is a condition called blepharospasm, which is a condition characterized by the persons rapid, uncontrolled blinking and even involuntary eye closure. One specialist tells me that it is a form of dystonia, wherein the nervous system signals the muscles to contract inappropriately. Towards the end of stage one, the blinking is accompanied by other quick facial changes such as eye rolling and severe grimacing."

The boy sat back down, while still rubbing his eyes. He started to rock back and forth, as if copying the woman. None of the three took any notice of Melanie and the general stood staring in.

Either they are used to being caged like animals, or part of the infection starts by changing the brain's chemistry, or they have no recollection of who they are, or where they are.

"They have bouts of cogitative moments, where they remember who they are and demand to know what is happening. Then, just as suddenly, they withdraw into themselves. It gets worse as the week draws on. By the end of stage one, they are mutes." The general stated, answering her unspoken question.

Melanie's faceplate was steaming up from breathing so hard. Instinctively, she went to wipe the moisture away, before realizing it was on the inside.

"Over here," the general said, while walking the short gap to the second pod, "is where you can see stage two."

Melanie followed closely behind. The type II hazmat suit was awkward to move in, and was making her sweat. Condensation was running down the faceplate.

The pod was identical to the first, but inside none of the five people was moving. It looked like they were in some type of coma. They were in different positions. A man in his early twenties was laid out on his back. A female child of about six was crouched in a corner. An older male and female, possibly in their seventies, was leant up against each other on a bench. Lastly, a female in her late thirties was laid face down on the floor. All were wearing the same one-piece medical garments as pod one.

Melanie had to stare hard to notice that any of them were breathing. There was just a hint of chest movement.

"During the second stage, which lasts two, sometimes three days, the host goes into a catatonic state, similar to a coma patient." The general raised a hand and pointed at the closest person to them – the man on his back.

"Have you noticed the eyes and throat?"

It was the first things she had noticed when she looked in. The eyes were slightly enlarged and swollen, with thick veins mapped across the forehead and cheeks – they look red raw, much worse than stage one. The throat was also different, looking bloated and inflamed, with the same engorged veins.

"The reason for the throat becomes obvious in the third pod."

This was the pod she was not looking forward to looking in. The sounds coming from it made the hair on the nape of her neck stand on end. She had been trying to block out the screaming and guttural noises since she had entered the contained side of the gym.

Something caught her eye. Inside the smaller high containment isolator unit, which was between pod two and three, a teenage girl of about fourteen was being dissected by a doctor in a type I hazmat suit, with his hands going into the until via thick rubber gloves. The girls head was right back, with her neck sliced open vertically, revealing the swollen insides.

Melanie moved over to the smaller chamber to get a better look.

The general noticed where she was heading and followed her.

The man was scraping tissue, to collect a sample from inside the enlarged throat.

"The neck muscles have completely changed, and the throat has widened." She muttered to herself. The general must have thought she was talking to him.

"Doctor Dresner is our otolaryngologists, an ear, and nose and throat specialist. He used to work at the Royal Devon and Exeter hospital in Wonford, obviously in the Otolaryngology department. A nicely located building, but simply too big to protect."

The general pushed a button on the unit, enabling him to talk to the doctor working inside.

"Doctor Dresner. Any new findings?"

The short, tubby doctor inside turned to the two figures stood outside the high containment isolator unit. He looked clumsy and hot in the bulky suit. The arms and legs were far too long for him, and the extra material seemed to weigh his arms down.

"Ah, general. Nothing new I am afraid. I'm just re-examining the masseter jaw muscles and the clavicular and sternal muscles." The doctor turned back to look at the young girl on the metal Gurney table. "Such a shame."

"Thank you doctor. Please continue."

Dr. Dresner simply nodded and pushed his hands back into the thick rubber gloves connected to the unit.

The general looked into Melanie's faceplate for the first time since donning the suit.

"I'm afraid the third pod is by far the worst," the general stated while leading the way.

Melanie followed closely behind. Her breath caught in her throat. She was completely unprepared for what pod three contained.

7

Noah
Newton Abbot
Courtney Street near Market Square
8:54 AM GMT

Noah stood motionless. In front of him, maybe thirty feet away, was the four yobs that set light to the building next to his flat.

They did not notice him; they were too busy heading across the street, while shouting and swearing at each other, and smacking objects around with their assortment of weapons.

Red hoody swung his head around, to avoid a tied-up carrier bag of rubbish that one of his mates had just kicked at him, and in that instant spotted Noah stood motionless with his two bags strapped to him, his gasmask on, and his hands at his sides.

"What 'av we here then, boys?" red hoody said while pointing the samurai sword in Noah's direction. His mates turned to see what he was going on about.

Red hoody looked to be in his late teens, possibly eighteen, or nineteen. He was skinny, and his clothes were dirty and hanging on him as if they were a couple of sizes too big. His white baseball cap was poking out from under his red hoody.

"What you got in the bag's mate?" One of the other yobs asked. He was much thicker set, looking slightly overweight, with a grey tracksuit on. The front of his zip up top was covered in what looked like blood, and it was dripping off the cricket bat he was holding.

"Yeah, what's in the bags asshole?" A small, runty looking boy asked who only looked about twelve, with a Manchester United tee shirt on, and he had a baseball bat resting over his shoulder against a black bomber jacket. The left leg of his grey tracksuit trousers was rolled up, for some reason, showing off his pulled up dirty white sock, and a tatty white trainer.

The last one in the group was much older, looking about thirty, but he did not say a word, simply stared, unblinking. Noah noticed he wasn't swinging the curtain pole like a weapon, but was using it as a walking stick. His baseball cap was pulled down low, so it was hard to see what he was staring at. He was the only one not wearing a tracksuit. Instead, he had on jeans and a long army poncho that went down to his knees.

The group of four yobs had turned towards Noah's direction, and was slowly inching towards him, while fanning out like a wolf pack on the hunt.

“My brother asked you a question, wanker!” Red hoody stated.

“I don’t want any trouble,” Noah said, which sounded muffled due to the gasmask.

“Well you found some mate,” red hoody replied, with a snort, while swinging the sword from side to side. It looked like a cheap replica, which the teenager had obviously tried to sharpen. “And what’s with the gasmask?”

Noah ignored the questions. He shifted to the side and swung the 22. air rifle off his shoulder, while swinging it around. He held it out, pointing it at red hoody’s spotty face.

“Come no closer.”

The four stopped.

“It’s just an air rifle, init,” the small runty looking kid said.

“It will still take your eye out from this distance,” Noah stated, while swinging it to point at the young chav with the baseball bat.

The boy hopped to one side. “Watch where you’re pointing that fucking thing!”

“Or it could do some real damage hitting you in the head. It has special pointed lead pellets. How would you like one rattling around inside your skull?”

“I said stop fucking pointing it at me!” The small lad was ducking behind his brother with the red hoody.

"You can only shoot one pellet at once, and when you reload, we will rush ya, like," the blood covered, tracksuit lad said.

"Yeah, just one bullet. But one of you would get it in the face. Would you be willing to risk it won't be you?" Noah said swinging the rifle to point at the person with the cricket bat. He also hoped using the word bullet would make it sound more threatening.

"Okay. Okay. You made ya point. We have no beef with you mate," red hoody said while starting to back away. "Just messing is all. No harm, no foul." Without taking his eyes of Noah, he said, "Come on guys, let's head over to Abigail's, and see if the dumb bitch is awake yet?"

Noah stood rock still, staring down the barrel, just to the side of the scope, watching them back off and head in the other direction.

The older person stood his ground. He was the only one who hadn't spoken. He gave Noah a long penetrating stare, and simply gave a nod, then turned to follow the others, limping slightly.

Red hoody shouted over his shoulder, "We shall see you around mate. You better sleep with one eye open, and your hand on that rifle."

The four headed across the taxi rank, and into the market precinct. The grey tracksuit lad smashed a window of a burnt-out taxi with the cricket bat.

Noah did not move until the group had disappeared around the corner. He then lowered the rifle. His arms ached from holding it up for so long. He did not swing it back over his shoulder, but kept hold of it. His legs were shaking from all the adrenaline coursing through his body. His nose was also running, but he had no way of wiping it without removing the gasmask.

Noah turned and started heading in the opposite direction, at a steady jog. He knew he would not be able to keep the pace up for long, but he wanted to get some distance between him and the yobs, in case they circled around.

A patter of rain started to hit the gasmasks faceplate.

I need to find somewhere safe and warm. Somewhere out of the rain.

Sweat was running down his face and back. He did not realize how unfit he was. Noah kept up the pace as he headed down Queens Street. In the distance, there were a couple of people running across the road, heading into a building. Noah crossed over the street, to keep distance between him and them.

It was a man and a woman. The man was holding a child of about two in his arms. The woman was pushing a pram full of black bin bags. The twenty something woman fumbled with some keys and got the door open. They scuttled inside, slamming the door behind them.

Noah jogged past wetherspoons. All the windows at the front of the pub were smashed. He could see that all the chairs and tables inside were thrown about as if by a hurricane.

He navigated around some chairs that lay in the street, along with a smashed up fruit machine that someone had dragged outside.

Every now and then, he would get the sense that someone was watching him. As he looked up, he would see a curtain twitch. Everyone was hiding, hoping for rescue, waiting for the cavalry to arrive, to save them from the wandering vandals and thieves.

Queens Street looked like a war zone. Almost every shop window was vandalized. He needed to get away from the shops. There were plenty of empty flats above them, but he did not want to risk having the shop beneath set alight again. He decided his best bet was finding an abandoned house where he could squat for a while.

Noah took the first right, heading up Kings Street, past a Cantonese restaurant. On the left-hand side was a long row of houses. If one caught alight they would all burn. On the right were large business buildings. A three-story mortgage company, a paint center, and a dance studio. All were unaffected by vandalism.

He slowed his pace. He was too exhausted to jog any further. His breathing was deafening inside the mask. The bags were digging into his shoulders, killing his back. He had only travelled the length of a couple of streets.

Maybe I will look for a shopping trolley or cart of some kind, he thought.

The rain was getting heavier. Water was running down the back of his neck. He needed to get out of the rain until the clouds passed, and he desperately needed a drink of water.

Between the Mortgage Company and paint center was a car park, with small outbuildings nestled at the back. Noah headed towards them, hoping to find a door or window he could get through.

I hope that there will be a toilet and the power would still be on.

He picked a small one-story building that had a steep pitched roof that was joined to the mortgage company's larger building.

Noah walked around the back down a small lane. It was the only way in or out. He was a bit worried that if he stayed here he would be cornered. However, he needed to rest, to take the bags off, even if it was only for an hour or so.

There were a few small windows, which he would not be able to fit through. The door looked flimsy, and with one good shove; the lock gave way, and the door swung open. The room was the company's break room. The area was almost twice the size of his burnt-out flat. He shut the door, pulled a chair across, and wedged it under the handle.

There were a few doors on one wall. He hoped one was a toilet. At one end of the room was a splattering of comfortable looking chairs, and a long couch, with a few tables, along with a vending food and drink's machine. A plasma TV was attached to a wall, next to the seating. At the other end of the room were a pool table, an Altered Beast video game, and an Indiana Jones pinball machine. In the middle, against the wall were a couple units with a sink, and a microwave.

Noah gave a long sigh as he took the pack off his back, and the smaller one of his chest. He was just stretching the knots out of his back when a voice said, "One wrong move, and I will put an arrow through the back of your head!"

8

Doctor Lazaro
Exeter University
The Gym, Bio-pod Area
9:07 AM GMT

Pod three was a slightly different shape to the other two pods; this one was thinner and longer, and sectioned into two units. The occupants were a lot different as well.

Melanie now knew what was making the animalistic sounds she had been hearing since entering the gym.

It was a little difficult to see who was in the first unit because the thick glass was covered in blood; smears and splashes of the crimson liquid saturated the sides. She could even see a tooth stuck to the glass in a blob of congealed blood. However, Melanie could just make out a figure crouched in one corner. It looked male, but that is all she could determine through the red smears.

"The male is forty-three," the general stated. "It's a little hard to tell, because of the mess." He coughed to clear his throat, and then his voice became business like.

"This is stage three. After the catatonic stage two, the host gains complete control once again, but the subject becomes animalistic in actions and appearance." Just as the general stated that, the naked figure lunged at the glass. With a loud thud, the body fell to the floor.

"Only one urge controls the subject at this stage – to eat."

The figure stood up and leant against the glass. His eyes were completely bloodshot, and swollen to twice their normal size, fracturing the orbits and pushing the cheekbones out. Thick veins that spread out from the eyes held the splintered bones and fractured skull together. His mouth had also swollen in size, rupturing the teeth, making them stick out in a jagged line. One of his arms hung tattered and ripped open, leaving flesh hanging from a splintered bone.

"The subject returns to a primordial state, concerned only with eating. Nothing else matters. To prove this point the subject has received no food, and because of this he has started to chew off his own arm."

Bile rose in the doctor's throat. She instinctively moved her hand to her mouth, but hit the faceplate of the mask instead.

"He looks almost like... like a... a..." She couldn't say the word. It just didn't sound real.

"Like a zombie?" he questioned. "Trust me that word has been bounced around quite a bit." He stared at the mutated human as he smashed himself against the glass, trying to reach the warm meat beyond.

"We've had researchers looking into everything associated with the word zombie. It first appeared in Haiti. The word zonbi referred to a person without consciousness and self-awareness, yet they were able to respond to surrounding stimuli.

"Sound familiar? However, the Haitian Vodou Houngans, or voodoo priests, use the puffer fish kidney, not plants." He looked at the malformed man, who was licking the blood off the glass.

"There are many strange and weird happening of ancient past, but none resemble anything like this. And if it has happened before, the people of the time did not know how to describe it in a way we would recognise." He shook his head slowly.

"In the second section of the pod, the subjects have been given food," the general stated as he shuffled along, while changing the topic. Then as an afterthought added, "The subject at stage three rips the clothes from their body. We are not sure why."

The second section had no blood covering its walls. Instead, it contained five people; an old woman, who looked about seventy, a skinny blonde woman in her late twenties, an obese middle-aged, balding man, and a set of male twins who looked about eight. All were knelt around the carcass of a cow. All their undivided attention was devoted to ripping and chewing the meat. Guttural groans of pleasure echoed around inside the unit.

"A subject will eat continually until the stomach has stretched to its absolute limit, then it will rupture. Even then, the subject will continue to eat until collapsing. Moreover, the host will eat practically anything, clothing, glass, dead animals, live animals, even people if they can get their hands on them. If it fits in their mouth, they will swallow it. They continually eat until the stomach ruptures then they return to the catatonic stage.

"In fact," he stated, "once the cow has been finished, if they still haven't hit stage four, and we supply them with no more food, they will turn on each other."

"That's when the genes start to multiply." Melanie asked. Her hands were crossed over her chest. She felt like she was intruding into something she should not be seeing. The people in there have families, people who love them, and here they were, having returned to a primordial state where they were not consciously in control of their actions, the parasitic gene was controlling them like puppets; using them as a host, to feed then disburse its seeds.

"The worst part is," the general stated, "the timeline from when the first documented case appeared in England, at The Royal London Hospital, and now, means over the next week there will be a huge incursion of stage three eaters all over England." He let the information sink in.

"Jesus," Melanie muttered. Then thought to ask, "How fast are they?"

"It depends on the person's age and health, before they were infected. If it is a young healthy person, then they can be fast and extremely dangerous. The older and fatter subjects are slowed down by either their size or ailing bodies.

"Also at stage three, a bite will also infect." The general pointed to the ceiling of the pod. "Look above them."

Melanie hadn't noticed it until it was pointed out, but floating above them was a hazy cloud. "Spores?"

"Yes," he stated. "A contaminated stage three subject discharges a small amount from their mouth, but not as much as they do at stage four." The general pointed to pod four.

"Finally we have stage four," the general stated while moving to the last pod.

Melanie's eyes held on to the two children who were feeding like rabid dogs, for a second longer, before she turned to follow the general.

Behind she could still hear the bloodied man throwing himself against the glass wall.

The last pod was the same as the first two. On the floor were three subjects. All were bloated almost beyond recognition. Two adult-sized bodies and one, which could have been a child, it was now hard to tell.

Her scientific mind took over as she concentrated on the closest body. It could have been a male, but due to the stretching skin and discoloration, and pus-like growths, it was impossible to tell. Pools of brownish liquid gathered around the bodies, possibly from emptying bowels.

"Once the body has filled with micro spores, and the skin has stretched to maximum breaking point; the body explodes and disperses the airborne seeds. This can take only a few hours, or a couple of days, depending on the host." The general pointed into the pod. "This is the first stage four subjects we have been able to study in a controlled environment."

"And anyone who breathes in those spores starts the cycle again." Melanie turned to look at the general. "We cannot stop this from spreading. People need to know the truth, so they can take the proper precautions."

"That goes way above my pay grade, I'm afraid." The general was shaking his head slowly. "But I do agree with you, people need to be warned."

Something caught the doctor's attention. She turned to look back into the pod. The body closest to them was vibrating. However, before she had a chance to draw the generals attention to it the body exploded, pouring guts and blood everywhere, completely covering the inside of the pod.

Melanie had fallen backwards, instinctively when the body popped. She lay on her back in the hazmat suit, trying to rock from side to side to get back up again. She could not believe how powerful the spore release was.

Suddenly, there was another explosion inside the pod. The airtight pod rocked on its foundations by the first detonation; the second expanded the sealed container to its limits. Cracks appeared in the glass. From her location on the floor, looking up, she could see black spores pouring out the minuscule cracks.

"General!" Melanie shouted, over the sound of all the lab technicians and other doctors running about.

The general turned to see what Dr. Lazaro was pointing at, when suddenly the third body exploded. The fine cracks now gave way completely, when the whole pod shattered, with glass flying in all directions. The general, who was still standing, was blown backwards, shredded by the glass fragments.

Melanie was rolled over by the percussion blast, and her left leg felt like it was on fire.

The whole gym was in utter chaos. An alarm bell pierced the air. Red lights flashed on the walls. Booted feet pounded the gym floor. Machine-gun fire reverberated around her.

What the hell is happening?

Rolling over to her left-hand side, she could see the third pod was also smashed open, by either the blast or the one-armed eating machine that had been slamming against the glass.

Was it an organized attack? Was there some kind of hive mind at work?

Bullets peppered the one-armed mans chest, but he kept on going, ramming into a soldier full on, his teeth ripping into the soldiers hazmat faceplate before they even hit the ground.

Melanie rolled over to her right, while trying to stand. The general was unmoving in a pool of his own blood. He did not look like he was breathing.

Gunfire echoed all around.

A new sound drew Melanie's attention. She turned her head just as the old woman – who had been ripping apart the cow – was crawling out of what was left of her pod. The woman's stomach was bloated to capacity, with bloody stretch marks around her belly button. Her demented red eyes were locked onto Melanie, as she used her hands to drag herself towards her next meal.

9

Noah
Newton Abbot, King Street
The Mortgage Company's Breakroom
9:31 AM GMT

Noah's first instinct was to put his hands up, just like in the movies. He was facing the door, while he removed the packs, so his back was facing the threat.

Jesus, now what?

"Slowly turn around. One false move and you become a pincushion." The voice was that of a female.

Noah turned slowly. He noticed the woman stood behind the couch.

She must have been hidden down behind it when I broke the door in.

She looked about his age, maybe a little younger, possibly nineteen – twenty at most. It looked like she had just woke up; her long red hair was all dishevelled and clumped up, and her black tee shirt was rumpled and creased. However, what captivated his attention was the technical looking compound bow, with the notched arrow aimed at his chest.

"This arrow can punch straight through you and pin your dead body to the door!

"I won awards at archery class," she stated.

"I didn't realize anyone was here. I was just looking for somewhere to crash. Some chav's just burnt my flat to the ground." He let that hang in the air. The arrow did not waver; it was still pointed at his heart.

"I was here first," she stated, almost childlike.

"I will leave. Just let me put my bags back on, and I will go."

"What's it like out there?" The arrow dipped a little.

Noah was a little taken back, having the conversation change from threats to polite chitchat in a heartbeat.

"Bad. The streets are empty. But almost everything that can be smashed up is. People seemed to be too terrified for vandalizing anymore, now there is nothing left to take. They seemed to be all hiding behind locked doors and drawn curtains. But there are a few gangs wandering around with weapons, threatening people. I had a run-in with four yobs ten minutes ago."

"How did you get away?" The arrow was now pointing at his feet.

"My rifle." His hands were still above his head, so he used a finger to point at the floor. His rifle had fallen over. "It's just a .22 air rifle, but it scared them enough to leave me alone."

"Are you a good shot?" One of her eyebrows rose a little. He noticed she had delicate features on her porcelain white, makeup-free face that had a splattering of freckles across her cheeks and nose. She was thin like a gymnast, and her arms didn't look strong enough to keep the string pulled for too long.

"To be honest, not as good as I would like. I've not had it long." He did not know why he was telling her that.

"Um, could I put my hands down; my arms are hurting, and it's been a weird day so far, and to be honest I don't know how much more shit I can take."

"Okay. First, take the gasmask off. I want to see your eyes – you can tell a lot about a person by their eyes." She released some of the pressure on the compound bow, but still held the arrow in place.

Noah pulled the mask off, and dropped it onto his pack. He used a hand to wipe the sweat off his brow, and then swiped it across his running nose.

She wolf whistled. "Oh, a pretty-boy huh?"

Noah didn't know what to say. He was sure if he commented on her looks when he first came in, she would have put an arrow through him.

"I'm Noah Morgan," he said, giving her his friendliest smile.

"Nicola Breslan. But I prefer the nickname Red." She lowered the bow all the way.

He could understand the nickname; her hair was stunning. It was not a ginger red, but a shining, flowing bright-red mane that cascaded down her back, and over her left shoulder.

"You woke me up when you kicked the door in," she stated.

"Sorry. Like I said, I didn't realize anyone was here."

"I will do you a deal. If you don't try and rape me, I will not cut your throat while you sleep." She returned his smile.

"Um, okay, it sounds like a deal."

"You take that end. I'm set up behind the couch." She stared at him for a moment. "With two people we can take shifts sleeping."

"Okay." Noah was too stressed from everything that had happened so far today, to think too hard about the situation. He gave her one last glance before dragging his large bag over to the pool table. Then he went and got the rest. When he looked back over, Red sat cross-legged on the couch, picking the dirt from under her nails with a seven-inch hunting knife. The compound bow rested against the couch next to her.

"I remember you from school," she announced. "You were two years above me in Knowles Hill."

Noah was placing his self-inflating mat on the ground. He did not answer her rhetorical statement; instead, he started unpacking his sleeping bag.

"I remember you weren't a dick like the other older boys. You never called me Ginger or anything cruel."

He looked over. She had put the knife away and was holding a packet of quaver crisp. She noticed he was looking at her food.

"I smashed the locks on the vending machines. You can just open the front and get the stuff out," she announced. However, before he could answer she was talking again. "And you worked in Asda, didn't you?" She questioned as she opened the crisp packet. "I have a good memory for faces."

"Yes, I did," Noah stated while placing his rifle on the pool table, facing the door.

"I used to work in Specsavers." She shrugged her shoulders. "That seems like a lifetime ago now." She munched on a crisp.

It was the most conversation he had had in almost three weeks. Red seemed like she was lonely and needed to talk to someone – anyone.

"The closest door to you leads back into the building. It is empty. The other door is a bathroom. There's a shower room on the second floor, next to some offices, for some reason."

Noah removed some tins of food from his bag. “When was the last time you ate some proper food, not just the junk food from the vending machines?”

Red cocked her head to one side, while thinking. “I’ve been here a week, and I didn’t have time to grab any food when I ran away from home. So a week,” she stated while pushing the last crisp into her mouth. She did not elaborate as to why she had to run away.

Maybe that is why she is so hyper, from all the sugar and Es she has been eating?

Noah removed his laptop.

“There’s no wi-fi here. Well, my phone doesn’t pick any up, when it’s working.” She scratched her bare foot.

Noah took off his coat and hung it over the pinball machine. It started to drip rainwater onto the wooden floor.

Noah untied his shoes and rested them next to his pack. He knew he should keep them on, in case he had to make a quick exit, but he was just so tired, and the boots were hurting his feet. The adrenaline from the last two hours had drained away, leaving him feeling as if he had just run a marathon.

“The TV works, but it only picks up the four channels, and they all have that boring army guy, rattling off that dull, ‘everything will be fine’ speech.”

Noah was leant on the pool table, looking over at her. Red seemed not to be able to relax; she was always moving, always doing something. The bow was on her lap, and she was rubbing it with a cloth.

"I used to do archery up at Forches Cross. Was top in my group." She turned the bow over. "Mum used to come and watch sometimes, when she was feeling well enough – on the good days." Red's head lowered. Her hair spilled down around her, hiding her face. Then just as suddenly, her hair flipped back over her shoulders with a quick flick of the head.

"She wouldn't have wanted to see me sad." She rubbed a hand across her face, to catch a few stray tears.

"What happened to your mother?" Noah asked, seeing that she was becoming upset.

"I can't talk about it yet. It's still too raw." She gave a loud sniff.

"No problem. Sorry to pry." Noah twisted his neck from side to side. The heavy bags did a number on his back.

"Do you mind if I grab a drink from the vending machine?"

"Go for it. I have drunk all the tango orange and sprite, I'm afraid." Her smile was back.

He walked over to the two large, hulking machines. With a small tug, the front of the drink's machine swung open. All the cans were in long rows. He grabbed a Dr. Pepper. He was surprised to notice it was cold.

"Still cold?"

"Yeah. Luckily, after I found the main junction box, all the power came back on. After a few attempts, I found the switch for the breakroom. If you want a shower, I will show you the switch that turns the whole floor back on. But don't worry, apart from the shower, I've made sure every light and computer and printer have been turned off or unplugged."

Noah was surprised that she had gone to so much trouble to say safe. She was unlike any female he had ever met.

"After I broke open the doors on the machines, I disabled the alarm and lights. So the chiller still works, but without the glaring light that can be spotted outside." She shrugged her shoulders.

"Without sounding patronizing, I'm impressed."

"My step dad was an electrician." She said no more.

Noah noted the past tense reference. He stood in front of the machine, holding the unopened can. He wanted to sit down, but the comfortable looking chairs were next to Red. He didn't want to presume he could intrude into her end of the room without being invited.

"Take a load off," she stated, pointing to the chair closest to him.

Noah dropped down with a sigh. He popped the lid and took a long drink, downing half the can. He rattled off a loud belch.

"Sorry!"

"Don't worry about it, does the same to me."

They sat in silence for a few minutes. Both seemingly unsure what else to say and they were both conscious of just how close they were sitting.

"So where are you headed?" she asked, breaking the silence.

"Headed?"

"I take it this wasn't your destination," she said, her hands waving around the room.

"I didn't really give it much thought, to be honest. I had to leave my flat on Union Street because some idiots set light to a building next door. And after I managed to get out, just in the nick of time, the pricks were outside, and I ran right into them. Then when I got away from them, I headed to the first place that looked safe, where they couldn't double back to find me." It was Noah's turn to shrug his shoulders.

"Do you think we could hold out here until the cavalry arrives?" She asked, obviously referring to the army, believing they would swoop in to save the day.

He realized she had said ‘we’. He ignored that for the minute.

“I don’t think the cavalry are ever coming,” Noah said. “There’s a video I think you need to see!”

10

Doctor Lazaro
Exeter University
The Gym, Bio-pod Area
9:34 AM GMT

All Melanie could concentrate on was the figure crawling towards her.

The naked old woman's bloodshot eyes were fixated on her. Hunger radiated off the deformed woman, who had resorted to quadrupedal movement to drag her deformed stomach across the gym's floor.

The alarm raged, bouncing off the walls. Gunshots echoed around the pods as the army tried to take down the other occupants of the third pod.

A scientist in a blood covered hazmat suit ran past. The two twins followed closely behind.

A firm hand grabbed the doctor on the arm.

"Are you okay? We need to get out of here," the voice shouted, as Melanie was manhandled to her feet. The voice was muffled by the hazmat's mask.

She could now see who was dragging her backwards. A soldier had her with one hand, while the other held the SA80 rifle, which was spraying bullets into the pod.

The old woman was hit repeatedly in the face, obliterating the back of her head.

"The general," Melanie shouted.

"He's gone ma'am. There's nothing we can do for him now."

The soldier dragged her backwards as she limped along on her aching leg. He was heading towards the hatch she had entered through.

The hatch was already occupied with ten soldiers in military hazmat suits. As soon as the mist was sucked away, the door opened and the men poured out, firing as they came.

"Has the doctor's suit been compromised?" one soldier asked.

"No sir," he stated. "I saw her go down. She was hit pretty badly in the leg by a container, but the suit is intact."

"Get her in the hatch. But not you soldier; your suit has been compromised. Once the area has been cleared, you will be evaluated."

"Yes sir."

Melanie was pulled into the hatch, as another doctor ran to join her. The soldier slammed a hand on the button to start the cycling sequence.

"Thank you," Melanie muttered in her mask, as the white mist washed down over her.

The gunfire was muffled inside the thick hatch, and the alarm seemed dulled.

Just as suddenly, the sounds intensified when the other side of the hatch opened. Strong hands lifted Melanie onto a waiting stretcher. The SCBA breathing apparatus was pulled off, and an oxygen mask shoved on.

She found herself inside a polythene tunnel, being checked over by nurses in hazmat suits.

"No rips, she's clean," a voice announced, as they stripped the hazmat suit off her and tossed it into a container with a yellow biohazard sticker on it.

"Get her out of here!"

With nauseating speed, the stretcher was hustled out into the vast openness of the gym, and pushed over to one side, near other uninfected casualties.

Everything happened in mere minutes. Melanie's head was ringing from the alarm and flashing lights, and the image of the general lying dead next to her.

The gunfire died away. The alarm switched off, but the red lights still kept flashing.

Melanie was staring at the high ceiling, trying to get her thoughts and emotions in order. Her leg was also throbbing with a dull ache.

I wonder how long I can lie here before someone makes me move?

She had not slept properly in days, and she could quite easily shut her eyes and sleep for the rest of the day; blocking everything out, and pretending she was at her parent's house, in bed, with her cat Pepper nestled up beside her.

My parents! Shit! They are out there, with those things everywhere. Melanie went to rise, to demand her parents be brought into the university, so they could be protected.

The media needs to know. The public needs to know what they will be facing.

Melanie went to sit up, to swing her legs down, and to find whoever was in command now the general was dead. She felt something touch her right hand. It was the folder she had shown to the general. It reminded her that there was a helicopter on its way to collect her, and take her to the base on Dartmoor. However, as she went to move a nurse jabbed an injection into her leg.

"That's for the pain, and it may make you a little drowsy."

Melanie was about to insist that she did not need any medicine, she just needed to see who was in command. As far as she knew only the general knew about her findings, and he was now dead. However, due to the painkiller and her exhaustion, she started to slip into unconsciousness.

However, just before her head dipped to the side, the alarm started to pulsate again, with someone shouting over the university's speaker system, "We are under attack! They have breached the barriers!"

11

Noah and Red
Newton Abbot, King Street
The Mortgage Company's Breakroom
10:06 AM GMT

Red had the laptop on her lap. The video Noah had downloaded onto the hard drive had just finished. Red sat with her hands clenched over her mouth; as if she was afraid she would scream and notify everyone in the area where they were.

"I know, right," Noah said.

Red's eyes snapped away from the screen to look at Noah. Tears streaked her freckle-covered cheeks. She removed her hand and sucked in a big sob.

"Fuck!" was all she muttered. "That was real, right?" she questioned.

"I think so. The fear in his eyes looked real."

"Shit!" she said, as she wiped the tears away with the back of her hand, and gave an unladylike sniff. She slowly shut the laptop, hiding the last frame of the camera, almost as if in respect to the death she had just witnessed. She placed it next to her on the couch, then sprang up, and started pacing back and forth.

"Jesus!" She muttered while running her hands through her long red hair.

"That's why I believe no one is coming. They are busy trying to sort out, or fight, or doing whatever it is governments do, in situations like this." He slowly shook his head. "They are most probably hiding," he added quietly. "I know if I had the resources I would."

"But things like that don't happen in the real world. How, how is that possible?" Red looked at Noah with a tear-streaked face, her tangled hair cascading around her shoulders – shoulders that were hunched as if a great weight was resting on them.

Noah felt terrible that he had shown her the clip, but she needed to know what the world was turning into, the dangers that were now stalking the streets.

"I believe it all started in Madagascar, with those nine or so loggers. When they were airlifted out of the jungle, they brought something with them. Something that is now spreading from human to human." It was Noah's turn to stand up. He picked up the laptop and took it over to the pool table. He turned back to Red.

"I'm not sure if it's airborne or you need physical contact. That is why I am using the gasmask." He had walked back over to the backpack, and picked up the mask.

"I had grabbed it by chance in the army-navy store; I didn't realize how valuable it would become."

"But I don't have one!" Red almost screamed. "What's going to happen to me?" She had dropped back onto the couch. The anger had instantly given way to depression. "I don't want to end up like that," she whispered while pointing at the laptop.

Noah stood for a moment, thinking.

"The paint center," he stated. "It will have filtration masks for spray painting. That would be as good, if not better than my old army castoff. And there would be goggles in their too, to protect the eyes." As he said it, he was pulling the mask back over his head.

"What are you doing?" Red stood back up.

"Going to get you some protection," he stated. "It's only across the parking lot. I will only be twenty minutes or so." Noah went to retrieve his knife from down next to his sleeping bag, and slid it into the sheaf on his right thigh. Then he pulled his boots back on.

Jesus, what am I doing? I have only known her for half an hour and already I am willing to risk going back outside for her.

He looked across. She stood with her arms crossed, still physically upset from the video. A tear ran down her cheek. She was slightly shaking too.

There is something about her. I remember her from somewhere, and I don't think it was from school. And is it a coincidence that the only thing I remember from my strange reoccurring dreams is the sense of the colour red?

"You would do that for me?" She wiped another tear away. "Why?"

He couldn't think of a good answer.

Her red hair. The flames consuming my flat.

"It's the right thing to do." He could think of nothing else to say. Anything else would sound cheesy and dramatic. The sort of line a guy would say while trying to get in a girls pants.

"You always were nice at school," she stated while looking at her feet.

He felt bad that he had no recollection of her from school. *With a head of hair like that, you think she would have stood out. But it was over five years ago,* he reasoned.

Noah picked up the rifle, double-checked a pellet was pumped and ready, and then swung it over his shoulder.

"Push the chair back under the instant I'm gone. Don't answer unless you hear my voice," he said, which sounded muffled because of the gasmask. He felt something else needed saying, but he did not know what. The whole situation was confusing.

"Be safe," Red said.

Noah simply nodded, removed the chair and slipped out the door, and closed it without a click. His shadow passed the small windows.

Red stood alone, with her arms wrapped tight around herself. Half an hour ago she had been by herself, and had no problem with it – preferred it even. Everyone close to her either left her, or hurt her. She had decided to strike out alone and survive on her own.

The pandemic had been the perfect opportunity to get away from the situation she was in, the ideal distraction for her to run. It was either leave, or kill. She had once had a younger sister. She had not done the right thing back then, and her sister paid the ultimate price for it. More tears flowed, but this time they were not caused by the video clip but from old memories.

Red picked up the compound bow and notched an arrow. She stood facing the door. She had never felt so alone in her life. She decided she no longer liked the feeling.

12

Doctor Lazaro
Military Merlin Transport Helicopter
Over the A380, Near Haldon Forest, Devon
10:27 AM GMT

The first sensation Melanie had was of vibrations running through her body. Her foggy mind associated it with being stuffed inside a tumble dryer. There was also muffled chatter, sounding like it was coming from a radio. However, the dominant sound was a kind of dull chop-chopping whirr.

She felt like she was propped up against something. Her mind was slow and muddled.

The drugs the nurse gave me. Her mind was slowly sorting itself out.

Flashes of gunfire and being wheeled along, sprung to mind. Blurred faces in military uniforms and naked, frenzied bodies running and attacking. It was all a haze of screaming and blood and bullets.

Melanie slowly opened her eyes. She was strapped to a seat with a red webbing harness. The cabin had two long continuous rows of seating against each sidewall. Grey squared padding covered the walls, with a metal-decked floor that was chock-full of gear in dark green containers interlocked together, and strapped down by green webbing. Around her were about ten or so soldiers in combat gear, covered in blood and gore, with another two on stretchers connected to intravenous drips. To the right was a hydraulic door that opened up the complete end. To the left was a hatch to the cockpit. Melanie's foggy mind realized she was on a helicopter.

"She's awake, Captain," a spotty soldier stated while leaning over her. He stunk of spent gunpowder and the acidic tang of blood.

Another, older soldier leant across from the right. "Thought we were going to lose you there for a minute. You were out cold when we found you."

With the chopping of the rotors and the vibrating of the cabin, his words sounded metallic and distant. He had to shout to be heard.

"We have orders to pick you up and drop you off at the research base on Dartmoor. We got there just in the nick of time; a large mod of naked..." He tried to think of a correct description, as his face screwed up from the recollection.

"Zombies!" Melanie mumbled.

"It's the only word that can describe them." He could not have heard her softly muttered word, but must have read her lips. He wiped at a cut on his forehead. "They were attacking the compound. There were maybe a hundred of them. It looked like an organized attack, if that is possible." He closed his eyes and looked like he gave a sigh, which was lost to the vibrating hum and chopping of the blades.

"I hope the information you have is worth it? We lost twenty good men back there, and the base has been overrun."

Melanie noticed the folder in a large industrial plastic, see-through Ziploc bag on her lap.

"It has the cure," she muttered, but her voice was lost to the background noise, and this time, he did not read her lips.

"First we have to drop some supplies off at the Britannia Royal Naval Collage in Dartmouth, and then we will take you to the research laboratory inside Dartmoor Prison."

A loud pinging sound started to echo through the cabin.

"Now what?" the captain said to no one in particular.

"I will check it out sir," the soldier who had first leant over her said. He unharnessed and headed through the cockpit hatch. Within seconds, he was back with a look of fear in his eyes.

"Brace yourselves everyone," he screamed, "we are going down!"

13

Noah
Newton Abbot, King Street
The Paint Center
10:39 AM GMT

Noah was knelt by the end of the breakroom building looking across the car park toward the paint center. There were only four cars in the car park, and all of them had been broken into – but not set alight. Rubbish littered the ground, with a shopping trolley thrown in for good measure.

The wind picked up, blowing mushy newspaper across the ground. There were faded red and yellow footprints among the rubbish.

Someone has obviously been in the paint center.

Noah could hear the rain starting to patter against the faceplate. His breathing was heavy and fast. Seeing the video for the second time gave him a surge of adrenaline.

He could hear a voice. He ducked back against the wall. It was coming from the street. Noah ran crouched over to the nearest car. He knelt behind an old style, red Renault Clio that had all its tyres slashed and windows smashed.

The voice became two, and rose slightly, as if in anger.

Noah peeked over the side of the car, looking through the back broken windows.

"I told you the world would end in two-thousand and twelve." The voice belonged to an old woman, pushing a shopping trolley full of clothes and tied-up bags.

"It's two-thousand and thirteen; ya fool, how could it end in two-thousand and twelve if we're still 'ere?" stated an old man in a long black trench coat and brown cap, with fingerless gloves, and a tatty brown canvass rucksack on his back. He used a long length of rusty pipe as a walking stick. He did not turn his head to address the woman, rather; he hobbled along looking straight ahead. They both looked like they were in their late eighties.

"It started then. It was a slow process. It's still happening." The old woman, who was dressed in an old style-cleaning smock, with her grey hair up in a bun, said. "Margaret, who's a dab hand on the internet thingy, said... oh what's that word she used? Connected! That's it, everything's connected."

"Poppycock!" He stopped walking, rested the pipe against his shoulder, and removed his thick, plastic rimmed glasses, to wipe off the rain.

"Margaret doesn't know squat; she doesn't even know how to use a calculator. The daft old bugger doesn't even know what day of the week it is half of the time." He replaced his glasses and started walking again. His feet shifted through debris that covered the middle of the road.

Noah had to smile to himself. Even with the end of the world just on the horizon, some people would never change.

"I am ninety-six years old, and I was born during the first world war, and also survived the second. There's no way a bloody virus is going to kill me off." He shrugged his shoulders, as if to say that is that.

They disappeared behind the wall of the paint shop, heading up the road, still arguing.

Noah strained his hearing. Apart from the old couple, there was nothing, just the wind, and the rain echoing a staccato sound on the car roof.

Noah gripped the rifle and headed across to the paint center, ducking and diving around the four cars. The sound of his breathing inside the mask was deafening.

The paint center was a two-story building. The front was the shop, and the back was the warehouse.

Noah headed down a thin back lane that led to the paint centers docking area. The front of the building look untouched, but the back was ransacked. A truck, parked up against the large back loading dock had its rolling back shutter open, with the contents scattered around the loading bay. Paint tins lay spilling their contents. The ground looked like a vast contemporary piece of art. Footprints of all sizes were scattered around in the paint, leading off in all directions.

The bay doors were wide open.

Paint tins were stacked on pallets four high. A row of cardboard boxes did not fare well from the rain; they had collapsed, spilling their contents of paintbrushes and tape over the loading bay, onto the back yard.

Noah climbed up a metal ladder the seven feet to the concrete loading bay platform. He stood listening. There was just the sound of the wind whistling around the warehouse and some loose cling film flapping on one of the pallets.

Noah headed in. There was row upon row of metal and wood shelving. He started checking them all. There were all sizes of tins, in every shade imaginable. Brushes, rollers, sponges, scrapers, trays, tape, and aerosol cans.

He inched his way along the wide aisles. Some were too high to reach. He craned his neck to check above. There was just too much stuff; he would have to check out on the shop floor.

A large double door, with plastic strips hanging down, led to the shop. Carts were abandoned with stock piled up. Vandals had ransacked the place. Shelving was tipped over, with dented and opened tins littering the floor. The place was huge. He had never been in it before, so he did not know the layout. He simply walked up each aisle, as if out on a shopping trip.

Bingo!

Noah found the car spray section, with all the aerosol cans. On a hook were a couple facemasks, cheap paper ones with elastic string.

No good.

Around the end of the aisle was the expensive equipment. A full-face filtration system with an attached electric pump breathing apparatus. *Too bulky.* Next to it was an insect looking, blue facemask that covered the lower half of the face. He grabbed the last one on the hook. There may have been more on the floor, mixed in with all the items that had been ripped from the hooks and knocked off the shelves.

Goggles. Goggles. Where are the goggles?

They were opposite. There was more of a choice, so he grabbed six pairs of various shapes and sizes, so Red could pick whichever was comfiest.

Sorted. Time to get back to Red.

Noah headed for the back of the store, towards the warehouse, planning to exit where he had entered, when he noticed the steps.

I wonder what's on the second floor? There might be a staff breakroom with food? he reasoned. *Best to check while I am here, save having to go out looking for more food when ours runs out.*

He caught himself thinking *ours*. He pushed it to the back of his mind. *Now's not the time for trying to work everything out. There is a time and a place for everything.*

Noah left the mask and goggles on the bottom step, inside a small box he found on the floor. He jogged up the stairs two at a time.

The warehouse was two floors high, but above the shop was a large selection of offices and the breakroom. Noah went through the fridges. There was nothing edible, and the kitchen was smashed up for good measure.

Noah found himself in the office of the store manager. Photos of his family were all over the wall. They looked happy and content.

A loud pulsating, chop-chopping sound made him move toward the window, as a helicopter flew over head. It had been the first one he had seen in weeks. When the outbreak had first started, they seemed to be forever flying overhead. This one though was streaming a trail of black smoke, and wobbling, as if the pilot was struggling with the controls.

He watched as it tried to hover in the distance, and then sink below the roofline, way too fast, twisting around in circles as it descended.

That would be near Courtney Park, he thought.

The sound of the helicopter receded, leaving an eerie silence. That is when he heard the wheezy breathing, coming from the next office.

14

Doctor Lazaro
Military Merlin Transport Helicopter
Courtney Park, Newton Abbot, Devon
10:46 AM GMT

Melanie's head was spinning. *Or is it the helicopter that is spinning?* She thought. She had to concentrate on not throwing up. She jostled hard against the webbing, as her body pitched from side to side. Then the sheer g-force the spinning helicopter was creating pinned her back against the grey padding. She could not move even if she wanted to.

A loud pinging alarm squawked around the confines of the hold.

A container broke free from the webbing in the center, flying through the air, catching a soldier in the face, crushing his skull. Pulp and brain matter sprayed over Melanie's face. Others shouted in defiance at death. Some sat praying, with their eyes clenched tight.

The helicopter was going down, and fast. Just at the last moment, the pilot pulled of some last minute maneuver. Whatever he did; it stopped the hunk of metal hitting with full force. The crashing jolt reverberated throughout the hull, twisting the frame, shattering glass and crumpling metal. The machine slid along the ground, churning up grass and mud, until some piece of the outer structure caught on something and flipped the helicopter over, making it roll a few times, making everything inside weightless, before coming to a grating halt.

Melanie was still conscious. Her body had not completely recovered from the drugs the nurse had pumped into her earlier, so she had been relaxed, making her body limper than normal, which saved her from serious contusions.

Others did not fare so well. The two soldiers, who were injured, and had been on stretchers, had been tossed about like rag dolls when the harnesses snapped. Melanie had seen them both shoot up into the air, smacking against the roof, when they first hit the ground.

The spotty soldier, who first noticed she was awake, and had raised the alarm, was missing his head; it was smeared along the grey padding behind him, and splattered over Melanie's face. It had all happened so quickly, his heart was still pumping blood out of his neck in a stream that sprayed across the ceiling.

Her arms were still held by the webbing harness, so she could not wipe the blood and gore from her eyes and out of her mouth.

Some part of the crumpled helicopter settled and moved slightly, making a loud grating sound.

The shock was wearing off. Groaning, and whimpering started to echo around inside the metal hull.

A couple of soldiers had unharnessed themselves and was checking on their companions. One was holding his hand over a chest wound, staunching the flow of blood from a piece of metal that was protruding from the mans chest.

Melanie could twist her head to one side, to see out the shattered side window. The crashed helicopter was resting up against some kind of bandstand, in the middle of a large park. She could hear water running from somewhere. However, what was most unsettling was the horde of ten or so creatures, that used to be humans, running along the ground, heading straight for the crashed helicopter and the warm bodies inside.

15

Red
Newton Abbot, King Street
The Mortgage Company's Breakroom
10:47 AM GMT

"He's gonna be fine," Red muttered to herself. "He's only been gone about ten minutes. It's a big paint center; he will be back any minute." Red stood facing the door Noah had left by, with the arrow notched and ready.

Why am I so nervous? She thought. *I've been alone for weeks.* She shook her head, spilling red hair everywhere.

A creaking sound echoed behind her, coming from the door that led off into the main building.

Fuck! She spun around; the arrow was now pointed at the door leading into the mortgage company. *He wouldn't have come back through the main building, would he?* Her hands were sweating.

Just the building settling, nothing more. Get a grip.

Then, there was another sound from behind the closed door. It sounded like something being dragged along the carpet.

Red used her forearm to wipe the sweat from her forehead, and then re-aimed the arrow at the center of the door. Her hands were trembling slightly, making the arrow wobble.

Suddenly, the muted sounds became a loud thud, as something hit the door from the other side.

Red jumped back a step, catching the back of her legs on the couch. She regained her balance and stood back up straight.

Shit, what if I missed a room and someone had been in there all this time? Impossible, I checked the place from top to bottom. The only other answer is someone has entered through a window or the front door.

Another thud that slammed the wooden door, shaking it on its hinges.

Fight or flight. Red had a choice, stand firm and wait for whatever it was to come crashing through the door, or run out the way Noah left, leaving behind all their worldly possessions, and try to find Noah.

However, before Red had chance to make a conscious decision, the door flew open, ripping it from the doorframe.

16

Noah
Newton Abbot, King Street
The Paint Center
10:48 AM GMT

Noah spun around; the breathing in the next room was loud and wheezy. He chastised himself for not noticing it when he first entered the room.

Images from the video filled his mind. He started to sweat. Noah raised the .22 air rifle.

What good would a small pellet do to one of those creatures? He thought. It was easy to scare a mindless chav, but senseless, animalistic beasts that look like they belong in a zombie movie, was a different matter.

Noah unclipped the hunting knife and held it in the hand that was balancing the rifle's barrel.

If the pellet doesn't work, I can use the rifle as a club, or swing out with the knife.

He inched his way along the wall. The doorway was the only way out, unless he wanted to jump a story to the concrete below.

There was a clatter of paint tins on the floor below.

Shit, how many of them are there? Maybe it is the yobs from earlier, and they have found me? He reasoned.

Then he heard the guttural sounds of something moving up the stairs, as if whatever it was could sense his presence, or smell him.

Another bang from downstairs, shortly followed by another. Whatever it was, there were a few of them.

Shit! I gotta run for it. Head along the hallway, check for another exit. I can't be cornered in this room.

It was need, not bravery that made him run out into the hallway. As he spun around the corner, he looked over his shoulder. Coming up the stairs was a naked male and female, both covered in dried blood and gore. The instant they noticed him they sprung into action, giving chase.

Noah swung the rifle over his shoulder; it would be no good on them. He ran with all his strength down the hallway. Images of the young man in the video flashed before his eyes.

An exit! Perfect.

Off, in the distance, Noah could hear automatic gunfire, peppering in short bursts. However, he did not have time to think about whether it was coming from those in the downed helicopter.

Noah slammed into the exit door at full pelt, swinging the door open. It led to a set of metal steps leading down into a thin back alley, to one side of the paint center. Noah stood looking down.

Fuck! No way!

Behind him, the two naked creatures charged, screaming a guttural, throaty roar, while ripping at the walls as they ran along. Below him, down in the alley there were mounds of bodies, all bloated and vibrating, ready to explode.

PART TWO: RUIN

17

Doctor Lazaro
Crashed Military Merlin Transport Helicopter
Courtney Park, Newton Abbot, Devon
Friday January 5th 2013
10:48 AM GMT

Melanie could see the creatures as they ran across the grass towards them. All were naked and covered in blood and filth. Some were young teenagers, who ran ahead of a few older ones. Their guttural cries pierced the air, making the hair on the nape of her neck stand on end. The sound of the helicopter crashing drew their attention.

Automatic gunfire sounded like metallic burps. One of the soldiers must have been surveying the area and noticed the advancing mass.

"Make a defensive wall," the soldier in command shouted over the screaming heading their way.

The crash, mixed along with the lingering drugs the nurse had given her, made Melanie weak and nauseated. If it were not for the crash webbing, she would have tumbled forward to lie stretched out on the metal decking.

The soldiers who survived the crash, and were conscious, were scrambling to get outside. Too many remained unmoving. There were probably only ten left capable of defending themselves.

Melanie was physically as well as emotionally drained. The last three weeks had been a nightmare, what with the world going to hell and all, but the morning she had been having was straight out of a horror movie.

"Rogers, to your left!" the officer shouted.

Gunfire vibrated the metallic walls of the helicopter's fuselage. The guttural sounds of what were once humans echoed around them. The crash, as well as the gunfire, was drawing more of them in. Melanie could not see how many because the small window gave a limited view across the park.

"I'm out!" a voice shouted over the sound of the gunfire.

"Me too!" shouted another.

"Coco, break the supplies open."

A soldier bounded in and pulled a knife from his belt, and proceeded to cut the webbing off some dark-green containers that were strapped to the metal decking. He tossed the lid back. It was full of ammo.

Melanie hung limply forward, held by the webbing. The soldier seemed to notice her for the first time.

"Hang in there Doc. We just have a little tidying up to do, and we will get you sorted." He gave her a smile. Sweat glistened on his young, stubble covered black face.

Melanie did not know if he was trying to lighten the situation by making a joke, or if he was the kind of individual who sees the best in every situation – the perpetual happy guy.

Coco grabbed an armful of ammo, gave her a wink, swung around, and headed out.

Cheers went up as the ammo was passed around.

"Oh shit!" another shouted. "Where are they all coming from?"

18

Red
Newton Abbot, King Street
The Mortgage Company's Breakroom
10:50 AM GMT

Red held the bow pointed to the gap where the door used to be before it was smashed from the frame. Nothing charged through. She expected one of those naked zombie type creatures. The bow trembled in her shaking hands. Instead, a large form of a man stood blocking the doorway. He wore a greasy grey overall and heavy work boots. She could not see his face because he was so tall the top of the doorframe shadowed it.

He's not naked? Went through Red's mind. *And he's not charging*. She pulled the arrow back harder. The bow shuddered in her hands.

"Stop making a mess, Lennie. Why'd you have to break everything?" said a female voice.

"Locked," a slurred male voice replied.

"Stand back, let's see what we 'ave 'ere then?"

The giant shuffled to one side, dragging his left foot along the carpet.

An old woman shuffled in. "Jesus girl, you gave me a fright." She raised a frail arm up in front of her face. "Mind pointing that thing some place else?" She had on a long brown dress that looked a few sizes too big for her – as if she had shrunk over the years – with a large thick, green polo neck jumper. She had no coat, just a couple of blankets tossed over her shoulders. Her greyish-white hair looked like it had been dragged through a bush backwards, and she was trying to impersonate a dandelion.

"Who are you? What do you want?" was all Red could think to ask.

"Now, now dear, no need for open hostilities, we are all victims 'ere." She shuffled into the room and plunked herself down into an armchair.

The giant of a man moved under the doorframe. He had to duck, and turn sideways to get through. Red noticed he looked about thirty. He had a wide, plain face, which was flushed red, like an oversized baby. He had a scruffy mop of black curly hair, large blank eyes, and thick wet lips, as if he continually ran his tongue over them.

Red lowered the bow and arrow a little.

"We were just looking for somewhere safe, is all. And for food." The old woman gave a loud sniff and wiped a sleeve across her nose.

"I'm Betty, and this here lummox is my grandson Lennie. Of course, his real names Able, but the name Lennie stuck after I read *Of*

Mice and Men. You know John Steinbeck's literary masterpiece?" Betty gave a smile, showing crooked teeth with lots of gaps.

"Say hi Lennie."

"Hi." Lennie moved forward to offer a handshake.

"I wouldn't shake it, if you wanna be able to use that bow again. Grip like a vice. Would probably shatter every bone in your tiny hand," she announced with a smile. "He doesn't know his own strength."

They did not seem like a threat. Just an old woman and her dimwitted grandson. Red lowered the bow all the way.

"My friend will be back any minute," Red said. It sounded like she was making out there was more on her side.

"That's his stuff over there I take it?" Betty asked. "Looks like the kinda stuff a man would carry."

"Yes. He will be back any second." Red still held onto the bow.

"Relax. Take a weight off," Betty said. She looked at the vending machines. "Mind if we eat some of your food? Pickings have been sparse as of late."

"It's not mine. But you're more than welcome to it." Red took a few steps back, away from the machines. She wanted to keep the giant in her sights.

Betty got up slowly, making a grumbling sound as she did. "Sorry, old bones. I should be at home relaxing at my time of life, not running around, avoiding bloody zombies, or whatever the naked things are." She shuffled over to the machine.

"You gotta pull the door open. Here let me." Red made a judgment call. The old woman seemed genuine, and not out to hurt anyone. She placed her bow and arrow on the couch. She then moved forward and pulled the front of the snack machine open. Red then took a step back.

"Hmm. Don't really like chocolate, but beggars can't be choosers." The old woman grabbed a bunch of chocolate bars and a few packets of crisp. After Red opened the drink's machine, the woman removed a handful of cans.

"Lennie, take a seat. Sit there." Betty nodded to an armchair. "But take the bag off first."

Like a slow moving tectonic plate, the giant of a man moved over. He slowly swung the large backpack off his back and gently placed it on the floor, and then dropped himself down into the seat. The chair groaned under his weight. It was a tight fit.

Betty deposited the snacks and drinks on Lennie's lap. "Eat up lad. Keep up your strength. Be a good boy for grandma."

It dawned on Red what the old woman had just said about the naked creatures.

"You've seen some of them?"

"Hmm. What was that midear?" The old woman straightened her back, and winced as it cracked like a row of dominos.

"The naked zombie type things, you just said."

"Yes dear. That's why we came into this building. After all that gunfire started in the distance, we saw a group of them running full pelt into the Paint Center next door."

Just then, the windows vibrated from concussion blasts. It sounded like something was exploding one after another.

19

Noah
Newton Abbot, King Street
The Paint Center's Fire Escape
10:51 AM GMT

Noah could not believe his bad luck. The bloated bodies that filled the alleyway blocked the only escape route. He could hear the naked, animalistic people chasing down the hallway behind him. With all his strength, he slammed the fire exit door shut. He could hear their bodies frantically slamming into the other side. It would not take them long to smash their way through.

Think fast.

He could not go down among the bloated bodies, because he had seen the result of their violent exploding, and he could not return the way he came.

Up!

A thin metal ladder was bolted to the wall, leading up onto the paint centers roof. Noah grabbed the rusted metal, and with the speed brought on by fear, he flung himself onto the ladder and started scrambling up it.

He could hear the screaming of those behind the door, as they collided with the fire exit. The sound of the metal hinges straining under the onslaught – along with the wet slapping of their bodies against the wood – sped him on. It did not take him long to swing his body over the lip onto a flat gravel covered section about four feet wide, and just in time too, because the door was ripped off its hinges and clattered down into the alleyway. He lay still below the lip of the low wall. He tried not to move because the sound of the gravel beneath him would give his location away.

The ear-piercing screams intensified when they realized they had lost their quarry. However, their screaming was drowned out by the sound of the bloated bodies as they started to explode one after another. The ground shook from the violence of the blasts.

Noah instinctively put his hands over his face, covering the gasmasks faceplate. Through the gaps in his fingers, he could see the blood, guts, and bones flying high into the air. As the fluids, meat, and bones started to be pulled back down by gravity, it left the deadly black spores floating like a slow-moving cloud of ash.

20

Doctor Lazaro
Crashed Military Merlin Transport Helicopter
Courtney Park, Newton Abbot
10:56 AM GMT

Melanie was jolted awake when a hand shook her arm. Bleary-eyed, she looked into the blood-covered face of Coco.

"It's okay; the bloods mine. I turned and caught my head on a sharp piece of wreckage," he stated, to ease her fears that he was not dripping contaminated blood all over her.

I must have blanked out; Melanie thought.

Coco was cutting the webbing from around her. She slumped forward.

I'm so weak. What the hell did that nurse give me?

"We've sorted out the worst of the critters, but stragglers are still heading our way."

The occasional sound of gunfire rung through the confines of the wreckage.

Four other soldiers were inside the crashed helicopter, salvaging what they could carry. They were just a blur in Melanie's vision.

Must have cracked my head good and hard.

Coco was shifting Melanie's thighs forward, and then gripped one arm firmly. "Sorry if this is a little undignified Doc, but we are moving over to one of the houses skirting the park, so we can create a better defensible location." As he said that, he pulled her forward and hoisted her onto his shoulder, using a fireman's lift.

Melanie's head swam as she was tossed over his shoulder like a bag of potatoes.

Coco did not seem to notice the extra weight of her body as he ducked under the twisted hatch and out onto the blood-soaked grass.

The January sky was like a slab of grey concrete, and the air was bitterly cold.

"Let's pick up the pace soldiers, more will be arriving any minute," the commanding officer shouted.

Even with the dull, overcast sky, everything was so bright to Melanie's eyes after the confines of the craft. Also, seeing the world upside down, while bouncing along, did not help with her nausea.

Soldiers fanned out into formation. Some were carrying containers between them. Others covered their run to the nearest house.

Melanie could see naked bodies littered all around the helicopter, with sprayed patches of blood fanning out from the cooling corpses. From her upside-down view, she saw a pond with the water fountain still working. A couple of naked bodies floated in the murky water, with red blossoms spreading out from their carcasses.

The sound of the soldier's utility belts and the stamping of their boots on the grass, along with their laboured breathing, filled the silence. No more gunfire echoed off distant houses.

"That one," the commanding officer shouted. The group changed direction like a flock of birds, heading towards a building that had what looked like a tower, one story higher than all the other houses around it.

As they hustled through a tall metal gate onto a redbrick driveway, Melanie noticed the sign stating it was a dental clinic. A few naked dead bodies lay face down on the road skirting the park.

So much death. So much waste of life, Melanie thought. *I need to get my findings to someone who can make a difference. Someone who can stop all this.* With that thought, she remembered the folder. She just prayed someone had grabbed it.

21

Red
Newton Abbot, King Street
The Mortgage Company's Breakroom
10:57 AM GMT

Red was worried. The explosions had stopped, but she just knew that they had something to do with Noah.

"You're gonna wear a hole in that carpet," Betty stated, as she tried to eat a mars bar with the few teeth she had remaining. Chocolate dribbled down her chin.

Lennie was happily consuming everything that was dumped in his lap. Empty wrappers littered around his boots. He slapped his lips and made content sounds as the chocolate was washed down with one fizzy drink can after another.

Red had noticed how he simply stared straight ahead, and he hardly ever blinked.

"Sorry about his manners. Never was a quiet eater, that one," Betty said. "He's got a good heart though." The old woman wiped the chocolate off her face.

"He came and found me," Betty stated.

"What? Sorry?" Red was deciding whether to go up a floor in the mortgage company building and see if she could see what was transpiring next door.

"I said Lennie came and found me, after all this started." She waved a hand around her, as if that could describe everything that had happened over the last three weeks.

"I was in an old people's home, up at Ford Park. I was there for almost nine years. They told me I was too old to stay in my own home. Incapable of looking after myself, as if I was some cripple or retard." She gave a gruff grunt.

"I am eighty-six and I have more wits about me than half those dotty teenage care assistants who were meant to be looking after me. Half of them couldn't even string a coherent sentence together. And they were always on their bloody mobile phones."

Red realized the old woman was just trying to distract her mind from worrying about Noah.

"Lennie was the son of my only child, Sophie." She had a faraway look on her wrinkled face. "I never did find out who the father was.

"Anyway, Sophie left him in my care. She just ran away one night, when he was two. She didn't leave a note or say good-bye or anything.

"When I got put into an old people's home he was taken into a special care unit in Torquay. They said he was to dimwitted to live on his own. They brought him to see me once a week." Betty looked across to her grandson.

"After all this palaver started he turned up at the home. He made his own way, walking about nine miles. Whether he broke out, or was left to fend for himself, I don't know. But he found me, and hasn't left my side since." A tear rolled down the old woman's face. "The big lummox."

Lennie was oblivious to the conversation. He was halfway through his eighth chocolate bar. Crisps were sprinkled all over his overalls.

While Betty had been talking, Red had collected all Noah's stuff together, packing it all back up, in case they needed to leave in a hurry when he returned.

Movement caught Red's attention.

Lennie stood up in one swift move. Some drink cans hit the carpet and rolled away. He dropped the half-eaten chocolate bar and clenched his chocolate-covered fists. Lennie seemed to be hearing something Red could not.

Then Red understood. She could hear the muffled sound of furniture shifting around through the gap where the adjoining door used to be. Something else was making its way through the structure towards them. Suddenly, a piercing, guttural scream echoed through the building.

22

Noah
Newton Abbot, King Street
The Paint Center Roof
11:01 AM GMT

Noah lay wedged up against the lip of the low wall for what felt like hours – but in reality, was five minutes – while he caught his breath. He could not hear any movement from below. Slowly, he rolled over onto his front and raised himself up to peer over the lip of the roof. Gravel dug into his elbows.

The alleyway looked like someone had tried to repaint it in shades of red and brown. It was hard to tell if any of the body parts belonged to the two creatures that had been chasing him, or whether they had returned inside. Blood ran down the walls, with larger chunks coming unstuck and dropping with a wet squelching sound onto the concrete below, like some cheap horror movie set.

His only choice was to head down through the guts and mess. The roof was a galvanized tin roof, which veered right up at an angle after the four feet of flat gravel. It was too steep to climb, and the noise his boots would make on the metal would attract unwanted attention.

Jesus, why didn't those teenagers set light to another building? I could be sat at home in the safety and comfort of my apartment; he reasoned. *But then I wouldn't have met Red.* He just realized the whole reason for heading into the Paint Center in the first place was to get Red a filtration mask, and he had left it in a box, inside, at the bottom of the stairs.

Fuck! I have no choice but to go back in.

Noah strained his hearing.

Nothing.

Slowly, he crawled over the wall and back onto the ladder with shaking legs. He had to hold on tight because the ladder was slippery due to being splattered with body fluids.

I hope Red is still inside the breakroom, and hasn't come outside to investigate the explosions. He looked down the alley. *Luckily, the January winds have swept the spores away.*

Noah stood on the fire escape looking back into the building. The remains of some naked body parts were splattered down the corridor. It was hard to tell how many people it had once been. The resulting blasts, of the bloated bodies in a confined alleyway, were phenomenal.

The inside of the gasmask was steaming up from his heavy breathing.

Cautiously, and carefully, so as not to slip, Noah made his way back along the corridor. On the floor, halfway down was his rifle. In all the frantic running and rush of adrenaline, he completely forgot about it. He was sure he had it out on the fire escape.

I must have dropped it when climbing the ladder and the blast blew it into the hallway; he reasoned. He picked it up, shook a glob of flesh off the handle, and hooked it back over his shoulder.

He strained his hearing. The building seemed deserted. With a little more confidence, he headed down the stairs.

The box had tipped over; the mask and goggles were on the floor. Quickly, he swept them up and ran toward the large back warehouse doors.

The yard was deserted.

Maybe the explosions scared the other zombies away. It still felt strange to use that word. It was such a surreal word that was used repeatedly in movies and books. The word did not belong in the real world. However, no other word better described them.

Noah jogged around the corner and across the small car park. He realized he had not heard any gunfire since he climbed up onto the roof.

Maybe that's where they have all gone, to investigate the new sound.

Just as he reached the small back alley, where the breakroom's entrance was located, the door flew open and Red ran out, closely followed by an old woman – who had her dress hitched up, so she could run – and a giant of a man who had to turn sideways to fit through the door.

The man then turned and lifted his huge meaty hand, and brought it down with enough force to crack concrete; he hit a head that just came into view. The deformed cranium of the naked female hit the floor with bone-crushing force.

"Run!" Red screamed when she noticed Noah.

23

Doctor Lazaro
Dentist Clinic
Courtney Park, Newton Abbot
11:06 AM GMT

Melanie swung from Coco's muscular back. She was slipping in and out of consciousness.

When the soldiers reached the building, they kicked the door open and fanned out inside to check there were no Blinkers, Stare-ers, Eaters or Poppers – the names the soldiers had labeled the four different stages.

After "Clear!" was shouted from each room, the building was determined to be deserted.

Melanie was propped up in a dentist's chair on the top floor of the clinic. Coco had sat her in the comfortable chair, and then stated he would be back after they had made the perimeter safe.

She then slipped back into unconsciousness. She was woken up by the sensation of water on her lips.

"Sip it slowly Doc," a scrawny twenty-something lad said, who was riddled with acne, and who had been sitting next to her on the flight. He poured a little water from his canteen into her mouth. “I’m Jimmy, the squad’s medic.”

“Don’t worry about me, see to your wounded,” Melanie muttered. Her mind flashed back to all the bodies lying motionless in the helicopter.

“You’re my only patient, Doc. The others were too far gone–” his words trailed off. He shifted. Melanie got the impression it was not from being in an uncomfortable position, but from the conversation.

Melanie could hear the other soldiers moving around furniture on the floor below.

“Only nine of us made it out alive. Including you.” Jimmy was rummaging through his medical backpack. He pulled out some cotton wool and poured a clear solution over it. As he dabbed it on her forehead, she stifled back a scream. She bit her lip instead.

“Sorry. You must have been hit on the head when we crash-landed. Just cleaning up the cut.” After the initial shock of the sting, she settled down as Jimmy cleaned the wound, and then placed a couple butterfly plasters over it.

“The wound needs stitches, but this will have to do for now.”

That explains why I keep falling in and out of consciousness, and why I feel so queasy.

“I gotta make sure you stay awake for a while, because of the bash on the head.”

Voices could be heard in the hallway outside. Two soldiers walked into the room.

"Doctor Lazaro, I'm glad you're still with us," the man stated. "I'm the leader of what's left of this squad. It's my job to get you safely to the Dartmoor facility." He gave a sigh. "I know I've not been doing too well so far, but hopefully I can redeem myself." He sat upon a stool by a work surface that was covered in dental instruments. He reached inside his jacket and pulled out the folder that was still inside the waterproof sleeve.

Melanie was relieved. *Thank God, at least I still have the documents.*

"I just hope whatever information you have is worth the sacrifices?" He just stared at the plastic sleeve, as if being able to read its contents. He dropped it onto the side.

A tall thin soldier walked into the room. He had long thin features, with large protruding teeth, as if they were too big for his mouth. "Captain, everything has been secured. The two entrances are barricaded, and all the windows on the lower levels are secure. And everything that could be salvaged from the helicopter has been brought to the building."

"Good." He rubbed a hand over his face. The action reminded Melanie of Brigadier General William Hay, before he was shredded by flying glass.

So many have died today.

“Rogers, get Echo to prepare food for everyone as soon as she finishes positioning her packages.”

“Sir, yes sir.” Rogers did not salute; he simply turned and went to carry out his orders.

“Captain,” another soldier said, as he came through the doorway. “Bull has the radio all set up ready for you. He’s talking to General Philips as we speak.”

“Tell him I’m on my way. And please assure him she’s fine.” He wearily got to his feet.

“Captain,” Melanie said.

“Yes.” He turned slowly. The crash left his body badly bruised.

“Thank you for rescuing me.” The images of the horde of naked creatures attacking the university flashed through her mind. She squeezed her eyes shut to blank them out.

“I’m sorry for everyone who has been lost.” A tear rolled down her cheek. “But trust me when I say that folder contains information that needs to reach someone in the Dartmoor labs.”

“It is that important?” he asked.

“It’s the cure,” Melanie stated. Even though technically it was not a cure, but a prevention, she did not think that mattered.

The room went silent as the ramifications of her statement sunk in.

"Jesus," Jimmy muttered.

"Captain," Rogers said as he walked back into the room. "We have a problem. General Philips said he has no more birds at his disposal; his other two are apparently not responding to radio contact. In addition, the three groups of Huskies that are on patrol – that he sent out this morning – aren't due to return from missions until tomorrow afternoon."

"So we're on our own."

"Yes sir. We have no back up and no transport. But on the plus side, we do have shitloads of ammo and firepower."

The Captain looked at his blood-flecked boots, while considering his options.

"Get Coco, Trev, and Franco ready. Within ten minutes, I want them out commandeering a vehicle big enough to transport us all."

"Captain." Another soldier strode into the room. "We have a problem." The soldier looked like a poster perfect image for the military; muscular frame, chiseled square jaw, with a flawless center parting in his dirty-blonde hair, even after everything they went through.

"What's the problem, Spice?"

"It seems we missed a small cloakroom when we cleared the building, and it has three Stare-ers comatose inside."

"Shit," Jimmy muttered.

“That’s not the worst of it,” Spice stated. “Two of them are children.”

24

Noah, Red, Betty, and Lennie
Newton Abbot, King Street
11:12 AM GMT

Red's warning echoed in Noah's ears as he tried to take in the situation. The old woman did not seem to be a threat; rather, she was also running for her life along with Red.

The huge man stood at the doorway, his hands covered in blood. Then he grasped the doorframe with both hands and with one leg, he kicked into the room. Noah could not see what he was kicking, but he knew whatever it was it could not have survived the impact.

"Run!" Red screamed again as she reached Noah. Red had her own cloth bag on her back, and she was struggling to carry Noah's. As she ran past, she pushed it into his arms.

The old woman was moving fast for her age, and as she also passed Noah, she screamed, "You deaf Sonny? Run!"

Noah fumbled with the large pack as he swung it onto his back, while keeping hold of the cardboard box, and running to catch up. With a backward glance, Noah noticed the giant was lumbering along with a limp, following them.

"Keep up Lennie," the old woman shouted over her thin shoulder.

A piercing, guttural scream echoed off the buildings as a naked female, and a teenage boy exited the breakroom, hot on their heels.

"Shit!" Noah muttered as the screams made him run even faster. *We won't be able to outrun them.*

The female was skinny, covered in filth and dried blood, with long matted blonde hair. She was running too fast and slammed against the wall. She skidded on the ground, as she ripped at the floor and wall with twisted, bleeding fingers while trying to get back up. The male teenager ran past her, straight at Lennie, who was at the back of the retreating group.

Fuck! Noah thought.

The huge man was just too slow.

Noah dropped the pack off his back and let it fall to the ground.

The rifle won't stop them, but maybe I could use it as a club.

Just as that thought passed through his head, the giant of a man stretched out a big hand and grabbed the shopping trolley that was resting on its side. In one swift move, Lennie twisted and swung the trolley in a large arc, pivoting on one leg as he twisted around. The trolley caught the naked teenager full force, knocking him sideways like a ragdoll. The body hit the Renault Clio like a bag of bones, and slid along the ground, unmoving.

The screaming female seemed undaunted and charged straight at the giant man. Lennie lifted the trolley above his head in both hands, and just as she reached him, with her bloody hands outstretched, Lennie slammed the trolley down with so much force; he twisted the metal frame. The female's body became unrecognizable. Blood started to pool around the crushed trolley and heap of dirty, mangled flesh.

Bloody hell, I'm glad he's on our side; Noah thought. Then added, *is he on our side?*

Red and Betty stopped running about thirty yards up the road.

"Good boy Lennie. You showed them," the old woman shouted. "Now get moving. Come on, stop staring, and catch up. More could be just around the corner."

Lennie turned, and with his blank stare stumbled past Noah as if he was not there.

"That's right, come on Lennie," the old woman prompted, as she leaned forward with her hands on her knees, catching her breath.

Noah hoisted his bag back on his back, and with one last glance at the two crushed bodies, he started to follow the giant.

"We need to get out of the road," Red stated, as they all grouped up behind a large blue van. “There could be more of them around.”

“I need a cuppa tea,” the old woman mumbled with a wheezing breath.

“Over here,” Noah stated as he walked to the closest house. The green front door was wide open. The front hallway’s carpet was soaking wet, and leaves, and rubbish had blown in from the January winds.

“We need to get out of the street.”

The others followed him in without a word. As they filed past Noah used his shoulder to wedge the door shut, which was tight because the wood had warped from the rain.

Noah walked down the hallway, past happy smiling faces in the photo frames. The others gathered in the large kitchen. Red dropped her bag and then slumped down onto a chair around a large, old style, kitchen table.

Lennie stood in a corner; blood covered hands limp at his sides. He stared, unblinking at the middle of the table.

The old woman pulled a dishcloth off the side and started to soak it under the running water. She then proceeded to clean the blood off her grandson’s hands.

Noah dropped his bag and then tipped the contents from the box upon the table.

“I have a mask and several goggles,” he stated.

Red was leaning forward, with her head in her hands; her red hair covering her face. With the sweep of one hand, she tossed her hair back over her shoulders.

“Goggles?” the old woman asked as she continued to wipe spots of blood off Lennie’s face.

Noah pulled off his gasmask and dropped it onto the table. He wiped the sweat from his forehead.

“Yes. What was chasing us seemed to be just one stage of whatever is happening to those who become infected. Eventually, they become bloated and pop, spreading black spores.”

“Is that why you wear a gasmask?” she questioned.

“It is.”

Red picked up the filtration mask and tried it on.

“But we only have the two masks. I didn’t know you would be joining us,” Noah stated. “But we have enough goggles for everyone.”

“We can grab more masks on the way past, once we decide what we are going to do,” Noah stated.

“Sit down Lennie,” Betty said, while pulling a stool out from under the table.

Lennie did not remove the bag, because he had not been told to, instead, he lowered himself down onto the stool. The wood creaked under his weight.

Betty dropped the blood-soaked rag in a flip-top bin and then washed her hands in the white porcelain sink.

"I believe the gunfire came from Courtney Park," Noah said.

"Probably something to do with the helicopter that flew over," Betty added.

"A helicopter?" Red questioned. She spun her head to stare at Noah. "You didn't mention anything about a helicopter."

"While in the Paint Center, I saw one flying toward the train station. But I think it was damaged, because it was trailing black smoke, and it went down spinning."

"There were obviously survivors if there is gunfire," Red stated.

"I know," Noah said. "And if their transport is too badly damaged, others will be coming to get them." He let that hang in the air. "That's why you are all going to stay here, where it's safe, and I'm going to find them, and get us rescued along with them."

25

Doctor Lazaro and the Squad
Dentist Clinic
Courtney Park, Newton Abbot
11:17 AM GMT

"Children?" The Captain asked.

"Yes, a mother, and her two children. One boy who looks about four, and a girl who looks about seven."

"Shit!" The Captain gave a long sigh, while holding the bridge of his nose in his hand. "I will take care of it personally." He went to exit the room.

"What are you going to do?" Melanie asked. She was too weak to leave the chair, and she was using all her strength just to stay awake.

"What needs to be done," he answered while not turning to look at her.

"But they are just children," she whispered.

The Captain stopped. He still did not turn around.

Jimmy was knelt by his medical supplies, packing them away. His hands had stopped moving, while he listened. He kept his head down.

Rogers stared at his blood-speckled boots.

"Do you want them to change while we are here? Do you want to take the chance that we will be safe?" He let the words hang in the air.

"The children are gone. They died the instant they were infected. Now they are something else. Just a means of transport – a shell."

The room went silent. They all knew the truth. They all knew how it had to play out.

Melanie closed her eyes. She knew, deep down, there was no other way. She had seen what they would become. The image of the twin children in the pod, ripping apart the cow, flashed in her mind.

The Captain left without another word.

Rogers closed the door gently as he followed.

Jimmy cleared his throat. "Don't go to sleep Doc."

"I'm not sleeping," Melanie stated as tears streaked her face.

"I know," Jimmy muttered. His hands were still in his medical bag, unmoving. Waiting.

Silence filled the room. A clock ticked on the far wall. A minute passed. A couple sniffs from Melanie seemed to be the only sound in the whole building.

The BAM, BAM, BAM, of the guns retort blasted throughout the dental clinic, echoing off the walls.

26

Noah, Red, Betty, and Lennie
Newton Abbot, In a House on King Street
11:21 AM GMT

"What do you mean you're going on your own?" Red's head flew up. "Do you think you're going out there on your own with those things around?" she stated while glaring at him.

"Without my pack, and on my own, I can travel faster."

Betty was rummaging through the fridge. There was nothing edible, just a large chunk of mold in the plastic bottom tray. She started going through the cupboards.

Lennie sat staring at his hands on the tabletop.

"I can cut through the back gardens, over the walls, and–"

"What, you don't think I can climb over a bloody wall?" Red interrupted.

"You will all be safer if you stay here. I–"

"I met you only an hour ago and already you're telling me what I can and can't do. You don't know me. You don't know what I'm capable of." Her own words seem to make her think for a minute. Red went silent. She lowered her head. Her hair cascaded down around her face.

They both sat in silence.

"Runner bean chutney. I haven't seen any of that in years," Betty stated, while rifling through a draw for a teaspoon.

"Tired," Lennie mumbled.

Betty had a mouthful of the chutney. She swallowed. "Do you need a nap, Lennie?" Using her sleeve, she wiped some chutney off her lips.

Lennie stood up. This was his way of answering her question.

"Let's see what we can sort out in the front room." Betty held her grandson's hand and led him down the short hallway.

"I can be there and back in twenty minutes," Noah stated. "I will go over back walls and through houses." He fiddled with his gasmask, turning it over in his hands. "If the army is there, they will protect us. That's their job." He sat in silence.

"I'm not useless," Red muttered.

Noah looked over his shoulder, down the hallway. "We can't drag them over walls; she won't make it." He shifted closer. "I need you to stay and look after them until I return with help."

Realization dawned that it was not about her being a girl, and slowing him down, but rather, he needed her to protect Betty and Lennie.

"Okay," she simply said.

Noah removed his phone from his pocket. He was surprised it was not broken. He had not checked it in hours. There was no signal.

"Does your phone work?"

Red removed an iPhone 5 from her pocket. She checked it. "No, there's no reception."

"Same here."

The mobile network was down, but there was another option – wi-fi. He checked to see if the house, or one around it still had the internet working, and if so, if their wi-fi was still on.

"Bingo!"

A few wi-fi networks were broadcasting. BTHub3-6SDK, SKY29781, Virginmedia1759781. The strongest was Simons_Place, and luckily; it was unlocked.

With a few swipes on his Samsung Note, Noah was on the internet. He used an app and called up Google Earth. Within thirty seconds, he was looking down at a view of the houses and streets separating him from the park. He now knew how to get to the park without having to travel along too many open streets.

With one click, he saved a picture of the map into his photos, for quick reference.

"He will be out for a few hours, bless 'im," Betty stated. "All this excitement has worn him out."

Excitement, Noah thought. *The predicament they were all in was many things, but exciting is not one of them.*

"Red is going to stay here with you and Lennie, while I go and get some help," Noah stated.

"That's nice dear." Betty started collecting tins out of a cupboard. She groaned as she lifted a large pot off a shelf.

Noah stood up and slid his phone into his pocket. He also checked the knife was secure on his thigh.

"I will quickly check upstairs to make sure everything's clear." It dawned on him that he should have checked right away, but he was a little preoccupied when they first entered the house.

"I will also see if there's a baseball bat or cricket bat or something I can use for a weapon." He knew his rifle was useless.

Betty was trying to get a tin into the electric tin opener, with not much luck.

"Bugger it." Betty muttered to herself.

Red sat around the table with her chin resting on her hands. She tossed her hair back while looking up.

"I will check upstairs with you," she said.

“I can manage, but if you want to drag some furniture across in front of the front door, that would be helpful. Oh, and close all the curtains downstairs, I will do upstairs.

“Okay.” She climbed to her feet and headed down the hallway. Noah could hear her trying to wedge a sideboard against the door.

A light snoring sound drifted from the front room.

Noah passed Red and headed up the stairs.

It was only a two-bedroom house. A kitchen and front room downstairs with a small toilet, with a master and single bedroom upstairs along with the family bathroom.

The first room he checked at the top of the stairs was the bathroom. It was empty, and the window closed. The single room was a child’s room, decorated in many tones of blue. It had airfix model airplanes hanging from fishing wire from the ceiling, with a thick airplane boarder running around the room.

Noah checked the wardrobe and cupboard. There was only a plastic baseball bat, which was next to useless as a weapon. He shut the curtains before leaving the room.

He moved toward the door to the master bedroom. It was wedged closed. As he slowly opened the door, a strong, putrid smell swept over him. He could also hear a low growling sound coming from the darkness.

27

Doctor Lazaro and the Squad
Dentist Clinic
Courtney Park, Newton Abbot
11:32 AM GMT

Melanie was not allowed to sleep, but she could rest her eyes.

Jimmy had asked if she required any tablets for the pain from the wound on her head. She had declined, stating she had enough medication swimming around in her veins already.

Jimmy then left her to rest, with strict instructions – once again – not to fall asleep. He said he would return within the hour to check on her.

Melanie could hear mumbled conversation through the old floorboards, but she could not discern the words. She heard one of the doors being unbarricaded so Coco, Franco, and Trev could go and find some form of transportation.

The door to her room slowly creaked open.

When Melanie opened her eyes, she noticed a woman decked in military garb stood in the doorway.

"Hi honey. Sorry to disturb you. I'm Echo." Her voice was soothing. She had striking cheekbones and piercing green eyes, and her mouse coloured hair was pulled up into a ponytail.

Melanie did not remember seeing any females on the helicopter. Then again, some of them were in full military body armour, along with helmets, so she could have easily missed her.

Melanie gave a weak smile.

"It's nothing fancy I'm afraid, just the standard military slops." Echo gave a wide smile, which highlighted the smear of dirt on her cheek. She walked into the room, carrying the food on a small metal dental apparatus tray.

She's tall, Melanie thought. *She must be well over six feet.*

Echo moved a stool over and placed it next to the dentist's chair. She gracefully slid on.

"How do you wanna do this? Do you want me to feed you, or can you manage it on your own?" Another smile.

"I got it, thanks." Melanie slowly raised herself up. Her body responded with stabbing pains through her muscles. She winced.

"The ride over sure did a number on you, huh?" Echo slid a stray strand of hair over her ear.

Melanie gave a grunt. "That's for sure," Melanie stated. She peered sideways at Echo, who was sat relaxed.

"You don't have a scratch on you."

"I have a few bruises, and my ears are still ringing, but I'm okay, all considered. Besides, it's not my first crash, I'm becoming a pro."

Melanie sat right up. She reached for the tray. The drugs were slowly wearing off. She was feeling less dopey with every minute that passed. The problem was, with the drugs washing away the pain from the head wound and bruises was amplified. However, she did not mind a little pain, so long as she was coherent.

"Two years ago a military cargo plane I was on had to ditch in the ocean just off the coast of Tunisia," Echo said while Melanie spooned some mysterious goo out of a silver packet into her mouth.

"Have you ever seen the film Cast Away?" She paused for a second to allow Melanie to respond.

Melanie simply nodded due to having a mouthful of food.

"Then you will have some idea of what a water crash is like." Echo shifted her thigh. "Some think it's easier than crashing on land. It's not. Water is just as hard when you hit it fast, and land doesn't pour in, filling the craft up." Echo smiled.

"The foods terrible, isn't it?"

Melanie swallowed a mouthful. "I can't work out what it's supposed to be."

"Best not to ask," Echo said with a smile. "It has all the nurturance needed to sustain a body. It's just they forgot to add flavour and a pleasant texture."

I wonder what her nickname means. And she's stunning, why would she join the army?

"Do you mind if I ask you a few questions?" Melanie said.

"Shoot, honey."

"Why did you join the army? Why a cook?"

"Everyone has to do something, right? I followed my father's example. And I do the cooking for the squad because the others can't warm a ration bag if their life depended on it, but I'm not the official cook; he's still on the chopper out there." She smiled again. "I'm the explosive's expert," she stated.

"Echo," said a voice from the doorway. A large black man stood filling the doorframe.

"Yes Bull."

"Firstly, the Captain wants to know how much longer it will take you to position your packages. And secondly, your fathers on the radio, he wants a word."

"Your father?" Melanie asked.

"Yes. General Philips is my father," Echo stated. She turned to Bull. "And tell the Captain

I'm all finished, the packages are all in position and ready to go."

That's why the General told the soldier to tell General Philips 'she was fine'. He was referring to Echo, not me.

Gunfire reverberated throughout the building.

Rogers appeared next to Bull. "Bull, Echo, downstairs now. We have more incoming."

28

Noah, Red, Betty, and Lennie
Newton Abbot, In a House on King Street
11:37 AM GMT

The growling was low, unlike the sounds of the naked charging creatures. It did not sound like a threat, more like a warning. Noah was not sure why, but he did not feel threatened by what was in the room. He slowly pushed the door open a little more.

The smell was almost overpowering.

The room had its curtains drawn, which made the bedroom dark and shadowy. He could just make out the large double bed. It looked like something was resting on it. Then, there was a movement on the floor.

Noah reached in and fumbled along the wall until he found the light switch. With a flick, the room's occupants were laid bare.

On the bed, under blankets with just their head's showing, were two adult-sized bodies and one child. On the bedside cabinet was a collection of prescription and over the counter medication bottles; all were empty. They rested next to a tipped over bottle of red wine and a small orange juice carton with a straw. The parents chose their own death rather than waiting to be rescued. They took their son with them.

Noah's attention drifted to what had made the growling sound. On the floor, protecting the bodies was a dog. It was a small scruffy terrier type mongrel, and considering the door was wedged shut, for God knows how long, since they committed suicide, it did not look in too bad a condition.

Noah knelt down.

"Come on. There's a good fella. No need to be scared," he said in a soothing voice.

The little dog's tail started to wag. It inched along the carpet then dropped back down onto its belly.

"Come on. No need to be afraid buddy."

The little dog looked up with frightened eyes. Its tail wagged across the carpet. It inched forward another couple feet, before dropping back down just out of Noah's reach.

"Come on, no one's gonna hurt you."

Its little tail wagged faster as it inched the last few feet to Noah's side. It rushed straight in, wedging itself against Noah's knee. It twisted to press as much of its body up against him, while burying its head. Its tail was a blur.

"There you go. You're safe now buddy." He rubbed the little scruffy dog. The dog relaxed against him.

Noah scooped the little dog up. The dog looked up with large watery eyes. It started to lick his chin and face.

“Good boy. Stop that. Good boy.”

With the dog in his arms, Noah checked the rest of the room. There was a large walk-in closet. Inside he found a set of golf clubs.

Perfect.

Noah pulled out four clubs of different sizes. Some with metal ends, others with large wooden ends. He had never played golf, and he did not have time to check what type of clubs they were. Now it did not matter. Now they were weapons.

He noticed a large plastic container on the floor half full of water, and one quarter full of dried dog food.

In one corner was where the little dog had gone to the toilet. The carpet was soaked in urine and lumps of excrement were scattered everywhere.

The little dog rested unmoving in his arms, simply happy to have physical contact once again. It stared around the room and gave a whine when it spotted its dead owners.

The room contained nothing else of use. With a strong tug, Noah wedged the door shut; once again, sealing their tomb.

Red moved a telephone cabinet and some chairs from the kitchen to wedge them against the door. It did not look like it would stop anything from getting through, but it kept her busy.

A low snoring drifted from the front room, and Betty muttered to herself in the kitchen.

"Here," Noah said as he passed the dog to Red.

"What the... Where the hell did he come from?" Red said as she took the terrier in her arms.

"He was locked away in the bedroom." Noah rested the four golf clubs against the wall. He leaned in a little closer. "Just make sure no one goes in the master bedroom, there are some bodies in there."

Red gasped. "Are they safe?"

"Don't worry, they're dead."

Red relaxed.

The dog wiggled in her arms. She twisted the collar and checked the nametag. "Charlie," she muttered. She then put the dog down. It ran straight into the front room.

Noah picked up the club with a medium-sized metal end. He gave it an experimental swing. It would do just fine. He carried it into the kitchen.

Betty had the gas stove on with a large pot resting on top. She continued to add tins to the mix. She hummed to herself as she prepared the food.

"I shouldn't be any longer than twenty or so minutes." He checked the knife on his thigh and grabbed the gasmask off the table.

"If I run into any problems, and I think I am going to be longer; I will text you via Whatapp." He turned to look at Red. "Have you got Whatapp on your phone?"

"Yes."

"The app doesn't use mobile networks, rather it uses the internet, and because that's working at the moment, we can still send messages to each other. Well, so long as I can find another wi-fi area, which shouldn't be a problem." He grasped the golf club in his right hand after slipping the gasmask on.

Red stood by the table. "You be careful out there," she said. She did not know what else to say.

"Once I'm gone, lock the door." Noah watched Betty pour a tin of sweet corn into the pot. *I hope the smell doesn't attract anything;* he thought. He wondered how sensitive the creature's sense of smell was, but he knew they needed hot food to keep them going.

"Keep the doors and windows locked and the curtains drawn. Try not to make too much noise."

Red stood motionless.

Noah stood opposite.

“Be careful,” Red said, as she raised a hand and rested it on his arm.

Luckily, due to the mask, she could not see Noah blush. Without another word, he slipped out the back door and across the small back garden.

“Be safe,” Red muttered, as she watched him climb up the back wall using a bench and shed, and then run along the top, out of view.

“Oh, don’t worry about him, he will be back with those army boys before this has even finished cooking,” Betty said, while stirring the large pot.

As Red stood leaning against the counter, watching the top of the wall, in case Noah came back, she let her mind wander. So much had happened in only a couple of short hours, she had not had chance to let her thoughts catch up.

Red closed the curtain that hung on the back door.

Noah had asked her to stay to look after Betty and Lennie. She had not had anyone counting on her for a long time. Not since her little sister looked to her to keep her safe from their stepfather. She had failed then, with devastating consequences. The ultimate price was paid for her mistake.

Red was pulled back to the moment at hand, when she could just make out the sound of gunfire starting up again in the distance. She was just about to mention it to Betty, when the sound of the front room window shattering made her spin around and run down the hall. She could hear the small dog start barking, and the sound of furniture smashing. Red snatched a golf club from against the wall as she entered the front room.

29

Doctor Lazaro and the Squad
Dentist Clinic
Courtney Park, Newton Abbot
11:49 AM GMT

Gunfire filled the building, reverberating off the walls and filling all the space with its deafening tattoo of sound.

The Captain shouted orders while shooting through the broken window that looked out onto the dentist's small car park.

They were down three men – who had gone off looking for transport. That left six people capable of defending their location, and an injured doctor with concussion.

The Captain knew the three gunshots could draw attention, but he had no other option. After securing the building, and shooting the three in the storeroom, they had stayed away from the windows and kept the sound to a minimum, hoping they had gone unnoticed after the first initial onslaught. But no such luck, it seems karma caught up with them.

The creatures filled the car park, pouring through the large iron gates. Their naked bodies bounded over abandoned cars, and slammed against the building like a tsunami. Frantic hands reached through broken windows; the jagged glass ran red with their tainted blood.

They were now all wearing military-grade gasmasks with built in communication devices. When they first crashed, and were attacked, they did not have time to retrieve them from the containers.

"Fall back," the Captain shouted over the sound of the gunfire and screaming creatures. Even though they could all hear perfectly well, due to the earpiece they were all wearing, force of habit made him shout.

"Get up the stairs. I want everyone on the third floor as arranged." The Captain walked backwards as he fired his handgun into the throng of thrashing arms that reached through the window.

Bull stood to the Captains left, with a machinegun resting against his large shoulder. He peppered the mass of bodies. However, just as one body fell below the window line, another took its place. The only reason they were not churning through was that too many were trying to get in at once. Even though they charged together, they were not organized.

There were only two windows in the large Waiting Room. Rogers and Spice covered the other window. Both conserved bullets by double tapping the trigger, and concentrating on headshots.

The animalistic, guttural screams filled the building, almost drowning out the gunfire.

The main entrance was a thick oak door. There was only a small pane of glass, which had an arm thrashing about through it. The door shook as bodies repeatedly slammed against it.

Jimmy piled more furniture up against a door that went into a large office. The creatures had obviously climbed through the window because they started to bang their bodies against the adjoining door.

"Captain they're in the office," Jimmy said.

Echo was running up the stairs two at a time to double-check the packages were in position.

"Everybody up the stairs now!" the Captain shouted, as he tapped Bull on the shoulder.

Bull stopped firing, then turned, and ran up the stairs.

Spice and Rogers gave another blast of gunfire into the window for good measure, and then followed behind Bull.

Jimmy tossed one more chair onto the pile of furniture and quickly gave chase.

The Captain was the last up the stairs, just as the first couple of naked bodies managed to squeeze past all the others and jump in through the window. Soon a steady stream was climbing in.

“Is everything ready Echo?” the Captain asked, as he raced up next to her.

“Ready for your word,” she stated.

They were all up in the top tower, on the third floor, in the room with the doctor.

They all put on their backpacks.

Bull helped Melanie put a gasmask on, and then he picked her up.

Rogers and Spice carried one large bubble container between them. The Captain and Jimmy carried the other.

The creatures could be heard running up the stairs, filling the rooms, looking for warm meat. They were only momentarily stopped by the chairs and desks crammed down the second-floor stairwell, tossed down by Bull and Rogers just moments ago.

“Now!” the Captain said.

Echo nodded, and then shouted, “In three, two, one.” She turned the switch on a device she held in her hands.

The blast shook the foundations of the whole building.

30

Noah
Newton Abbot
Between King Street and Fair Field Terrace
11:51 AM GMT

Noah stood on a garden bench, and then jumped onto a small shed, which he used to climb the ten-foot wall at the bottom of the short garden, which was awkward while holding onto a golf club.

On the other side were two large apartment buildings, each with grass around them and a winding road, with lots of parking spaces.

The drop on the other side of the wall was further than the side he just climbed. Scanning the wall, he noticed a lamppost twenty feet away. Noah ran along the top of the wide wall, dropped the golf club down first, and then shimmied down the lamppost.

The place seemed deserted. A few abandoned cars littered the road and a couple on the grass. Suitcases were left were they fell. Some were open, with clothes and belongings spread around them.

Windows were broken on the apartment buildings, with the curtains hanging out of some of them. It was hard to believe that all this could happen in a mere three weeks. It looked like the area had been abandoned for years. The scene reminded him of old war movies, where people had deserted areas quickly, due to an advancing army.

Noah knew someone who he used to work with who had a grandmother that lived here. The two buildings were small old people's apartments. Somewhere they could still have their own independence, but someone could keep an eye on them.

Noah raced across the road, onto the grass, and along the side of the closest building. He glanced into a couple of windows as he ran past. The first few were empty. The third had someone lying on the carpet, next to a tipped over TV; they were bloated beyond recognition.

Noah did not stop; he kept running at a steady pace.

The road led around to the complexes entrance out onto Fair Field Terrace. Noah crouched down next to the wall, while checking the road was clear.

Behind him, a loud explosion destroyed the window – and part of the wall – of where he had just glanced into. He could see the cloud of black spores pouring out of the hole.

His breath was deafening inside the mask. Sweat poured down in the inside of the faceplate.

With another quick check each way, Noah sprinted across the road, down a small alleyway, next to an electrical hardware shop. He came out in a small back alley, behind a row of houses.

A screaming sound made him stop. He crouched down behind a wheelie-bin, with the golf club held across his chest. Noah peered around the large green bin and saw a naked middle-aged man running up the alleyway, chasing a dog.

Noah ran across the short alley. He kicked at a gate, making it fly open. He sprung inside and swung it shut. He rested his back against the wooden gate. He was now inside a small concrete patio area, at the back of another house. Staring through the windows, he did not see anyone. The back door was open and swinging back and forth in the wind.

Inside there was blood everywhere. It looked like a few people had bled out. However, there were no bodies.

Noah did not stop to check any rooms; he ran straight through and out the front door and onto Prospect Terrace.

He crouched down behind a new shaped yellow beetle. A commotion drew his attention up the road. A group of eight or so naked creatures was gathered around something in the middle of the road, feasting.

Noah searched across the street. A couple of houses had their front doors open. One house, halfway up the road, was on fire, belching thick smoke high into the air.

Noah sprinted straight across and into the closest, jumping over the skeletal remains of a man while doing so. He did not stop, but charged straight through, jumping over a chair and around a table. He rammed the backdoor with his shoulder; it flew open, taking one hinge off the door. Once again, he was in a small courtyard at the back of a house.

Movement caught his attention. A naked, dirt covered teenage girl was crouched in the corner, with her back to him. She was ripping apart a small animal of some kind that she had pulled from a wooden hutch.

In a few leaps, he ran along a raised flowerbed, up onto a large water container, which had a pipe from the gutters running into it, and then he jumped onto the wall, and without knowing how far a drop it was, he soared over, before the creature realized he was a bigger, warmer meal.

Noah landed hard, knocking the wind from his lungs. It was only about eight feet, and he rolled as he hit the ground. He did not stop to catch his breath; he simply scooped up the golf club he dropped and carried on running.

Noah could hear gunfire start up in the distance again.

It started to rain, hard and fast. It cut visibility down due to saturating his mask. He had to keep wiping the faceplate with the sleeve of his coat.

Noah realized he was in some kind of large yard, with an old wooden building to one side. A road led out onto Devon Square. Without a backwards glance, he raced along it.

Across the road was a large church, with a towering steeple that could be seen right across the valley. Around the church were grass, trees, concrete, and parking spaces.

Noah darted across the road and into the bushes.

The gunfire was continuous now, and louder, which was almost drowned out by the pouring rain.

Noah was soaking wet and cold. He looked around. There were larger open spaces here, so he would be more vulnerable, but he had to risk it to get to the park. The rain was in his favour, because it was so heavy.

A roaring sound drew his attention. It was a large, white lorry, driving along at the end of the road, heading towards the park. He was too far away to catch their attention, or to see who was driving it. It did not look military; it looked like the sort you would rent for the day to move house.

The sound of the lorry was drawing the attention of some naked creatures that were running behind it. They could not catch it, but continued to follow in the same direction.

Noah ran around the circumference of the church grounds, keeping to the tree line, giving him plenty of cover to duck down behind if he needed to.

Suddenly, a naked figure appeared directly in front of him; he did not see him approach. The eyes caught his attention first, how big they were, and bloodshot, with veins mapping out from them across the checks. Then he noticed the wide stretched mouth, with twisted broken teeth jutting out in all directions. Time seemed to slow down as he soaked in every detail.

Noah did not have time to think; his reflects took over, as he swung with the golf club with all his strength. He hit the old man directly in the head. One minute the naked creature was lunging with outstretch arms, the next he was flying sideways as if being hit by a speeding car. Blood splattered his faceplate, which was washed clean by the pouring rain within seconds.

Without a backwards glance, Noah ran full pelt across the grass, onto the road, and down a junction. The road opened up onto Courtney Park.

The park was large and on a slight incline. There was a children's play area inside a fence, a large pond with a bandstand next to it, and many benches, trees, and plenty of open space. Around three sides were housing, and one side had a main road, with a public toilet and a large train station.

One thing was there that was out of place – the crashed helicopter. It had churned up a large trench, leading to the bandstand, which the twisted hull leaned against. All around it was naked, dead bodies. Blood and gore was everywhere.

Noah crouched behind a small silver Fiat Punto.

He could see where the military was, mainly because it was surrounded by a frenzy of naked creatures. Noah was just deciding how he would approach, or even get to them to let him know he was there, when two things happened simultaneously; the white lorry turned a corner, and an almighty explosion blew fire and dense smoke out of the windows on the bottom two floors of the building.

31

Red, Betty, and Lennie
Newton Abbot, In a House on King Street
11:59 AM GMT

Red ran into the room, not knowing what to expect.

Lennie sat on the couch, protecting the small terrier by hugging it, while rocking back and forth. The dog was whimpering with its head buried under Lennie's arm.

The cause for the smashed window was arms thrashing around, trying to get at the warm bodies inside. It looked like a twenty-something woman, with short black hair. She screamed and grunted while trying to force her way in through the splintered wood and fragmented glass of the window.

Without thinking, Red ran forward swinging the golf club with all her might, similar to using a baseball bat. The end connected with the middle of the woman's forehead; the sound it made was like dropping a watermelon onto a slab of concrete. The naked female shot backwards into the street, landing on her back. Blood pooled around her deformed head. She did not move again.

Screams echoed up and down the street, as more naked creatures headed towards the commotion.

Red pulled the curtains shut, hoping to bide them some time.

There are so many of them all at once, Red thought. *For the last week or so, I thought it was quiet because everyone was hiding, waiting for rescue. But in fact, they were already infected, and slowly changing in their own homes.*

Red swung around. "Lennie, stand up. Go to the kitchen," she shouted.

The giant of a man did not move he just rocked back and forth with his eyes shut tight. The little dog's tail wagged with the sound of a human voice.

"Lennie, move right now."

The man opened his eyes and looked up, as if registering Red for the first time.

"Lennie take the dog into the kitchen. It needs your help."

This seemed to wake the man up. He stood, turned, and headed down the hallway, while muttering, "Protect little doggy."

It sounded like a few creatures were fighting outside, but Red dared not open the curtains.

She quietly closed the front room door and looked around for something to wedge it shut. She noticed a dog lead on a coat hook. She wrapped the lead around a banister rail, then through the hoop and then pulled as hard as she could, and managed to wrap the lead around the front room door handle, and click the link closed over the rigid lead. She then ducked under the line and moved down the hall to the kitchen.

Betty stood over Lennie, checking he was all right. The little dog stared around, wide-eyed at the strangers in its home.

"One smashed the front room window. There is a few outside, fighting among themselves. Or possibly eating the one I just knocked out," Red said as she moved around the table. She checked outside. The yard was empty. There was no way Lennie or Betty would be able to climb the ten-foot wall.

"Don't worry dear," Betty said. "Noah will be back soon with those men with the guns. They will save us." She gave a toothless smile, to reassure Red, as she used a big wooden spoon to stir whatever was in the pot.

A ringing timer went off.

"Turn that off," Red said while trying to dash to the timer to stop its ringing.

"Oh, just another ten minutes and dinner will be ready," Betty said as she moved over and switched off the timer.

I don't think Betty is playing with a full deck of cards; Red thought. *How can she be so calm?* She looked at Lennie as he rocked back and forth, while stroking the small dog.

Just then, a guttural scream echoed throughout the house as the creatures started to pour into the front room. The door rocked as bodies slammed against it. The dog lead held. Then the front door started to shift, knocking the furniture over that Red had piled against it, as arms reached in, smearing blood over the wallpaper and door.

Red pulled the curtain on the back door aside and swung the door open. She looked up at the roof of the kitchen, which was an extension from the main part of the house. It was flat with a railing around it.

"Upstairs," Red said as she ran back in.

"What was that?" Betty questioned.

"Both of you, upstairs now. I have a plan," Red said.

Neither of them moved.

"Lennie, go upstairs, and take the bags with you," Red repeated.

Lennie looked over to Betty, while he stayed seated, stroking the dog.

"It's okay Lennie, do as Red tells you," Betty said while wrapping the blankets back over her shoulders.

"Shame," she muttered, as she left the food on the stove.

Lennie held Charlie under one arm, while swinging Noah's bag onto his back, he then picked up his and Reds in the other large hand.

Betty led the way along the hall. It was a struggle for Lennie to crawl under the stretched dog lead, but he managed it.

The creature's blood covered arms flailed around faster through the gap in the front door, when they heard movement. Their screams intensified.

The door leading to the front room shook from the multiple impacts. The sound of furniture smashing resounded from the closed room.

Red watched Betty and Lennie make their way up the stairs, and then she moved over to the stove. She turned the gas off, so the flame went out, and then turned on all four-gas hobs and the oven. Gas hissed into the kitchen.

Red started rummaging through the draws. She found what she was looking for. She pulled a chair over and wedged it against the table, and put the electric gas lighter on the floor, and with some duct-tape, she found in the same draw, she taped it to the floor, rammed up against the chair so it would not slide backwards.

Perfect, Red thought, as she grabbed a carrier bag off the side and tossed what was on the table into it. She then squeezed through the gap in the door, and pulled the kitchen door shut. She then ducked under the dog lead, swung around the banister post, and sprinted up the stairs two at a time, while avoiding the gap next to the front door. One creature was halfway through, crawling down over the piled up chairs and telephone table.

Lennie and Betty were in the master bedroom. Lennie crinkled his nose up against the rancid, pungent smell.

"Over here," Red said as she barged between them and ripped the curtains to one side. Dust motes filled the room. There was a double door leading out onto a small patio built on top of the kitchen extension. With a kick, the doors swung open.

It started raining hard.

Red opened the bag she was carrying. Inside was her filtration mask and goggles, along with spare goggles for Lennie and Betty. She put hers on.

"Here," she said, while passing the largest goggles to Lennie, then another to Betty.

"Pull your jumpers up, to cover over your mouth and nose," she instructed.

They both slipped on the goggles and pulled their clothing up to cover the lower half of their face.

"Good, now quickly, outside," she said.

"Poor devils," Betty muttered as she looked down at the three corpses under the blanket.

"There isn't much time," Red shouted.

The front door gave way under the onslaught, and as the creatures rushed in, the first couple slammed into the dog lead, pulling it from the handle.

"Out!" Red screamed, and she pushed Betty outside. Lennie stumbled after them.

The patio had wobbly concrete slabs, made slippery by the rain, with a small metal bistro table and two chairs that the rain pinged off. A few plant pots filled the corners.

"Over the rail, onto the roof next door," Red shouted, as her red hair plastered to her face.

The roof joined to the house extension next door. However, the other roof had no patio, just a tiled apex. There was a dip of about four feet down.

Lennie tossed the bags over, then, while still holding onto the dog, swung a leg over. Once he was on the sloping roof, he had no choice but to put the terrier down, while he reached over and lifted his grandmother over.

Red swung her legs over and ducked down below the roofline, and rested her back against the wall.

"You might wanna duck down too," she stated.

Lennie held onto Charlie as he crouched next to Betty.

Red could hear an explosion in the distance. It sounded louder, and different from when the bodies popped. She gave it scant attention; she would have an explosion of her own within seconds, to contend with.

They could hear some creatures running straight up the stairs. Others ran along the hallway, slamming into the kitchen door. The door flew open and hit the electric lighter, which was tapped to the tiled floor. A small flame sparked to life, igniting the gas that filled the kitchen.

The blast incinerated the naked bodies and blew their dusty remains back along the hallway. The fireball filled the corridor, running into the front room and up the stairs; consuming everything in its path.

32

Doctor Lazaro and the Squad
Dentist Clinic
Courtney Park, Newton Abbot
12:07 PM GMT

The whole dentist building shook. The sound was deafening. Thick smoke and dust poured up the stairs, filling the top floor. The building settled, with large cracks running along the upper-level walls. The two floors below collapsed onto themselves, due to the charges placed by Echo. Small, isolated fires burned in the remains of the lower levels.

"Everybody okay?" the Captain asked through the gasmasks communication device. Thick dust swirled around him, making it difficult to see anyone.

A series of affirmative answers returned, stating everyone was fine, apart from their ringing ears.

"If we give it a minute, most of the concrete dust will settle, due to its weight," Echo announced.

Even as she said it, they could see the heavy, grey dust starting to slowly fall like a thick fog.

There was no more animalistic screaming coming from anywhere in the house. The blast momentarily took care of the mob of eaters.

"Is our exit ready Echo?" the Captain asked.

"Yes sir. I blew the hole at the same time as the main blast."

"Then let's move out. I'm sure this has sent out a calling card to every creature within miles."

The Captain waited for Echo to lead the way. She swung the door open, making dust swirl across the ground and back up into the air.

They walked down a short flight of stairs, from the high tower room, down onto a landing. The stairway leading down to the next level was gone, having collapsed down along with the two floors below. All that could be seen was smoke and rubble, with an odd piece of wood sticking out here and there, along with a dentist's chair and the remains of a light unit. There was no longer any color to anything; it was all grey due to the concrete dust.

Echo walked past the remains of a door, which was all twisted and splintered. In the room, adjoining the house next door was a gaping hole – their exit.

They filed through into the top level of the house next door, straight into a large bedroom. The bed was pushed up against the far wall, and the rest of the furniture was reduced to splinters due to the explosives used to create the hole. The bed sheets were burning, along with the curtains and some of the carpet over in the far corner. Everything was also covered in a thick film of grey dust.

They all moved through the room and down some stairs to the next floor down.

The Captain removed a small walkie-talkie from his pocket. “Coco, are you there, over.”

“Reading you loud and clear Captain. I take it you’re in the next house, as arranged if you came under attack. Over.”

“Roger that, Coco.”

“We have just pulled onto the road surrounding the park. Over.” The air filled with static for a moment. “I have a visual on the house. Move to the east-facing window on the first floor. Over.”

“Roger that, Coco.” The Captain placed the walkie-talkie back into his pocket.

“Coco and the others have returned with our transport outta here,” he stated.

They followed him into a medium-size bedroom. It looked like it was a spare room, for visitors. It had a magazine feel to it, as if to impress those who came to visit. The effect was wasted on the people who just walked in.

Echo walked backwards at the rear, in case the house was occupied and a naked creature came charging at them.

The Captain placed the container on the ground and moved over to the large bay window. He could see a large white removal's lorry heading around the circumference of the park, racing through the torrent of rain.

In addition, there was a multitude of naked creatures heading in the direction of the sound of the explosion, and the rising column of dense smoke. There must have been at least fifty or so charging in their direction, with more appearing from adjoining roads and houses as he watched. They looked like they had just been pulled from a shipwreck, naked and soaking wet. A few skidded and fell on the wet grass, and like feral animals, they scurried to regain their footing.

The white lorry cut the corner of the park, bumping over the curb and across the grass. Some of the naked creatures changed direction, heading for the lorry when they saw it. The lorry hit two head on, as they ran directly at the moving vehicle, as if being able to stop its momentum. They disappeared under the front tyres with an explosion of blood and guts.

"Help me with this," the Captain said.

Jimmy, who was stood closest, helped lift the firmly wedged sash window. Below was a large bay window, with a small area covered in beaten lead. Jimmy got out first, and the containers of ammo and equipment was passed to him. Then Bull passed Melanie through. She stood, leaning against the wall, covering her sensitive eyes from the dull sun. There was not room for anyone else; they would file out when the lorry arrived. The rain soaked them within seconds.

The lorry did not seem to slow down as it mounted the curb and smashed through a low wooden fence, and then rip its way through some flowerbeds, and up onto the short front lawn. The lorry skidded to a halt, scraping along the lower bay window.

They now had a large white platform to climb onto.

Jimmy climbed across, through the pouring rain onto the slippery surface that was echoing a tattoo of sound from the downpour.

Bodies slammed into the sides of the truck, jumping, trying to reach the meat above.

Coco, Trev and Franco did not bother lowering the windows to fire at them, there was just too many and would be a waste of ammo.

Everyone was now on the lorry's roof, squatting down as low as possible, spreading out their weight.

Coco had thought of everything; a rope was tossed from one window, then over the roof, and back through the passenger side, and then tied down. Those on the roof had something to hold onto.

Just as the Captain slammed his hand on the roof, to announce they were all on, a screaming drew their attention back to the window they had just climbed out of.

A naked male ran through the bedroom. He could have climbed through a broken window, which shattered during the explosion, or he could have been in the house all along. He dived through the open window, hitting Rogers and Spice, wrapping his arms around both, while sinking his deformed teeth into Rogers' neck. All three tumbled over the side of the lorry, into the throng of creatures below. It became a feeding frenzy – like chum thrown to circling sharks.

Unaware that two of them had fallen off the roof, the lorry revved and pulled away, crushing creatures as it moved.

Everything happened so fast.

The Captain twisted and pulled his gun from its holster. As the truck skidded along the gardens, knocking down fences before bumping back onto the road, the Captain took aim and fired, first to clear some of the naked creatures that were ripping into them, then just another two shots, one through Spices forehead, and one through the back of Rogers' head.

33

Noah
Newton Abbot
Courtney Park
12:14 PM GMT

Noah was crouched in the bushes watching the creatures run past. He could see the white lorry mount the curb and cut across the garden. He witnessed the soldier's climb on the roof, and two of them being knocked off. The lorry then drove off in the opposite direction, away from him.

I will never be able to catch up with them; he thought. *Especially with all the naked creatures chasing them.* Then he had a crazy idea.

What the hell am I doing, he reasoned, as he stood in the pouring rain, behind a bush, stripping off his clothing. He knew it was a risk removing the gasmask, but he had no choice.

He heard a dull explosion from the direction of where he left Red and the others. He ignored it. *Not everything that happens has to have something to do with them*, he thought.

The screaming intensified as the lorry revved and drove off down the road.

Noah concentrated on the moment at hand.

If I cut across the park, I may be able to reach the lorry in time.

He was shaking due to the rain and the cold and being stark naked. He left his clothes in a wet pile, and rested the golf club on top. He pushed his hands into the mud and smeared it over his face and in his hair and over his pasty white body.

Naked, screaming creatures ran past with their feet slapping against the cold, wet tarmac.

Noah pushed aside the bushes, jumped up and ran out onto the road, screaming, following the throng of charging creatures.

Most of the naked bodies were heading towards the remains of the house on the corner; there was a large group on the front lawn.

Noah ignored them and started running straight across the park, heading towards the lorry. He was in luck, as well as the creatures completely ignoring him, there was a car turned on its side, blocking the lorry's exit, and due to there being a thick fence around a bowling green in the park's corner; the driver had no choice but to turn around and head back across the park, directly towards Noah.

34

Red, Betty, and Lennie
Newton Abbot, On a Roof
12:16 PM GMT

The gas explosion ripped away the side of the building, destroying the kitchen and half the wall. The wall they crouched down behind had twisted and buckled, but intact. Small chunks of bricks and stones rained down around them, pinging off the roof tiles. Thick smoke mingled with the heavy rain.

The small dog whined in Lennie's arms.

Betty had her head forward with her hands over her ears.

"Time to go," Red had to shout over the ringing in her ears. The mask muffled her voice. As she stood, she could see how devastating the blast had been. Part of the house had collapsed onto itself. The back wall was also gone, blown out onto a back parking lot.

"Let's go," she said. "We should be able to climb down here no problem." The wall collapsed leaving part of it behind. It would be tricky, but not too difficult to climb down.

In the distance, she could see a thick column of dense smoke rising into the grey sky; mirroring the one she had just created.

Slowly, and carefully, they climbed down the rubble. They stood looking across towards two large apartment complexes.

"We should find somewhere to hide," she stated.

Lennie stood cradling the dog, while holding the other bags. Betty stood mute, with a little blood trickling from both ears.

"Let's go, we don't wanna be out in the open for too long." Red walked at a brisk pace toward the closest building.

The other two followed.

I'm gonna have to let Noah know where we have gone. If he returns and sees the destroyed house, he would think the worst. I will look for somewhere with wi-fi and send a message with Whatapp; she decided.

They needed to get inside, out of sight. The place looked abandoned, with all the smashed up cars and littered belongings.

Red noticed a golf club on the ground. She bent to pick it up. It was scorched black, but otherwise okay. *It must have been tossed by the explosion*, she mused.

"In here," she said.

They were near the closest buildings front entrance. From the intercom system, she could see there were sixteen flats in the block. The chances of running into anything inside seemed much greater because so many people had lived here. However, she knew it would be riskier standing around outside.

The front glass double doors were smashed and hanging open. Blood pooled on the worn carpet and splattered up the wall near the entrance. There was no corpse near it. Red found it hard to believe that someone who had lost that much blood could still walk away.

“In here.” Red moved into a flat that had the door wide open, and was slowly knocking against the wall from the wind blowing along the corridor.

While Lennie and Betty stood just outside the doorway, Red ran around the small flat, to check it was empty. It was not. A bloated body lay on the double bed in the small bedroom, with another bloated body, covered in puss lying on the floor, after possibly rolling off the bed. Both were moaning in pain, and vibrating, as if her presence had triggered off some kind of reaction.

Red swung around to shout a warning to Lennie and Betty, but before the words left her lips, both bodies exploded simultaneously.

Betty slowly got back to her feet; the blast tossed her backwards. Lennie was groaning to her left, with the small terrier stood next to him, licking his face. Bits of plaster rained down from the ceiling.

Betty felt dizzy and disorientated. The air around her was filled with black spores, which was being sucked out the front double doors by the strong wind. Even though her nose and mouth were covered, she still held her breath.

Lennie slowly sat up and picked up Charlie.

"Stay here Lennie." Betty slowly walked through the doorway into the small flat.

The blast was so powerful it had stripped the wallpaper off the walls, and blasted the wooden floor black in places. Glass was sprinkled everywhere from the shattered windows. However, what was most disturbing was Red's motionless naked arm, lying on the floor, poking out from the bedrooms doorway.

35

Doctor Lazaro and the Squad
Newton Abbot
Courtney Park
12:18 PM GMT

Melanie was soaking wet, cold, and frightened. The lorry was bouncing, wheel spinning and skidding along the wet grass. She was lying on the roof of the lorry, holding onto a rope for her life. She could hear the naked creatures screaming around her from all directions. With her other hand, she held onto her jumper, because underneath was the plastic sheaf containing the folder, and all their hope.

The Captain knelt holding onto the rope with one hand and a container with another. He kept seeing the look of horror on Spice's and Rogers' faces as they were being ripped apart.

He knew he had no choice; he knew he had to shoot them, stop their suffering. He just hoped that when the time came, someone would do the same for him.

The truck jolted to one side, making them all leave the roof for a split second before they slammed back down. The driver had to swerve around the rut churned up by the helicopter.

The rain pelted the windscreen hard, blurring Coco's view as he tried to miss bins and ditches. He did not bother avoiding the naked creatures. Blood constantly splashed up over the windshield.

"Get back to the road," Trev screamed.

"What the hell do you think I'm trying to do?" Coco yelled back, while swinging the wheel to one side to avoid a shallow dip and a tree root.

Franco looked like he was going to throw up at any minute. He did not look like he could get any paler.

The truck bounced up onto a wide concrete path that ran along side the large pond. Suddenly, the front wheel dipped, and then caught something. Within a fraction of a second, the truck tipped over, tossing everyone from the roof into the pond. It skidded along, after spinning around when hitting the thick pond wall. It slid along the wet mud, churning up grass. It halted when it slammed into a large oak tree.

One minute Melanie was bouncing on a truck roof, the next she was under water. Her head broke the surface.

Jimmy was floating face down in the water next to her. With what little strength she had left, she rolled him over. She could not tell if he was breathing.

Bull pulled himself out of the pond. His machinegun was clipped to his armoured jacket so it hung by his side. He shook the water from his eyes and gripped the weapon.

The Captain pulled himself out next to Bull. He could hear Echo's voice off to the right.

The creatures caught up with the crashed lorry, and were charging straight at them.

"Doc," Echo shouted, as she pulled Jimmy over to the edge of the freezing cold pond. With the Doc's help, Echo rolled Jimmy onto the wide concrete edge of the pond. Melanie started to give CPR while stood it the water, leaning over him.

A loud creak announced Coco had kicked the twisted door open. The truck was wedged against a tree on its left-hand side. As Coco slowly pulled himself out, he noticed Trev and Franco were not moving.

"Shit!" Coco shouted.

However, he did not have time to check them, because the screaming of the naked creatures running towards them drew his attention.

It had all happened in a mere minute. One moment they were free and getting away, the next they had crashed into the pond and was surrounded by a frenzy of charging creatures that would give no mercy and leave none alive.

36

Noah
Newton Abbot
Courtney Park
12:19 PM GMT

Noah could not believe what he had just witnessed. The lorry had tipped and slammed into the pond before skidding along to hit a tree.

He halted in his shock, before continuing to run again. The rain pelted his bare body.

The naked creatures that charged past him completely ignored him.

The survivors of the crash gathered around the pond firing into the mass of charging creatures.

Even with their hopeless predicament, they were still his and the other's best chance of survival.

As he got closer, he slowed down and started shouting, so as not to be shot by mistake. He waved his arms and screamed, "Help me. I am not one of them. I need your help." He was close enough to get their attention.

A female soldier knelt on the pond's wall, next to woman giving CPR to another soldier.

The soldier raised her rifle and pointed it directly at him. Their eyes locked.

"I'm not infected. I need your help," he screamed, just as Echo pulled the trigger and fired.

PART THREE: INFESTED

37

Noah
Newton Abbot
Courtney Park
Friday January 5th 2013
12:22 PM GMT

Noah closed his eyes and waited for the inevitable bullet that would end his life. He could see the image of the soaking wet female soldier taking aim and firing, and he knew it would be the last image he ever registered.

It's not fair; his mind screamed as his bladder emptied from fear.

There was so much he wanted to do and achieve during his life. Find his soul mate. Fall in love. Create a life. Grow old while watching his grandchildren play. He was too young to die, to have his body left among the twisted naked creatures, to rot, to be forgotten, and be picked at by scavenging birds.

His mind did not flash thousands of past images in slow motion, as you hear some people state, when they have a near-death experience. His mind shot forward calculating all the things he would miss.

However, the logical side of his brain screamed back, *who are you to survive, when all around you lay dead or dying. You're no-one special. You have no more right to live than all those who have already been changed by the spores and who have turned into animalistic hunters. You're nobody – an orphan with no family or friends. You have no special gift that the world needs to save humanity. You're a loner, who locked himself away in a small flat, closing the world outside. The world doesn't need you – no-one does.*

I do want to live; he screamed back.

Noah's eyes were still closed tight. He could see images of Red – her smile, the way she flicked her hair back, her graceful movements. He was shocked when he realized that the grandchildren he visualized had flaming red hair. He had never believed in love at first sight, but he had only known her for about three hours, and already he was dreaming about a future with her in it.

I should never have left her. Now I will never see her again.

All these thoughts took mere seconds.

The rain hammered against his cold, naked body. He could feel the mud beneath his numb toes. The wind against his goosebumps skin.

Nothing happened. No bullet slammed into his head or chest.

Noah opened his eyes and saw the female soldier firing repeatedly in his direction.

Surely, she cannot be that bad a shot. Maybe the mask is affecting her aiming.

Then realization dawned – as he felt the air of the passing bullets on his bare skin, and creatures toppled all around – she was protecting him.

Noah scrambled forward, jumping over a twisted, deformed body, and dodging another as it slapped the earth facedown.

"Down by the wall," the female screamed as she concentrated on the charging mass, peppering them with bullets. Her hand slammed into the side of the SA80 rifle; the magazine fell away. In a swift, reflex move, she grabbed another from a pocket on her thigh and forced it in place. She pulled back on a lever, hit a section on the top, and continued firing.

Noah ducked down below her line of sight and scampered along on hands and feet to the short wall; he forced his wet, naked body up against the freezing cold concrete surface.

Gunfire echoed around him.

Noah could hear another woman screaming, "Come on Jimmy, breathe, damn you!"

As Noah turned back towards the park, he realized just how many creatures were heading towards the pond – it was no longer just a handful, there were hundreds.

38

Red, Betty, and Lennie
Newton Abbot
In an Old Peoples Flat
12:23 PM GMT

Betty headed into the flat over the sticky carpet and then onto floorboards, where Red's arm lay protruding from the bedroom's doorway. Betty scanned the room for danger. There was blood and guts everywhere, up the walls, and over the remains of the furniture. Part of the ceiling collapsed due to the blast, and the large double glazed window was blown out.

Betty slowly lowered herself down on arthritic knees. Her hand went to a vein on Red's neck. She still had a heartbeat.

Red lay on her back, covered in blood and gore. Her hair was matted, and her clothes ripped and torn. However, she had no visible cuts or protruding bones from the exploding bodies. Her mask was still on, even though it had a fracture in the faceplate.

Black spores danced around what was left of the ceiling as they were pulled up to the next floor and out the smashed window by the strong wind.

"Lennie!" Betty called, sounding all muffled due to her top being pulled up over her mouth and nose.

Lennie slowly lumbered in while rubbing his back below the backpack, where he had been tossed backwards onto it.

"Pick her up Lennie," Betty said. Betty stood back to give her grandson room to move.

"Put her in the bath."

The small flat's bathroom was cluttered with lots of pink frilly things. Pink mats upon the floor, with a pink cover over the toilet seat, and a pink shower curtain and toilet roll holder and towels. It strained the eyes. It seemed too ordinary after what had happened in the other room.

"Lay her down softy, there's a good boy."

Lennie slowly lowered Red into the bathtub. Before he left, Betty wiped the blood off his sleeves and hands the best she could.

"Take off your overall and toss it down by the toilet," she said.

Lennie slowly removed the backpack and took off the sodden grey overall. He then moved into the small flat's hallway in jeans and jumper. He then rummaged through his backpack, removed his spare overall, and pulled it on. He liked wearing overalls; it made him feel like a real worker, like Bob the Builder.

Betty then went and wedged shut the front door, and pulled what was left of the bedroom door shut also. She closed the curtains in the front room, even though the window was smashed; it still stopped anything from looking in.

"You sit on the floor there, Lennie, and look after Charlie."

Lennie slowly lowered himself down, blocking the front door from opening, with Charlie snuggled under his arm.

Betty found some black bin bags in the kitchen then returned to the bathroom and shut the door behind her. The water still worked, as she turned the shower on and started to wash the blood and spores off Red's body, clothing and out of her long red hair.

Red did not respond to the sensation of the warm water washing over her.

The bathtub filled with murky water, swirling around Red's body and down the plughole, as Betty cleaned off the mess. She removed the tatty shirt and trousers with a pair of scissors from the medicine cabinet, leaving Red in her skimpy underwear. She cleaned off the blue trainers as best she could. She removed the filtration mask and cleaned it off only after she bagged up all the tatty clothes in a black bin bag. The bathroom seemed safe; the spores in the bedroom had drifted upstairs through the collapsed ceiling and out the smashed window.

The bathroom did not have a window, but it did have a powerful fan in the ceiling, sucking everything up and away. The fan vibrated and was a little noisy, but she had no choice; the light would not work without the fan kicking in as well.

Betty then wiped the bow and arrows clean that lay close to Red's body when she found her. The golf club she had been holding in her hand was twisted by the blast, and the head had snapped off. She rested it next to the bow and arrows; it would still come in handy as a weapon.

Betty looked into the medicine cabinet's mirror. Her dandelion hair swirled around her head. The goggles made her eyes seem huge and bug-like. She pulled them down around her neck. She gave a long sigh. She could hear Lennie playing with the dog. The dog's nails tapped on the floor as it rushed about.

I'm eighty-six, and I'm stood in a stranger's pink bathroom, surrounded by naked zombie type thingies, which either try to eat you or explode over you, and I'm washing blood and gore off a young woman's unconscious body that I only met this morning. And just think I could be stuck in the old people's home, crammed in a smelly rocking chair watching bloody Murder She Wrote *reruns. All the while, the dimwitted care workers – who are telling me what to do when they are young enough to be my great grandchildren – meander around giggling at their phones like schoolchildren about something or other that's been posted on Facebook.*

Betty ran a wrinkled hand through her white hair. She winked at herself in the mirror and smiled.

This beats crappy daytime TV any day of the week.

She then went to search for some new clothes for Red.

The bedroom was a right off, and even if there were clothes in there; they would be shredded by the exploding bodies and drenched in blood.

Betty asked Lennie to shift over so she could go down the hallway to check out some other flats. She did not like the idea of wandering from flat to flat, but she could not leave Red in just her underwear.

When she opened the door, she noticed Red's backpack in the middle of the entrance-way.

Huh, what are the chances of that? Betty thought to herself. She picked the bag up and returned inside.

The only clothes were a pair of jeans and two tee shirts and underwear, but it was clean. It also had a photo of Red and another female, who looked like Red but a few years younger, with an older man and woman stood between them. The woman looked like Red's mother. It was hard to tell if the man was related because his face was obliterated by being rubbed over with a black pen until the photo disintegrated.

Strange, Betty thought. She tucked the photo back in the bottom of the bag.

Betty then went through Lennie's bag and found a dark-blue jumper with a rainbow across the front that dwarfed Red, but would keep her warm.

With Lennie's help, after drying Red and dressing her, she moved her to the front room, laying her on the long couch that still had its protective plastic wrapping over it. After shaking one of the blankets that rested over her shoulders, she laid it over Red's motionless body.

Betty noticed the lump on Red's head when she washed her hair. She perched on the couch next to Red and held her small pale hand.

"Come on dear, time to wake up now," she muttered. She began to rub Red's hand. It was so cold.

The strong wind made the curtains flutter. Betty got up and pulled them tight, while wedging the heavy china angels on the windowsill into the corners to stop the curtains from flapping around.

They didn't help much; she thought as she looked at the statues of the angels. *Where's our God's now?* One china angel held a sword as if ready to defend the weak.

Betty was raised a strict Catholic. She was marched to church every Sunday in her best, regardless of weather or illness. However, unlike the other old people at Mount Pleasants Old Peoples Home, who seemed to grow more religious as their years mounted up and the time to finally find out got closer, Betty grew further away from believing there was a supreme being. In her opinion, there was just too much suffering and hatred in the world.

Marquis De Sade made her mind up when she read one of his books. He wrote, *I think that if there were a God, there would be less evil on this earth. I believe that if evil exists here below, then either it was willed by God, or it was beyond His power to prevent it. Now I cannot bring myself to fear a God who is either spiteful or weak.*

Betty agreed wholeheartedly with his statement, and it forever changed her view about God.

When the outbreak had first started, the TV channels and radio airwaves was full of preachers, priests, and evangelists screaming their beliefs, stating God had judged humanity due to his sins, his violence, his ignorance, his unrepentant ways.

On the second week, as the pandemic spread, and the infected jumped from millions to billions; people started to gather at the high places. Fires sprang up on the peaks around the world, with people screaming in every tongue. They made sacrifices to the Gods, of every type of animal, including human, trying to appease their anger. However, no Gods answered. There was no divine light – no celestial cure. The crowds thinned, and eventually dispersed under the knowledge that they were completely on their own.

The sound of Lennie playing with Charlie in the hallway, as the small dog scurried around, brought Betty back to the present.

Abruptly, the little dog froze while sniffing the air. It moved over to the door, and continued sniffing along the gap at the bottom.

A rubbing sound echoed around the small flat, as something scraped up against the other side of the door.

Charlie started growling, and the fur on his neck stood on end.

39

Doctor Lazaro, Noah, and the Squad
Newton Abbot
Courtney Park
12:26 PM GMT

"Doc, how's he doing?" Echo shouted over her shoulder, as she continued to pump bullets into the charging mass of naked creatures while quickly swiping water off her gasmasks faceplate.

"He's breathing, but only just," Melanie responded, while placing Jimmy in the recovery position. Her body ached and shook from the cold water.

Jimmy coughed up the water from his lungs, and now lay upon his side, unconscious. His mask flew off in the crash. She could not find it in the murky, churned-up water.

Melanie might be cold and aching, but the freezing water succeeded in waking her up. It was just the kick she needed to shake off the last effects from the drugs the nurse had pumped into her, and apart from a banging headache, she felt almost normal.

"Behind you Bull," the Captain shouted.

Bull spun around, while firing round after round. A naked middle-aged man plunged into the pond behind them, after tipping over the green railing that ran along one side. He floated to the surface with a blossoming red halo around his head.

"There's just too many of them," Bull screamed back, as the torrential rain poured down his faceplate.

The ammo container that was on the roof along with them bobbed up and down on the choppy ponds surface.

Coco stood braced against the truck's door. There was no point checking on Franco and Trev, because the low-lying branches had punched through the windscreen and then through them.

So far, the creatures had ignored him, and were charging towards the gunfire.

Coco checked the truck's cab. He could not see his machinegun; all he could see was splintered branches, ruined flesh, and lots of blood and pulp. He only had a Browning's pistol on him. He unclipped the handgun and held it in his cold grip. The rain pinged off the truck's metal surface. He was soaked to the skin.

He saw the naked male running and screaming towards the others. It was a neat trick, making the creatures think he was one of them. Pity it would not work for everyone.

Coco could see the Captain and Bull to one side, with Echo and Doc to the other, with

Jimmy lying between them. However, he could not see Spice or Rogers.

Coco jumped down onto the wet grass, and ducked behind the overturned lorry. He needed to reach the others; he stood a better chance if they all remained together.

At least, the rain is working in our favour; he thought. *The downpour will stop the spores from floating around.*

Just then, a female child of about eleven changed direction and ran straight at him. The rain washed away the blood and dirt; she looked almost normal.

Coco raised his gun.

This is someone's daughter. Someone raised her, loved her, and taught her right from wrong. Now she's a delivery device for a fucking plant!

Coco watched as the thin naked child jumped the curb, racing across the slippery grass with guttural screams emanating from her wide throat. Her eyes were twice the size they should be, with veins holding her fractured skull together. Her throat was bloated and red, with a large deformed circular mouth with ruptured teeth protruding in all directions. Her features were pure animalistic; no human emotions remained – just hunger.

Coco pulled the trigger. The bullet went through her open mouth, exploding out the back of her head. She thudded to the grass, slid along, and hit a tree root. She lay unmoving, bleeding out.

"Forgive me," he whispered.

"Doc, get that ammo container open, we need more bullets," the Captain shouted.

"On it," Melanie screamed back. She felt like she should be doing more.

I could be holding a gun at least. I have never fired one before, but how hard can it be – point and shoot. I've watched someone do it a thousand times in the movies. Hell, people are doing it right in front of me.

She waded through the freezing water. The rain was hard, splashing up into the faceplate. It was difficult to believe she was in a chest high pond about the size of a tennis court; it felt like she was in the ocean.

Melanie reached the bobbing container and started to drag it to the side. She tripped on something, possibly pondweeds. Her head went under for a second. It also felt like something large brushed up against her leg.

How big are the fish in this pond?

Gunfire echoed around her, distorted from the water in her ears. She managed to reach the wall. She could not lift the container out by herself; it was just too heavy, so she wedged it against the wall with her body and fumbled with the metal catches. She managed to swing the lid open after the second attempt. It was full of ammo magazines. It also had a few weapons held against the inside of the lid by webbing.

Echo stood up, while still firing, and jumped over Jimmy's body, and walked along the wall to Melanie.

"Those," Echo pointed, before returning her finger to the trigger.

Melanie pulled five magazines from the container and started filling Echo's wide pockets.

Echo slapped her gun; the empty magazine fell over the side of the wall, clattering onto the concrete path.

"Another," Echo screamed, without taking her eyes off the approaching mass.

Melanie smacked a full mag into her hand.

Within seconds, Echo was firing again.

"Get the same type over to the Captain and Bull," Echo shouted over the sound of the rain, wind, and screaming creatures as she made her way back to Jimmy's side.

Melanie gripped the container and then waded through the water over to the other two. Once again, something large brushed against her leg. She glanced down just in time to see a golden-red, scaled back. She felt relieved; she half expected a creature to leap from the water.

"Here!" Melanie screamed while stacking magazines next to the Captain and Bull.

"Thanks," Bull shouted.

The Captain concentrated on the charging creatures.

Melanie fumbled with the webbing, and finally got a Browning's pistol free. She turned it over in her hands. *It looks so easy when they cocked and loaded it on the TV,* she thought. She gripped the top and pulled it back. It was harder than it looked. With effort, she finally got it cocked. It was also heavier than she thought it would be. She gripped it with both hands.

"Behind you," the Captain shouted. He had evidently witnessed what Melanie was doing in his peripheral vision.

Melanie spun around.

A bloated thirty-something female, who had obviously already been feeding, was wading across the pond towards them with her arms outstretched.

Melanie raised the gun in both hands.

She's already gone. She's been taken over by the host virus. She's just an empty shell being used for transport, nothing more. She will kill and eat me without a moment's hesitation.

Melanie's finger gripped the trigger. The heavy gun shook in her cold grip.

The pouring rain bounced back up from the choppy ponds surface.

I have no choice. I have no choice. I have no choice, she repeated like a Tibetan mantra.

The naked female thrashed across the pond towards her.

Melanie aimed, closed her eyes, and pulled the trigger. Nothing happened.

"Release the safety," Bull shouted. "It's a little lever on the top."

Melanie fumbled with the gun. It was so heavy, and her hands were so cold. She found the lever and twisted it. She gripped it again in both hands and pointed it at the thrashing female.

BAM!

The first bullet hit the female in the shoulder, spinning her around. However, it did not slow her down.

BAM! BAM!

Two more shots, one in the chest and one straight through the females left eye. The woman tumbled backwards, and floated on the water, surrounded by her own expanding ring of blood.

"You're a pro, Doc," Echo shouted. "Remind me not to piss you off now you have a gun."

Melanie grabbed some magazines from the container, and then slammed it shut. She did not know how many bullets were in each magazine, or how to change it once it ran out; but one-step at a time.

Melanie lined up the sights and pulled the trigger again. Another naked body hit the grass.

It is just like an arcade game; she reasoned, while trying to divert her mind from the fact that she was shooting real people.

"We need to pull back into a building again. We are sitting ducks out here," Bull shouted.

The charging horde was unrelenting. They were appearing from side roads and from across gardens and out of smashed windows and broken doors.

Noah was freezing cold, crouched up against the ponds slimy wall. His body was shaking uncontrollably.

A hand appeared over the lip of the wall holding a handgun.

"You still alive down there naked guy?" a voice called.

"What?" Noah was at the first stages of hypothermia, and his mind was finding it hard to concentrate on anything other than screaming at him about the cold.

"Do your hands work?" the voice screamed down.

"I-I-I g-guess," he stuttered with the cold.

"Then stand the hell up, take this gun, and bloody well help us!"

Noah climbed to his feet. "I'm cold and naked," he mumbled in defense. He saw the female soldier that had saved him holding a gun out with one hand, while still firing the rifle with the other. She also looked cold and wet.

Noah was not cowering and hiding due to nerves; he did not want to bundle up into a ball and hope the world sorted itself out. It was just that he was so cold, numb, and lethargic, and it was such a relief to be near someone who could defend him with real weapons, that all the adrenaline that had been keeping him going all morning had washed away. He felt completely drained. He was too tired to even be embarrassed that he was stark naked in front of a female stranger.

"Do you think they give a shit if you're cold, wet, and naked? Do you think that will stop them from ripping you apart and eating you while you're still alive?"

Noah reached for the gun with wet, muddy hands. An image of Red, Betty, and Lennie came up in his mind. They were counting on him to save them.

Stop feeling sorry for yourself.

"Is it all ready to go?" he questioned, while spitting water from his mouth.

"Just point and shoot."

Noah spun around, and was once again overwhelmed with the amount of creatures charging at them. He lifted the gun in both hands, aimed it at a naked skinny man – who had his right arm missing – and fired. Years of video games had honed skills he never knew he had in the real world. The bullet hit the man right between his disfigured eyes.

"Now that's what I'm talking about," Echo shouted.

As if he was playing *House of the Dead*, Noah used only one bullet per creature; all were headshots. Noah concentrated on those closest to him. He only had a handgun, and he did not know how far the bullets would go and still be deadly.

Movement by the crashed truck caught Noah's attention. He almost pulled the trigger, then he realized the man had army clothes on. The black man sprinted across the gap, firing at the creatures as he ran.

"Glad you could join us, Coco," Echo shouted. "Where are Trev and Franco?"

"They didn't survive the crash," he stated, as he turned and continued firing.

Echo said no more, she just concentrated on taking down one creature at a time; she would mourn them later with a bottle of Jack.

It seemed hopeless. It almost felt like every creature in the area was heading in their direction. For every one they shot; three more ran around the corner.

We need a miracle to survive. We cannot keep this up for long. Even with the container, we will eventually run out of ammo, Echo thought. She was so tired and cold. Her fingers were going numb, and she had to concentrate on just pulling the trigger. Her bullets were already going wide because the rifle was becoming heavier with every passing minute.

Melanie managed to pull herself out of the pond. Her legs were almost numb from the cold. She leaned over Jimmy, checking he was still breathing. Every now and then, she would aim and pull the trigger, taking a creature down. However, the gun was getting heavy, and it was difficult to see the blurs of pink flesh running along due to the rain lashing against her mask.

The Captain was shaking from the cold. His body was so numb he could no longer feel his limbs. A moment ago, he rattled off a long blast on the machinegun, not because the two figures charging towards him warranted so many bullets, but because his numb finger would not let go of the trigger.

A beeping sound drew his attention. It was not loud, just out of place among the screaming and gunfire. The beeping was coming from the field radio strapped to Bull's back.

"Captain," Bull shouted. He was unsure if the Captain had heard the beeping over the noise around them. Bull spun around to give the Captain access to the radio.

The Captain pulled the headset away from the waterproof casing. He forced it over his head.

"We need backup!" he screamed at whoever was on the other end of the military line.

40

Red, Betty, and Lennie
Newton Abbot
In an Old Peoples Flat
12:49 PM GMT

Betty was on her feet and at the door in seconds. She lifted up the small terrier and Sshhhhed it, and then gripped her hand over the dog's snout to stop it barking. Charlie froze in her hands as if aware a predator was close.

Lennie seemed to understand something was wrong as he placed both hands over his mouth, as his eyes stretched wide.

Outside the scraping continued on the door. Then suddenly there was a thud as something hit the floor hard. Then nothing.

It did not sound like the frantic movements of a naked creature, which if it had heard them, it would be flinging itself against the door and blaring like a wild animal. It almost sounded like someone was injured.

"Take the dog," Betty whispered.

Lennie took Charlie and held him close.

There was a spy-hole set in the door. Betty twisted her neck to put her eye to the lens. The fisheye lens distorted everything. There was a figure on the ground, but it was hard to tell anything else.

"Shift over," she said quietly.

Lennie shuffled along the floor, allowing Betty to open the door a little, very slowly.

The dog started to whine.

As she cracked the door an inch, Betty could see two slippered feet pointing in her direction. It was an old man.

Betty quickly swung the door open, and was about to run out to help him to his feet, when she noticed he was staring at the ceiling with wide deformed eyes.

Infected! her mind screamed. She shut the door quietly, locked it and put the chain across, and then got Lennie to lean his bulk against it.

We need to get somewhere safe; this place is obviously riddled with the different stages. She wondered how long it would be before the old man turned, stripped off his clothes and started hunting for flesh.

She put a finger to her chapped lips to signal Lennie to sit quietly. Betty moved back into the front room to check on Red. She was still out cold, but her hands had warmed up, and she had a bit of colour in her face.

Betty was deciding on what to do when a loud noise startled her. Beyond the door – out in the building's entrance hall, where the old man lay – an animalistic sound echoed around the confines of the corridor.

Betty ran to stand next to Lennie.

The dog was whining, with its head buried under Lennie's arm. Lennie sat rocking back and forth with his hands over his ears.

Betty looked through the spy-hole.

Outside, three creatures had found the comatose old man and were ripping into his body. The fisheye lens distorted their naked bodies as they set about chewing off his skin.

Betty pulled away from the lens, while fighting back the urge to vomit, as the sound of tearing flesh and snapping bones echoed around the small flat.

41

Doctor Lazaro, Noah, and the Squad
Newton Abbot
Courtney Park
12:51 PM GMT

"We are at your six. We have room for two on the bird. Over," the voice stated.

Suddenly, the pond's water was not just choppy; it was a tempest, as a large military helicopter came to hover overhead. It was the same type as their crashed chopper – a Merlin Transport Helicopter. In addition, suspended below the large helicopter, on thick cables, was a utility flat bed husky all-terrain vehicle.

The pilot hovered over the road and released the lines. The thickset vehicle bounced as it dropped a half meter to the tarmac, crushing a fallen creature. The cables whipped and snapped around. One cable decapitated a creature and severed a leg off another, until the cables settled on the wet road.

"Captain, we will help you clean up a little. Roger." As the voice said this, the helicopter moved forward to hover overhead. The large .50 mm miniguns suspended beneath the cockpit started to whine and spin, they then started churning out thousands of rounds per minute. The pulsating sound was deafening.

The bodies of the charging creatures no longer tumbled over; the larger powerful bullets obliterated them. Heads disintegrated and limbs evaporated, as the helicopter arched around in a circle, mowing everything down with devastating accuracy. The .50 mm bullets churned the earth up; mud flew high into the air, mixed with blood, and shattered bones. Tree trunks cracked open, and tree limbs severed and fell to the wet ground, as pine needles filled the air along with spraying blood.

The squad lowered their weapons, as they were no longer needed. They gathered together. They could not talk though because of the sound of the machineguns suspended above. Steam rose from the ponds rough surface as thousands of hot casings landed in the cold water.

The Captain had to use hand signals to get the squad's attention. He motioned to Jimmy and Echo as the Doc started to get him ready to load aboard.

Melanie was expecting it, but it was still a relief when the Captain pointed at her. He outlined a square with a finger, meaning the folder. Melanie pulled up her jumper; the folder was inside the waterproof sheaf, tucked into her waistband.

Then realization dawned that she was going to leave behind the people who had sacrificed so much to protect her. Four people died within the last hour, and eleven at the university. In addition, Jimmy was unconscious with pasty white skin, and his breathing was shallow.

The helicopter pulled back. Compartments opened in the underbelly, and three sets of double large wheels lowered down on hydraulics. It landed next to the husky, on the road skirting the huge park.

Everyone fanned out; guns raised, ready to pick off any stragglers. There were one or two, but it seemed like the vast wave was quelled for the moment.

The Captain walked forward a little as the large back hatch slid open, revealing a collection of civilians sitting strapped in. A soldier – one of the four aircrew – jumped to the ground and jogged to where the Captain was standing.

"Captain." The soldier saluted.

The Captain gave a halfhearted salute in return; his arms were aching and cold, and the rain still lashed down.

"General Philips managed to contact us and divert us to your last-known position, via the transponder on your helicopter. Luckily, we were transporting civilians and a husky when they were eventually able to contact us." If the soldier had noticed the crashed helicopter, all twisted and spread across the ground behind them, he did not mention it.

"You said something about having room for two?"

"Yes sir, the General wants his daughter to be one of them, so the other will obviously be the individual you were sent to pick up."

"I'm not going! Jimmy needs medical attention, and this may be his only shot at an evac," Echo said while wiping water from her faceplate.

"I have my orders," the soldier stated.

"I don't care about your orders," Echo said, spinning away from the Captain to confront the soldier.

Gunfire echoed behind them as Bull took down a lone naked runner.

The soldier flinched. He was nervous and unhappy that he was stood in the rain, surrounded by so much death. In addition, he was a little concerned that he was not wearing a gasmask.

"Doctor Melanie Lazaro was our main objective. She has important information."

Melanie stood next to Coco, who had Jimmy in his arms.

The soldier nodded at the Doc and pointed to an empty seat.

"First class to Dartmoor Prison," the Captain said.

Emotions boiled to the surface. There was so much Melanie wanted to say. There was so much she wanted to thank them all for. She realized how much life had been shed in her name, for her sake, and a simple folder. However, as she went to open her mouth, she could not think of any words. Everything seemed so inadequate.

"We shall see you soon," Echo said, while resting a hand on Melanie's arm. "We will take the armoured husky, and we should rendezvous at the base within the next hour or so."

Melanie flung her arms around Echo and squeezed tight. Then she hugged the Captain. She still had not uttered a word. She then muttered thank you into the Captains ear. She then turned and jogged to the helicopter. Tears streaked the inside of the mask.

"Private Philips," the soldier said, motioning for Echo to follow the doctor.

"Sorry you have the wrong person," Echo said.

"Pardon?"

"No Private Philips here." Echo stood ramrod straight, with her rifle at her side.

The Captain did not say a word.

The rain pounded the tarmac at their feet. The soldier could have pointed out that her name was stitched onto her jacket, or that he had seen a picture of her, sent along with the orders. Instead, he said, "That's what your father said you'd probably say." He spun around to Coco.

"Place him on the floor by the hatch."

Coco carried Jimmy to the waiting helicopter.

"The husky is fueled and the remote controlled 12.7mm machinegun is fully loaded."

Gunfire announced another creature had been gunned down.

The Captain nodded.

"I have three friends, waiting to be rescued," Noah stated.

The soldier had noticed the naked twenty-something man stood to one side, holding a handgun over his groin, but decided it was not his problem.

The Captain nodded. "We will collect them on the way."

Coco loaded Jimmy, making him as comfortable as possible.

"Hopefully we shall see you soon," the soldier stated as he saluted for the last time.

"Any message for General Philips?" he asked looking at Echo.

"Tell him I will see him shortly." Echo turned to look over towards Melanie as the Doc bent over, fussing with Jimmy.

The soldier turned and jogged back; he jumped up and slid the hatch shut. The wind picked up as the blades kicked up a notch. The helicopter ascended slowly, leaving the Captain, Echo, Bull, Coco, and Noah to watch it leave them all behind.

The Captain wasted no time. "Bull, prepare the vehicle."

42

Red, Betty, and Lennie
Newton Abbot
In an Old Peoples Flat
12:57 PM GMT

Betty could not block out the sound of the creatures eating outside the front door.

Lennie sat hugging Charlie, while rocking back and forth. The small dog was shaking in terror.

They could not leave via the front door, and the windows were too high off the ground for them to safely climb out. In addition, the shattered windows had jagged edges sticking out, and there was no way they could get Red through.

The only option was up. The bedroom ceiling had collapsed, and with a little effort, they could climb to the flat above. Betty had decided that if they made it to the roof, they could barricade the door, and it would be the perfect location to spot Noah's return. From the high roof, they would be able to see the old ruined, burning house, and the location Noah disappeared in. That is if the rain was not pouring too hard.

While the creatures fed outside, with the wet sound of tearing flesh, and the content moaning of wild animals getting their fill, Betty tapped Lennie on the shoulder and motioned for him to follow her.

They quietly made their way into the front room.

"Put your pack back on, and give me the dog," Betty whispered. She then emptied the few remaining items from Red's bag into Noah's. It was heavy, but with Lennie's help, she struggled to get it on. Betty looked at the dog and then placed it on the carpet.

Lennie gave her a hurt look, possibly afraid they were going to leave Charlie behind.

"The little blighter has four legs; I'll be damned if I'm gonna carry the lazy bugger," she whispered.

Lennie slowly picked Red up. She looked like a china doll in his thickset arms, resting against his large chest.

Betty hooked Red's bow over Lennie's wide shoulders, and wedged the arrows into the top of his pack. Betty picked up the golf club minus a head, then walked over and shoved open the bedroom door, and led the way up the collapsed wall, furniture, and ceiling rubble. It was tricky going for Betty with her arthritis, and heavy bag – which she contemplated on just shrugging off her shoulders, but she managed to pull herself up onto the first floor, into a hallway leading into another front room. She just hoped that whatever was in the bag was important.

Lennie's large feet found easy footing in the masonry rubble. The little dog bounced and danced around their feet.

The flat was empty. A lot of the furniture was missing, and clothes littered the floor, as if the owners had packed up and left in a hurry.

Betty stood looking out the spy-hole onto another corridor. The fisheye lens only showed a few meters to either side. Betty pressed her ear to the door.

Slowly, she cracked the door a little. Stale air rushed in. She pulled her jumper up more. She turned to check Lennie's goggles and jumper were in place, and that Red's mask had not slipped to one side.

Betty poked her head out of the doorway. The hallway was empty.

Now which way?

To one end, she could see an elevator and stairs. She strained her hearing.

Nothing.

Without warning, the small dog shot out from between her legs and pelted down the corridor. The terrier bounded along, whipping passed doorways. It reached the end of the corridor, sat down, and started scratching behind one of its scruffy ears.

Betty waited for a few seconds.

If there were any naked creatures around us, in one of the rooms, then they would be chasing the small ball of fur, trying to snack on the little flea ridden mongrel.

There was no sound of crashing furniture or pounding feet.

Betty slowly inched out of the doorway and headed towards the small dog, which was standing, wagging his tail, with its little pink tongue hanging out its mouth.

Lennie trailed along behind.

A soft murmur issued from Red's lips.

Betty did not have time to check on her; Red would have to wait until they were all safely on the roof.

There were flat's on either side of the hallway. A couple of doors were shut, but three were open. Betty walked passed them slowly, inching along, while gazing in, waiting for any telltale signs that there was life within, and whether that life was actively seeking food.

So far, so good, she thought.

The small ragtag group reached the stair-well at the end of the corridor.

Just as Betty was about to pull the heavy fire door open, the small dog cocked its head, its ears pricked up, and it started to whine.

Betty could sense something was wrong.

The small dog started growling.

Unexpectedly a loud explosion rocked the floor, as a wall halfway down the corridor collapsed into the hallway. Black spores danced in the concrete dust filled air.

Bloody hell, there must have been a bloated body just inside the flat, and as we passed we set it off.

Betty gripped the fire door and swung it open. The spores drifted along, heading towards them because of the suction of wind up the stairwell.

"Lennie, quickly!"

Lennie turned Red sideways so as not to whack her head on the doorframe. As he darted through, Betty was quick to follow as she pulled the door closed. However, the fire door mechanism caught as is slowed the door down to stop it slamming.

Betty looked through the small glass pane as the black spores rushed along the ceiling, churning toward the open door. With just a few meters to go, the door clicked shut.

Betty almost sank onto the floor with relief. However, in the haste to get the fire door shut, she had not noticed the little dog was growling, with its body pointed down the stairwell.

The screaming echoed off the stark stairwell walls, reverberating up the levels. Then, there was the sound of bare feet slapping against the steps, heading up the stairs.

43

Doctor Lazaro
6,000 Feet over Newton Abbot
Heading Northwest to Dartmoor
1:11 PM GMT

Melanie was wrapped in a warm blanket, and found herself inside a helicopter for the second time that day. In all the mayhem, and rescue, she forgot about the last flight and its outcome. Her hands gripped the webbing that held her in place.

Jimmy was still unconscious and strapped to a stretcher on the metal floor. The soldier put an IV drip in his arm.

Melanie looked around. This time, instead of being full of soldiers in military combat gear, the hull was full of civilians – men and women of different ages. They all looked like parents because they all had one child sat between or next to them.

It did not make sense. None of them were injured, or looked sick.

Why are they being transported to the Dartmoor military base?

The dull throbbing of the blades reverberated through the metal hull and against her back.

Melanie peered out the small window. The last time she had looked out a similar window, naked creatures were charging across the grass towards her. She could not see anything through the grey, pouring rain.

She turned to stare at the closest woman who sat to her right.

The healthy woman looked about twenty-five; she was Caucasian and had long silky mouse coloured hair with piercing blue eyes. She was dressed in neat, casual, ironed clothes. She was holding the hand of a little girl who was her spitting image.

Melanie leaned forward.

The woman noticed Melanie was going to say something, so she leaned sideways. The woman's clean hair cascaded around her spotless cashmere jumper and expensive coat.

"Who are you all? Why are you being taken to the Dartmoor military base?" she shouted to be heard over the roar of the rotors.

"I am the same as everyone else on the flight," she stated, while smiling, showing off her perfect white teeth. "I am part of the Adam and Eve project."

44

Noah and the Squad
Newton Abbot
Courtney Park
1:13 PM GMT

Noah sat in the back of the Husky along with Coco and Echo. Bull was driving with the Captain in the command seat.

As they were preparing to leave the park behind, along with their four fallen comrades and the crashed helicopter and truck, Noah introduced himself, and thanked them for their help. He then explained where he had left his clothing.

The park seemed deserted, with just a handful of naked creatures feeding on the remains of the dead. Now there was no gunfire, there was nothing to attract their attention.

The Husky pulled up next to a bush near a large church. Noah jumped out, followed by Echo and Coco. They took up a protective stance. Noah appeared from behind the bush dressed in soaking wet clothes, with his mask on. He left the golf club on the ground now he carried a gun.

Noah climbed in first, with Coco and Echo to either side, so they could use the glass firing ports in the windows if they were attacked.

With Noah's directions, they left Devon Square behind and headed down Queen Street. The truck maneuvered around the burnt out, abandoned cars, and piled up debris.

As they passed a pizza restaurant on the left, a naked creature ran out of the open door and hurled itself at the truck's bonnet.

Bull never stopped; he continued on, running over the naked woman. The truck bounced as it crunched over her body.

"Down there," Noah said as they slowly drove up King Street.

"That one," Noah said while pointing.

"Coco and Echo, take Noah in to retrieve his friends. Bull and I will stay with the truck."

The Captain was not sure why he was taking time to help the young man and his friends, especially when there was a whole town full of people that needed his help. However, he would do what he could. If he could save just a handful of people while making his way to the base, he would.

Then again, he reasoned, *with the amount of creatures charging us at the park, this man and his friends might be all that's left in this dead town.*

As the truck rolled to a stop, Coco and Echo jumped from the vehicle, with their weapons up and ready at their shoulders.

Noah climbed out slowly. He could not believe how fast, agile and alert the soldiers were.

They must be just as tired and wet as I am, he thought.

He knew something was wrong as soon as he saw the front of the house. When he had first spotted it, he had not registered the devastation. The front room window was blown out, with black scorch marks up the wall, with burnt, twisted curtains flapping against shards of glass. The front door was pushed in, with blood smeared everywhere.

Please God do not let that be Red's blood.

Coco took the lead. Slowly, he climbed over the barricaded front porch area and stood motionless, listening in the hallway.

Noah climbed in second, with Echo protecting their backs.

"God!" Noah whispered as he stepped into the hallway next to the stairs. All the wallpaper was burnt off the walls. The carpet was still smoldering. There had been a quick, flash fire. Bodies littered the hall, all twisted and black, with sticky puddles of boiled body fluids gathering around each one – the flash fire had crisped the outside, leaving the inside to slowly drip out.

It was impossible to tell if any of them were Red or Betty. However, Noah was confident none of them was Lennie; they were all simply too small. If Lennie was not here, then there was a good chance the other two were not either. In addition, he could not see any burnt clothing – all the corpses were naked.

With the smoke rising from the charred bodies, they were all glad they had gasmasks on.

Next, they moved into the kitchen.

"There," Echo pointed with the rifle's barrel. They could see the gas lighter melted to the floor from the blast that had engulfed the house and had blown the kitchen wall into the backyard.

"This was rigged," Coco stated.

It was good news. Someone had orchestrated the fire, so there had been planning, so they could have had time to escape. So hopefully the bodies in the hallway were not the people they were looking for.

"Report," the Captain said over the communications devices embedded inside Coco an Echo's gasmasks.

"We are still checking. It looks like they are gone after they set a trap for a bunch of eaters," Echo said.

"We are going to check upstairs," Coco stated.

Upstairs was deserted, apart from the three bodies in the bed. Smoke still lingered from the fire, but little was damaged, just mostly scorched. They found the bedrooms patio doors wide-open.

"Here." Echo pointed.

Down over the side against the wall was a dog collar.

"Charlie," Noah said. "It belongs to a dog we found inside the house."

Noah looked down over the collapsed wall, over across the parking lot toward the old people's housing.

"They're in there," Noah stated.

Just as he said that, an explosion shattered the windows on the second floor within the building closest to them.

45

Red, Betty, and Lennie
Newton Abbot
In a Stairwell at the Old Peoples Flats
1:24 PM GMT

"Quickly Lennie, go up!" Betty shouted.

The screaming intensified. Bare feet could be heard slapping against the tiled stairwell.

There were only two floors for the creatures to race up, which they seemed to be doing with the phenomenal speed of rabid wild animals.

Lennie was in front, jogging up the stairs two at a time, with Betty close behind.

"Bugger this," Betty said, while shrugging Noah's bag off her back. Whatever was in it was not worth dying for.

The creature's bodies could be heard slapping against the walls as they hurled themselves around the stairs, only one flight below.

We will never make it in time; Betty thought. *I'm too old and Lennie's too slow. At least, we will be together at the end.*

Charlie though seemed to have realized the situation was different. He was no longer shaking with terror, or hiding; he was standing his ground, growling. Then in one bound, he was gone, shooting down the stairwell.

The screaming intensified when the creatures spotted the four-legged meal.

Lennie was breathing hard when he reached the fire exit to the roof, and with a mighty kick, he sent the door swinging open.

Betty was close behind.

Lennie stood in the pouring rain while holding Red in his arms.

Betty was in the process of swinging the fire door closed, just as Charlie shot through like a bullet from a gun. He had only confused and distracted them for a few seconds, but that was all that was needed to allow them to reach the door.

Betty checked the door. She held the metal shaft of the broken golf club, but here was nothing to force it into, to wedge the door shut. Her eyes scanned the roof; there was not a scrap of heavy furniture to barricade against the exit.

"Put Red down," Betty shouted.

Lennie lowered Red's comatose body onto the wet roof, and then shrugged the packs and bow from his back.

"Wedge your shoulder against the door Lennie," Betty screamed, just as the first creature rammed the exit.

Lennie ran and slammed against the door.

The creature's body had obviously hit the door bar, because it was swinging open, with a grasping arm thrashing around from the side.

Lennie hit the door like a freight train, forcing the door closed so hard it severed the arm just above the elbow. The arm twitched on the ground, while Lennie used all his strength to hold them back. However, many creatures were flinging their bodies against the other side of the door.

Betty looked around again. There was nothing on the roof, no covered areas, no large air-conditioning units, no air vents, and no small storage unit, nothing; the roof was completely exposed. They were trapped with nowhere to hide.

46

Doctor Lazaro
6,000 Feet over Dartmoor
1:27 PM GMT

Melanie was confused. The woman said no more and had returned to simply sitting, waiting to arrive at their destination.

The phrase, Adam and Eve sounded ominous. Whenever a biblical reference was given to something, it always took on a completely different meaning. To Melanie, the words invoked something new – a new beginning. With everything, that was happening throughout the world it sounded out of place and surreal, almost menacing.

After a few minutes, she removed her gasmask. She felt stupid wearing it – it felt wrong sat wearing one when everyone else looked so normal. She placed it on her wet lap. Rainwater gathered around her trainers.

Melanie looked around. These people seemed prepared for something. This was no thrown together group this was organized. They all looked content, not scared, and confused. These people knew exactly what was happening and where they were going and why; and that scared Melanie even more than if they were all crying and scared senseless.

Melanie had no idea how long a helicopter flight would take from Newton Abbot to Dartmoor. She knew the Moors were a vast four hundred square mile national park. She also knew that the Ministry of Defence owned large sections of the land, using it as training grounds for soldiers and weapons.

Living in Exeter, she had been to Dartmoor on numerous occasions. The scenery was beautiful, rolling hills, rambling brooks, and waterfalls, vast tracks of woodland and spidery ferns, and massive outcrops of rocks on the peaks, pushed up by violent upheavals millions of years past.

She went many times as a child during wintertime to play in the snow. The snow was only ever a dirty sprinkling in Exeter, but on the moors in was deep and pure white. Thousands invaded the moorland when it snowed. Parents stood in thick jackets watching their kids play on sledges. The sides of roads and car parks were wedged tight with vehicles.

In the summer months, climbers converged on the large rocky outcrops, and the rolling scenic hills attracted walkers of all ages. The moors were a welcome break from the over-crowded cities and towns; a place people could go to unwind and relax.

Melanie had many happy memories of the moors. Just two weeks before all the madness started; she had gone on a long drive over the moors just to relax and clear her mind. She parked in an area called Badgers Holt and walked down the riverbank. She had a picnic in the car, because it was too cold to eat outside.

Melanie stared at the blurry grey clouds out the small window. Rain pelted against the hull.

So much has changed since that day. So many have died and were dying. The world would never be the same again.

Melanie realized something had changed. The helicopter had slowed down. It was no longer heading forward, but downward.

They had reached Dartmoor Prison, England's largest top-secret military base.

47

Red, Betty, and Lennie
Newton Abbot
On the Roof of the Old Peoples Flats
1:36 PM GMT

Betty did not know how much longer her grandson could hold the door against the onslaught. The creatures did not seem to be tiring. She had no idea how many were throwing themselves against the door. For all she knew, the stairwell could be full down all three flights of steps.

Lennie's large feet would slide backwards an inch or so, as he pushed back each time the bodies slammed against the exit. Lennie was big and strong, but even he could only last for so long. He was soaked through to the skin. Every ten seconds or so he would spit out a mouthful of rainwater. His eyes were squinted tight as he used every ounce of his strength to stop the door from opening.

The little dog was at his side, barking continually, as if offering his support.

Betty was knelt on the wet gravel that covered the flat roof, with Red's head on her lap, while she held a corner of the blanket on her shoulders over Red's face.

Red had regained consciousness and was mumbling something. Her eyes flicked open, only to shut again due to the stabbing pain in her head.

Betty could not hear what Red was saying because of the screaming creatures, the pouring rain hammering on the roof, the wet slapping sound of the bodies hitting the door, and Charlie's constant barking.

However, Betty would swear Red kept mumbling, "I'm sorry Jasmine."

Two explosions rocked the roof beneath them. The screaming intensified.

The door was crashed into so hard an arm managed to poke through the gap. The owner of the arm seemed unconcerned when Lennie slammed the door back against it. The bloody arm franticly slapped against the door, searching for whatever was blocking the way.

Betty's head jerked up, she could hear an engine approaching.

Lennie could hear it too, his head shot up, and his concentration lagged for just a split second. However, a second was all it took to give the creatures the edge they needed. The next slam jerked Lennie off his feet, sending him sprawling backwards to land next to his grandmother and Red.

Charlie sprinted over to protect them, barking at the open door.

The door hung open on broken hinges as five eaters ran out onto the roof, directly toward the three warm lumps of meat.

Betty instinctively used her body to protect the young injured woman, as the closest creature lunged like a wild animal, knocking Betty backwards away from Red. The crazed naked teenager then sunk its deformed teeth into Betty's upraised forearm.

48

Noah and the Squad
Newton Abbot
In the Old Peoples Flats
1:38 PM GMT

Echo fired three bullets; each hit the back of a head, taking down three creatures. Coco's shots stopped the two remaining eaters, one of which was crouched over an old woman. They both then fanned out to secure the area.

Noah ran passed them out onto the roof; he jumped the naked, twisted bodies that were still twitching and raced to Red's side.

"Is she hurt?" Noah asked, thinking they had arrived too late, and Red had been bitten.

"Am I glad to see you," Betty said, wincing in pain as she rolled the dead body off herself. She used the blanket to wrap over her arm to hide the teeth marks.

Lennie was slowly getting to his feet, while hugging Charlie. The dog was enjoying the attention.

"Red was knocked unconscious in a flat downstairs. A couple of poppers exploded in a room she had just walked into," Betty announced. No one had noticed she was bitten; they presumed the look of pain upon her face was due to arthritis and old age, or being soaking wet and cold.

Noah and the two soldiers had just set a couple of poppers off themselves as they made their way up through the building, following the sound of the screaming creatures. They presumed the three had climbed down the demolished wall and went to hide in the closest building. The explosion on the second floor of the old people's home had confirmed there was someone inside.

Echo had updated the Captain and Bull, and stated they were heading down over the remains of the back wall to check the structure.

Noah gave Echo directions to pass on to the Captain, so Bull could drive around to meet them.

Once they entered the closest block of flats – where the explosion had occurred – they heard the animalistic screaming coming from the stairwell.

"We have a vehicle outside; they are going to take us somewhere safe," Noah explained.

Noah saw Betty physically sag from relief as tears ran from her eyes. Noah noticed she was cradling her arm.

"Are you okay?"

"I'm fine, just a little bruised nothing to worry about." She kept her arm hidden beneath the thick blanket. It did not feel right. It was not aching, as a savage bite should; rather, it was tingling as if a small electrical current was passing through it and working its way along her arm. She knew she was infected. She did not know how long she could hide the bite or the effects for, but she needed to make sure Lennie was safe first; she knew her grandson would never leave her side, so she had to try to keep it together until they reached the safety of the prison.

Echo was now knelt by Red. "Is she able to walk?"

"Lennie had to carry her up here because she was unconscious. She seems a little better now though," Betty stated.

Red's eyes seemed a little unfocused, but she smiled when she recognized Noah.

"Let's get them all downstairs before more eaters arrive," Coco said.

Noah picked Red up. It felt right having her body pressed up against his.

I will never let her out of my sight again; he thought, as he carried her down the stairs following Echo, with Coco at the back.

"Can someone grab that, it's mine," Noah said as they pushed passed his large rucksack.

"Sorry, I tried to carry it, but it was just so damn heavy," Betty stated. She did not feel like talking, but she had to keep up the pretence that she was fine.

Coco picked it up and swung it over his muscular back.

They reached the Husky without any incident. There was not enough room for everyone inside the vehicle. Lennie sat in the open flat bed with the bags, with Coco and Echo stood next to him, leaning against the roll bars that wrapped around the flat bed. Red, Noah, and Betty sat in the back of the cab, with Bull driving and the Captain still in the command seat.

A group of four naked creatures ran from around a corner. They did not bother wasting ammo. The Husky drove off leaving the creatures running behind. They soon lost them at the first corner.

“Next stop, Dartmoor,” the Captain announced.

49

Doctor Lazaro
Dartmoor National Park
The Helipad at Dartmoor Prison
1:44 PM GMT

Melanie was unloaded in the pouring rain along with the rest of the passengers and hustled over to a squat building on the roof of the prison next to the helipad.

She watched as Jimmy was placed on a stretcher and rushed to the prisons hospital by a hectic group of military doctors and nurses.

The passengers moved in silence along the corridor, disappearing through some double doors following a group decked in military attire.

After all the commotion, hustle, and bustle, the corridor seemed too quiet and abandoned now they had all gone.

Melanie was left standing with an armed escort in the eerie silence, with a puddle of rainwater gathering around her.

The tall soldier said nothing. He stood ramrod straight with his hands behind his back, with a pistol at his hip.

She was left waiting in the corridor for half an hour. There were seats, but she was too pent-up to relax. She tried to engage the soldier twice in conversation. She was beginning to think he was a mute.

"Am I at least allowed to use the toilet?"

The soldier nodded once and pointed to a door three doors down the corridor. He followed her to the toilet, and waited outside.

The toilet was eight feet by eight, with a toilet and a sink to one side. There was a large cabinet. Inside were green surgical scrubs.

Melanie stripped out of her wet clothes and left them in a pile. She used the soap dispenser and washed her body as best she could. She filled the sink with warm water and washed her hair. She then used a couple scrub tops to dry her hair and body. She tossed them onto her wet clothes. She used the toilet, and then dressed in warm dry scrubs. They felt so good against her skin. For the first time in hours, she was warm and dry and felt almost human again.

Melanie picked up the folder in the sheaf; it was the only possession she had on her, apart from a thin gold necklace. Her purse and mobile were still resting on her desk in the university.

She gazed into the mirror and saw a bedraggled twenty-three year old female dressed in green medical scrubs. Melanie did not recognize herself; she looked like she had aged ten years in half a day. She unlatched the door and returned outside.

If the soldier was confused by seeing her in different clothes, he said nothing.

"Ah, you must be Doctor Lazaro?" A man said who had just pushed through a door that required a pass card. He wore a long white lab coat over faded brown corduroy trousers and an old olive-coloured cardigan over a brown button-down shirt. He was deathly thin and looked about fifty, with a terrible brush over of white hair, and pale loose skin.

There was a racket outside as a group of technicians finished refueling and checking the helicopter. It took off and disappeared into the hazy thick clouds.

"My name is Doctor Albert Hall; I am responsible for the bio lab. Then, as an afterthought added, "I know; my parents had a strange sense of humour when it came to naming their children." He held out a hand.

Melanie was having the worse morning of her life. She was confused about the people on the flight and worried about the soldiers she had left behind. With everything that had happened, and how long she had been left around waiting with a mute guard; she did not feel like being polite and shaking hands while enjoying chitchat. She ignored the outstretched hand.

"Who were those people on the helicopter with me?"

"Ah, I see. I understand; you've had one hell of a morning," Doctor Hall said as he shouldered the heavy door open that led outside.

Melanie followed.

The soldier stayed in the warm building.

Doctor Hall lit a cigarette. He lifted it up as he said, "You'd think with everything that's happened that I would be allowed to smoke inside. Nope. People still get upset about smoke drifting into their airspace. Anyone would think I was blowing spores in their direction." He gave a chuckle. He blew smoke out of his nose as he pressed his back against the concrete wall, while trying to stay dry under the inadequate covering over the door.

The doctor gave Melanie a quick side-glance. "So you're Doctor Melanie Lazaro. Born May 2 1990 to Edward and Margery Lazaro.

"It was soon discovered, after you took the Cattell IIIB Test that you have an IQ of 157, and considering the world-renowned physicist Stephen Hawkins is 160; it's not too shabby. You also aced the Cognitive Ability Tests. You excelled at school and were years ahead in all your classes. At the age of ten, you were recognized by the National Association for Gifted Children and Children of High Intelligence and moved to a specialist school for the gifted in Manchester. You passed all your exams with a string of A+'s and at the mere age of thirteen, you were accepted into Cambridge University where you studied three years for your BSc degree in Biomedical Science, and three and a half years for your PhD. I might add that you are one of only four people ever to be accepted into Cambridge at such a young age." He blew a plume of smoke out his nostrils.

"And while others in your classes – who were many years your senior – were struggling to simply fulfill their coursework, you wrote extra papers on subjects such as DNA sequencing, which were published by science journals the world over." He took another long drag.

"You could have worked anywhere. You had offers of jobs from all over America, Europe, and South America, and yet you picked Exeter's University of Biomedical Sciences Department, to be close to your parents, and even moved back in with them." He scratched at a mole next to his eye.

"You were a golden ticket for Exeter University. They were swamped with grants once word spread. You–"

"I know my history," she snapped. Melanie was a little taken back that he knew so much about her. "What's my past have to do with anything?"

Doctor Hall stood silent. He continued to blow smoke out into the pouring rain.

Melanie stood under the covering; she did not intend to get wet again after just putting on dry clothes. She noticed the large yellow stains on his two fingers that held the cigarette.

They stood in silence for a minute.

He obviously was not going to tell her why he knew so much about her, so she asked the same question from a few moments ago. "Who were the people on the flight with me? One said something about Adam and Eve."

Doctor Hall pulled long and hard on the cigarette. He flicked it into the rain. For a moment, he just looked straight ahead. The only sound was the thrashing rain hammering against the helipad.

"They are part of a secret that dates back over one hundred years. A secret our government, and many others the world over, has been hiding from the general population." He turned to look at her. "Those people are our last hope and our species salvation."

50

Noah, red, Betty, Lennie, and the Squad
Between Newton Abbot and Bovey Tracy
In the Husky Heading Towards Dartmoor
1:52 PM GMT

Bull kept the Husky well under the truck's maximum speed of 70 mph. He did not have a choice; the roads were congested with abandoned vehicles and littered objects, and numerous corpses.

The noise of the truck caught the attention of the naked creatures that were wandering, looking for food. Even though the truck was way too fast, they still tried until they were left behind.

Noah sat hugging Red, whose head rested against his shoulder. She was still groggy from being knocked unconscious, but her strength was gaining with each passing mile.

Betty looked like she was sleeping, with her head covered over with her blanket and resting up against the thick bulletproof window. She looked her years, curled up to one side.

Lennie sat hugging Charlie, keeping the small dog dry with his body. There was a large piece of tarp in the back of the truck, and Lennie had it wrapped around him. He had his head uncovered though, because he liked to see the scenery around him, and he liked the sensation of the wind and rain blowing through his hair. He had never been allowed to sit in the back of a truck before. He did not want to miss a thing.

Echo and Coco were knelt next to Lennie, with their rifles ready to be used at a moment's notice.

The Captain sat with a small device on his lap; it looked like a controller for a game's console, with a screen on it. It was, in fact, the remote for the large machinegun on the roof.

It did not take long to reach the A38, a four-lane dual carriageway, which was deserted. There were plenty of vehicles wedged up against the embankment or middle reservation, but none of them was moving. All the cars that had been packed weeks before, and drove away from their homes had either reached the destination they intended, or were abandoned along the way when the petrol tank ran dry. Petrol stations ran out of fuel during the first week of the pandemic.

Bull pulled off the motorway up onto an incline leading to a large roundabout. Drumbridges roundabout led to Bovey Straights, a long stretch of straight road over a mile long, with woodland to each side.

In one field, as they passed, Noah could see a group of six or so naked creatures eating what looked like a horse. There was so much blood it was hard to tell. He looked away. He could also see naked blurs running through the woods to either side of the road, attracted by the unfamiliar sound of the large engine.

On the outskirts of Bovey Tracey, or otherwise known as the Gateway to the Moors, there was an industrial park with a large building in flames. It had been set alight within the last few hours, or something had eventually broken-down from lack of human intervention. The flames danced along the roof. Windows shattered as thick black smoke poured from every broken window. The air smelt of burning plastic.

Bull kept on driving, navigating around groups of abandoned vehicles. Sometimes he had to use the truck's powerful four-wheel drive to go over grass embankments, or over curbs and along pavements. On a few occasions, he had to reverse and find an alternate road.

At one such point, where about twenty cars all seemed to be in one large collision, Bull was reversing to go up over and around a grass verge, when a group of about thirty creatures seemed to appear from nowhere. The group was a collection of all ages and sizes, from a female child who looked about nine, up to an old man in his eighties.

"Shit!" Bull said while jamming the gear in place. He was not worried about those in the truck, because the armoured shell and windows would deflect even a landmine; he was worried about the three in the back without protection.

The Captain could hear Coco and Echo firing into the mass of surging bodies.

Lennie pulled the tarp over his head.

"Down," the Captain shouted into the microphone in his gasmask, as he used the remote to spin the automatic machinegun around on the roof.

Coco and Echo ducked as they heard the guns motor kick in.

On the handheld unit, the moving creatures were outlined in red by the most up-to-date military technology. Within seconds, it marked the targets, their speed, and their predicted trajectory. With one simple press of a button, the 12.7 mm bullets ripped into the flesh of the charging mass, starting with the closest and fastest. They were literally cut in half. In was over in less than a minute. The hot bullet casings pinged down onto the wet tarmac.

Bull continued reversing over the shredded bodies; it was a bumpy ride.

After another roundabout, they found themselves heading along narrow hedged crowded lanes.

Red was alert now, and staring out the window. She had not spoken to Noah, but simply snuggled up against him, as if seeking his body heat.

Noah still had his arm around her, as if protecting her from harm.

Betty had not moved in a while. She sat in the corner with her head covered, curled up against the door and window.

The truck raced along the narrow lanes.

A few cars were abandoned along the route, but the truck managed to squeeze through. At one section of the road, where the lane was thin and a car was wedged up against the hedge; Bull had to shunt the car along, crumpling the side panels of the silver Honda Civic so the truck could grind through.

The scenery started to change over just a short distance as the truck started to climb in elevation. The grass became a short hardy moss, covered in bracken and ferns. Hedgerows gave way to old stonewalls, held together by gravity and age. Trees became shorter and robust and covered in moss and vines. On the tall hills, massive jutting out granite boulders the size of houses and some five stories in height looked over the landscape.

The truck drove over stone bridges that spanned a diversity of waterways, from large, wide, fast flowing rivers, to trickling streams and brooks.

The trees seemed to clump together the higher they drove, as if seeking company. Large tracks of woodland covered the sides of the rolling hills and vales that created long valleys. There were lone houses and farms here and there, surrounded by old stonewalls and barns.

The truck zipped over cattle grids, making the vehicle vibrate.

Noah noticed some naked creatures running in the distance. Some were in groups of ten or more. The most disturbing thing was they all seemed to be running in the same direction. If anyone else had noticed, they kept it to themselves. Noah just hoped it was a coincidence, because they all seemed to be heading in the same direction as them.

51

Doctor Lazaro
Dartmoor National Park
On the Roof of Dartmoor Prison
2:28 PM GMT

"Please follow me," Doctor Hall said. He turned to the soldier.

"You're dismissed. I will take Doctor Lazaro from here."

The guard simply nodded, turned, and walked away, disappearing through a swinging door.

"Ah, is that your findings?" he asked while eyeing the plastic sheaf.

Melanie was still trying to work out what he meant by 'our species salvation'.

"Sorry?"

"Your findings."

"Yes." She seemed to wake up from her daze. "I found the position where the host strain latches onto the human DNA," she stated while flicking the folder with her wrist.

Melanie looked at the folder. So many had died because of its contents.

If only General Hay had sent the information via the internet before he took me on a tour of the gym, then all of this could have been avoided. But he wasn't to know a horde was on its way to attack the university. The squad had already been diverted from their supply mission, and they had no idea why I was so important.

"Interesting," Doctor Hall said. "Of course, we have never tried to find a cure. It was just too impractical once the full implications of Clarkson's discovery came to light."

Doctor Hall was leading the way along the corridor to a thick door with a swipe slot next to it. He pulled a passkey from his top lab coat pocket.

"What do you mean; you've never tried to find a cure? And who is Clarkson? What discovery?" Melanie asked as the doctor swiped the card, and the door hissed open.

Doctor Hall step into the elevator. He ignored her first question and answered the second.

"Clarkson was a British explorer working for the British Museum in London," Doctor Hall said as if Melanie needed to be told where the vast museum was located. "In 1898, he found something that changed the way we look at the world."

Melanie stepped into the lift. "I've never heard of Clarkson before." She noticed that three sides of the lift were made of thick glass.

"Few have. His findings were covered up by the British government and reclassified as top-secret." With another swipe of the card, a panel slid across to reveal a scanner. Doctor Hall placed his nicotine stained hand on the surface. A green line ran up and down the screen. With a beep, tumblers could be heard falling into place, and then the elevator engaged and started to descend.

"Clarkson was in Tibet, in an area nowadays referred to as the Plateau of Tibet in the Himalayas, in an uncharted valley between Lhasa and the Bhutan border, looking for antiquities to fill the new White Wing that had been completed at the Museum in 1887. He had no specialty, like all the explorers of the time he used his British credentials to bully his way into countries and paid off officials, so he could send back artifacts to his employers."

The lift was still descending. Melanie had no idea how fast, but it had passed the nine stories of the prison long ago; she was sure they were now deep underground.

"On June 25th 1898, along with his large accompaniment of sherpas and aids, Clarkson discovered an undocumented valley high up in the Himalayas on the border of Bhutan. There, in that deep valley, after they spent two days walking through caves and thin ravines, the fifth pod was discovered."

Melanie was about to ask what he meant by 'pod', when the lift seemed to break free of the concrete walls around them, as the lift started descending down a glass shaft. Melanie was gobsmacked at what stretched out before her eyes.

52

Noah, Red, Betty, Lennie, and the Squad
Dartmoor National Park
In the Husky Somewhere near Widecombe-in-the-Moor
2:31 PM GMT

Red turned to look at Noah. She had a nasty bruise down the left-hand side of her face where she had been tossed against the doorjamb. She still felt dizzy and nauseated. She did not say a word. Nothing needed to be said – for now. At the moment, they both just needed to hold on and have someone close.

Red's mind wandered back to just before the pandemic broke out. Life was hard and getting harder. Her mother had passed away just two months before from cancer. It affected them all differently. It was so hard to see her fade away.

It was not like a car crash, where the news was a shock and devastating, and final. Cancer was slow and lingering. Her mother had stage four lung cancer. Ironic considering that neither she, nor anyone else in the house, smoked. Red could see her mother getting weaker and weaker, and thinner. The chemotherapy was slowly killing her. It would be a toss-up between which killed her first, the chemo, or the cancer.

Finally, her mother decided the chemo was not working and refused any more treatment. Now it was simply a matter of waiting.

Her stepfather – who took over raising the two children when her father died in a car crash when Red was ten – sunk deeper and deeper into the bottle, while watching his wife fade away before his eyes. At first, Red felt sorry for him. He was still the breadwinner, having to feed them all. The government helped a little, but the money did not go very far.

After five months, her mother died in her sleep in her bed. She was riddled with sores and as thin as a skeleton.

Within two weeks, things got even worse.

Her stepfather drank more than he ate. He seldom went to work, and he sat all day in front of the television with old photo albums of his wedding day.

Red had to hold the household together. She had to drop out of college to get a job to support them all because the bills were mounting up. Her dreams of becoming a primary school teacher had to go on hold.

Jasmine, her twelve-year-old sister, had no one else to look after her. Their stepfather was a wreck and because their mother was an only child, there were no aunties or uncles to ask for help. The grandparents, on her mother side, had both passed away years earlier. The drunk was all they had.

Red starting working long hours in Newton Abbots Specsavers labs. She worked the polishing machine, where the cut lenses for the glasses went after they were fined. She stood in front of the polishing machine for hours on end, swapping the tools over and placing the lenses in the correct position while checking the PSI pressure and the machines speed. She worked extra hours to rake in as much money as possible.

One night, after Red got home late after a long fourteen-hour shift, her life got even worse.

Her stepfather, Colin, was not asleep in his normal chair, with the TV blaring and an empty bottle in his hand. At first, she took it as a good sign. For weeks, he slept in the chair, only moving to go to the toilet, or grab a rare bite to eat, or a fresh bottle.

Maybe he was pulling himself back on his feet; Red remembered thinking. That was until he stumbled down the hallway into the front room. He was naked and crying. He had blood around his swollen groin and on his hands.

Red dropped the bag of groceries she had collected on the way home.

"What have you done?" she screamed as she ran passed, knocking him to the floor, as she headed to her sister's room.

Her sister lay in bed on her back, with her nightie pulled up over her face. One leg hung off the bed. There was blood everywhere.

"NOOOO!" Red raced to her side.

Jasmine was dead. Suffocated by a pillow her drunken stepfather held over her face as he raped her.

She had two choices, leave, and phone the police, before he returned and tried to hurt her, or make him pay.

Red stared at her sister's broken, bloody body. Slowly, like an automaton, Red walked to her bedroom. She was not thinking straight; it was almost an out of body experience. Red unhooked her bow from behind her bedroom door. She notched an arrow, with her sister's blood still over her hands, and headed for the front room.

Her stepfather was on his back with his hands over his face, crying.

"I'm so sorry Jasmine," he screamed. "You look so much like her!"

Red ignored his shouting and pulled back the bow.

He must have realized she was back in the room, because he struggled to raise himself on his elbows, while staring at her through his tear-streaked, drunken, bloodshot eyes.

"I'm sorry," he muttered, while spittle dribbled down his stubble covered chin.

Red released the pressure, and watched the arrow go through his right eye, pinning Colin's head to the TV cabinet.

In the background, on the TV, the BBC was reporting on an outbreak of a serious virus in South Africa.

Red ignored the television. She went to the kitchen and filled a bowl with warm soapy water, and returned to her sister's bedroom. She slowly cleaned the blood from her sister's battered, limp body, as tears blurred her vision. She changed the sheets and her sister's nightie and laid her back in the bed. She then kissed her sister on the forehead.

Red then packed a few items of clothing, and filled the rest of the bag with food and three heavy two-liter bottles of water. She pulled an old sleeping bag from the bottom of her wardrobe, and then swung her bow and arrows over her shoulder and left.

The last thing she did was dial the emergency services on the house phone and left the phone off the hook. As she walked out the door, she could hear the operator ask what service was required: police, fire brigade, or ambulance.

Red had no idea where to go, or what to do. She slowly walked from her home on Barton Drive and headed into the nearby Bakers Park woods. She remembered an abandoned stone shack she found years ago with her sister, hidden by clinging vegetation.

For five days, she hid, with her phone turned off, avoiding the world, consumed by her grief. On the sixth day, when her water and food ran out, she emerged from the woods to give herself up. However, the world was in chaos, as if her innocent sister's death was the catalyst that changed everything.

53

Doctor Lazaro
Dartmoor National Park
Below Dartmoor Prison
2:32 PM GMT

Melanie stood with her mouth hanging open as the lift continued its momentum.

"It was first started back in 1957; it took twenty-four years to complete. Luckily, there was a vast network of caverns riddled throughout the granite bedrock, which were enlarged and shaped. The prison above served as misdirection, enabling enormous amounts of materials and personnel to move back and forth without causing suspicion."

The elevator finally stopped, and the door hissed open. Melanie stepped out of the lift into a cavernous chamber.

"There is room to house two thousand people, with enough food and supplies to last twenty years. There is a freshwater spring providing unlimited water for consumption, washing, and irrigation."

Melanie looked up. A vast dome stretched into the distance. It must have been over two hundred foot high. Only a couple of thick glass pillars connected to the ceiling, which was the elevators that joined the underground bunker to the building above.

From her location, she could see lakes, large parks, numerous housing complexes, and colossal multistory buildings. It was an underground city. The buildings looked dated, as if she had been transported back to the seventies.

"There is just a handful of technicians down here at the moment, preparing the facility and checking everything is working properly. For the last thirty-two years in has only had a skeleton crew running it. That changed three weeks ago when it became the country's top priority." Pride radiated from his voice.

"I have been working here, collecting, and archiving data for thirty-two years, from when it became operational."

Then as an afterthought added. "The two hundred adult candidates and their one hundred children are still in the building above, getting their final checks. Of course, along with support staff, doctors, scientists and military personnel, the number bumps up to just over a thousand. This leaves room for the candidates and their children – once they are of breeding age – to multiply.

"The support staff, and soldiers have all had their tubes tied – so to speak. They do not want everyone interbreeding down here, just the final selected candidates and their offspring.

"It is believed that over the twenty years, at a fixed rate each year, with the candidates, their children, and grandchildren, when they come of age, the number should be up to around the two thousand capacity once it is safe to return topside."

Melanie turned three hundred and sixty degrees, so she could take in the whole view.

"I can't believe this has been here all this time. Has it a name?"

"It is the Ark," Doctor Hall announced, pride radiating from his voice.

"The Ark?"

"Our salvation." He turned and started to walk towards a five-story building.

"If you follow me, I will explain everything."

Melanie followed the thin doctor into the old style, large squat building, along white corridors and through laboratories. The outside of the building was dated, but the inside was a different matter.

"There is everything here mankind will need to start over," he said as he led the way.

"The seeds of every known plant, fruit, and vegetable have been collected. Every known animal has its DNA frozen and stored. Every known medical cure and procedure, every known book, document, and scroll – everything that we have accomplished, discovered, and created, or recorded in the last few thousand years – has been digitally stored, and physically – where possible – for future generations."

They walked through a vast chamber that must have been in the center of the five-story building. It had tens of thousands of small sealed doors running up the walls, behind thick glass. A robot with four arms, on long metal cables that allowed it to move to any location in the chamber, was lifting an object from a container that rested on the floor, up into an open hatch.

"Everything a civilization would need to continue its species is here. And America, China, and Russia, as well as many other nations have their own versions."

They passed into another smaller lab. A group of about fifteen technicians was entering information into computers.

"Just last minute data entry," he said.

Doctor Hall reached out a hand.

"The file please, Doctor Lazaro."

Melanie passed it to him.

"It will be scanned and entered into the computer. Your cure will be studied at depth in the coming years by a collection of Britain's top scientists and doctors who will live down here with the Adam and Eve finalist." He noticed the look on Melanie's face.

"Your named was short listed as a possible candidate. We add and delete the doctors and scientist on a yearly basis. You would have been called to a government building in London within the next few months for vetting to see if you have what it takes to be picked for the Ark.

"But don't worry, now you're here when we return to the surface I will have you checked over." He gave her a smile. "You may still be picked to live down the rabbit hole." He gave her an even bigger smile. "And because of your IQ, profession, age, and health, you may not get sterilized but might even get the chance to become a breeder!"

54

Noah, Red, Betty, Lennie, and the Squad
Dartmoor National Park
In the Husky Somewhere Near Princetown
2:36 PM GMT

The Captain was concerned. The amount of naked creatures running across the moorland was excessive. There were not enough populated areas across the region to warrant so many of them. It did not make sense as to why they were all out here, and heading in the same direction. He was getting a bad feeling in the pit of his stomach.

Bull drove the truck down narrow lanes, over bridges, and through a steep valley. They passed through small villages with just a handful of houses. At first glance, they looked normal. However, there were always telltale signs – a broken window, left luggage, or an abandoned car parked haphazardly. Then, as the sound of the engine moved through the hamlet, the creatures would run out of the buildings.

At one valley, they witnessed a large cloud of spores lazily rolling up the hills through the woodland.

Echo was cold and tired. She could not wait to reach the safety of the prison and the warm barracks. She wiped rain from the masks faceplate.

Not long now, she thought; the prison was just around the next valley in the small town called Princetown.

She hoped Jimmy was okay and responding to treatment. She also knew her father would give her an earful when she returned.

Echo knew about the underground bunker. She was relocated there two years ago and placed in the Captains squad by her father. Up until today, she had never fired her gun in combat. Her squad simply ferried supplies to the large government compound. She never truly believed the bunker would ever be needed.

Coco had a banging headache. The straps of the gasmask were digging into the side of his head. However, the last thing he would think of doing was loosen the thing, not after everything he had seen.

Almost there, he reasoned. *I can take it off soon.*

Coco could not believe the day he was having. It was supposed to be a simple drop off and return mission – routine. Then they received the priority redirection to the university. One helicopter and one truck crash later, with fifteen casualties, with possibly another if Jimmy did not make it, and here he was. He could not wait to get back behind the thirty-foot tall, four-foot thick walls of the prison.

Just give me a hot cup of coco and my bed, he thought; every inch of him was cold and ached. When people first heard his nickname, they presumed it was racial and referred to his skin colour. In fact, it was due to his unusual habit of drinking coco as if it was tea or coffee. A nickname his older brother gave him when he was eight, and it had stuck ever since.

Lennie still had the tarp over his head. He had lost interest in the surroundings after the horde had attacked them on the outskirts of Bovey Tracy. He sat beneath the heavy tarp hugging Charlie while scratching the little dog under the chin. He still liked it in the back of the truck, but he was starting to miss his grandmother.

In the distance, the towering North Hessary Tor communications mast, bristling with satellite dishes and antenna, soared six hundred and forty-three feet into the sky, which land-marked Princetown from miles around.

Betty was hot – very hot, but she dared not pull the blanket off her head. She could feel the spores moving through her body; changing her. If they found out now she would be dumped by the side of the road, and Lennie would refuse to leave her. She would try to hide it for as long as possible. She was an old woman; no one thought it strange that she had *slept* since getting in the truck.

Betty tried to keep her eyes shut, but she could not stop blinking, and her throat was raw.

"Almost there," Bull announced, just in case the three passengers in the back had never been to Princetown before. "Just over the next hill," he stated.

And about time, Bull thought. He was hungry and cold. *And once I get there, and get down into the bunker; I will not have to leave again for twenty years. I will be safe. And how hard will it be to look after a group of placid breeders.*

The truck drove over an arched stone bridge. A collection of naked bodies floated face down in the watercourse; they obviously drowned in the powerful rapids up the river, while trying to cross.

The Captain was wet, and his left knee was killing him. The supply run was supposed to a simple there-and-back mission. He was meant to drop off supplies to the Britannia Royal Naval College in Dartmouth, and return with twenty candidates who had been collected at the Naval College awaiting safe transport. Instead, he had lost fifteen of his squad and was returning by truck with four random civilians and a dog. He knew they would not be allowed to enter the Ark, but at least they would be safe behind the four-foot thick walls of the prison, at least there; they had a chance.

At least I'm brining Echo back to her father. I would hate to think how the General would react if I had lost her along the way.

Princetown is the highest elevated settlement on the moors – the unofficial capital – which is why it was chosen for the underground bunker. There were only two roads leading into the small town, and Bull was driving along the one that crested the brow of a hill, before running down into the valley.

Bull slammed on the brakes.

"Jesus!" Bull shouted.

Everyone, apart from Betty hiding under the blanket, and Lennie under the tarp, could see why Bull had skidded to a halt.

Coco and Echo's view was the best, stood up in the back of the truck.

Below, in the distance, stretched out around the bowl of the valley was Princetown. It was a small town with a square and housing in long neat rows. The prison dominated the view; a large collection of tall imposing granite buildings set out orderly inside the soaring walls. Outside the fortification were numerous bulky warehouses and a large car park.

However, this was not what made Bull slam on the brakes. Thousands of naked bodies were converging on the small town, running across the fields and down the streets, all heading towards the large circular prison, as if being guided by a hive mind to the same location.

55

Doctor Lazaro
Dartmoor National Park
Below Dartmoor Prison in the Ark
2:38 PM GMT

"Picked?" Melanie asked, as the technician was scanning her findings into the database.

"Yes. Not everyone is automatically chosen due to education and breeding, there has to be a complete physical as well. They wouldn't want someone with a heart defect, or diabetes to get through the screening." Doctor Hall swung a chair around.

"Once Brigadier General Hay contacted General Philips and announced you had found a blocker; it was cleared to bring you and your findings to the Ark." The thin doctor chuckled.

"No one seriously thought anyone would actually succeed in finding a cure. The centers all over the country were there simply for show, to calm the population, to make it look like the government was doing something, while the Ark was being prepared. Even though the Ark was kept on standby, no one knew one of the pods would be activated.

"Please sit, we shall wait for the scanning to finish, then you can check the document over to double-check everything is in place."

Melanie was tired, hungry, and confused. She just wished the nightmare would end.

She sat on the chair and rested her face on her hands. Realization was slowly sinking in.

"The government has known for decades," she mumbled into her hands.

"Oh yes," Doctor Hall said, thinking Melanie was talking to him.

"It's the worlds best-kept secret. For obvious reasons," he stated. "Just think of the panic that would ensue if everyone knew what was happening. As far as they are concerned, this is just a pandemic, which would be over in weeks, like the swine or bird flu. Moreover, as they watch the TV, they believe it will not affect them. It's just numbers and reports on the news." He stopped to think for a second.

"Mind you, I think they would have worked it out by now. However, it is too late to do anything. Everything is in place."

"You said all the governments know?" She looked up with tired eyes.

"Not all, only those who are allies with the countries in question, or who know about the pods."

"You mentioned Clarkson found the first."

"Yes, in the fabled Shangri-La, high in the Tibetan Mountains. He obviously didn't know what it was, and luckily an avalanche hundreds of years prior had closed the valley off from the outside world, so when one of the sherpas touched the black, pulsating pod, and released the spores, it didn't spread any further than the enclosed valley.

"An expedition was sent to discover what happened to Clarkson and his crew the following season. None returned. Their location was left with a village elder down at the base of the valley in case of trouble. That group also vanished without a trace. But now the British government knew their general location.

"A third team was sent, this time they were accompanied by a group of soldiers, in case the last two groups had been attacked by bandits. At the time, outsiders rarely visited Tibet.

"It was a complete fluke that when the third group entered through the winding tunnels, out into the hidden valley that one of the soldiers was wearing a gasmask, due to suffering chest pains because of the high elevation. He thought breathing through the mask would help his lungs. It saved his life, and he was able to return to sound the alarm."

Technicians were milling about; they had obviously finished their assignments.

"If you have finished, make your way to the elevators, and you will be taken back to the surface," Doctor Hall announced.

A group of nine people left the room. They all seemed glad to be able to return to the world above.

Melanie found their nervousness odd.

"Archeology was just gaining ground and becoming popular. That's when references to other pods started to make sense. The Egyptians painted images of it inside their temples and pyramids. The Mayans carved likenesses of it at Chichen Itza. It was also found referenced at Teotihuacán, in Mexico. At Angkor Wat in Cambodia. On one of the fifty tonne sarsen stones at Stonehenge. At the Puma Punku temple in Bolivia. In the Temple of Jupiter, in the Bekaa Valley of Lebanon. There is even a glyph of a pod in the Nazca Lines, in the Nazca Desert in southern Peru. Even Babylonian stone tablets referenced it. And more recently at Gobekli Tepe in southeastern Turkey. All the ancient civilizations seemed to know about the pods and inscribed or carved warnings for future generations.

"It was later found out, while excavations were carried out, that some of the ancient temples and pyramids were built over the pods to protect mankind and stop the spores from spreading. One is beneath the Great Pyramid of

Giza in Egypt. The second is inside the Pyramid of the Sun in Teotihuacán in Mexico. The third is inside the temple at Angkor Wat in Cambodia. The fourth was discovered in a vast sealed temple cave in the Northwest Territories, near Great Bear Lake in Canada. The fifth is at Groom Lake, Nevada. You may know it as Area 51. Stories of crashed alien crafts and top-secret military black ops are just smoke screens to divert people from the truth. The American government has been studying the pod since it was discovered in July 1947.

"Four had been located by ancient civilizations, and sealed away beneath thousands of tonnes of stone. Clarkson found the fifth in Tibet, and a well digger found the sixth in Nevada. However, the ancient scripts and carvings described seven Seeds of the Gods.

"The first registered reference to a pod was found in Sumer, an ancient Sumerian city. The Sumerian legend, The Epic of Gilgamesh, referenced one on a clay tablet." Doctor Hall seemed happy to impart his accumulated knowledge. It was so rare to find someone who had not been completely briefed.

"Nebuchadnezzar wrote about the pods, calling them the Temples of the Seven Lights of the Earth."

Melanie was astounded that with so many pods in the world, that the story had not leaked.

“There were even references found in the Dead Sea Scrolls discovered in 1947 at Khirbet Qumran in the West Bank. The Great Isaiah Scroll, one of the seven original parchments, called them ‘Seeds of the Lord’. Other fragments, in Hebrew, Aramaic, Greek, and Nabataean, written on parchments and papyrus and even engraved in bronze, also referenced the ‘Seeds’.

“Books that were not canonized into the Hebrew Bible, such as the Book of Tobit, Wisdom of Sirach, Psalms 152, Jubilees and the Book of Enoch all referenced the ‘Seeds’ God had placed on the earth.

“The Book of Enoch, sections obviously never released, even stated the ‘Great Flood of Gods Seeds’. This, some believe, to be the Great Flood, which wasn’t water, but a pandemic that wiped all living things of the face of the earth, apart from those inside the Ark.” Doctor Hall was enjoying giving the hidden history of the world.

“The governments that knew the secret have had teams of specialist searching for the last pod for sixty-six years. A group of loggers in a deep valley in Madagascar found it first.

"The rest, as they say, is history." Doctor Hall's fingers were twitching, possibly his nicotine habit was kicking in. He was a long way away from where he could smoke.

"Bunkers started being organized when the world's population started growing, and mankind started expanding out into new regions. It would only be a matter of time before the last pod was found by someone who had no idea what it was, and touched it."

"Finished," the man sat at the computer said.

"If you would like to scan through the–"

A loud ear-piercing siren filled the room.

"What the hell?" Doctor Hall said as he walked over to a phone on the wall. He picked it up and pressed a quick dial button. He used his free hand to cover his other ear, so he could hear what was being said.

"What's going on?" The doctor listened. His face paled. He slammed the phone down.

"We have to return to the surface; the prison is under attack."

"Return to the surface? Surely, we are safer down here?" Melanie said while getting to her feet.

The technicians who were left in the room were running to the elevators.

"It doesn't work like that. Only those who have been chosen are allowed to stay in the

Ark. They will be starting to get them underground within the next hour." The thin doctor was heading towards the exit.

Melanie was jogging along behind.

"I'm not going aboveground if we are under attack," she stated and stopped dead.

The doctor spun around. "You don't understand, only those chosen have had the injection needed to survive in the Ark!"

"Survive what? You said there was no cure for the spores?"

"The injection is not to counteract the spores. Only time locked away below ground, while the spores decimate the surface, eventually mutating from one species to another, until the whole planets surface has been wiped clean.

"The injection is because the whole underground bunker has been fitted with a system that will release a fine mist into the air ducts, which will affect everyone who hasn't had the injection. Once the Adam and Eve finalists, and their support staff and protective soldiers, have been sealed underground, the gas is released to kill off any unauthorized technicians or hideaways. Only a chosen few can survive the end of days."

PART FOUR: THE ARK

56

Noah, Red, Betty, Lennie, and the Squad
Dartmoor National Park
In the Husky Looking Down Over Princetown
Friday 5th January 2013
2:41 PM GMT

"This can't be happening," Bull said as he slammed his palm against the steering wheel.

It's right there. Safety and a cushy babysitting mission for the next twenty years. Right on the other side of those walls, Bull thought. *Sod's-fucking-law!*

The Captain just sat staring out through the windscreen at all the naked bodies running full pelt towards the large circular walls of the prison. Unlike Bull, who was selfishly worried about his comfortable future, the Captain was more concerned with the questions: *What made them all come here? Is there a hive mind at work?*

Coco could not believe his eyes. He stood in the back with Echo, looking down over the countryside, with the wide-open landscape marred by the running creatures.

We are so close. It is right there! He reasoned.

Why didn't I get on the chopper; Echo mused? *Oh well, it is not going to be as boring as I first thought.* She scanned the hills around the prison. The naked creatures were converging from every direction; like metal shavings drawn to a powerful magnet.

Noah tried to peer between the seats, but Red was asleep on his shoulder, recovering from a concussion. He could see why they had stopped. However, he was wondering why there was a problem. Yes, there were thousands heading towards the prison, but it is built like a medieval fort, there was no way they would get in unless they were let in. If he was driving, he would put his foot down and drive through the lot of them.

Betty was aching all over. It felt like the blood in her veins had turned to acid. The pain was making her grit her teeth. She had to stop herself from screaming out. She was blinking so hard and fast, that her eyes were raw and bleeding.

Not long now, she thought. *Just get us to the prison, and get Lennie inside, even if it means leaving me by the roadside.* Betty knew she was becoming delusional from the spores, because she could hear voices in her head. She pulled the blanket tighter around herself, and stifled a whimper.

The Captain formulated a plan.

The main prison entrance was an arch into a courtyard, with building's housing the guardhouse and delivery point. The main gateway was double walled, and you had to drive through a squat building, leading into the prison, then out onto the main road that led straight into the main hub building that all the others fanned off from, like spokes from a wheel. The core hub building was where the main lift for large loads was situated for transporting materials down into The Ark.

“Head around to the far side. Get us to the museum,” the Captain said.

Dartmoor prison is the only prison in the country with its own museum. Rooms full of documents, manacles, weapons, memorabilia, clothing and uniforms, and information about famous prisoners, as well as photos and paintings of the prison going back to the year it was built, in 1806, to house the prisoners of the Napoleonic War and the thirty-two month war of 1812, between America and the British Empire.

“There is an old tunnel from the prison’s rectory to a hidden entrance in the museum. Apparently, the prison’s chaplain was not a hundred percent convinced his congregation were fully repentant, and required an escape route just in case.

“We will use the tunnel to get us to the rectory, and then we will be right next to the hub building,” the Captain stated.

A series of gunshots announced a couple of creatures had ventured too close to the truck, and Echo or Coco had taken them down.

To Echo the infected seemed different, they were not so interested in feeding as reaching the prison. She only shot the three running by, in case their hunger kicked in, and they swung around to attack. She realized it was a waste of ammo, because one of the creatures was not killed instantly, her shot hit the middle-aged woman in the neck, but rather than turning and attacking, she was still trying to crawl in the direction of the prison, smearing a long pool of blood along the road in her wake.

"I've got a bad feeling about this," Echo said over the microphone on her mask.

No one answered, but they all knew what she meant.

Bull wedged the gear in place and pulled away from the grass embankment. He circled out wide to run over the crawling creature; there was no need for her to suffer, she had been someone's daughter, wife, and sister once. He showed a little mercy as he drove the truck over her disfigured head.

Noah grimaced in the back, as the head audibly popped like a watermelon.

Betty gave a groan from under the blanket.

Noah presumed it was because she was sickened by the sound of the head popping. He did not realize it was because she was slowly changing into something they were all running from.

57

Doctor Lazaro and Doctor Hall
Dartmoor National Park
Princetown
Below Dartmoor Prison in The Ark
2:46 PM GMT

Melanie stood her ground, unmoving. Her hands were clenched at her sides.

"We have to get back to the surface, so they can start to prepare the Adam and Eve finalists, and get them safely below ground," Doctor Hall stated. He could not understand why Doctor Lazaro was not running for the exit.

"You're going to kill everyone you don't deem fit to live down here?" Disbelief poured from her voice as it raised a few octaves. Her head slowly shook from side to side.

"There is only so much room." He flapped his arms, as if in an exasperated manner. "You would have us take up precious room, on, on," he stumbled on his words, trying to describe his disdain for such a thought, "on, those unworthy?"

The technicians were no longer around; they had run to the lifts as fast as they could.

"Unworthy!" She took a few steps closer to the skinny doctor. "You will fill The Ark with perfection; with only those genetically, emotionally, and highly educated?" She took another step closer.

"Of course! Why would we make space for those who never applied themselves to a specific field of research – to the uneducated?"

"Because everything needs balance. You are filling this bunker up with mindless drones; people who will jump at your every order. There is no individuality. You have bred and beaten their humanity out of them." Her arms flew up into the air.

"I sat with a helicopter full of these people – our so-called salvation. I felt no emotions emanating from them, nothing. They are simply produced for breeding – just mindless cattle. We cannot rebuild a world with people like that!" Her arms dropped back to her sides.

"Why aren't you in the lift, Doctor Hall?" a voice boomed.

Melanie swung around. There was a large wall of monitors against the far side of the room. A man's face filled them all.

"General Philips, we were just leaving, sir." Doctor Hall seemed to shrink in size, as if the stare of the general sucked the life from him.

"Doctor Lazaro." The head nodded in her direction, as if giving a courteous bow.

"Once you are topside bring Doctor Lazaro to the main control room." The head turned, as if the connection was about to fadeout. However, as an afterthought, the head turned back and said, “Better hurry Doctor Hall, you don’t want to be trapped down there when the door seals shut.” The image started to fade, leaving a glimpse of a smile on the Generals lips. It then flicked off, leaving a bank of monitors showing only static for a second before turning off.

“What does he mean; you don’t want to be trapped?”

Doctor Hall held up his hand, displaying his nicotine covered fingers.

“Because of my thirty-year habit; which I just can’t seem to quit.” His face showed regret for a few seconds. “As well as a few other things.” His hand rubbed down his face, in a show of quiet defeat. “I have been deemed unworthy of a place in The Ark.”

58

Noah, Red, Betty, Lennie, and the Squad
Dartmoor National Park
Princetown
Main Street
2:47 PM GMT

The town looked like a disaster site.

They drove through the town along Two Bridges Road; a road hedged in by rows of housing, with small front gardens. There were smashed windows, with curtains blowing in the January breeze. Wet paper littered the streets and gardens, along with rubbish, abandoned vehicles, and dropped luggage.

The road gave way to a few cafes, a handful of pubs, and a souvenir shop. Clapboard signs lay blown across into the road.

Bull slowly drove along passed the Railway Inn on the left, and then took a right at the Jubilee Memorial, and a huge cream building that looked like a stately mansion, with its towering columns and balcony with two large wings, which is, in fact, the Princetown Visitors Centre, right next to the famous Plume of Feathers pub.

The left wing of the visitors centre had collapsed due to fire, and the once cream coloured walls were cracked and covered in soot.

Bodies littered the wide pavement, in different states of decomposition.

Bull navigated around a body of a child and his mother.

Naked creatures were running down the main street, heading towards the prison.

The truck was ignored.

Then it hit Echo; *none of them are screaming. They are so quiet. Why?* There was only the sound of their laboured breathing and the slapping of bare, bleeding feet on the wet tarmac.

Bull drove slowly down the main street, passed the shops with their smashed out windows. There was a large green to the right, with another memorial.

The creatures ran straight past them, unconcerned with their presence, as if they were driving along with a crowd of naked marathon runners.

There was a primary school on the right, with a large, brightly coloured hopscotch snake painted on the ground, surrounded by congealed puddles of blood. There was the Prince of Wales's pub on the left.

Bull gave it a quick glance. It was his local pub. He, along with a few others from his old unit, used to drink there. They told the locals that they were stationed at the Merrivale Range, one of the three military training areas located on this side of the moorland. However, none of the locals cared where they came from, so long as they cause no trouble, and poured money into the area.

Princetown was a small community, with a gossip network that would impress the CIA. Rumours of army personnel staying at the prison have been circulating for decades. However, no one cared what they did up there; it was full of prisoners after all.

The road started to run up hill slightly, and pass a long row of identical houses on the right. Through the gaps in the houses, the prison started to rise up like a medieval fortress.

Naked creatures climbed over hedgerows and through gardens, and ran along the road. They were clumping together now there were so many of them close to the prison.

The houses were becoming spaced out, with more trees and grassland scattered around, as they approached the main entrance to the prison. Then after a short stretch of just trees and long, low stonewalls, the area opened up as the front gate loomed into view.

There was a dark stonewall about fifteen feet high, with a towering arch leading to the main gate. There was another wall, over twenty feet tall, with the principal gateway under a thirty-foot tower. The gap between the two walls is about thirty feet of flat concrete, kept clear of vehicles and people with concrete bollards and the latest surveillance CCTV cameras.

However, today it was not clear; it was chockfull of naked creatures, all clawing at the walls and wooden gates; it was a mass of undulating, blood and grime covered, bodies.

59

Doctor Lazaro and Doctor Hall
Dartmoor National Park
Princetown
Below Dartmoor Prison in The Ark
2:51 PM GMT

Melanie was shocked. "You have been here, working for over thirty years, and you don't even get a space in The Ark?"

Doctor Hall seemed more embarrassed than upset. "I made my peace with that decision many years ago." He looked down at his hands. "It's not just the smoking habit; I also have seronegative polyarthritis, an autoimmune disease where my own body's immune system is attacking my own tissues." He rolled his skinny shoulders, as if to say, *what can a man do; it is what it is?*

"Anyway," he said, squaring up his shoulders, as if recovering from a moment of weakness, "we best get topside." He turned to head for the exit, seemingly uncaring if Melanie decided to follow or not.

The shock of finding out that a man, who had given the best part of his life for the project that would save his corner of the world's species, was wearing off. Melanie's loathing for the people responsible for the project was growing with every passing minute.

With one last look around the large data input room, she started to follow the thin doctor outside.

The view of the underground city still filled her with awe the second time she gazed upon it, from the entrance into the bio building. She noticed for the first time where the light originated. Above, covering the arch of the dome, were millions of triphospor lights, beaming down with the intensity of the sun, enabling the vegetation to grow.

"How is The Ark powered?"

Doctor Hall was just a few steps ahead of her. He turned.

"Nuclear, or course. The reactor is four hundred feet below us. It has been upgraded numerous times, as technology perfects the process of gaining power via the use of sustained exothermic nuclear processes to generate heat and electricity."

Melanie noticed that he was not looking at her while he talked; rather, he stared at a thirty-foot tall weeping willow that was on the edge of the nearest park.

"I planted that tree thirty years ago. I ate my lunch next to it, then under it, everyday since."

He turned without saying another word, and headed for the lift.

As Melanie got closer to a different lift from the one they descended by, she noticed two soldiers stood by the open doors.

"We were taking too long, and General Philips is not a patient man," Doctor Hall mumbled from the corner of his mouth.

The soldiers said nothing as they all climbed into the lift.

Melanie looked out the glass walls as they soared above the manufactured terrain. Buildings perched surrounded by manicured gardens and parks. Lakes glistened from the artificial light. Trees swayed in the air-conditioned wind.

Doctor Hall said she would be vetted for a chance to live the next twenty years down here. She wondered if the feeling that it was all fake would fade with time.

She looked across to the doctor. He seemed to have shrunk in size within the last few minutes, as if the knowledge that he would not get to live in the underground city was eventually sinking in.

He may realize that after thirty years of working down here, creating it, making it a possibility, that this could very well be the last time he ever sees it.

Then it dawned on her that just like Doctor Hall; this might be the last time she looks out across the city – a city that could cocoon her from the madness and death above.

60

Noah, Red, Betty, Lennie, and the Squad
Dartmoor National Park
Princetown
Main Street
3:04 PM GMT

Bull drove past the mass of undulating bodies, all seemingly clawing at the stonewalls with bloody hands. The creatures were oblivious to the truck roaring past so close.

"I don't see how they are going to make a difference," Echo stated over the mask's microphone, as she looked down at the naked bodies from her advantage point in the truck.

The Captain agreed with her.

It does not make sense. It seemed like a hive mind is in control. How else could they all suddenly decide to head for the prison at the same time, while ignoring everything else? However, if that were the case, he decided, *then how would making all the creatures scratch at the walls accomplish anything?*

The truck had to slow down, due to a petrol tanker having jackknifed, blocking off most of the road.

"Jesus!" Coco shouted.

The tanker took up the Captains attention, while they shunted a small Smart Car out of the way, so they could squeeze the truck through the gap. He swung his head around; trying to see what alarmed Coco.

“What are they doing?” Echo said.

The Captain could see a large number of creatures, that was close to the prison walls to the right across the road, had all turned on each other. Or, it would be correct to state, had turned on a few. A handful of creatures did not defend themselves as those around them ripped them apart.

“It doesn’t make sense,” Coco announced. “They have been ignoring us, and everything else, and then suddenly they start to attack each other?”

“Shit!” the Captain announced. “We haven’t got long. Get us to that museum Bull, we need to get inside.”

“I don’t understand,” Echo said.

With a final shove, the truck pushed the small car out of the way.

Behind, the creatures continued gorging themselves on their own kind.

“You know what happens once they are full, and their stomachs rupture?” The Captain let the statement hang in the air.

“They become powerful, exploding bombs!” Echo stated.

"Something is controlling them. How else is this possible?" Coco said. "They are actively planning on breaching the prison walls!"

61

Doctor Lazaro and Doctor Hall
Dartmoor National Park
Princetown
Dartmoor Prison in the Hub Control Room
3:05 PM GMT

The lift did not go to the helipad; rather, it led directly to the main control room of the military part of the prison – the hub building.

The two soldiers stepped out of the lift and stood with their backs against the wall on either side, allowing the two doctors to walk past into the large room.

The room is the size of a tennis court, designed in a semicircle, filled with tables in semicircle rows, on tiered steps, all facing a huge wall sized bank of monitors. Each table has its own collection of monitors and phone. Soldiers sat monitoring the television news feeds, the internet, mobile, and landline phones, as well as CCTV camera feeds. The whole of the country is being monitored. The hum of machines, the ringing of phones, and the buzz of conversations fill the room.

Melanie stared at the large main screen. The wall is sectioned into almost a hundred different feeds; the monitors around the edge of the display are from street surveillance cameras, mounted up high, looking down across the carnage of dead bodies, littered about among smashed up cars and trashed shop fronts. A dozen different cities scattered all across England, now all looking the same – abandoned and dead.

There is what looks like a riot in Trafalgar Square. However, there is no police to quell what seems like an angry mob, which is, in fact, people, running for their lives as naked creatures swarm from side streets, almost looking like the people have been herded together for the slaughter.

The main section of the large wall sized screen though is taken up by camera images from around the perimeter of the prison. Melanie could see what looks like thousands of the infected swarming towards, and around the towering stonewalls. The creatures were climbing over themselves to reach the impenetrable, thick walls. It seemed like a hopeless endeavor.

"Look!" Doctor Hall said, while nodding toward an image in the top left of the main display. "They are eating each other!"

Melanie watched in morbid fascination as groups knelt around in circles, consuming their own kind. However, unlike the previous attacks she had witnessed, this spectacle seemed organized. It did not make sense.

"They are planning on breaching the walls," a voice stated, a matter of fact.

The two doctors turned to see a tall man in his fifties, decked in a military uniform, marching towards them from a sliding door to the right of the large room. Through the open door, Melanie caught a glimpse of an oval table.

"We all know what happens once they gorge themselves senseless."

A small group of people scurried along behind the General. A couple were in military uniforms, showing rank. Others wore doctor's lab coats. A few looked like office staff, donning blouses and tight fitting skirts. Some carried paperwork, other's computer tablets, or walkie-talkies. None of the nine people were talking.

"At the rate they are devouring the meat; they could be ready to explode within..." he stopped talking, waiting for one of his aids to fill the silence.

A tubby, balding man in his mid-forties, who was sweating as if just having finished a marathon stated, "Um, we have witnessed – that is, test results coming from our labs all over the country, state, that the process can be reached, that is, in the perfect conditions, within twenty minutes. Um, sir." He gulped loudly, and then wiped some sweat from his top lip.

The General turned to stare at the feasting horde. “And I would say that is the perfect conditions, wouldn’t you?”

The General swung around. “Doctor Simi, what is your estimate for having all the finalists injected, screened, and ready to send down into The Ark?”

The doctor was slim and short, with Asian characteristics. Her hair was so black and straight it looked like an oil slick down her back.

“Doctor Banks stated she would be ready to start sending them down within the next three hours.” She stood ramrod straight, holding a clipboard to her flat chest.

“Unacceptable!” the General stated. “I want them all underground, and sealed off within the hour.” He stared at the doctor. “Well, why are you still here?”

The doctor turned slowly, ignoring the General’s mood swing. She strolled off towards a sliding door, without saying a word, and apparently without much haste.

“Baker,” the General said, while quickly scanning the wall of screens.

A man in military uniform stepped forward, saluting. “Sir, yes sir!” the man barked.

"Forget the rotations; I want every available soldier holding a weapon within the next five minutes!" He was still looking at the creatures feasting next to the soaring walls. "Get them up on the towers, targeting those groups of eaters."

"Sir, yes sir!" The soldier strode off to carry out his orders.

The General turned to stare at Doctor Hall.

"I see you've made a friend?" he stated with a smirk. "Wife number two maybe?"

There seems to be history between them. The General doesn't like him much, Melanie thought.

"Doctor Lazaro, if you would be so kind as to follow me." He turned and headed back towards the sliding door and the office beyond. His group of supporting staff parted to allow him passage.

"Oh," he said over his shoulder. "You might as well join us Doctor Hall, seems you have nothing better to do."

62

Noah, Red, Betty, Lennie, and the Squad
Dartmoor National Park
Princetown
Dartmoor Prison Museum
3:09 PM GMT

The road snaked out past the prisons towering walls. To the right across the road was a large warehouse complex, where the food supplies were located. A forklift truck was on its side, with a pallet full of baked bean tins spilt across the concrete.

The large warehouse doors were wide open. No one was around; as if there had been a warning of the approaching horde and everyone had run for cover.

There was a big white house on the left with the front door and windows sealed with planks of wood nailed to the frames. There was even a car on the drive with a protective covering over it, as if it would protect it from the end of the world, and after someone would simply throw back the cover and use it as if nothing had happened.

“There it is,” the Captain said.

On the left was a blue sign attached to an old stonewall, stating the museum was in the next group of buildings.

A row of imposing structures ran along the left-hand side of the road. It looked like a converted barn, very old and solidly built.

Red was awake, and sat up. She no longer leaned against Noah. Her head was pounding like a kettledrum, but apart from the headache, she felt a lot better. She watched out the front windscreen as the truck pulled into the car park. Gravel crunched beneath the wheels.

In her deluded, comatosed state, she thought of nothing else apart from her sister, Jasmine. How she let her down. How she had spent almost every waking hour working to support them, when it should have been her stepfather's responsibility. She felt no remorse for what she did to Colin. She would do it again in a second, if given the chance. Red wondered if her sister's body was still in her bed. Or did the police arrive to sort it out before the world turned to shit?

Noah did not know what Red was thinking. For the last half an hour, she was snuggled up against him. Now she sat staring through the front windscreen. He wanted to reach for her hand, but decided against it. After all, he had not even known her for a whole day yet.

Red did not talk about her family. He decided she would when she was ready. She had dodged the questions he asked in the mortgage company's breakroom.

We all have history; he reasoned. *Some sadder than others.* He watched her face as she studied the museum out of the window.

There were a handful of creatures flinging themselves against the museum's front door. The infected ignored the truck as it pulled up outside.

I will never hurt you, Noah thought looking at Red. *But would you hurt me?*

Betty made a whimpering sound.

"Are you okay Betty?" Noah asked, leaning across Red to touch Betty's arm.

Betty recoiled away from his touch.

Gunshots resounded across the car park as Coco and Echo killed the ten creatures near the museum. None of them turned to defend themselves.

"This is getting creepy," Echo said into her microphone.

"Their whole body language and aggression levels have completely changed within the last hour or so, as if something has clicked, and taken over," the Captain stated.

Lennie noticed they had stopped, and pulled the tarp off his head.

The small dog wiggled out of Lennie's grasp and jumped to the ground. He peed up against a tyre. Charlie then shook his coat, as if shaking off water, and stood wagging his tail, waiting for someone to do something.

Echo walked over to one side, so she could cover everyone while Coco dragged the bodies away from the doorway.

"The entrance to the hidden tunnel is in the 'Black Museum' section," the Captain stated. He stood stretching the kinks out of his back.

Bull slammed his door shut. He did not feel like crawling down a hidden tunnel. In the distance, he could see the prison. Safety was just on the other side of those towering walls.

But for how long? He reasoned. *At least when I get down inside The Ark, and it is sealed, all this would be just a bad memory.*

Noah helped Red out of the truck.

Red seemed fragile, as if her swagger had faded. Her smile and happy countenance was replaced with a scowl and squinting eyes.

Lennie slowly climbed out of the back of the truck. He stretched, making him look impossibly tall. He dragged his backpack across the bed of the truck and shrugged it on. He stood motionless, waiting for instructions. He wiped a large hand across his nose, smearing snot up his sleeve.

"Nana," he muttered softly, looking through the thick window where his grandmother sat hunched under the blanket.

Noah noticed Betty had not attempted to move out of the truck. He opened her door.

"Are you okay Betty," he asked.

Betty groaned.

"Betty?" Noah said, as he raised the edge of the blanket.

63

Doctor Lazaro, Doctor Hall, and General Philips
Dartmoor National Park
Princetown
Dartmoor Prison in the Hub's Boardroom
3:12 PM GMT

Melanie followed the General into the large, what looked like a boardroom. There was an oval mahogany table in the center of the room, with more monitors all around the walls.

The accompaniment of assistants all filed in behind Doctor Hall.

Melanie noticed that at the far end of the room was the podium used for the government recording, which was televised, on a loop, every thirty minutes.

"Coffee!" The General barked. "Would you like a drink?" he asked, looking at Melanie, while ignoring Doctor Hall.

"Please." Melanie was so thirsty her throat felt raw. She had swallowed what seemed like gallons of rain and pond water over the last few hours, but she still felt parched.

"Milk, two sugars, please," she simply said.

“So you have found a blocker capable of stopping the infection from spreading?” the General asked.

“Yes,” she simply said. The seat was so comfortable; she felt like leaning back and closing her eyes.

“You know; we tried to make an antidote from the pod the Americans have. However, once the chemical makeup of the pod was checked against the pod buried under the Great Pyramid in Egypt, we found they were different. We realized, after checking them all that they all held a different strain of the same virus.” He leaned back, sipping from a cup that was placed in front of him.

“So we decided a blocker was a no go.” He shrugged his shoulders. “If all six pods had different chemical variants, it would mean the seventh would be distinctive also. And because we do not know its location, we could not collect a sample.” He lowered the cup.

“Of course, now we have a blocker; the transportation network needed to distribute it is non existent. Most roads are blocked with wreckage. I’m afraid we are at a point beyond repair.”

His assistant stood near the edge of the room, pent up, as if ready to move at a moment’s notice. Some were tapping away on tablets or scribbling on clipboards.

Doctor Hall listened as he sat with his elbows on the table, with his face in his hands. He looked exhausted. He was also dying for a cigarette.

"Our only hope is to crawl into our bunkers and wait underground while the world is cleansed by the spores." He motioned to the monitors. "The infection has progressed too far for your blocker to have any use. But it will be studied over the years to come."

Melanie had not said a word since the General started his speech. She could not understand why she was here in the office with him, and why he had taken the time to talk to her. Besides, she was only going through the motions now. She was weary and hungry, and she listened with a heavy heart. Her parents were out in the chaos. She was not naïve; she knew they had no more of a chance than anyone else did out there.

The General changed direction.

"That is why I had you brought here; I want you as part of the scientific team who will study the information gathered about the pods. You will have complete clearance, and use of all the equipment in the extensive laboratories. And of course, a free ticket to sit out the end of the world."

Melanie did not say a word. She was sick of the mention of the pods and their infection.

The world as she knew it was gone, in the process of being wiped away by the black spores. The human race will never be the same again. Her head twisted sharply, looking over at the General.

"On one condition," she stated.

"I think getting a free pass and food and lodgings for the next twenty years is payment enough."

"I want my parents with me. Bring them to The Ark." She stared the General down.

The General turned to nod at an assistant. The woman pressed a button on her tablet. The screen on the wall in front of Melanie switched from a view from the prison walls; to an image of the street her parent's house was situated.

"This was taken by the same helicopter that was sent to rescue you mere hours ago."

The image was a still shot, all blurry. It showed the row of houses where she grew up. Where she played as a child, and where she moved back, to be with the ones she cared for most.

"The reconnaissance camera was recording continually; it gives us a better understanding of what is happening out there." He pointed at the screen. "This is a still shot of when the helicopter flew over your home."

The whole row of houses was burnt to the ground. It was hard to pick out which house used to be her parents. The towering column of smoke rose high into the air.

64

Noah, Red, Betty, Lennie, and the Squad
Dartmoor National Park
Princetown
Dartmoor Prison Museum's Car Park
3:14 PM GMT

Noah jumped back. "What the fuck!" He grabbed Red and pulled her away from the truck.

Coco and Echo swung around, expecting a creature to be running from their blind spot. Both weapons honed in on the problem – Betty.

"Step back everyone!" the Captain shouted. "Don't fire!" He waved a hand at Coco and Echo.

The blanket lay on Betty's lap, uncovering her head and shoulders. Her head lulled back, showing her blistered eyes and swollen cheeks, with veins mapping over her face. She blinked repeatedly. A groan emanated from her raw lips.

The only sound was the gravel under their feet. Then the small dog started barking and backing away.

"She must have been bitten while they were attacked on the roof!" Echo said.

"Surely she knew she would change? Why endanger us all?" Coco stated.

The reason had just noticed his grandmother.

"Nana?" Lennie's voice had a pleading quality to it. His simple mind could not comprehend what was happening.

"Keep him back!" the Captain shouted.

Lennie was fixed to the spot; he could see his grandmother, but could not understand what was happening to her.

"I can feel it..." Betty muttered. Her bleeding tongue smeared blood over her lips. A bubble of blood popped in the corner of her mouth. Her face was a mask of pain.

"What did she say?" Echo asked.

"I can feel it in my head..." Her hand tried to wipe the blood away, but it fell limply back onto her lap.

The Captain stepped closer. "What did you say, Betty?"

"It is buzzing around... I can feel its hunger, its wants... its plan for mankind..."

"What did she say?" Noah asked, also stepping closer.

Red was crying softly, with her arms hugging herself.

"You can feel what, Betty?" the Captain asked, taking another step closer.

"Nana?" Lennie muttered again. His large eyebrows were creased together. He was slowly working the situation out.

"There is a force behind everything... I can feel it entering my mind... I can feel it pushing, taking my memories..." A bloodstained tear rolled down Betty's wrinkled face.

"A force?" the Captain asked.

Everyone was listening intently.

"It knows everything... All the accumulated knowledge of those infected..." She coughed; blood sprayed onto the truck's ceiling. "It knows where we are trying to hide... It will not allow any to live!"

65

Doctor Lazaro, Doctor Hall, and General Philips
Dartmoor National Park
Princetown
Dartmoor Prison in the Hub Control Room
3:17 PM GMT

Melanie was dumfounded. The image on the screen was like a kick in the chest.

Dead! They are both dead!

The General seemed to switch back to the problem at hand. He had passed along the bad news, and as far as he was concerned, that was the end of the situation. He moved the topic along.

"We have been in constant communication with our American allies." He waved a hand in the air. "You obviously saw the vast mast as you landed?" He was referring to the telecommunication pole, with which the base could send and receive signals worldwide.

"Our friends in Groom Lake, America have said their pod has changed."

This had Doctor Hall lower his hands away from his face.

"Changed, how so?" Melanie asked. She was struggling with grief, but a small part of her mind had recovered from the shock, and she knew her parents would not sit around while their house burned down. Deep down she knew they were still alive.

"The pod started emitting a high frequency wavelength, the kind never before registered." He took another sip from his coffee. "We have just received confirmation from Egypt, Mexico, Cambodia, Canada, and Tibet, that the other five pods are also sending out a previously unknown radio frequency." The General looked up at a monitor showing a view across a deserted city center.

"Of course, we don't know if the seventh pod, the one that started all this mess, is doing the same, because as of yet the location of the pod has not been verified." He slowly shook his head. "Apparently, when the loggers were airlifted out, they were in no fit state to tell anyone where they had found the damn thing." He drained his cup.

"If these pods are sending out frequencies, this could be the reason the creatures behaviour has changed, and why they are attacking strategic locations," Melanie said.

"We need to destroy the pods," Doctor Hall stated.

"Thank you Doctor Hall, that much we have worked out for ourselves. Please give us some credit." The General pushed the chair back with his legs as he stood. It was almost as if he was only talking to them both while he took a few minutes to drink his coffee.

"As we speak B2 stealth bombers are already in the air. The six pods we know the locations of will be destroyed within the hour. The seventh is being hunted down using satellite-inferred topography and teams in a search grid on the ground."

"But you said the pods are buried under thousands of tonnes of rock, inside pyramids and temples," Melanie said. "Why can't the people in the locations destroy the pods themselves?"

"Anything could go wrong. Some small part may survive and release another strain. That is why the American president has sanctioned the use of tactical nuclear warhead strikes!"

66

Noah, Red, Betty, Lennie, and the Squad
Dartmoor National Park
Princetown
Dartmoor Prison Museum's Car Park
3:19 PM GMT

"You can hear it in your head, can't you?" the Captain asked.

"Hear what?" Noah questioned. He was ignored.

"It knows everything... Every human changed has contributed to its knowledge... It knows every secret, every hiding place..." Betty muttered. Blood dribbled out of the corner of her eyes.

"That's why all the creatures are here; it sent them!" the Captain stated. He swung around, as if a thought had just accrued to him.

"Bull, get that door open. Now!"

"A hive mind is at work," Echo muttered.

Bull used the butt of his rifle to smash away the lock.

"Nana?" Lennie muttered softly. He took a large step forward.

"Take him. Save my grandson." Betty grimaced as pain filled her body.

"Nana?" Lennie's voice raised a few octaves.

"Everyone into the museum. We haven't much time!" the Captain shouted, while searching around.

"We can't just leave her," Red stated.

"It's too late for her now," the Captain said softly. He placed a hand on Betty's arm.

"If you want, I can end the pain?" the Captain whispered.

Noah started pulling Red towards the museum's entrance.

"It's not fair," Red screamed.

This effected Lennie, who started shouting Nana repeatedly.

Charlie's barking echoed around the car park.

"No Captain... Lennie will never leave with you if you hurt me." She tried to focus in on Lennie's face.

"Go with them, you big lump," Betty muttered.

However, Lennie had a different idea.

"No Lennie. Stop!" Betty tried to shout, but her voice was cracking from the pain.

"Leave her Lennie, we need to get inside," the Captain stated.

He was knocked backwards by a powerful push to the chest by Lennie's large hand, and before anyone could stop him, Lennie scooped his grandmother up into his arms.

“Please, Able,” Betty muttered, using his real name for the first time in years. “Go with them. Leave me... Please.” Bloodstained tears streaked her face.

Then they attacked. A horde, called by the hive mind started pouring over the walls and bushes, heading for the truck.

“Everybody in the museum, now!” the Captain hollered.

Coco and Echo stood either side of the entrance, shooting at the crowd bearing down around them.

Bull was pulling Red into the museum, while shooting his rifle with his free hand.

Noah had hold of Red’s hand and was pulled along with her.

Lennie just stood next to the truck, while hugging his grandmother close to his chest. Sobs racked his large body.

“No Nana. No Nana,” he screamed over and over.

The creatures ignored the giant for the moment, and concentrated on those trying to get inside the building.

67

Doctor Lazaro, Doctor Hall, and General Philips
Dartmoor National Park
Princetown
Dartmoor Prison in the Hub Control Room
3:22 PM GMT

"Look, the first plane has reached its destination," the General said as he pointed to a large screen against the wall.

An aerial image showed a black and white scene from the underbelly of the plane. In the distance stood the imposing triangular silhouettes of the three pyramids. The B2 stealth bomber was approaching from the East, and the sprawling city of Cairo stretched out below. Apart from a few columns of smoke rising from burning buildings, the city looked unaffected from a distance.

"The pod is located in the Pyramid of Khufu, in a secret subterranean chamber thirty-three meters below the Queens Chamber," the General said. "Out of the one hundred and thirty-eight pyramids located in Egypt, of course it would be under the largest."

The sound from the cockpit echoed through hidden speakers.

"Roger that control. The order has been confirmed. The package is away."

Melanie was now standing, with her hands in front of her face.

There may be thousands of survivors hiding in Cairo, waiting to be rescued. They have no idea they are about to be incinerated. A tear rolled down her face.

On the screen, silently, a bay door opened and a missile lowered on hydraulics. Without fanfare, the missile ignited and accelerated away from the belly of the craft, in the direction of the pyramids. The B2 then banked and headed in the other direction, accelerating to its maximum speed to outrun the blast radius.

The image then changed to a view from an EP-E3 reconnaissance plane, circling thirty thousand feet over the target. The view was straight down, with the three pyramids looking like square blotches on the sand.

The boardroom was eerily silent.

The image stayed fixed on the area around the pyramids, looking like a satellite photo, not a live feed. Suddenly, the image changed. In a split second, it went from buildings, pyramids, and sand, to a white circular, oscillating, expanding light. Then the image went blank – overloaded by the glaring light.

"Bingo!" the General shouted, making Melanie jump. "One down, six to go."

68

Lennie and Betty
Dartmoor National Park
Princetown
Dartmoor Prison Museum's Car Park
3:24 PM GMT

The creatures churned around Lennie, ignoring him holding his grandmother in his arms, the prey they were after were much faster, and more likely to get away.

Charlie was dancing around Lennie's large feet, barking and growling at the passing creatures.

Slowly, without rush, the heartbroken, giant of a man, with the mind like a child, walked off towards the road. He paid no attention to the direction; or the screaming of the squad, and the blasting of gunshots behind him, he simply stared down at the bleeding face of the only person in the world that cared about him.

Lennie had no concept of death, of being nothing. He did not know about heaven or hell, good or bad, right or wrong; his life was simple. All he cared about was the fragile body he carried in his muscular arms.

"No Lennie... Put me down and run..." Betty said in a weak voice, while coughing up a glob of blood. She blinked so fast it looked like she was having a seizure.

"Get away from here..."

"Nana is gonna be okay," Lennie muttered while hugging her close to his chest. He did know when someone was poorly.

Lennie started singing slowly, concentrating on the words; it was a nursery rhythm Betty sung to him as a child, whenever he was sick. "I woke before the morning, I was happy all the day, I never said an ugly word, but smiled and stuck to play,"

The banging of the creatures behind stopped. Their focus was changing. They could not reach those behind the sealed door, but they could get to the man walking along the road. The sound of gravel crunching under stamping feet echoed around the car park.

"Run Lennie... run...!" Betty whispered.

"Nana is okay. Lennie is here. Lennie carry you home Nana." He rubbed his cheek against her face, as she used to do to him when he was ill as a child while she sung *A Good Boy* nursery rhythm.

Lennie continued to sing softly in a relaxed tone. "And now at last the sun is going down behind the wood, and I am very happy, for I know that I've been good."

The feet pounded closer.

"Grandma loves you... and always will..."

"Nana loves Lennie. Lennie loves Nana." A big smile spread across his face, as he hugged her close. He could feel her eyelashes brushing blood against his cheek.

Lennie rocked her gently in his arms as he continued to sing. "My bed is waiting cool and fresh, with linen smooth and fair, and I must be off to sleepsin-by, and not forget my prayer."

Betty cried tears of blood, as she used her last ounce of strength to kiss her grandson on the cheek.

Lennie seemed oblivious to the creatures charging at them. He cradled his grandmother like a newborn baby. He continued singing. "I know that, till to-morrow I shall see the sun arise, no ugly dream shall fright my mind, no ugly sight my eyes."

The first group of creatures hit him in the back, making him trip forward, releasing his grip on his grandmother – Betty flew forward. As he was crawling towards her, a crowd of savage eaters sunk their teeth in, ripping and shredding his overalls, trying to reach his flesh.

Lennie did not understand what was happening. He tried to roll, to get them off. He grabbed one creature and crushed its head in his hands. Another he swatted away. But there was just too many.

Betty rolled on her back. She could not close her eyes; her blinking would not allow it. She watched as her grandson vanished under a pile of frenzied, naked, biting, creatures.

Charlie jumped and snapped, biting and scurrying around, trying to get the creatures to leave. They ignored the small pest; they had a bigger meal to contend with.

Betty cried tears of blood, as her grandson tried to crawl towards her, even from under the pile of furious, chewing creatures.

Charlie gave up barking and lay down next to Betty, his small head resting against her arm. He whimpered constantly, while shifting his back legs as if deciding to run or stay.

"Nana..." This time is was faint. Lennie was confused and in pain, and losing a lot of blood.

Betty was grateful for the dog; where he lay was right in her line of sight – she could no longer see her grandson dying.

She also hoped he died quickly, and they left nothing of him, because she knew when she changed, and became an eater, he would be the first thing she would head towards – that is, right after the small dog.

The sound of ripping flesh and cracking bones drowned out the dogs whining.

Betty muttered the last lines of the nursery rhythm, "But slumber hold me tightly till I waken in the dawn, and hear the thrushes singing in the lilacs round the lawn...

"Nana loves you... I will see you again soon..."

69

Noah, Red, and the Squad
Dartmoor National Park
Princetown
Inside Dartmoor Prison's Museum
3:25 PM GMT

Noah stumbled as he ran backwards through the museum's door. Red tripped, but kept her footing, as she released her grip on Noah's hand, and shook Bull's hand off her arm.

Gunshots continued to echo around the confines of the room.

"Get the door secure," the Captain shouted, as he walked backwards, firing at the charging mass.

Echo sprang back, closely followed by Coco.

With a final blast of his rifle, that removed the top of a naked, young male teenager's head, Coco swung the heavy door shut.

"The lock has been smashed off, get me something I can wedge the door closed with," he said to Echo through laboured breaths.

Echo scanned the area around the front door.

The museum was a large, long room, with a high ceiling with thick wooden beams. The floor was skimmed, painted grey concrete.

There was a main aisle through the middle of the room, with displays to either side.

"Here," Echo said, as she grabbed a long piece of wrought iron, which was hanging on some pegs, it was two inches thick and was part of some original section of prison bars on display.

Coco wedge the bar through the two handles.

The creatures smashed themselves against the thick glass panes. The glass held – for now.

"This way," the Captain announced as he headed down the wide aisle.

Noah stared through the mass of thrashing creatures. He could not see Lennie or Betty in the car park. He turned and followed the others.

There was a section of keyring's and hand painted objects to the left. To the right a visitor could get their photo taken, like an old mug shot. The Captain did not check to either side, but headed towards the display cabinets at the back of the room.

Even given the situation, the room seemed depressing, as if the objects contained within held the despair of the inmates, as if their emotions had saturated the very concrete and metal.

The Captain led them to a section containing glass cabinets, chockfull of weapons created by the inmates – axes forged from metal, knuckledusters, knives, shivs, shanks, spikes, and nails, an array of items created to kill or maim. The section was called the 'Black Section,' a nickname given to the illegal weapons made by the prisoners.

"Here, help me Bull." The Captain stood next to a tall case. Inside, a dirt-smeared manikin – with a terrible fake, lopsided beard – was dressed in a prisoner's uniform dating back to 1916 that looked like the material from a badly sown, coarse, itchy sack. A sign hung around the manikin's neck, stating he was a Conscientious Objector, one of the eleven hundred confined in the prison for refusing to fight in the First World War.

Noah realised the banging on the front door had stopped. The silence was even scarier than the creatures tossing their bodies against it. He tried not to think about Betty and Lennie.

Red was twisting and turning, checking every direction, as if frenzied; biting bodies would fly out of hidden corners at any minute.

"Grab the edge," the Captain instructed.

Together, after a few tugs, the paint chipped away around the edge of the case that was resting up against the stonewall. The Manikin tipped over and hit the glass, sending out a spider web of fractures.

As they tugged, the case swivelled on hinges unused in decades. Stale air escaped from the dark tunnel.

The soldiers reached for their torches. Four beams stabbed through the darkness.

They filed in, one at a time. Then, with the large rusty handle, Bull tugged the case back into place. The dull sound of shattering glass announced that the manikin of the prisoner had managed to break through the glass.

"Let's keep moving. We need to get into the hub building before the walls are breached."

As they raced down the tunnel, which was just a little too low to stand up straight, they could hear the banging commence on the front door. The eerie sound of metal sliding, and then hitting the concrete floor, was followed by the sound of the creatures pouring into the museum.

70

Doctor Lazaro, Doctor Hall, and General Philips
Dartmoor National Park
Princetown
Dartmoor Prison in the Hub Control Room
3:29 PM GMT

Melanie was dumfounded. There was so much life being wiped out by the spores, and now they were dropping nuclear warheads all around the planet.

"Good work everyone," the General said. "The next target will be Tibet."

Melanie still had her hands before her face. Disbelief radiated off her.

Tibet! her mind screamed. *Wasn't it Buddha who said something like, 'the body is simply a means of transport for the soul, but it corrupts the spirit?'*

She was not religious in anyway. She wanted to believe there was an all-powerful being out there that set everything in motion. However, as a scientist, she believed in what she could see and touch. Nevertheless, she did believe the physical erodes the metaphysical, similar to Buddha's saying.

If God does exist, how could he stand by and allow us to nuke sections of our planet, even with everything that is going on?

"General," one of the soldiers said, who was talking into a walkie-talkie. "We have activity in one of the tunnels running under the prison walls."

"Really?" the General asked, sounding curious. "Patch us through."

Melanie turned, along with Doctor Hall, happy to have a distraction from the destruction going on across the globe.

The soldier pointed to a screen against the wall, while talking into the walkie-talkie. The screen flickered, then, after the static faded, and the horizontal lines stopped running up the screen; a group of fuzzy people could be seen, via night-vision cameras mounted on the tunnel walls, making their way through the darkness, with thin beams of light to aid their progress.

"Ah, ladies and gentlemen, I believe my daughter has arrived."

71

Noah, Red, and the Squad
Dartmoor National Park
Princetown
In a Tunnel Under Dartmoor Prison
3:33 PM GMT

"Crap," Echo muttered, as she hit her head for the third time. "How much further? I'm gonna brain myself before we get there."

"We have moved under the road, the warehouse, and I think we are under the main prison wall as we speak." The Captain kept his torch pointed down.

"All this for a Chaplin, in case he got spooked?" Bull muttered.

They all ignored his question. They were thinking about Betty and Lennie, and how they had abandoned them. They all knew there was nothing they could have done.

Red was once again holding Noah's hand. She squeezed it so tight he was afraid no blood was reaching his fingers.

Coco gave them his torch, and Noah pointed it at Red's feet, guiding the way. Noah was not claustrophobic, but the tunnel was making his blood run cold. It felt even more depressing than the museum.

"Hello daughter!" a voice said over the soldier's headsets. "I will roll the welcoming mat out for your arrival."

"Hello sir," Echo replied. Her voice changed from her cocky attitude to respectful tones.

"Ah, Captain, I see the twenty soldiers I sent on a simple mission have reduced to four, along with two hitchhikers."

"I'm afraid you're breaking up, General Philips," the Captain said, a hint that he did not want to speak to the General. He switched the radio off. So did the other three.

They walked through puddles and over chunks of rock, which had fallen away from the wall. The beams of light crisscrossed the tunnel.

The Captain almost warned the General that the walls were about to be breached, but he knew the General would already know what was happening.

A concussion boom echoed down the dark tunnel, quickly followed by a series of others. It sounded like a firework display rattling off in the distance.

"The main attack has started," the Captain shouted, to be heard through his mask now he had turned the microphone off.

The Captain shined his light against the closest wall. Cracks had appeared, running down the wall, with dusts and small stones raining down from the roof of the tunnel.

72

Doctor Lazaro, Doctor Hall, and General Philips
Dartmoor National Park
Princetown
Dartmoor Prison in the Hub Control Room
3:34 PM GMT

"The walls are breached," a soldier stated.

No one needed to be told, they could all hear the loud booms that shook the room they stood inside. The monitors on the walls flickered. The lights dimmed for the briefest of moments before flaring back up.

"Are the men not in position, like requested?" the General asked, spinning around to confront one of his advisors.

"Yes sir." The soldier looked nervous. "They have been firing on the crowds since you gave the order."

"I've heard no grenades or missile launchers exploding?" His eyes pierced the officer.

"We thought it might damage the walls to use explosives so close to the perimeter."

Melanie could see the officer gulping.

"Do you really think that matters now?" The General hollered. "Unleash everything we have. Try to contain them near the walls, while we get the people underground." He turned and marched out of the room.

Melanie and Doctor Hall followed the General and his group of lackeys.

The main control room was in chaos. There were people shouting orders, with others running back and forth.

Melanie noticed the main bank of monitors. It showed the walls had collapsed in several areas. The hordes were pouring through the gaps of tumbling masonry. Soldiers stood in rows, firing into the mass of undulating bodies.

Large M2 Browning machineguns stood on tripods at intervals along the line. Their destructive .50 caliber bullets shredded everything in their path. The creatures behind climbed over the remains of their companions.

"I want those people injected and underground now!" the General screamed. He then sprung around to the two doctors. "Doctor Hall, get Doctor Lazaro over to the preparation area, and get her injected and send her underground with the first batch!" He sprung around.

"Heather, go with them and get yourself injected and underground. Oh, and make sure Doctor Hall doesn't screw this up."

Heather was one of the people who followed the General around like a lost puppy.

She looked flustered, as if she believed her place was in the main building, helping to direct operations, not baby-sitting two doctors. She had shoulder length blonde hair and a kindly face. She could have been anything from forty to fifty, and could have passed as a midwife in a maternity ward of any hospital, if it was not for her expensive taste in clothes – she wore a Dolce and Gabbana cream blouse and an auburn, knee-length Fendi skirt, with Manolo Blahnik shoes.

Melanie had also noticed that Doctor Hall had been flicking glances over at the woman since they entered the control room.

“My names Heather Kennedy.” She held out a hand to Melanie, while giving Doctor Hall an evil glare.

With all the shouting, the booms of explosions, and the muted sound of gunfire through the walls, Melanie found it strange that this woman wanted to shake her hand.

“For god’s sake Heather, we haven’t got time for fucking pleasantries,” Doctor Hall said through clenched teeth.

Heather dropped her hand before Melanie could grasp it.

“Jesus, Albert, do you always have to be such a cock!” She marched off towards a set of sliding doors, not caring if either of them was following her.

"You'll have to excuse my ex-wife; she always was such a bitch!" Doctor Hall stated, as he took a cigarette out of the packet from his breast pocket. He followed Heather out into the hallway, while lighting the cigarette and inhaling deeply.

"What?" Doctor Hall said as Melanie caught up and walked along next to him.

"I think a little cigarette smoke is the least of everyone's problems."

73

Noah, Red, and the Squad
Dartmoor National Park
Princetown
In Dartmoor Prisons Chapel
3:41 PM GMT

"Bull help me," the Captain said, as he wedged his shoulder against a wooden barrier. However, just as they were both about to push, the hidden entrance swung open.

"Bull," a voice said. A soldier stood in the glaring light from the exit, which was a wooden panel in the small antechamber next to the main chapel.

"Clint?" Bull said.

"I've been sent to take you directly to the General," the soldier stated. He looked at the six people exiting the tunnel.

"Only four of you made it back, along with two civilians?" Clint asked. He was young and tall, and covered in masonry dust.

"It is crazy out there," Echo said as she pushed by, glad to be out of the claustrophobic tunnel.

The booms of exploding poppers were much louder aboveground. The rat-a-tat-tat of gunfire echoed around inside the chapel, with the screams of dying soldiers mixed in. Different blasts could now be heard, not the dull popping of bloated bodies, but the sound of grenades and missile launchers.

"The way is clear for now, but they are swarming into the prison through multiple breaches." The soldier pushed open the thick chapel door. The sounds tripled in loudness.

The chapel was close to the back wall, which was breached. However, even though the thick wall had caved in, a tall security, metal linked fence was still holding the swarming creatures back.

The chapel's back door exited onto a forty-foot compact dirt area, used for storage that had a few smaller stone huts against one side, along with a long polythene greenhouse. A thin concrete path led to the back of the hub building, next to a row of what looks like prison warden houses.

A line of soldiers stood in the dirt, firing repeatedly through the fence, cutting the creatures down.

The Captain noticed what was happening.

"Stop firing!" he hollered. The sound of the rifles and large M2 miniguns drowned his cries out.

The Captain could not understand how the soldiers were so blind. The horde was climbing on the dead, using them like a mound, and now they could reach the top of the fence. They swarmed over.

74

Doctor Lazaro and Doctor Hall
Dartmoor National Park
Princetown
The Preparation Area in Dartmoor Prison
3:42 PM GMT

"You know you're not meant to smoke inside?" Heather said over her shoulder, without bothering to turn around.

Doctor Hall simply ignored her, and his next exhalation was even louder.

Heather returned the favour and ignored him.

The sound of fighting was dull but could still be heard through the thick walls. The muted explosions vibrated through the soles of their shoes.

"The Preparation Area is in the center of the building, right above the main lift shaft," Heather explained for Melanie's benefit. "Sadly though, almost a hundred Adam and Eve Finalists failed to arrive as scheduled. The General believes either their helicopters crashed, or they simply never got the chance to board."

The long white hallway ended in a series of three thick doors. Heather pulled a card from her clipboard and scanned it on the center door. It hissed open.

Doctor Hall flicked his cigarette to the floor before following the two women inside.

Melanie found herself inside another contamination vault. The memories of the last one rushed back. She used a hand to steady herself against the cold metal wall.

A white mist hissed from vents in the ceiling, enveloping the whole chamber. Powerful fans kicked in, and the mist was sucked away.

As the thick door slid open, screaming filled the vault they just stepped out of.

"What the..." Heather's words died on her lips when a naked teenager, who was saturated with blood and masonry dust, tackled her, knocking her sideways like a ragdoll.

Melanie was pulled back by Doctor Hall, just as a group of creatures noticed them.

Doctor Hall slammed his hand on the close button. The door gracefully slid shut. The creatures slammed against the thick metal door.

Through a small window, Melanie could see that one side of the large room had collapsed, with creatures pouring through. The handful of soldiers were already dead, with the remains of the Adam and Eve Finalists – men, women and children – being ripped limb from limb. It was a blood bath.

Her view was partially blocked when blood was smeared over the thick glass by a naked arm. She jumped when the hiss of the white mist filled the room, blocking her view out of the window.

75

Noah, Red, and the Squad
Dartmoor National Park
Princetown
Outside the Dartmoor Prison Chapel
3:45 PM GMT

"Run!" the Captain screamed.

The fence was starting to buckle under the mass of bodies trying to climb over. The creatures surged across the compact dirt.

"Into the hub building," Coco shouted as he led the way along the thin path.

The fence finally gave way. The creatures tipped, rolled, and then righted themselves in one move, while racing towards the soldiers.

Coco and Bull ran along the path, with Red and Noah close behind. Echo and the Captain jogged backwards while firing into the mass of surging bodies.

The line of soldiers fragmented; they knew they had no chance against the multitude racing towards them.

Noah gripped Red's hand as if both their lives counted on him never letting go. Suddenly, movement caught Noah's attention out of his peripheral vision. He instinctively stopped running, pulling Red to one side.

Naked bodies were pouring over the walls on either side of the thin pathway.

They were blocked in.

76

General Philips
Dartmoor National Park
Princetown
Dartmoor Prison in the Hub Control Room
3:46 PM GMT

The General could see, via the bank of monitors, that every major part of the prison's main wall was breached; creatures were pouring in by the thousands; all called from miles around by some higher, hive mind.

He just received confirmation that the Tibetan, Cambodian, Canadian, and Mexican pods had been tactically nuked. The Americans had evacuated Groom Lake and had remotely detonated a controlled nuclear device to destroy their pod. The only one remaining was the Madagascan pod – the cause of all the trouble.

The American president had given up waiting, and had approved complete blanket coverage of thermal nuclear warheads over the two hundred and twenty-two thousand square mile island of Madagascar. All eighteen Ohio-classed ballistic missile submarines had been diverted with their seventeen hundred warheads. It was estimated that it would take two days of nonstop firing to complete the mission. The projected twenty-two million casualties (if that many were still alive) would be chalked up as casualties of war.

The General was glad one world leader had the balls to do something.

The British Prime Minister, David Cameron, and his cabinet members, were hiding down inside a bunker one hundred feet below the Northwood suburb of London. Normally, it was the control center for the Combined Task Force 345, which was England's control room for its four Vanguard class submarines. However, it was taken over to keep the British government running.

The Prime Minister and cabinet members, along with their families, were supposed to relocate to The Ark five hours ago. The reason for their delay was unknown, due to not being able to reach the Northwood bunker.

The General did not care if the Prime Minister was dead or alive. In his opinion, Parliament members come and go, but military leaders stay the duration. He had been in the army for almost forty years; he had seen eight different Prime Ministers inside number ten Downing Street. He ran the most important British secret bunker, not them. They would come and take a tour, umming and ahhing about how big and expensive it was. Then they would leave and never come back. They never truly believed they would ever need to use it.

As for the Queen and royal family, within days of the word pandemic being broadcasted, and the boarders being closed, they had all vanished. He had heard rumours that they were on a large luxury yacht in the middle of Loch Lomond in Scotland. They could all drown for all he cared.

The control room was in complete chaos. A live video feed, from the Preparation Area, showed that the creatures had entered the main part of the building and was in the process of killing England's hopes for future repopulation.

It seemed hopeless.

Soldiers and civil servants were abandoning their posts. It was only a matter of time before the whole complex was overrun.

The General casually walked through the chaos of screaming and crying, and headed to his private office. His attendants had long disappeared.

The General walked around his luxurious office, with walls filled with books, and photos. He sat behind his large antique desk that once belonged to the Prime Minster, William Pitt the younger.

He stared at a photo of Echo and her mother Jane, who died when Echo was five.

The General pulled open a large bottom drawer and removed a black box. He pressed his thumb against a scanner that clicked and the lid slowly opened.

Outside, in the main control room, people were screaming louder. The creatures had broken in.

Inside the box was a small device with a simple keyhole. The General pulled a chain from around his neck. A key hung from it. Without any rush, the General inserted the key, pushed his thumb against another scanner, and turned the key. A piercing alarm resounded throughout the whole prison.

"T-minus twenty minutes," a robotic female voice announced over the tannoy system, cutting through the alarm.

Explosives positioned around the grounds would level the complex, leaving the underground bunker unaffected.

The General seemed way to calm, as if on the verge of a breakdown. His whole military career was connected to The Ark. Everything he had been working for, for his entire working life, was collapsing around him.

His left eye twitched.

From the same drawer, he then removed a small case. He placed it on the desk. Inside was an injection system – the antidote for the gas. Without fanfare, he picked the device up and forced it into his neck. With a hiss, the fluid was in his system.

The General stood and brushed down his uniform. While ignoring the screaming on the other side of his office door, he strode to a bookcase and pulled down on a book – Z *Wars* by Max Brooks, which was his idea of ironic, and the bookcase slid open.

Somewhere in the prison, his daughter was fighting for her life. He had to find her and his sister, the only two surviving members of his family, and get them into the bunker.

The General disappeared down a hidden tunnel.

77

Doctor Lazaro and Doctor Hall
Dartmoor National Park
Princetown
The Preparation Area in Dartmoor Prison
3:47 PM GMT

Melanie was back out in the hallway, breathing hard. She felt like she was going to have an anxiety attack. She leaned forward with her hands on her knees.

"This way," Doctor Hall stated, as he walked across to another door.

Melanie noticed he held a metal, silver, bubble briefcase in his hand. She wondered where it had come from.

He must have snatched it out of the room.

Muffled sounds of screaming and gunshots echoed around the stark white walls. Distant concussive booms vibrated the floor and walls. The explosions sounded like they were getting closer.

"They're everywhere!" Melanie muttered.

"Now, now, Doctor Lazaro, let's not give up so easily." Doctor Hall swiped his card. The door swished open. The hall was only three meters long and had a lift at the end.

"Shall we?" He held his hand out for her to go first.

"What? Where?" Melanie blurted.

"The safest place in this country – below our feet, underground."

"We can't, have you forgotten about the gas?" Tears of fear ran down Melanie's cheeks.

"That, midear, will no longer be a problem," he stated while swinging the briefcase in his hand.

"T-minus twenty minutes," the speakers announced, as the alarm rang through the hallway.

"What now?" Melanie asked.

"To the bunker. And by the sounds of it, we'd better hurry."

78

Noah, Red, and the Squad
Dartmoor National Park
Princetown
The Greenhouse Tunnel
3:50 PM GMT

Eaters scrambled over the wall, launching themselves through the air, slashing, and swinging their arms.

One hit Bull in the chest, knocking him backwards, to land hard on the concrete path. The wind was punched from his lungs, as his arms flew to the sides, releasing the rifle. The back of Bull's head cracked against the ungiving surface. In his dazed state, he tried to bring his arms up to protect his face, but the creature was just too fast.

So this is how I die! Bull thought, as the deformed face of an adolescent male, with bulging, bloodshot eyes and a twisted, overstretched maw of a mouth, flew straight at his face.

Bull disappeared under a pile of frenzied naked attackers. His bloodcurdling scream filled the alleyway, then cut off into a wet gurgling, choking sound.

Coco stood back, firing at the bodies climbing over the wall.

The Captain and Echo could see what was happening to Bull, but they had problems of their own. Now the fence had collapsed a mass of creatures were surging into the grounds. The soldiers vanished under the piles of undulating bodies.

"Here!" Noah shouted to Red. He picked up a stone and tossed it through a window of a long snaking tunnel that led to the greenhouse.

While Red used a stick to rake the fragments of glass from the sill, Noah pulled his handgun free and shot a child of about eight in the head.

"Noah!" Red screamed.

Noah turned to find Red already through the window, holding her hands out to him. He ran and dived through.

The tunnel joined the greenhouse with a large building. Ignoring the feeble sided polythene greenhouse, they sprinted along the tunnel towards the stone building.

Noah could hear the squad outside fighting for their lives. He felt bad for leaving them, but his priority was to protect Red. Also the alarm ringing, with the robotic countdown sounded ominous. In any movie he had ever seen, a countdown never ended in anything good.

At the end of the tunnel was a thick door. With Red's help, he swung it open. The room on the other side held something they were not expecting.

79

Doctor Lazaro, Doctor Hall, Noah, and Red
Dartmoor National Park
Princetown
The Gathering Room
3:51 PM GMT

The lift did not go all the way down to The Ark, but stopped in the large Gathering Room, a chamber with a large lift that took all the provisions down to the bunker.

There was no one around. If someone was supposed to be operating the lift, they had obviously run away.

The chamber was cavernous, with walls of shelving holding stacks of pallets. Parked machinery was up against one wall – an industrial hedge trimmer, a large, motorized lawnmower, a mechanical lift for possibly reaching streetlights.

As Melanie followed Doctor Hall towards the large lift platform, a door swung open and two people raced through.

Noah and Red barged through the door. They skidded to a halt, while scanning the room.

Noah noticed two people and raised the handgun.

"We are unarmed," Melanie shouted, which echoed around the chamber.

Doctor Hall raised the metal briefcase, possibly hoping it would deflect bullets.

It was a standoff for a few seconds until they all realized they were all uninfected.

Noah and Red ran towards the two strangers.

"I recognize you," Noah stated, looking at Melanie. "You were up to your chest in water, resuscitating a soldier. You left in the helicopter."

"Naked man!" Melanie said. "Where are the Captain and the others?" She knew this young man was with them when she was whisked away. If he was here, so should they be.

"They are outside, fighting the creatures. We had to run," he said, embarrassed at leaving the others.

"We have to hurry," Doctor Hall stated. He was standing next to a series of buttons on a raised dashboard.

"That's far enough Doctor," General Philips said, as he stepped from behind a set of shelving. The General held a gun pointed at the doctor's chest.

80

Doctor Lazaro, Doctor Hall, Noah, Red, the Captain, Echo, Coco, and General Philips
Dartmoor National Park
Princetown
The Gathering Room
3:56 PM GMT

"Father! What are you doing?" Echo's voice stabbed through the silence.

The Captain and Coco followed Echo into the chamber. They shot their way out of the alleyway, and then jumped through the window Noah smashed. They had to leave Bull's body behind.

"T-minus ten minutes!"

"Glad you finally made it, daughter." The Generals gun did not waver.

"What are you doing?" Echo repeated, taking a few steps closer.

"Lower your gun," the Captain said.

"I do not take orders from underlings, Captain."

"We are all on the same side," Melanie stated. She was confused as to what was happening.

"Where is Heather?" the General asked.

"She didn't make it," Melanie replied.

"I was talking to Doctor Hall." The Generals grip tightened on the gun. His left eye twitched.

"What do you mean; she didn't make it? Where's Aunty Heather?" Echo asked. "Uncle Hall?"

"He's not your uncle, not anymore!" the General screamed.

"The Gathering Room is compromised. She was attacked and killed," Melanie said softly.

The General coughed, and twisted his neck, making it click. "Pass the case to my daughter, please, Doctor Hall."

The Captain nodded to Coco, who slowly started to drift over to the right.

"The case, Doctor Hall." The Generals voice was cracking. Sweat started to pour down his face. He twisted his neck again.

"It's over," Doctor Hall stated. "The base is overrun. The Adam and Eve Finalist are all dead, or dying." He let his words hang in the air.

"We can all survive this. In the briefcase is the antidote to the gas. We can all go underground. We can all live on."

"Not you, Doctor!" The General took another step closer.

"Listen to him," the Captain said. "Let's inject ourselves and get underground."

A smashing sound echoed down the tunnel.

"Too many have died today," Echo muttered. "Please father."

"He ruined your aunt's life. He made her miserable."

He has a screw loose; Melanie reasoned.

"My sister should be going down there, living on, not you!"

"Put the gun down, General," the Captain said.

"I am tired of your demands," the General muttered as he swung the gun around and fired a bullet into the Captains chest.

81

Dartmoor National Park
Princetown
Dartmoor Prison
3:57 PM GMT

The prison was completely overrun. Creatures swarmed every hallway and room. More churned through the breaches in the walls.

Bodies lay uneaten, as the horde of infected searched every part of the prison for anyone left alive.

Computers lay tipped over next to cooling corpses. Blood gathered into congealing pools.

The hive mind knew the humans were preparing to hide below ground. Every infected human's memories were added to the collective knowledge of the hive. Every secret known.

However, what the humans failed to realize was, the pods did not contain the knowledge – only the spores, every single infected human did. Billions of minds connected. Each brain filled to capacity with information. Each mind capable of controlling every infected person. The only way to stop the sharing of information was to destroy every infected creature.

Once enough time had passed, to make sure as many people were infected as possible, the pods started to send out a frequency that tuned all the creatures into one directive, the eradication of all human life.

The spores would spread, consuming every human. Then once they were all infected, exploded, and the spores multiplied, it would mutate, infecting other species. The land and sky would be wiped clean. Mother Nature would recover from the human scourge, and in time, the world would heal, and the evolutionary chain would start all over again, when, given time, something else would crawl out from the sea, which has been the case, on the fertile third planet from the sun, since the dawn of time.

82

Doctor Lazaro, Doctor Hall, Noah, Red, the Captain, Echo, Coco, and General Philips
Dartmoor National Park
Princetown
The Gathering Room
4:01 PM GMT

"T-minus five minutes!"

Coco fired. The bullet spun the General around. The gun flew through the air. The Generals body hit the concrete with a loud slap.

"Dad! Echo shouted, while running over to his body. The bullet went clean through his shoulder.

The General rolled over.

The Captain slowly got to his feet. His armour stopped the projectile, but it still winded him.

"Calm down, it was just a warning shot. If I wanted the Captain dead, I would have shot him in the head." Sweat dripped down the Generals face. Blood soaked his uniform around his shoulder.

"You, on the other hand," the General said, as he reached for the gun on the floor with his left hand and pointed it at the doctor again.

"We only have five minutes to inject ourselves and get below ground!" Doctor Hall stated. "Please everyone, step forward." The doctor knelt down and opened the bubble briefcase. Inside were rows of injection devices.

"Did I say you could move?" The General was coughing, with sweat soaking his uniform's collar.

"T-minus four minutes!"

"Father please, we need to get underground," Echo pleaded, while using her hand to staunch the flow of blood.

"I said, don't move!" The gun went off again, this time hitting Doctor Hall in the chest. Unlike the Captain, the doctor had no body armour to stop the bullet.

Coco stepped forward and fired again.

"No!" Echo screamed as she rolled her father around. The bullet that was intended for him hit Echo in the neck.

"Echo!" Coco dropped his rifle and ran over.

Melanie leaned over the doctor. Blood bubbled on his lips.

"You're going to be okay," Melanie muttered, while cradling him in her arms. She jerked when she felt something stab her leg. She looked down and saw that with his last ounce of strength, the doctor had stabbed an injection into her leg.

"T-minus three minutes!"

Noah stood in front of Red, blocking her with his body. Everything was happening so fast. He was confused as to what was going on. However, in all the chaos, he realized the injections were important somehow. He grabbed Red's hand and dragged her over to the two doctors.

Bare feet could be heard running down the tunnel. The creatures then poured into the chamber.

The Captain rattled off bullets.

"Coco! Coco! I need your help!"

Coco was cradling Echo, who had blood spurting from her neck wound.

"What have you done?" the General screamed.

The Captain fired at the door, cutting down the advancing creatures. He knew his bullets would soon run out, and in the time he needed to change the magazine, they would be upon them.

In all their stress and panic, and for losing Bull, they had forgotten to secure the door.

The Captain took a few steps backwards. He slapped his hand down on the button to start the lift.

"T-minus two minutes!"

Noah grabbed an injection from the case and forced it into Red's arm. He stabbed himself in the leg with another. He then grabbed Red and pulled her down next to him. If he was about to die, he wanted to be holding onto Red.

Creatures were pouring through the door.

Echo let out her last rattling breath.

Coco seemed to wake up.

"You bastards!" he screamed as he picked up his rifle and walked towards the advancing creature's firing into the mass of bodies.

The lift was descending fast.

Melanie held her hand over the wound in the doctors chest.

"It's no use," he muttered. His eyes rolled back a little. "A cigarette."

Melanie pulled the packet from his pocket. She placed one in his mouth. The lighter was inside the carton. She lit it for him.

The cigarette rested limply on his dry lips. He did not have the strength to take a deep breath and inhale the smoke. His eyes rolled back as his last breath left his body.

Red and Noah embraced each other.

The General lay hugging his daughter as the lift dropped down below his line of site. Echo had stopped moving; even her blood had stopped squirting now her heart had stopped pumping.

"No! No! No!" the General muttered. "It wasn't meant to end like this! It wasn't meant to end like this," he muttered like a Tibetan mantra.

"T-minus one minute!"

The lift was accelerating faster.

Noah could hear the gunfire far above. They must be at least fifty feet below the ground level, and still moving fast. As he looked up, the ceiling started to close, with large metal blast doors grinding together.

The Captain stood next to Coco; they both fired into the horde piling in through the doorway. Behind, the Captain could feel the thick metal doors grinding shut through the soles of his boots.

"T-minus thirty seconds!"

The Captain knew he could not join them on the lift. The creatures would simply pour over the side after them, allowing many to reach the lift before the doors closed. And even though most of them would die in the fall, it would still mean the spores would succeed in getting inside the bunker.

Coco was in a daze from shooting Echo. His face was contorted in rage as he fired. Then his rifle clicked. He had used all his bullets. He turned it around, hefting it like a club and ran at the closest creature.

The Captain continued firing; even though he knew in a few seconds they will all be incinerated. However, even with that in mind, he wanted to die knowing he had personally killed as many as he could with his own two hands.

"T-minus five... four... three... two..."

Noah could feel the lift shake as a loud boom shook the shaft.

Aboveground, the towering prison walls were flattened as the detonation sent out a sonic donut ring as the buildings were incinerated. The vast communication mast swayed, as the thick cables snapped, then slowly, as the metal melted under the heat, the pole tumbled down.

83

Noah, Red, and Doctor Lazaro
Dartmoor National Park
Princetown
The Ark
4:07 PM GMT

The lift descended, breaking free from the concrete tube, entering the widest of the glass shafts.

Noah and Red were gobsmacked. Below them was a vast city, with buildings dotting the landscape, with manicured lawns, lakes, and trees swaying in the artificial breeze.

"What is this place?" Red whispered while walking over to the edge, looking through the thick glass.

"It's a secret bunker build by the British Government. It can hold two thousand people, with enough food, water, and power for them all for twenty years. The three of us can survive here for the rest of our natural lives." She looked down at the body of Doctor Hall.

I will bury you under your weeping willow, she thought. So, *in the end, you did get to stay down here*. Tears dripped off her chin.

Melanie looked down over the city.

With over one hundred years of preparation, all the British have to continue our corner of the world is one male and two females!

Her leg was going numb under the doctor's dead weight. She gently moved him to one side, and rested his hands over his chest, then closed his eyes.

I will spend every minute creating a cure, not a blocker, in case any of the pods have survived. I have a lab, the equipment, and all the time in the world. Humanity will never have to go through this again.

Red stared down over the calm, surreal city.

I do not deserve this; Red thought. *My sister should be here, not me, not after what I have done. How can I ever be happy with Jasmine's ghost holding onto my heart?* She looked sideways at Noah, who had come to stand next to her.

I like you, but can I live the rest of my life with you, imprisoned in a fake world? She decided she had twenty or so years to find out.

Noah noticed Red looking sideways at him. He turned to look at her.

I know it was you in my reoccurring dreams. I dreamt of the colour red – your hair. It was a sign!

He gave her a smile. Then he looked over his shoulder and asked Melanie, "What's the city called?"

However, it was Red who answered, as she reached for Noah's hand. "We shall call it Home."

* * * * *

Now we return three weeks to the beginning of the outbreak and see how each of the main characters survived up until the point when all their lives crossed paths.

* * * * *

NOAH`S STORY

Noah Edward Morgan

Twenty-one-year-old male
Flat 17b, Union Street
Newton Abbot
South Devon
England

Works at Asda Newton Abbot on the Provisions Aisle as a shelf stacker.

1

Saturday 15th December 2012

The Day of the Outbreak

The alarm jolted Noah from his dream. With a slam of his hand, the clock flew from the bedside cabinet.

Every night for months, the same bloody dream. He struggled to remember anything from the dream that made him toss and turn every night, and soak the sheets in sweat.

The colour red! It was all he could remember. What the colour symbolized he had no idea. He had Googled what the colour represents if it was in your dreams. One dream interpretation site stated: *Red could represent courage, passion, and emotional relationships. Red also represents the colour for danger. Red signifies energy and vitality, action, fire, blood, anger, and dominant sexuality.*

To get a better understanding of the mindset of the people who wrote the information, he entered the word sandwich. For some reason, to see a fish sandwich in your dream means you have a conflict between your spiritual beliefs and what is practical. He tried another random word. A hamster supposedly represents underdeveloped emotions. He decided to skip any more research.

Noah squinted his eyes at the clock.

6:35 AM.

Jesus! And it's a Saturday!

He hated the early-morning shifts. He was not a morning person.

Asda was the only place hiring when he lost his job at Blockbuster. So maybe he did let off a few too many customers who brought the DVDs back late. *But,* he reasoned; it *was a big company; they wouldn't mind.* Obviously, they did.

He had to take whatever was going, he needed the money. He had no savings and little education. Being an orphan, he did not have parents to send him to college, just a system that booted him out as soon as he was legally old enough to look after himself.

Noah groaned and swung his feet off the bed. He rubbed his hands down his stubble-covered face. He would have to shave today. He was told if he went in looking like a homeless person again he would be sent home and docked a day's pay.

Jane, his supervisor, was such a bitch. Super Jane they called her behind her back; always rushing about, mostly when management was around.

Simon and Jean were both away this week. Why Super Jane let them both have the same time off; he will never know. It just meant more work for everyone else. And of course, ever since the misunderstanding, where Noah thought the freezer was empty, so he closed it on the way to lunch, only to find, when he returned, that he had locked Super Jane in there for almost an hour, he now found he was marked down for all the early shifts for the next week.

Super Jane. Super Bitch.

Noah snatched up the TV remote and flicked it on from standby. He did not care what was on; he just liked the sound of people talking; it made him feel like he was not alone.

The channel was set to CNN. He loved to listen to the America news network. Everything was so dramatic and sensationalized. And, if he was honest, he liked the sound of their accent.

"...In other news, a group of nine loggers were airlifted out of a work site next to the Nosivolo River in Marolambo, Madagascar, and taken to Cape Town, South Africa, after apparently suffering from some unknown malady.

"Reports are sketchy at the moment, but what is known is within eight hours of the helicopter leaving for the Mananjary Airport, eighty-one miles away, the Madagascan government declared Marolambo, in the Atsinanana Region, in the Province of Tamatave, a quarantined area. All twenty-six thousand residents are said to be under house arrest.

"Also, the city of Mananjary, Fianarantsoa, where the plane took off from, has also been quarantined, with an estimated twenty-eight thousand civilians under house arrest.

"As the news comes in, we will update you."

Tens of thousands under house arrest. And I think getting up at 6:35 AM is bad. Then again, if I was under house arrest, I wouldn't have to go to work.

Noah contemplated phoning in, saying he was ill. However, unless he took a doctor's note in, he was docked a day's wages. At first, they believed him, and even paid him for a few sick days. However, they soon realized after working there for almost a year that he had a few too many upset stomachs.

The worst thing about his flat was that the toilet was downstairs. He lived above a fish and chip shop, and shared a back door with them. After entering his flat, next to the stairs, was his freezing cold toilet. Last year, one of the pipes burst because it froze.

He started the shower, turning it on piping hot, while he sat on the toilet, letting the steam warm the room. The whole bathroom was covered in tiles, including the ceiling, and was an off-white colour with mold growing in the grouting, regardless of how much he scrubbed the things with bleach.

He rested his head on the sink as he sat on the toilet, and with a jolt realized, he had fallen asleep. He napped for ten minutes. His routine was to the minute, and if he did not rush, he would be late for work.

Noah rushed his shower, and then shaved over the sink. He did not like shaving; the razor gave him a rash for the rest of the day. Nevertheless, for some reason, Super Jane would rather see an unsightly, raw rash than a little manly stubble.

After shaving, and cutting himself twice, he raced back upstairs. He grabbed a gaudy-green and black shirt off the couch. He sniffed under the arms. It looked like an elephant had slept on it, but he did not have time to iron it. In fact, he could not even remember where the iron was. It also had a tidemark around the collar.

Who would see that if the top button was done up?

His black trousers were just as bad. They even had a small rip in the back on the pocket line. However, he was dead set on buying the new Call of Duty MW3 X-Box game, and he could not afford new trousers as well, not when the game cost forty quid and it was over two weeks until the next payday.

His black shoes were so scuffed they almost looked grey. He did not own shoe polish or brushes. He used a greasy dishcloth, which was draped over the dirty dishes in the small sink, to give them a quick wipe.

Noah checked himself out in the mirror next to his desk. He was five feet six inches tall, and skinny as a rake, with what looked like a runner's body. No matter what he did to his light-brown hair, it always stuck up everywhere. Some people paid good money to make theirs look as causally scruffy as his. All he had to do was wake up, shower, and then ignore it.

Noah pulled on his coat.

The TV was showing images of a deserted city.

Possibly, one of the two cities in Madagascar, Noah thought, but gave it scant attention. Just as he was about to flick the TV off, the scrolling line across the bottom announced that Cape Towns International airport and surrounding three-mile area was under quarantine.

Jesus, they always overreact; he thought, as he grabbed his wallet, mobile and keys off the table and headed to work.

2

Noah sat in the breakroom for his forty-five-minute lunch break.

His morning was hectic.

Saturdays were the busiest day of the week. Just keeping the milk stocked up was a full-time job by itself, but he had to keep one whole side of the aisle stocked.

Customers complained when the milk ran down, and they had to reach back to get the jug from the bottom of the trolley.

People are so lazy; they want everything handed to them nowadays.

He rushed to fill up the yogurt, the cheese, and packaged meat sections. However, it was a hopeless task. The large cages, full of products, would have to be on a conveyor belt to keep up with demand. But they weren't. He had to walk to the chillers, out the back of the store, fill the cages by pulling the stock off the shelves and pull the heavy cage back out onto the shop floor, then unpack, stack, and tidy as he went.

Halfway through a cage he would have to rush back to grab more trolleys of milk.

Also, customers would ask where a product was, even though each aisle had the contents written on huge hanging signs, and he wasn't allowed, due to company policy, to just point and grunt; he had to personally walk the customer to the exact location on the shelf.

Noah sat looking down at his lunch. Shepard's pie with peas and gravy. It was one of the few good things about working for a large food outlet; the meals were crazy cheap. He only snacked at home, and ate all his main meals at work.

He had twenty minutes left on his break, so he sat gripping his Samsung Galaxy Note.

He did not check his Facebook page, as everyone else seemed to do every ten minutes, because he did not have one.

Noah did not have any family, due to his mother dying when a car hit her when he was young, and he never knew his father, and subsequently; he had worked his way through Social Care as an orphan. Therefore, he had no family to chat with, and upload photos about. He did not even have any real friends, just a couple of people he worked with.

Society would class him as an introvert. However, he was not too big on tags.

Therefore, instead of checking out what people were currently complaining about on their Facebook pages, he sat checking the Sky News App.

The top stories were: Child Abuse Web Images Must Be Blocked; Three Britons Killed in

Welsh Helicopter Crash; Mosque Blast Suspect Held Over Woman's Death, and hidden away next to Superman and Batman Battle in Man of Steel 2, was South Africa Closes its Boarders Due to Quarantine.

Noah clicked on the link.

Whatever was infecting the loggers was spreading fast. The report stated that there was concern that Mananjary, and Cape Town International Airports were not shut right away, and the potential for the virus having hitched a ride on one of the one hundred and seventy-eight flights, which had taken off since the loggers arrived, could be a potential time bomb waiting to happen. It finished by saying that unlike the bird and swine flu, this might become a real pandemic.

With a few minutes left of his lunch, he quickly checked out who would be playing Batman in the new Man of Steel Movie.

The rest of his day was even worse.

Noah crushed a finger between two cages. Tipped over a trolley of two-pint semi skimmed milk, splitting four of them all over the docking bay area. In addition, he accidentally hit a middle-aged man in the shins with a trolley; he spent twenty minutes in an office filling out accident paperwork, in case the man sued.

By the time 4 PM arrived, he was dead on his feet.

His day was made even worse when he popped into the local Game Store and found they had run out of Call of Duty MW3, and would not be receiving more until Monday.

Noah walked home with his head down, trying to keep the bitingly cold December wind out of his face.

It was almost dark already, due to the early nights. The colorful Christmas decorations swung across from building to building down the main shopping streets.

Noah did not bother with Christmas. He had no tree or decorations at home. Why bother when it was just him? No one had ever been in his flat, apart from his landlord. The computer game, when he could get hold of a copy, would be an early Christmas present to himself. He could honestly say he had never received a Christmas card in his life.

"Hi Noah."

"Hi Roxi. How's life?" Noah asked as he walked through the back door that he shared with the chip shop, while trying to get his keys ready.

Roxi was a washed-out middle-aged rocker chic who worked part-time in the chip shop. Her hair had been dyed so much over the years it was hard to tell what colour it was supposed to be. It looked like brittle, nicotine yellow straw. She was a little on the plump side, which was held in place with tight, worn jeans and a tee-shirt with a band called *Bam Margera and the Fuckface Unstoppable.* Her bingo-wing arms had faded tattoos of wolves, bears, flags, and children's faces. She had more studs and rings in her face than looked healthy, and probably made putting on makeup difficult. She held an apron in a hand that had a least ten rings on it, and a wrist weighed down with bracelets, which sounded like a percussion orchestra falling down a flight of steps every time she moved.

"You know love, same old, same old," she stated, while blowing smoke into the dark, cold sky.

Noah had nothing against Roxi; it was just she could talk for England. If he didn't get his door open straight away, he would be stuck chatting with her until Eric, the chip shop owner, came out to see what was taking her so long.

Roxi spat out a bit of tobacco from her rolly and gave a cough that sounded like an old diesel engine starting up.

She had a good heart, and raised seven children on her own, but she was oblivious to other people's time and needs. She was one of those people who just does not know when a conversation should end, or to take a hint when you are not interested, and she never listened to the other side of the conversation; she simply waited for you to finish talking so she could carry on with what she was saying.

"Did you hear the news about Ronald?"

"Gotta run Roxi, I'm expecting a phone call any minute," Noah lied as he swung the door open before she could utter another word.

The flat was cold. It had no central heating, and he could not afford to keep the small electric heater on all day. The flat had a coin meter at the bottom of the stairs, which the landlord emptied once a month. Noah was sure it was set wrong, and he was paying too much for electricity.

He switched on his laptop, letting it boot up while he flicked on the kettle for a cuppa tea. He undressed, tossing his work clothes onto the couch. He knew he should pop to the launderette, that was only a few shops away down the street, but he just could not be bothered. He decided he would do it tomorrow.

He sat at his battered desk with his pajamas, and a thick nightgown and slippers on, and a plate with a few slices of toast with plain Philadelphia, vanilla and strawberry jam.

The TV was on in the background. CNN was covering what they had simply named The Virus. Cases of outbreaks were now popping up in major cities with international airports, all over the world.

Noah muted the TV as he slipped his gaming headset on. He logged onto his online *Steam* account and booted up one of his favorite games, *Left 4 Dead;* an apocalyptic zombie shoot 'em up. He would play on his laptop until he could get hold of the X-box game he wanted.

In the virtual world, he ran around an abandoned fairground, shooting zombie clowns and pedestrians. Three other players ran at his side as he battled, shot, and bludgeoned his way through the levels, leaving a mass of carnage in his virtual wake.

3

Sunday 16th December 2012

Day 2

Sunday was Noah's day off. He eventually rolled out of bed at just after 11 AM. He spent thirteen hours playing a variety of PC and X-box computer games. He moved only to go to the toilet and to make toast or fill his coffee cup.

In the background, unheard due to his headphones, the news reported the spread of the virus. At the last count, nine countries had confirmed cases.

Even though so many people were being infected, and across so many countries, the news seemed a little sparse on the details. Whenever an outbreak was registered and confirmed, the military – in whichever country concerned – swooped in and took over, quarantining the area.

The Public Health, an agency of the Department of Health, was giving out a few details. If you felt dizzy and nauseous, with constant blinking of the eyes, which form a bloodshot clouding over the cornea, then you were to phone an emergency number set up for your individual County.

A new organization called The UK Plan for Rare Diseases, which had only just been passed through The Commons, and was run by the Department of Health, was being inundated with inquiries.

The Health Minister Lord Howe gave a news conference, telling people to use the numbers for their particular area.

Even though, as of yet no confirmed cases were reported in the UK.

However, that did not stop over twenty thousand calls an hour blocking up the emergency phone lines. Anyone who had a headache or a cold was trying to get through.

Bruce Keogh, the Medical Director for the NHS, backed-up Lord Howe, and went on the BBC News at Ten asking people to stop phoning 999 and use the number for their district.

A scrolling bar rolled across the bottom of the TV screen stating the number for Noah's area. The English Riviera Centre, in Torquay, was being used for the county of Devon.

Noah missed all of this while he played computer games. A few of the gamers commented on the virus while waiting to respawn, but they were soon told to shut up and concentrate on the game.

4

Sunday 23rd December

Day 8

The week got worse.

Noah struggled with the week of early mornings. In addition, because of two people being away, and it being so busy, Noah had to work on his day off.

Super Jane had been busting his balls all week, stating if he went any slower, he would clot. He noticed, apart from walking around pissing people off, that she never actually did any real, physical work. She had also commented on his clothes again, saying he looked like he slept in them.

The supermarket was busier than the normal Christmas rush, what with it being the last shopping day before Christmas. People were spooked about the outbreak that was spreading across the world, and they were starting to horde food and drinks.

Some were even wearing respiratory paper masks. One old man even walked around doing his shopping wearing an old-fashioned scuba diving breathing apparatus, with the big goggles covering half his face, and a large air tank on his back. Noah had even looked down at the floor, expecting him to be wearing flippers, but he wasn't.

No one talked about anything else. It consumed every TV station and conversation.

By the end of the first week, seventeen countries had confirmed cases. However, the World Health Organization had still not classed it as a pandemic, because as of yet, apart from severe side effects, no one had died from the virus. Nevertheless, that did not stop people from panicking.

The food was flying off the shelves faster than it could be restocked. The supermarkets were having trouble keeping up with demand. The shelves were starting to have large gaps. The frozen-food section was practically empty.

Fights would start over the last carton of long life milk, or a packet of cereal bars.

One couples trolley was full of cheap dog food and two-liter bottles of Asda's own lemonade. Noah hoped they had a dog.

While walking home on Friday, Noah could not believe how deserted the streets were. There were no people ambling along, window-shopping. No prams full of screaming children. No one sat on the public benches. No street performers filling the pedestrian precinct with their renditions of famous songs. No teenagers slamming around on battered skateboards, trying to impress a ring of girls sat on the ground. Even the roads were empty of cars. All that seemed to be around were lorries and vans trying to keep up with the food demands.

Most of the shops were closed by the time Noah finished work. Normally, they stayed open beyond 4 PM – if they had opened at all. The only shops that were open were the food outlets.

The public waste bins were overflowing, with rubbish piling up and blowing through the streets. The wheelie bins were wedged up against the houses, also unemptied with black bin bags thrown up against them. Animals had ripped bags open; household waste was scattered across the pavements and roads.

The five-minute walk home seemed surreal, as if he had walked onto a movie set.

The strangest thing was the silence, as if everyone was holding their breath. No music blared from open windows. No conversations carried on the breeze. Mainly, because every window was closed tight.

Noah was glad to get home.

The chip shop was closed for the last two days. It was normally bustling with activity, with the owner Eric rushing around while Roxi stood outside smoking.

He rarely had to use the key for the back door, because it was normally open. The hallway was deserted and cold. It seemed like a tomb without people rushing around, and the sound of the people preparing the food, and the hissing of the large fryers, and the pinging of the microwave.

Noah's flat seemed even emptier than normal. The muffled sounds from the shop below were always a background noise. He had not realized just how much he noticed them until they were not there anymore.

Noah ignored the computer games for the night, and instead watched the news on the TV as CNN kept him updated on the worldwide virus outbreak.

Apparently, so the reports were stating, the contaminated person, after the rapid eye blinking and disorientated state, then falls into a coma. Tens of millions were infected across the world.

America had football stadiums, and convention centres converted to hold those in the comatose state because the hospitals were overflowing. Every large public space was being utilized to hold the contaminated.

America had closed its borders and was under marshal law. Strict curfews were in place to stop people mingling and spreading the disease.

As of yet, Great Britain was virus free. Being a small island had its benefits.

Noah switched over to the BBC. There were riots in London, Manchester, and Bristol. The police was spread too thin.

Ambulance workers were on strike; their unions wanted more money and better working conditions, and apparently, decided that now was the best time to make a point.

The firefighters were just managing to keep up with the fires spread by the rioters. There were rumours that they too were about to strike.

The parliament was in session. They were deciding on whether to implement Marshal Law. The police force was at breaking point.

Only once in British history had the army been brought in under Marshal Law. In 1918, the army was called in to cover for the police when they went on strike over pay and pensions. The lack of police on the streets had caused chaos, with violence and looting, which lasted four days until the army restored order.

If the reports were correct, Marshal Law would be implemented, and the army would be on the streets within twenty-four hours.

Noah flicked channels.

CNN was reporting that Monaco – the second smallest nation after the Vatican, and the most densely populated country in the world, with over forty-two thousand people per square mile – was as of yet uninfected. Their boarders were closed, with all two-hundred and fifty-five of their standing army defending their checkpoints.

The Vatican also closed its doors to the world, when the faithful needed it the most. The walled in enclave, which is landlocked inside the city of Rome, was allowing no one entry. The basilica and obelisk, in Saint Peters Square, looked down upon an empty expanse of concrete. Normally full of worshipers, it now held only silence.

Pope Francis is said to have announced in an official press release, “I am praying for every single individual in the world.” However, apparently he did not want any of them anywhere near him.

Noah flicked back to the BBC.

The BBC had a specialist in. He reminded Noah of his old history teacher. The bearded, middle-aged expert was trying to describe the spread of the virus. He talked about the Basic Reproductive Rate or RO for short. The RO depended upon three major factors, the duration of the contagion, the infectiousness of the viral organism, and the number of susceptible individuals with whom the infected subject comes in to contact with. In short, if the RO is greater than one, then the disease will continue to spread.

It was getting late. He realized he had been watching the news channels for hours.

Noah flicked off the TV.

Tomorrow will be Christmas Eve. He had no tree with presents underneath. No one to come around and be with him. Tomorrow would be just like any other Monday.

As it turned out, today would become the last real normal day he could remember, because on Monday the 24th, the virus reached the shores of England.

5

Monday 24th December 2012

The Day the Virus Reached England

Day 9

Noah crawled out of bed at just after 11 AM, and flicked the TV on while he made his first coffee of the day. Everything, as they say, turned to shit.

The Royal London Hospital had announced a young woman, who had just returned from a holiday in Cancun, Mexico, was showing all the signs of the symptoms. Within three hours, another case was registered in Manchester.

Christmas Eve this year seemed like it was not going to be a good one.

Within eight hours, all flights were grounded, with all the airports and docks closed, along with the Euro tunnel. England quarantined itself – no one in or out.

The queen appeared on TV, asking that no one panic, that everyone must stay calm and trust in the government that had everything under control.

The army was out in force, in all the major cities, strictly enforcing the curfew. No one was allowed to leave their homes during Christmas Eve, Christmas Day, and Boxing Day.

It was announced that a window for collecting everything a household would need would be open on Thursday the 27th. However, the window was only open for ten hours, between 10 AM and 8 PM.

Noah could not believe what he was hearing. Everyone was under house arrest. No unsanctioned movement outside the home was permitted.

A crashing sound made Noah wander over to a window. Down on the main street, a group of chavs was breaking into the local branch of The Halifax Building Society. The building's alarm blared.

Idiots, Noah thought. *Everyone knows all the money is locked away, and there is no way a bunch of yobs would have the skills or tools to crack the banks safe.*

Another crashing sound made Noah look the other way, up the street. The metal shutter, which protected the windows of Iceland, was ripped from the front of the building by a chain that was wrapped around a Renault Mégane's tow bar. A middle-aged man and woman jumped from the car, and with a crowbar, the man broke open the door. They raced inside, along with two teenagers that could have been their children. Another alarm bell pierced the air, mixing along with the first.

The family ignored the klaxon and ran back and forth, tossing armfuls of food and bottles of drinks into the back of the car.

Noah expected the police to rush round the corner, but none appeared.

The BBC announced that there was rioting in London, Glasgow, Bath, Plymouth, Leeds, Birmingham, and Sheffield.

The News showed Leeds Town Hall, with the army and police opposite an angry mob – bricks and bottles sailing from one side to the other. The mob chanted that they wanted the cure, as if the government was holding back on them.

It flicked to an image of police and rioters fighting in Birmingham's Victoria Square right outside the Council House Building. Some were even standing in the fountain. The news reporter felt the need to point out that the fountain was the largest in Europe and was known locally as '*Floozie in the Jacuzzi*'.

Police on horseback pushed back a group of teenagers that were tossing paving stones. In the background, Antony Gormley's famous Iron Man Statue stood imposing and unaffected.

The sound of a large sheet of glass hitting the pedestrian walk made Noah turn back to the window. Three of the large windows of

Iceland shattered and fell in a glistening waterfall. From where he stood, it looked like a wheelbarrow full of diamonds spread over the ground.

The family jumped back into the Mégane. It wheel spun as it disappeared around a corner.

A chair sailed through the bank's window, bouncing as it rolled across the ground.

Noah dialed 999 on his mobile, to report the incidents. A busy signal was all he received in reply.

Suddenly, the power cut out. The TV died. Everything in the flat went silent, making the alarm bells outside even louder.

Noah stood by the window. He watched the teenagers run from the bank. They carried nothing with them. They disappeared down a side street into the market.

The power came back on. The TV clicked to stand by mode.

How can everything change so suddenly? How can normal become unreal in such a short space of time? Noah thought, as he picked up the remote and turned on the TV.

CNN announced that America was calling for international aid. Millions were in a comatosed state, with tens of millions more reported to have the first stages of the virus. However, every other country was in the same situation. Those that were not affected were closing off their boarders and hoarding provisions. No one was in a position to offer help.

It dawned on Noah that he would not be able to go to work. He was meant to fill in on Boxing Day, one of the busiest days of the year. But how could he if he was not allowed to leave his home?

Noah walked to his small kitchenette. The shabby collection of units held little food. The old fridge gurgled and chugged as it tried to keep cold a packet of ham, a pint of milk, and half an uneaten pizza. He never really kept any food at home because he ate his main meals at work.

He rummaged through the cupboards. A tin of spaghetti bolognese and a chicken and mushroom pot noodle.

He walked over to his table and picked up his wallet. Eleven pounds and fourteen pence. With just enough in the bank to buy the computer game he wanted. His wages would not go in for another eight days. He had the tokens for lunch at work in his wallet, which he brought on the first of each month as soon as he was paid. However, they were just useless pieces of paper, unless he was at work.

Noah needed food.

He only had one option left.

Noah picked the keys off the hook by the door. The owner gave him a spare set of keys for the chip shop in case of an emergency, like the alarm going off or a water leak.

Noah stood in the chip shops kitchen. Two large chest freezers rested against one wall. They were full of fish, sausages, chicken nuggets, burgers, and pies. On the shelves were packets of dried gravies, sauces, salt, pepper, herbs, flour, batter mix, and rows of tins of mushy peas. In a large blue tote bin rested the cut up chips in cold water, stacked next to it was large industrial bags of Maris Piper potatoes.

There was enough food to feed him for months. Nevertheless, he was aware that none of it was his.

Surely, Eric would understand. Anything I eat I will pay for.

Noah did not own a deep-fat fryer, and there was no way he could spark up the huge chip fryers in the shop just to make one meal. On the shelf was a stainless steel Delonghi deep fryer. He did not know why they would need the smaller fryer, possibly to cook smaller, messier items that would dirty the oil of the larger fryers.

He took the fryer upstairs with a large tin of peanut cooking oil. He was a little surprised that the oil was made from nuts, so he read the label. Apparently, the peanut oil had a higher smoke point, whatever that was. It was also suitable for vegetarians.

He set the fryer up on his small work surface, and headed back downstairs.

He only had a small fridge with no freezer, apart from a small shelf at the top that could fit a tray of ice cubes in. He took up a packet of fish, sausages, a few pies, and burgers. He found a plastic bucket and transferred some chips into it. He changed the water, which was looking a little brown. He presumed the chips were meant to be used a few days ago, but due to Eric not opening the shop, they were slowly going off.

I am doing him a favour eating them; he reasoned, as he poured the oil in and turned the fryer on.

Noah sat eating fish and chips while watching the news. The batter was a bit of a disaster, but he had never made it before. It was edible, but a little floury. He had no tomato ketchup, so he grabbed a handful of sachets.

A report that a boat, that was trying to leave the harbor in Portsmouth, was fired upon. The coastguard stated that, so far they had found nineteen bodies in the wreckage.

A doomsday group in Scotland committed mass suicide; all twenty-eight in the cult were found with plastic bags over their heads, including the nine children.

A police officer, in the armed unit in Stoke-on-Trent, took his firearm home and shot his eight and eleven-year-old daughters, then his wife, before turning the gun on himself.

A family in Norwich was found dead in their garage inside their minivan. They had all died from asphyxiation due to a pipe being connected from the exhaust into the back window.

There was a thirty-six car pileup on the M1.

One man in Swindon decided to end it all by train, parking his car on the tracks. He succeeded. However, he also caused an intercity 125 to derail and tumble down a steep embankment onto a busy roundabout at Great Western Way on the B4289.

Noah spent the day flicking back and forth between news channels. No news, as they say, is good news.

6

Christmas Day 2012

Day 10

The world was not in a celebrating mood.

Tens of millions the world over were infected with stage one and two. No one knew what would happen next. What would stage three be like? Death?

Noah was overloaded with news from around the world, so for a change, and instead of playing computer games, he decided to watch something other than the news on the TV.

The BBC series Planet Earth was showing. Sir David Attenborough was talking about ants.

This will take my mind off everything; he decided. Noah settled down with a plate of cold sausages.

The bullet ant was acting strange. Attenborough explained that it had walked over a fungus. The fungus – *Opiocordyceps unilateralis*, of the Cordyceps family – bores into the ant's body. Over a two-week period, the fungus takes over the ant's nervous system and brain.

If the other ants in its colony notice it is infected, they remove it as far away as possible.

The fungus, once it has completely taken over the ant, releases a chemical to make the ant leave the colony and climb to the understory vegetation of the tropical rainforest, which provides the perfect platform for when the spore-producing stem grows out of the back of its head.

The stem can take up to three weeks to grow – looking like a long alien antenna with a bulbous end – before it is ready to explode, releasing spores that will affect any ant in the vicinity. One infected ant can wipe out a colony of over eight million.

Noah felt uncomfortable; the growth looked disgusting.

Attenborough went on to explain that there were thousands of different types of the fungus, and each one specialized in a different type of species. He stated that it was good for the environment, because it stopped one species from becoming dominant. Stating that the more numerous the species the more likely it would become infected, keeping the numbers down.

The program unsettled Noah. He flicked channels. The Snowman was showing on Channel 4. The twenty-six minute animated film made him forget about the world outside his walls.

He remembered watching the film when he was young, living in Ash Leaf Children's Home.

He used to dream that one Christmas a magical snowman would turn up to take him away. When it snowed, he made a row of snowmen. No snowman with a green hat and scarf ever came and rescued him.

When he needed pajamas, from the hand-me-downs, he even went for a pair that had blue and white stripes.

"*Walking in the Air*," drifted from the TV.

Just as the film was finishing a news flash report scrolled across the bottom of the screen. It stated that forty-one hospitals across Great Britain had confirmed cases.

Outside Noah could hear cars screeching up and down the pedestrian section of town. He did not bother getting up to look.

Probably, idiot boy-racers taking advantage of the situation, knowing the police were too busy with other things.

Noah flicked off the TV. He could not get away from the news even if he tried.

For lunch, he ate more chips and a steak Pukka pie.

He was not allowed out, and even though there were people milling about, he knew the instant his foot touched the pavement a police car would turn the corner. He rarely left his flat when he was not working, and now he was not allowed to he felt as if he needed to.

He booted up his laptop and scrolled through some of his downloads.

Noah only had ten gigabytes on his Virgin account each month, and because he liked to download, he had found a way around it. He loaded up his laptop with downloads, from Piratebay, and when he was at work, he piggybacked on their Wi-Fi. He left his laptop turned on in his bag in his locker, downloading all the time he was working.

He had a few new movies he had not seen yet, and he hoped they were not cam copies. He also had a season called Doomsday Preppers.

The American program was about a group of people who believe the world, as we know it will soon change. They believe that either a financial collapse of the economy, solar flares, nuclear war, a pandemic, super-volcano's, global warming, or a vast array of other catastrophes will cripple the world, making survival difficult unless you are ready. That is why they are called Preppers, because they spend time and money preparing for the end of the world.

The first episode of the eleven part series was called: *Bullets, Lots of Bullets*.

The first words spoken by the voiceover man were ominous, "*Across the country there is a growing darkness. The belief that the end of days is near!*"

The man's low voice made the hairs on the nape of Noah's neck stand on end.

He watched the first episode that covered a couple that lived in Texas inside welded together metal shipping containers. They believe we are overdue for a polar shift, which will wipe out billions of lives and send the world back into the dark ages. They spend on average fifty hours a week storing food. They have enough to last two people for twenty years.

It would come in handy being them right about now, Noah thought.

The second story was about a man prepping for a huge earthquake. He lives off the land, cooking greens he collects that most people would class as weeds.

The third story was about a woman who believes there will be a worldwide oil crisis.

Noah decided they all seemed slightly crazy, someone you would meet, and your first impression would be that they were not quite right in the head – not all their lights were on.

Of course, the way things were panning out; they may be the only ones left standing at the end of it all.

Noah spent the day watching all eleven episodes, and made notes in a small notepad. By the time he finished he had a list of things he needed to fill what was called a bug out bag

– a survival bag that had everything in it you would need to survive for anything from twenty-four to thirty-six hours, if you had to get out quick.

By the time he went to bed, he had completely forgotten it was Christmas day. All he thought about was survival techniques and equipment, which he had a feeling he was going to need very soon.

7

Boxing Day 2012

Day 11

Noah did not sleep well. It seemed like a conveyor of cars turned up, sometimes a couple at once, to load up on stolen food from Iceland. He wondered if Asda was the same.

He could hear people fighting, glass smashing, and people shouting. Then at around 4 AM the red glowing light filtered through his pulled curtains. Someone set light to the flats above the Vodafone shop.

Noah watched in morbid fascination for over two hours. No fire trucks turned up. The fire did not spread. By the time he looked out in the morning the fire had turned the top two flats into a smoldering heap, sagging down over the phone shop. Blackened masonry and mortar littered the street.

He was feeling queasy because of all the fried food he had been eating over the last few days. He would kill for a salad.

During the night, a few other shops were broken into. Boots Chemist was a big favorite, with everyone trying to get hold of any kind of drugs. Also Carphone Warehouse and a sandwich shop – buns littered the street, and it looked like someone had tried to get the cash machine out of the wall at the HSBC bank. They failed.

He stood at the window at just after 10 AM drinking a cup of coffee, while watching a couple lad's jogging down the high street with a large plasma screen television. The plug rattled and skipped on the ground between them. The teenage at the back tripped and went down hard on the TV. The screen did not shatter, but it was pushed in, with a spider web of cracks reaching out from one corner. They both stood looking at the ruined screen – swearing like state troopers – then as one they simply walked away, leaving it in the middle of the pedestrian walkway.

Two motor bikes sped around the corner, screaming into the street. One rider had half a brick in his hand, as he passed the key cutting shop; he tossed it at their window. The large pane shattered, raining down glass. A revolving display cabinet tipped over, rolling out onto the street, lighters, silver cups, and photo frames sat in the pebbles of glass. The bikes roared up the road.

The worlds going mad!

As he watched, an old green Morris Minor reversed up to Iceland. An old couple slowly climbed out. They looked around, to check no one was near, and then they ducked into the shop. Moments later, they returned with a trolley full of food and drinks. They proceeded to fill the boot, as if it was a normal shopping expedition. The food was even in carrier bags. The old man even returned the trolley back inside.

He did not see one single police car. Luckily, the alarms switched off after a couple of hours.

It started to rain, a heavy beating rain that soaked everything in minutes. It poured down in sheets, with the wind whipping it against his windows with a rhythmic tattoo.

Noah booted up his laptop and turned the TV on.

There was no other news apart from the pandemic. It filled every station.

The Hospitals were inundated. Thousands waiting to be seen. The authorities told them all to go home; they were at risk gathering in such large numbers. However, no one listened. Riots broke out. Hospitals became war zones. They were angry people with nothing to lose.

Noah watched one news clip where a young mother held a crying child in one arm as she tossed a brick with the other.

Police officers on horseback held back youths bent on fighting. All they needed was an excuse, and this seemed as good as any – any reason to fight the system.

The next main gathering area was outside chemists. Fights would break out simply over a small box of paracetamol.

The BBC had three specialists around a table with a presenter. Each specialist described what they thought will happen, and how to take precautions. Each gave different answers to the questions, and it ended up as an argument.

Noah sat shaking his head as he watched a woman lean across the table and slap a tubby bearded man.

And these people are supposed to be calming the population.

BBC 2 was playing a series of movies in theme with the virus: *Contagion, 28 Weeks Later, Children of Men, I Am Legend, Outbreak, Quarantine, Doomsday, 12 Monkeys, The Stand, and The Andromeda Strain*, and at the moment *28 Days Later* was playing.

A little insensitive, he thought.

Noah started flicking through the channels. Suddenly, the same message was on every channel.

A thin man in his fifties decked in a military uniform stood in front of an important-looking podium – with some kind of British government logo on with a lion and a unicorn on either side of a shield supporting a crown – was addressing the camera.

"Do not leave your home. Do not try to leave the cities and towns. Stay put. Keep calm. The government is doing all it can to sort the situation out. Keep your families together and seal all windows and doors. Do not go outside! Do not approach anyone who looks infected!"

The message was on a loop, and played for a few minutes before the channel flicked back to the news.

Noah's mobile phone alerted him to the fact he had a message.

Who would be checking up on me? he wondered.

He did not recognize the number. The message read the same as the man just announced on the TV. It was an automated message sent to every mobile phone in the country. A link connected to a government web page that showed the same news clip. The text message said 'do not reply' at the end.

Noah clicked on Google on his laptop. He found out that the British government could control all news outlets, from radios, TVs, satellite channels, Social Network sites, and mobile phones.

The one used on his mobile was called Cell Broadcast Emergency Alert. The government recognized that the mobile phone is one item that most people carried with them at all times, and was the most efficient way of getting information to millions of people at once.

Ofcom – the UK communication regulator of all TV, radio, fixed line, telecom, mobile, plus airwaves and wireless devices – stated that eighty-two million people in the UK have mobile phones. Ninety-four percent of adults own one. The number of TVs registered in the UK is fifty-two million. Over forty-four percent of homes has DAB Radios. It listed that fifty-five percent of adults used social network sites daily. Every one of these channels would have been utilized to spread the message.

Every adult in Great Britain, in one form or other, would have just seen the same message as he had.

Noah clicked on another link, one listing the British Governments ability to take over all the communication devices, when the link for connection ended. A blank white page appeared with the message 404. It was the standard HTTP response code indicating there was a problem communicating with the server.

Noah pressed the back button, to return to Google, thinking there was a problem with the link. Google was also down.

How can Google not be responding?

He had used Google for as long as he could remember.

With the top search bar, which he seldom used, he typed: www.bing.com, the second largest, Microsoft owned search engine. It was still working. He reentered the search parameters. The same list appeared, but over half the list was faded, to show the link was inoperative.

Within the last few minutes, the government started to regulate the Internet.

What are they trying to hide? Keeping people in the dark will just make the situation worse.

He ate more chips with two saveloy sausages. He liked the way the skin-popped when he bit into them.

The message with the man in military uniform flashed up on his TV every thirty minutes, interrupting whatever was on. He also received a text every thirty minutes as well.

The text got so annoying, that he clicked on the ‘Spam’ filter option on his phone and blocked the number.

The heavy rain outside kept people indoors, doing a much better job than the absent police.

The power went off twice. The first time only lasted a couple of minutes. The second time it was off for twenty.

Noah was bored with sitting indoors. Tomorrow he was allowed out between 10 AM and 8 PM. He would go to work to see what was happening. To see if he still had a job, or was it ransacked like Iceland.

The rain drummed on his windows.

At least nothing will burn in this weather; he thought. He had a new fear that some idiot would set light to the building, trapping him inside.

He read the notes he made while watching *Doomsday Preppers*. He put the list on the side. Tomorrow he would see if he could find any of the items to make a survival Bug Out bag.

Tomorrow he would become just like the people he had been watching out of his windows.

8

Thursday 27th December 2012

Day 12

Noah was up earlier than normal, at just after 7 AM. His job at Asda was supposed to start at 7:30, but because of the curfew, he would have to wait until 10 AM.

He was dressed in his work clothes, just in case, by some miracle, Asda was unaffected by the looters, and they had not ransacked everything. He had his doubts. What he was witnessing outside his windows was just the tip of an iceberg.

However, by 9:30 the streets were packed. He had never seen the pedestrian area so full of people.

It was a complete frenzy outside.

Noah ate some cold sausages in a sandwich. He then took an old scarf and wrapped it around his mouth and nose. He then hooked an empty Oakley backpack on before leaving the flat.

It was cold and wet. The rain had stopped, but heavy, dark clouds promised more to come.

Rubbish littered Union Street, which people had thrown out of their windows, rather than letting it stink out their home. Black bin bags were ripped open with food, plastic bottles, and mushy paper littering the streets.

People were pushing and shoving through the crowds. Everyone was in a hurry.

Almost everyone had some type of cloth or medical paper mask over the lower half of their face.

There were queues for the cash machines, with people trying to take out as much as their savings as possible. Fights broke out because the person in front was taking too long, or someone tried to jump the queue before the cash runs out.

Noah realized that most of the shops were not open, but had been broken into, and people were simply walking off with whatever they could carry.

It was chaos.

People screamed and shouted. There were pushing matches, which turned into fistfights.

Noah walked by a teenager running and kicking at the door of an Oggy pasty shop.

Cars were parked everywhere, the boots and doors open, with people filling them up with whatever they could find.

A large shop window was shattered, with pots and pans shining in the weak light.

He had to shoulder his way through the crowd. People jostled him from side to side.

Every shop had been broken into, even property retailers, which had nothing edible or of value, unless someone wanted to carry off an outdated computer.

Noah peered inside the Rightmove estate agents. The place was destroyed inside, with computers broken and on the floor, with tables upturned and smashed.

People were using the outbreak as an excuse to vandalize, just for the sake of it. Noah was confused as to why people would want to spend so much time and effort destroying things.

At the end of the street was St Leonard's Clock Tower. Noah remembers the tower from a school field trip.

It was the site of a church, built in 1220 on the meeting place of three main roads. It is said that King Richard I, after suffering misfortune following his third crusade, had prayed at the spot where Saint Leonard was martyred. He decided to dedicate churches throughout England to the name of the Saint. In 1836, the main chapel was demolished, leaving the tower standing.

Noah was happy to see that even though the shops around the tower were ransacked, with windows smashed and metal shutters twisted and broken, that the tower stood unaffected, like a sentinel against time and suffering.

He remembered going inside the thin tower, climbing the winding stairs to the second level where the bell ropes hung down like dead vines. There were chains and manacles hanging from the walls, and stocks for the head and hands. He was only a child of ten when he went in, and the place seemed magical and dark at the same time.

As Noah turned the corner, he could see that Asda was looted.

The car park had vehicles parked haphazardly, with the driver trying to get as close to the building as possible. A truck had driven over the pedestrian bridge, through the barriers and then straight through the main doors, into the building. It was obviously damaged in the ram raid, because it was still there, inside.

People were everywhere, running around pushing trolleys full of food and drinks.

Noah pushed his way into the building.

The racket of people shouting, arguing, and fighting resounded in the high ceiling building – the clamor of white noise was uncomfortably loud. The lights were off, but the large front windows let dull light in.

To the right was the tobacco counter. It was the first area people had emptied.

Noah walked over.

Clothes littered the floor, along with dropped chocolate bars and food. He scooped up the chocolate bars and put them in his pack.

People had already rummaged through the litter and fallen display cabinets around the tobacco counter, and had wandered off looking for larger things to steal.

Under a twisted shutter off the cabinet was a roll of lottery scratch cards. Noah put it in his bag. He knew they were now useless, but it would be interesting to scratch them off.

You never know; he thought; the *world could return to normal within a few weeks, and these might be worth something.*

Noah uprighted a small trolley from off the floor.

It felt strange seeing the place he worked, in the process of being ransacked and destroyed at the same time. He had childishly daydreamed about the place being hit by an asteroid, or a raging fire, or picked up by a tornado and dragged across the town, too many times to count.

On the ransacked provisions aisle, which only had a handful of items that was either squashed or spilt open left on the shelves, Super Jane stood screaming at people. His supervisor was defending her workplace. She was dressed in her impeccable, ironed work uniform, and was shouting at people to put things back.

As he approached, pushing the trolley, she was trying to take objects out of a woman's arms. The younger female kneed Super Jane in the crotch, which made Noah wince.

As he approached, Jane was climbing back up from falling into a refrigerated shelf unit.

"Noah!" She stood up, rushing to his side. "You're late! Now you're here you can help me. People are stealing everything!" She had a slight deranged look on her face, as if something had finally snapped and reality was hanging by a delicate thread.

Her eyes drifted down to the trolley.

"You as well?" She took a step back.

"That is it! That is the final straw!" Her eyes were wide and penetrating. "You're fired, Mr. Morgan. Fired!"

Noah slowly walked off, leaving his ex-supervisor screaming at other looters.

We all deal with things differently; he reasoned. *Some try to hang on to what they know. Reality can be hard to adjust to.*

After almost an hour of forcing his way through the crowds, defending his stolen food and cartons of cranberry juice – the only drinks left on the shelf – he eventually made it back out into the cold morning air.

He kept the trolley, using it to haul his goods, rather than trying to carry everything home.

People looked into his trolley as he passed. As of yet people were not interested in stealing off each other, only looting the shops and businesses around town, but he knew that would soon change when the food became scarce. He needed to get the provision's home as quickly as possible.

A family passed; the father carried a microwave, the mother a Dyson vacuum cleaner, the son a mini hi-fi system, the two young daughters a large boxed up Sylvanian Regency Hotel between them.

Noah did not see one single police car or police officer. It is as if they had all simply vanished. Newton Abbot had a large police station just two minutes walk away. He wondered where they all were.

The town was complete anarchy. Windows were still being smashed, even though the doors had been prized open. It was if people were smashing things up just for the sake of it.

Noah wanted to get the stuff home before someone tried to steal it off him. As he passed a haberdashery shop, he noticed a green striped curtain on the wet ground. He picked it up and tossed it over the food in the trolley.

Pushing the metal cart over the rubbish was awkward and difficult. He almost tipped over the shopping trolley on four occasions.

With sweat dripping from him, he eventually reached his back door. It took him three trips to get all the food upstairs, using a cardboard box out of the large blue rubbish bin in the alley.

He left the trolley by the back door.

After arranging the food on the side in the small kitchen, he gulped down some cranberry juice, and ate two croissants out of a packet of four.

Noah emptied the lottery scratch cards and chocolate bars from his bag, and slung it back over his back. He had stuff he needed to find. He had to head back out while he still could.

A woman's scream from outside froze him to the spot. It was the shriek of physical pain. He ran to the window. Down in the street a skinny, middle-aged man was kicking a woman on the ground. People around them ignored the fight, leaving a clear space, as if they were rocks in a river.

9

Noah had to rush through the chip shop. To run around would take too long. He fumbled with the keys to the door from the shop into the back of the building. He had two deadbolt locks to open. As he swung the thick door open, he got the keys ready to open the front door. However, he did not need them; the front window was smashed, with a public bin resting on the glass.

He could hear the woman still screaming.

He was not a violent person, or someone who involved themselves in someone else's troubles. However, if he did not intervene, he was sure the man would kick the woman to death.

The street was still busy. People were keeping away from the man. They continued to rob the shops, running off with armfuls of loot. Nevertheless, no one came to the woman's aid; they pretended they could not see what was happening.

"Leave her alone," Noah shouted as he rushed out of the smashed window, pushing past people, and then barging into the mans back, knocking him over the woman. The man went down hard, face-first into the concrete.

Noah was ready to punch if necessary, but the man just rolled over.

"What the fuck are you doing?" The voice was not the mans, but the woman's who was being kicked.

"Leave my husband alone," she screamed, as she slowly, and painfully got to her feet.

Noah was confused.

The mans face was bleeding, with blood pouring from his broken nose.

The woman pushed Noah in the chest with both hands.

"He was hitting you... He-he..." Noah stuttered.

The woman pushed him again, and then turned to help her husband to his feet.

"You fucking animal. Look at what you did!" she screamed.

"He was kicking you!"

"Mind your own fucking business!" she hollered as she put her arm around her husband, and they started walking off down the street. Him bleeding and her limping. She talked to him softly, as she held a tissue over his nose.

What the hell?

Noah stood staring at them walking off.

People are going crazy!

The crowd closed back in, filling the empty space. The sounds of the street returned, as if the void had been filled.

Noah ducked back through the broken window. He was not alone. Two teenagers were inside, heading through the open door into the back of the chip shop.

10

The teenagers did not look too old. They were possibly sixteen, maybe seventeen. He was older, but they looked thickset for their age, and they were both taller than he was. If he tried to fight them both, he could get hurt.

They wore the clothes of skateboarders, loose tee shirts and hoodies, with the strange skintight beige trousers with baggy crotches that made the person look like a child wearing a nappy. They both clutched skateboards.

He only had one chance to get them out. The looting was in full swing, but he hoped the mindset of the people was still cautious. Give it a few more days and things would change; people would get even bolder, but he hoped that it was still unnatural for people to act so brazen.

"Hey! What the fuck are you doing in my shop?" he shouted at their backs.

The two teenagers jumped.

"Get the fuck out now, before I grab my cricket bat!"

Noah shouted even louder. "Hey, Steve, Mike, Lou, Adam, we have two punk kids down here in our shop!"

"We don't want any trouble; we thought it was empty man," the tallest lad said.

"Steve, Mike, Lou get down here quick! Adam, bring my bat!"

"We're going man. It's just a big misunderstanding." The two teenagers looked around for a way out.

"Get the hell out before Adam gets down here with my willow-wood bat!" Noah stepped to the side so the lads could get out.

They both looked wide-eyed and scared, and unmoving.

"Now!"

They jolted and started running for the smashed window.

Noah watched them join the throng of bodies outside. A man ducked under and stepped into the shop.

Noah rushed into the back room, swinging the thick door shut, slamming it and clicking both deadbolts into place.

That was close.

He checked the back door was locked. He decided he needed to do something to make his flat safe.

11

Noah worked through the afternoon. He carried four large blue plastic bins upstairs from the storeroom. He used the hose from downstairs, connecting it to his kitchen tap, and after placing the four bins, one in each corner of the room, he filled them to the brim with water. He then wrapped industrial cling film over the top.

He could not carry a freezer up the stairs, so he took another blue bin upstairs and only filled it up quarter way. He then sealed frozen food into plastic bags and dropped them into the cold water. He hoped they would last longer than being left out in the open.

He packed his fridge to the brim and turned it up full.

Most of the tins and packet food and sauces he carried upstairs, along with two large tins of cooking oil and three large bags of potatoes.

Even though it was almost freezing outside, he was in his tee shirt sweating.

He stood on his fire escape looking at the ladder mechanism. As far as he was aware it had not been lowered in years. It took a couple of hard kicks to loosen the rust, until the lever twisted and the ladder slid down with an ear piercing grating sound.

Noah returned inside and filled a bowl with the used oil from the fryer. He poured it over the mechanism, and down the lever.

After rifling around in the cupboards, he found what he was looking for, Eric's tools. With six-inch nails, he proceeded to nail the door to his flat shut. He then, with great difficulty, dragged a large old-fashioned cupboard across his door, hiding it from view.

As he was catching his breath, leaning against a wall, someone started banging on the back door.

Shit!

He silently moved over to the door.

Suddenly, the sound of keys jingled in the lock. However, the person could not open the door because Noah had wedged a chair under the handle.

"Noah, are you there? It's just me, Roxi!"

"Roxi?" Noah said, while pulling the chair away.

Outside Roxi was with her three oldest children.

Noah could see her old white Renault Scenic parked in the back lane.

"I didn't know where else to go for food. All the shops are empty. We have just come from Tesco's." She stood with her children huddled around her. Noah noticed another sat behind the wheel in the vehicle.

"Of course, there's plenty here." Noah stood back, allowing them entry, as if he was some kind of guardian, and they needed his approval to be able to step inside.

He helped them carry frozen food, tins, and potatoes to their minivan. There was still plenty left.

After they had stacked up as much as they could, with the children sat balancing stuff on their laps, Roxi turned and gave Noah a hug.

"Thank you Noah, I always knew you were one of the good ones." She stepped back. "God bless you, and may he watch over you." Before Noah had chance to reply, Roxi jogged to her vehicle and jumped in. All the children waved as the car drove away.

He then wheeled in the wheelie-bins and proceeded to empty them all over the cupboard and shelves. He scattered frozen fish and all the other frozen food that was left everywhere. Hopefully, when it thawed out it would start to stink.

Noah locked the back door, and forced the chair back under the handle.

He then proceeded to trash the storeroom, making it look like someone had already rummaged through everything.

By the time he had finished it was dark out, and the streets only had a few people milling around. The streetlights did not come on. The local council was trying to stop people from wandering the streets.

Noah listened at the door for a few minutes to check no one was in the shop. Once he was sure he was alone, he opened the door slowly. He locked it from the shop side, in case anyone came in. He then proceeded to toss everything combustible out into the street.

By the time he climbed the fire escape, and wound it back up, it was almost 6 PM.

Noah was dirty and exhausted.

While he took a shower, the power went off. He was covered in shower gel. The shower was electric. He stood shivering in the dark waiting for the power to flick back on. It did after about a quarter of an hour.

Noah spent four hours cooking pies, sausages, and burgers. He stacked the cook food on plates and trays and covered them in tinfoil. He did not know how much longer the power would last, and if it did switch off for good, he would have no way of cooking the food. At least cooked he could live on it for a while. Cooked and old was better than raw.

As the food cooked, he watched another fire glowing over the top of the nearby flats.

He had not turned the TV on all day. When he did, only a few stations were broadcasting. These were interrupted every thirty minutes with the emergency broadcast.

One news flash stated that everyone was to stay inside. No one was allowed out for any reason. The next day put aside for venturing out to restock on provisions was in four days on Monday the 31st.

Downstairs, in a cupboard, Noah found an unopened packet of four silver duck tapes. Standing on a chair, he taped over all the gaps in his two windows, down the outside and around each pane. He even walked down the stairs and taped around the nailed shut door.

Noah noticed a blue Volvo was idling down on the street, with a family he recognized who lived opposite, running back and forth, filling the car to capacity with everything they loathed to leave behind. When it was full, the family squeezed in and then slowly drove off.

Noah spent four hours on the internet, trying to find out what was happening around England and the rest of the world. Google was still not working, and most of the links on Bing were broken.

With a flat full of the smell of fried meat and chips, Noah crawled into bed exhausted. He watched the glowing red from a fire flicker across the ceiling, wishing that he had someone he could hold, someone who could whisper in his ear that everything will be all right. He drifted off to sleep to dream about the colour red.

12

Friday 28th December 2012

Day 13

It was 5 AM and Noah was already up, stood at the window eating a cold steak pie with one hand, while holding a coffee cup in the other. He watched people outside fighting in the early dawn light over what little food was left in Iceland.

Noah had a list of things he needed. Regardless of the curfew and house arrest, he had no choice. At the rate people were ransacking shops, if he did not go today there would be nothing left.

He finished the last bite of the pie and rubbed a hand down his stubbled face.

He wrapped a scarf around his nose and mouth, then grabbed his rucksack and climbed out the window, pulling it down shut after, leaving just enough room to get his fingers in to open it later. He lowered the ladder most of the way, leaving a ten foot drop at the bottom. He climbed down and lowered himself to the last rung before dropping to the concrete. When he returned he would use a bin to reach the ladder.

It was still dark, and would be for a while. The streetlights were off. He carried a small torch. He hoped the batteries lasted.

He looked both ways when he moved out of Union Street onto Courtenay Street.

A few people were up early like him, or had been out looting all night. Three men and a teenage girl were loading boxes from Carphone Warehouse into a white van. One man stopped and looked over at Noah.

Noah kept his head down.

The man flicked his cigarette in to the street and returned to what he was doing.

Noah stood outside Iceland looking in. The place was empty. They weren't any food left inside. What was left of the shelving and freezers was destroyed.

He carried on walking.

Around the corner, an old woman strolled by in her dressing gown and slippers, walking her small Scotty dog. She paid no mind to the chaos and destruction around her.

A silver Subaru Impreza, with a blue dragon motif down the side roared down the road, dodging the obstacles and then skidding around the corner. It vanished from view, even though he could hear it racing away into the distance.

Noah's breath billowed from his mouth. It was very cold. There was even a few ice patches on the pavement.

He moved from the pedestrian Courtenay Street onto the longer Queen Street.

The Christmas lights hung stretching from building to building. A few had fallen, or had been pulled down. All were off but one. It had an image of a train made out of green bulbs, the train flashed on and off. The whole street lit up green, before being plunged back into darkness.

Cars were vandalized. One was even smoldering from a fire that had gutted it, leaving a smoking shell.

Shops had their contents spilling out onto the streets as if they had been tipped on their side and shaken. Things too heavy to carry or broken remained where people had dropped them.

Noah stepped back into the kicked open doorway of a betting shop, when he heard a group of chavs running from one side street out onto the road. He could hear them shouting at one another – boisterous and drunk.

“Did you see that bitches face?” one voice shouted.

“You showed her Carl. That bitch has been broken!” a whiny nasal voice stated.

Noah could not see the yobs who were speaking because he was ducked down behind a tipped over fruit machine. Betting slips covered the floor.

The group ran past the window, shouting and laughing and kicking at objects on the road.

Noah did not want any trouble. He waited until their voices faded.

The shop he was headed towards was just over the road.

Millets front window crunched under his trainers. The place was ransacked, but most of it was still here, just all over the floor.

The first thing Noah looked for was a better light. He found a Petzl Tikka Plus 2 headlamp on a hook on the wall. He pulled it on and switched on the bright LED beam.

Noah kicked his way through the camping gear.

He found a black and grey Vango Pumori seventy-liter backpack.

One hundred and ten pounds that will do nicely.

He stuffed his Oakley bag into it. He rummaged around until he found a four-season Deuter Exosphere -8 sleeping bag. He chose it because it had a one hundred and sixty pound price tag; he decided if it was that expensive it should be good. Next, were a two-man Vango tent and a Thermarest Prolite 3 regular sleeping Mat. Again, he picked it because it was ninety pounds.

He found it strange that to connect with nature and sleep outside, under the stars was so expensive.

As he was kicking around, he found a waterproof cover for the backpack. With the light he read the label. He was amazed that backpacks costing well over a hundred pounds were not one hundred percent waterproof, and that they required covers costing a further forty quid.

Noah stuffed the sleeping bag and tent into the backpack. He then rummaged around and found a hard plastic Spork – a spoon and fork combo, cooking pots in a sack, and a small Coleman Sportster 2 gas stove.

As he was rummaging through the gear, he was amazed at what things people would buy to go camping. There were things like inflatable solar lights, remote control tent lights, a two-way spirit level, tent carpets, hanging remote fans, and solar panels for recharging phones. He thought that the whole point of going camping was to get away from the hustle and bustle of the day-to-day life, not take it all with you in a smaller, more expensive form.

He put a Goal Zero 10 Adventure solar recharging Kit in his pack.

Over in one corner was a tipped over display of Wayfarer pre-cooked boil in the bag meals. He picked up chilli con carne, all day breakfast, chicken tikka and rice, chocolate pudding, and a load of others, which he was surprised to see, had a three-year shelf life. He filled the remainder of the bag with as many as would fit in. There were still about twenty packets left, so he grabbed a small daypack and filled it up.

He climbed the stairs to the second level. Upstairs was the shoes and clothing.

Most of the items had been tossed around, just like downstairs. Apparently, camping gear was not high on people's lists of things to steal. He felt that once the seriousness of the outbreak sunk in, people would be racing to the shop.

He found a comfortable Scarpa Cyclone GTX right walking boot in his size. It took him ten minutes to find the left boot on the floor. He left his tatty trainers on a bench.

It was starting to get light outside.

Next to the counter was a door.

Noah stepped over the broken cash register and stepped through the door. It led to a collection of rooms. A large storeroom that was ransacked, a toilet, and an office.

The office was littered with paper. The window was broken, with the cold wind blowing in, whipping the paperwork around. The large table was pushed against the wall, punching a hole in the plasterboard. The computer screen was smashed on the floor. Someone had spray painted a tag on the wall in red, after knocking the pictures off. It looked like the initials S.N.O but it was hard to tell due to it looking like a four year old wrote it.

Noah pushed the litter on the floor around with his new boots. There was nothing interesting.

There was another open door in the office.

Inside was a small cupboard. Boxes sat on the shelves, full of paperwork. Whoever opened the door had not bothered to throw all the boxes to the ground. They were probably too tired after trashing both floors and the office.

Noah noticed something sticking out over the top shelf; it looked like a bit of black plastic.

Using the lower shelves as a ladder, he climbed up. He was shocked to find an air rifle. He propped the rifle against the wall and climbed higher. He found some pellets, air canisters and two hunting knives.

Bingo! Bear Gryll's eat your heart out.

Noah carried the objects to the office table and laid them out.

The engraving on the barrel stated it was a XS78 CO2 .22 air rifle. There was a 3-9x50-mildot telescopic sight connected. The four tins were full of umarex AirForce 5.5 mm pointed lead Pellets. The canisters were 12-gram double-charge C02 cartridges. The two knives where eight inch hunting knives, with matt black steel blades – anything over three inches was illegal in the UK.

Noah decided either the manager had a business on the side selling illegal knives, or they were part of his private collection. Whatever the situation, they were his now.

Noah lifted the rifle and tried its weight. He placed it on his shoulder, looking down the sights. It felt comfortable.

He checked there was a pellet in the barrel, and that the C02 cartridge was full.

Noah pointed the rifle out the door down the hallway. He fired. The gun made a cracking, hissing sound. Walking to the end of the corridor he noticed the lead pellet had gone through the plasterboard and was somewhere inside the wall.

Excellent!

Noah returned and reloaded the rifle, and then put the pellets and cartridges in the bag and pulled it back over his shoulders.

Carefully, so as not to trip on all the gear scattered everywhere, Noah made his way out of Millets.

He had just one more shop to visit. He hoped it was not ransacked too.

13

The bag was heavy. He also carried the smaller bag in his left hand and the rifle in his right. He was sweating from the effort.

The shop he was heading towards was right at the end of town, in the cheaper rent area.

There were more people milling around.

The sky grew a little lighter as dawn was breaking.

Noah walked along, stepping over rubbish bags and littered objects. He had to walk out on to the road to walk around a VW van that was smashed through a butcher's shop window.

He did not have to walk along the pavement, because there were so few cars around, but old habits were hard to break.

An Oasis song drifted down from the flats above a Pound Shop. The song was *Where Did It All Go Wrong?*

Noah thought it was ironic.

The front of the Pound Shop was smashed with the cheap merchandise scattered everywhere. Noah kicked a large mug that had *The Worlds Greatest Dad* wrote on it.

He watched the mug as it skipped over the concrete before smashing.

Noah did not know who his father was. His birth certificate simply stated unknown. His mother died before he was old enough to ask. He never knew what it was like to have parents. He had never called anyone mum or dad. He lived most of his life in Ash Leaf Children's Home, a seventeen-bedroom building that had no character and few luxuries and held sixty-eight children between the ages of three and eighteen. The home sat on the outskirts of Exeter and was surrounded by rolling fields. Mr. Keller ran the facility; he was a middle-aged, obese man who treated it like a business, and thought about the children as a commodity. He would walk by without a look or a word, as if the children were dumb animals.

Noah would sometimes sit in his bedroom, which he shared with three others the same age, and look out onto the fields. Horses grazed and ambled in the distance. He used to daydream that his father was a cowboy, and that the huge house was theirs and all the other children living there were people his family took in.

He made the mistake of telling someone this once, when he was nine, when they asked him why he spent so much time looking out the window at the horses. The other children teased him for months. The younger children would bow or curtsy when he was near. The older kids simply beat him up. Even a few of the care workers snickered when they heard the story.

Everyday was the same. On weekdays, he would wake with the bell that announced he was to rise, wash, and get ready for school. He would eat food in a huge, cold hall, sat in the same seat on a wooden bench that ran in long lines, similar to the ones in Hogwarts. However, there was no magic or happiness here, and no tables full of steaming, bubbling, and spilling over plates of mind-boggling food. Breakfast was porridge – watery and tepid. The evening meals were set, seven different meals each day – they never varied until he was thirteen.

The local councils care section was taken over, and an inspection stated the building was unfit for habitation, and the children were malnourished. Things changed. The building was completely renovated, and Mr. Keller was out and Miss. Sung was in.

At first, things seemed like they would get better. Miss. Sung seemed much nicer than the cantankerous Mr. Keller did. However, he soon found out Miss. Sung was much, much worse.

In the distance, a boom made him look up, pulling him out of his daydream. Over the top of the buildings, way off in the distance, a mushroom cloud of smoke announced where the explosion had taken place.

He had no idea what it could have been. So long as it was not near him, he honestly did not care.

Noah walked passed his old workplace, Blockbuster; it was almost empty. A few DVDs lay on the carpet, or out on the street, but everything else was gone. Shelves leaned against one another as if someone had played a giant game of dominos.

A car was smashed against the wall next to the Orange phone shop. The burnt-out shell left black scorch marks up the wall, and melted the plastic frame of a window above.

There were some cars driving along the main Avenue, near the memorial statue. Three cars were in a row, each full to capacity with the people's belongings. Ropes held more property on the roofs. One pulled a trailer that was overflowing with furniture. The cars leisurely picked their way through the obstacles on the road. They slowly disappeared heading toward the train station.

Noah crossed the road, crossing over the bottom section of Devon Square.

He was on the main food strip where all the takeaways were situated, or 'takeout alley' as it was called by the locals.

On the strip along the road, there were three Indian restaurants, four Chinese, a Nepalese, KFC, two chip shops, and a kebab shop, as well as an off license. All were looted and vandalized.

What Noah was after was a small shop, tucked away between an independent solicitor and an artist's supply shop.

The door was kicked in, shattered glass crunched under his new boots. Noah stepped into the small Army Surplus Store, which had been there for decades.

The shop smelt of used socks and mothballs. Old army clothes hung from circular racks – jackets, jumpers, and trousers. A few items were tipped onto the floor, but the shop was mostly untouched, apart from the cash register, which someone had smashed open.

There was old style, thick green sleeping bags made from duck down, in a pile. Noah picked one up. It was heavy and smelt of mold. He decided to stick with the Millets sleeping bag.

Everything had an air of moldiness about it, as if the room had not been aired in years. Noah tapped a finger on an old metal, battered helmet that looked like it had a bullet dent in it. It all felt like it should have been thrown-away years ago.

The walls were made out of green wood with thousands of holes in it, and in those holes hung hundreds of hooks. On those hooks were camouflaged ponchos, camo netting, canvas bags, pouches, holdalls, shemagh scarves, berets, thick woolen socks, and thick green belts. One wall held scuffed boots in a row. Another was filled with pots, pans, shovels, buckets, and canteens. The small shop had everything a survivalist would need to start a small army. It was just it was all outdated and tatty. Years ago, they were the place to go if you needed something sturdy and good value for camping. However, nowadays it was cheaper and better from places like Millets.

Then something caught Noah's attention, a gasmask. It was on a long metal hook next to fake I.D dog tags and army badges. Even though the tags and badges looked fake, the mask looked real.

Noah moved over to the counter.

On the counter was karabiner clips, an assortment of buttons in a large glass jar, trouser ties, strips of Velcro, small plastic bottles of oil, plastic mirrors, camo cream sticks, Para cord, small button compasses, olive whistles; a midge head net, and some waterproof notebooks.

Noah collected some things and put them in his bags that rested against the counter. He probably would not use half of it, but better to have it, not need it, than need it, and not have it.

He kept hold of the air rifle. It was loaded and ready to fire.

To the right of the counter was a smashed display case. From the looks of it, it once held a collection of knives. It was empty. He noticed blood on the glass and some splattered on the carpet.

Probably, from when they smashed the glass, he reasoned.

It looked wet.

How long does blood take to dry?

He shrugged and ignored it.

To the left of the counter was a manikin dressed in a full woodland gilly suit. Noah contemplated taking it; it would be perfect for hiding anywhere there was shrubbery. However, when he tried to lift it, he realized how heavy it was. Camouflage came at a price – weight. He decided to leave it; he had enough to carry already.

Noah reached up for the old-style mask. There was a plastic bag taped to the head strap that had a bundle of spare filters inside. He rested the rifle against the wall and tugged down his scarf, and then pulled the mask over his head. It stunk of rubber. He took it off and tossed it on to his bag.

He looked around one more time, and was about to grab his bags, to get ready to leave, when he noticed part of the back wall was slightly open.

As he walked closer, he noticed it was a concealed door leading out into another room.

Noah pulled the door open a little. Inside was not a storeroom, as he expected, but a small room with a kitchenette to one side, a chair and table, and an army cot bed against the back wall. The bed had an old man on it. His hands where on his stomach, with blood pooling between his fingers and onto the floor. The man's head turned in Noah's direction.

"Help me!"

14

Noah rushed to the bleeding mans side.

"What happened," Noah asked while kneeling down and trying to work out what to do. He missed the first aid course at work, even though, Molly, the first aid woman still gave him the certificate.

The old shopkeeper lay on a small cot that was just wide enough to fit him on. The sheets were saturated with blood. His wrinkled hands were also covered in blood and were pressed against his abdomen.

Noah pressed his hands against the mans, simply because he did not know what else to do. He looked around for anything else to press against the wound and stop the bleeding. He quickly scanned the room.

Apart from the kitchenette, table, chair, and bed, there was a door, possibly leading to a toilet, and a set of stairs leading upwards. Noah had not noticed the stairs when he first walked in because he could not see them from his original position.

The room was where the man ate his lunch or made a cup of tea, or took a nap while the shop was quiet. It was small, neat, and a little sad. It suggested a lonely man with no family and few friends. It reminded Noah of his own flat. He hoped the man had a nice flat on the floor above.

Noah jumped up and started opening the doors under the sink, looking for a first-aid kit, while smearing the man's blood everywhere. Then it dawned on him, there would be one in the shop. He returned to the store, searching the walls. A few hooks had a collection of different-sized kits hanging from them. He ignored the old army kit that looked dated and impractical, and grabbed a little red nylon bag with a white cross on the front.

Noah rushed back to the injured man's side.

Was this an accident? It looked like a stab wound! Not that Noah was an expert, but he did watch a lot of TV and play way too many computer games.

Blood dribbled from the corner of the old shopkeeper's mouth.

Noah could not remember if it was there just now, or if the man was getting worse.

Well, Noah reasoned; he *certainly wouldn't be getting better.*

Tears streaked the old mans face. A face worn with wrinkles and time.

Noah fumbled with the small first-aid kit, trying to get it open, but it was slippery due to the blood. Noah wiped his hands on his jumper.

He had no idea what he was doing.

The man tried to speak but started coughing instead. Blood speckled Noah's face.

"He's still here!" the man mumbled as his eyes rolled back in pain.

"What?" Noah said.

Just then, as if the universe timed everything just right, a floorboard squeaked upstairs.

Noah dropped the first-aid kit and spun around. Someone was walking down the stairs.

The air rifle.

It was next door, leaning against the wall by the till.

The man coughed behind Noah.

In front, a skinny man in his mid thirties appeared at the foot of the stairs; he was carrying a gilded box in one hand, and a long hunting knife in the other. He was dressed in a dirty blue tracksuit that had a white stripe up the side. His fingers were covered in gold sovereign rings; a thick gold chain hung from his wrist poking from his tracksuit sleeve, and there was an even thicker chain around his skinny neck. He had a blue bandana around his head, as if he was a gangster wannabe.

Noah was knelt, staring up at the man.

The man was using the knife to try to prize open the ornate object, which he presumed was a jewellery box. He had obviously not heard Noah talking, and at present; his eyes were focused on his pilfered prize.

The man looked too skinny to be healthy, as if his body had been ravished by sickness. As he stood there his left eye twitched and his body jerked. Around his nose and mouth was covered in small spots and a red rash.

A druggie!

"That's a lot of shit you've got up there!" His shoulder twitched.

"What's in the box, gramps?" the man asked while sniffing, as he raised his eyes to the cot.

The druggie's hands froze when he saw Noah kneeling on the floor. His brows creased, as if trying to get his addled brain to work the new situation out.

Both did not move a muscle. Each weighing the other up.

Then, in a flash, Noah sprang forward and shot toward the door to the shop, scrambling through.

The man reacted a second too late, dropping the box and diving at Noah as he shot through the doorway.

Noah tripped and dropped to the floor, skidding under a circular clothes rack that held stale smelling camouflaged shirts and jackets.

The man burst through the door, throwing it open with an arm. He was a second too late to see Noah drop to the floor.

The shop was crowded with supplies. It was obvious Noah was on the floor somewhere.

"I'm not gonna hurt you mate!" the man said. "Let's chat. The old guy was already dying when I got here. I didn't stab him or nothing, like!"

Noah could hear the man slowly walking around the room, moving among the rails.

Noah gripped the metal pole of the clothes rack he was hiding next to, and lifted it with all his strength, ramming it towards the druggie's voice.

There was a clink of metal on metal as the man slashed out with the long knife. He hit the pole as it slammed against his chest, pushing him backwards into the wall.

Noah was running on adrenaline as he forced the man back with all his strength.

The man screamed in pain.

"Ya bastard! I'm gonna gut ya, ya fucking cunt!"

Noah let the pole go, after one last push, and raced between the clothes racks towards the counter.

The man was in a pile on the floor, under the jackets, with the clothes rack on top of him. He struggled to free himself.

"I'm gonna make you bleed bitch!" the man screamed, with a voice full of rage and hatred.

The man tossed the rack to the side while shouting abuse. He was about to stand when he noticed Noah stood over him, pointing a barrel at his face.

"Whoa, whoa! Let's not be hasty geeza!"

"Shut up!" Noah shouted.

The rifle shook in his grip.

The man dropped the long knife, which Noah noticed had blood on the end.

The druggie's face changed from rage to a smile, which showed gaps in his rotting teeth.

"Look, there's been a big misunderstanding, like." His brows wrinkled in thought. "Is that just an air rifle?"

Noah swung it around and brought the butt down hard against the druggie's blue bandana.

15

Noah pushed his fingers against the druggie's neck. There was a heartbeat. He was worried he had hit him too hard.

Using some green army belts, Noah tied the druggie up, and laid him on the floor.

Taking his rifle with him, Noah rushed back to the old mans side.

It was too late. During all the commotion and fighting, the bleeding man had died.

Fuck!

Not that there was anything he could have done.

Noah crossed the man's hands over his chest, and pulled a blanket off a chair and placed it over him.

He felt like there was something he should say, or do. However, he did not know what. Noah did not know of any scriptures, and would have felt like a hypocrite if he recited any anyway.

He felt wrong leaving the man on the cot, but what else could he do; he couldn't drag him to a strip of mud, and bury him.

Noah noticed the ornate box the druggie had been carrying was smashed open on the carpet. Photos had spilled out. He picked them up, noticing it was a black and white, faded photo of a young man and woman on their wedding day. There were a few others of the couple, as they grew older. It was obviously the man and his wife. On the back of one it read, *My Effle, always in my heart.*

Noah placed the photos back into the box and rested it under the man's hands.

Noah decided to check upstairs, just in case there was another victim.

The upstairs was even sadder than the small room downstairs.

The shopkeeper was a hoarder.

There were four rooms on the first floor and two of them were filled to capacity.

The front room had papers, magazines, books, boxes, plastic containers, toys, old machinery, old electrical goods, rolled-up carpets, stacks of picture frames, with a variety of object's spilling out of cupboards and chests of drawers, and stacked on tables; all piled up to the ceiling.

The bedroom was crammed full of cardboard boxes. The ones on the bottom of the piles were moldy and had collapsed under the weight of the ones above. A double bed was pushed into a corner, with boxes leaning precariously over it. The bed was covered in dark stains and had a pile of dirty army sleeping bags piled on it, with a collection of old pillows. Half of the bed was covered in soiled Styrofoam eating containers.

In the bathroom, the floor was covered in plastic bags in all different stages of decomposition, with soiled toilet paper everywhere. The lid on the toilet was up, and the bowl was jet black with mold. There was a clear space just in front of the toilet were the old mans legs would rest. He did not want to check the room too closely.

The kitchen was appalling. Rubbish bags filled the floor, with waste spilling everywhere. They were all waste high, with an almost clear, lower path leading to the cooker. Trash was piled on the stove, with just one ring visible. One corner was full of empty bottles of every description. The sink and the area around were stacked with every dish, cup, and bowl the kitchen held, all dirty and growing fungus.

At least he kept downstairs clean and clear, Noah thought. For some reason, he felt like defending the old man.

The smell was getting to him, so he had to return downstairs.

Noah stood looking down at the figure under the blanket. He wondered how someone could become a hoarder. How someone's life amounted to what they could stack and hide away.

As he left the room, he closed the adjoining door. He did not know what would happen, and how the whole virus situation would play out, but he hoped the old man would be found and given a proper burial.

The druggie was snoring.

Noah wondered how he could have found the ornate box among all the accumulated junk.

Noah stared down at the unconscious man.

The man was a murderer; he had stabbed the shopkeeper over whatever was in the till and a few knives. He deserved to die. However, Noah was not judge, jury, and executioner.

The belts were not too tight, with a little effort; he would be able to escape. He decided he would let karma deal with the druggie.

Noah walked out of the shop and headed home.

16

Noah was drained physically and emotionally by the time he dragged a large bin over to reach the ladder and climb the fire escape to his flat.

He dumped all the stuff on the small two-seater couch. He then spent half an hour under the shower, while scrubbing the old shopkeeper's blood off his hands and face.

After he downed a cup of strong coffee, and ate a couple of cold burgers and sausages, Noah set about sorting out the gear he found.

By the time he finished his bug out bag was ready. It had the packaged food, sleeping bag, roll mat, tent, cooking gear, a waterproof jacket in a small pack, the two hunting knives, and everything else he would need if he had to get out quick. He went and filled the canteen with fresh water and hooked it to the front of the bag.

He laid a pair of camouflaged trousers and a green tee shirt, with a dark-green jumper on the bed.

In the street outside, he could hear people shouting and fighting. He did not bother to walk over to the window to see what was happening. It was becoming an hourly occurrence.

It was only 11 AM. Even so, Noah stretched out on the bed and took a nap with the TV on in the background.

Noah awoke to a quiet flat. The power was off. He did not know how long it had been off for. He checked his watch. It was 2:14 PM.

He had a cold sausage sandwich. The bread was a little stale, but it would have to do.

He stood at the window watching a teenage woman pushing a pram down the pedestrian precinct. Instead of a baby, it held a full black bin liner.

Noah's mind wandered back to when he was first called to Miss. Sung's office. His daydreaming earlier had brought the whole incident back and opened raw wounds – wounds that had never truly healed.

All the children, including Noah, were feeling much happier, they had better, varied meals, and the walls did not have peeling paint and dry rot. Activities were arranged, so they could get some exercise in the fields around Ash Leaf Children's Home. They had a room full of paint supplies and games. It was as if Christmas had come early.

However, there were rumours that the older boys were called to Miss. Sung's office regularly. The older boys whispered between themselves and made rude gestures with their hands, and exaggerated hip movements. But Noah was naive and shy, and hardly talked to the older boys at the home.

Then on a cold April night, on Noah's fourteenth birthday, just after supper, Noah was sent for.

It was 8 PM, and the other children were washing and preparing to retire to their rooms, where they could read until 9 PM, when the lights went out.

He stood in his pajamas and nightgown, waiting in the long stark hallway.

Miss. Sung looked rosy cheeked when she opened her office door for him to enter.

She was a fifty-one-year-old short pudgy woman – not big enough to be called fat, and not thin enough to be called healthy. If she were a touch taller than her five foot four inches, then she would have looked average. As it was, she looked stumpy. In addition, she always wore bulky pastel coloured felt dress suits in yellows, pinks, and purples, with gaudy big jewellery and thick, colourful glasses on a dainty string. Her nails were longer than was practical, and her skin looked weathered and stained from her chain-smoking habit.

Noah noticed half a bottle of red wine on her desk. He also noticed her grey hair, which was always in a tight bun, was loose and spilling down her back.

"Noah Edward Morgan, isn't it?" Her painted on eyebrows rose.

"Yes Miss. Sung."

"Please take a seat. And please, call me Helen."

Noah went to sit on the straight-back chair facing the desk. He was trying to think of what he had done wrong.

"Not there... here," she announced, as she took a seat on a long leather studded couch next to a bookcase. She patted the leather next to her while kicking off her bright green high heel shoes. She gave a wide smile showing yellow teeth.

Noah nervously took a seat; sitting ramrod straight, and as far away from Miss. Sung as physically possible.

"Scoot on up, why are you sat so far over?" she purred, lowering her voice.

Noah scuffled along. He felt uncomfortable. Everything felt wrong. The hair stood up on the nape of his neck.

Miss. Sung put one arm around Noah's shoulders.

"There. We are both friends here, aren't we?" She leaned in a little.

Noah remembered her breath stunk of red wine and cigarettes, and her body stunk of makeup and sour sweat.

An hour later, he was ushered from her office. She grabbed his arm and leaned in close and whispered in a threatening voice, “Nothing happened here tonight! You understand Morgan?”

For some reason he vividly remembered that her lipstick was smudged.

Noah simply nodded. He just wanted to crawl under his sheets and pretend nothing had happened.

He was a teenager; he had daydreams and wet dreams about how his first encounter would be like and how it would feel.

It was not until he was a little older that he truly understood what rape meant – what had truly happened to him.

He was never called back to the office; obviously, he was not what she was looking for, there were older boys who willingly participated. She did not want to waste her time with someone like him.

Four months later the police turned up and dragged a kicking and screaming Miss. Sung away. Everyone at the home was interviewed, but Noah stated he was never called into her office, and did not know what happened to those who were. Apparently, two other male care workers were also arrested. Noah was just glad he was never called to one of their offices as well.

Noah shook his head. The people who were meant to be there for him, to raise and protect him were the ones who hurt him the most.

Noah took a sip of coffee.

Over the top of the buildings, there were many columns of thick grey smoke bent by the December wind.

Across the street, a window smashed. A chav could be seen rummaging around in the room.

The power came back on.

Noah closed his curtains and sat in front of the TV.

The BBC News announced that America had regulated all its outgoing news channels. They believed that the British government would soon follow suit, and within hours, all live news coverage would be halted. The reporter finished by asking what was the governments of the world trying to hide.

Noah settled down to a day of channel surfing.

17

New Years Eve 2012

Noah saw the New Year in when he made his way to the toilet after being woken up by fireworks. Noah checked his watch and realized it was a brand-new year. It then dawned on him, that with everything that was happening, there was at least one person out there celebrating the New Year.

He went to the window and watched some lame fireworks fizzle out over the top of a few buildings in the distance. He wondered about the mentality of the person who lit them. Were they being optimistic, or were they a little crazy.

The streetlights had not worked in weeks. There was a full moon, and few clouds.

Something caught Noah's attention. In the distance, there was a naked man running across the road at full pelt. It was hard to make out any details, and the man soon disappeared round the corner.

Noah shrugged it off. It was either a drunk, or a religious fanatic. He saw clips about them on the news, new groups turning up, singing prayers, and lighting fires on the hilltops.

It reminded Noah of the prophecy which was supposed to end the world on the 21st.

On the other hand, maybe it did happen; Noah thought. *Maybe the virus hit its high point on the 21st, and it became the point of no return for the human race.*

He scanned the dark street.

Dogs started barking in the distance. He ignored them and returned to bed.

18

Thursday 4th January 2013

Day 20

Noah had not left the flat in over a week. The encounter with the druggie made him cautious of stepping back outside.

He spent the rest of the week watching TV, surfing the web, playing computer games, and eating unhealthy amounts of fried food, while watching the world outside his window grow even more dangerous as gangs started to roam the streets.

Everyone realized that they were on their own. There was no longer any police to defend the weak. It was everyone for themselves.

Noah opened his window a fraction and practiced with the air rifle, hitting different targets across the road, and down the street.

The TV was down to just a couple of channels, and they were showing mainly repeats. The news had dried up, with only a few new reports each day, and they seemed almost scripted as if the government was trying to keep something from the public.

There was no news whatsoever regarding other countries. The only short clip regarding another country came on the fourteenth day, when the news reported that the World Health Organization had classed the virus as a pandemic.

No shit Sherlock.

The internet was next to useless. Google was working again, but only spasmodically. Ninety-five percent of all links were broken. Sometimes the internet connection didn't even work.

His mobile reception was just as bad, and only worked half the time.

On Wednesday morning, a group of about forty naked people, of all ages, covered only in ash and mud, walked down the road, all carrying makeshift crosses, while singing hymns about redemption. From his window, Noah could see that a few of them even had blood running down their faces from crowns pushed down on their heads made of thorns. In addition, some of them had what looked like raw whip marks down their backs.

During the day, there were more columns of smoke rising over the buildings. Either more buildings were burning, or people were lighting large bonfires just as the news had described.

Noah spent hours watching Doomsday Preppers over and over. When he eventually had to leave the flat, he decided he would head towards Dartmoor. There were plenty of rivers and streams and vast amounts of sheep, cows, and horses wandering the hills. Meat would not be a problem. He would become a survivalist hermit, living off the land.

I have been on my own, for as long as I can remember, never counting on anyone else, why change now.

He settled down to sleep thinking that tomorrow he might leave the flat again. Maybe go and look for some more food, while there were still some to find.

What will tomorrow hold for me?

When he eventually dropped off to sleep, he dreamt of a future where he was not alone. Where he had someone to love and hold. Someone to share his dreams and fears with. Someone he could grow old with.

He dreamt of the colour red.

RED`S STORY

Nicola Arusha Breslan

Nineteen-year-old female
317 Barton Drive
Newton Abbot
South Devon
England

Works at Newton Abbot Specsavers, as an Optical Technician.

1

Saturday 15th December 2012

The Day of the Outbreak

Nicola Breslan's hand swung in an arc and whacked the alarm clock. It read 6:15 AM.

"Just ten more minutes!" she muttered as she rolled over and buried herself under the thick duvet.

Work was a fairly new concept to her. Going from being a lazy student of leisure, to the main breadwinner of the household was a shock to her system.

In addition – along with the shock to her system with having to support her sister and stepfather – was anger. It smoldered inside her. Each early morning, each long day at work, each bill that dropped through the letterbox stoked the flame.

She couldn't understand how adults didn't go crazy with all the responsibilities – working, bills, cleaning the house, shopping, and a thousand other small things that all built up into one huge heavy cloud that hangs over their heads. The fact she was only nineteen did not help.

She decided she should be enjoying herself.

Before the devastating news of her mothers' illness, she was a student, studying BEd (Hons) Primary Education with QTS in Plymouths University of St Mark & St John. She always wanted to become a primary school teacher. She was on her third and final year before she was given special permission to pause her education due to her mother's illness. The window for her to resume her studies in the university was fast approaching, and she saw no way of being able to return.

She loved it at university. Living on campus, going out with friends, getting drunk, sleeping in, dating, making mistakes, and arguing with her mum over how much money she was wasting.

Whereas she was the one earning the money now, doing the overtime, adding up the bills, and watching someone who was meant to be looking after her, waste all the funds.

Nicola's mother died two months ago. She was diagnosed with lung cancer, and she slowly watched her mother battle the disease until it took her from them, over a lingering five-month period. She was diagnosed too late; she already had stage-four cancer. They tried chemo-therapy, but it was simply going through the motions. There would be only one outcome.

It was bad enough that she had lost her mother, with the devastating realization that she was not around anymore – sometimes it didn't seem real. However, she knew it was. She stood at the front row of the funeral service with her arm around her twelve-year-old sister's shoulders.

Her stepfather Colin was the cause for her building problems and smoldering anger. Colin completely broke down after the funeral. He stopped working. He was an electrician, and used to work hard, providing for them all. Now he was a drain. When he wasn't sleeping, he sat drunk in front of the TV.

Colin was forty-six and short with tuffs of hair to either side of a bald head, with a large paunch, which was getting bigger each week due to his binge drinking. He was now so unfit, that just getting up and stumbling to the toilet made him break out in a sweat.

Nicola took the first job she was offered, an Optical Technician for Specsavers. The work was repetitive, doing the same thing all day long. She stood in front of the fining and polishing machines, padding up tools with different fining pads, depending upon the type of lens, and positioned them in the large machines. As the outdated piece of equipment ground down the lens to its particular thickness, she was changing the pads on another set of tools. She swapped the jobs from one machine to another, a conveyor belt of work, continuous and mind-numbingly boring.

Even so, she could not let her mind wander too much, because she had to keep her eyes on the tools. There were thousands of different metal tools, each a particular curvature, and she had to check each one against the job sheet, to make sure that the man, whose job it was to place them in the tray, had picked the right ones.

The job was messy and cold. The fining machine poured cold water over the tools as they fined, and the polishing machine poured a thick white polishing cream over them after. She had to wear rubber gloves to protect her skin. In addition, the optical laboratory had to be kept cold – very cold, to keep the lens stuck to the metal blocks with the blue wax.

As she worked she got covered in freezing cold water and polishing liquid, and she could see her breath billowing out in front of her.

However, the money was good, and she had no choice.

The alarm blared again, announcing another five minutes had passed.

6:20 AM.

Nicola could not remember the last time she had a lie in. She rolled back over after whacking the alarm clock for the second time.

She did not have to be at work until 8 AM, but she had things she needed to do before she could leave for work. Jasmine needed breakfast, and even though she was old enough to sort it out herself, it was the one thing in the morning that Nicola liked to do.

Their mother used to have a spread each morning, to prepare them for the day. She missed a big breakfast when she was at collage. Mainly, because hangovers and food did not mix well first thing in the morning.

Also, if she did not sit and watch Jasmine eat, she knew she would leave the house hungry. She was worried. Jasmine had lost over a stone since their mother had passed.

Slowly, like a mummy raised from an ancient tomb, Nicola shuffled around her bedroom, getting ready for another fourteen-hour work shift.

As she exited the bathroom, she could hear Colin snoring, recovering from another day of binge drinking. She did not know what time he got up, probably around midday, whereupon he would grab a case of beer and go and sit in front of the TV, with his wedding album on his lap.

Nicola lightly tapped on Jasmine's door and popped her head in.

"Wakeup sleepyhead! Time for school!"

"It's Saturday!" a muffled voice stated from under a pile of Justin Bieber bed sheets.

Nicola pulled her phone from her jeans pocket and checked the screen.

"Huh? Oh!" The days were blurring together. A bad sign she decided.

"Okay. I knew that!"

"Yeah right!" The mountain of sheets moved to a new position. A thin pale leg hung from underneath over the side of the bed.

"I will see you tonight, Jasmine. And don't forget, tomorrow we will put the rest of the Christmas decorations up." Nicola wanted to go and hug her, ruffle her hair and tell her how much she loved her. However, Jasmine stated that she was becoming too smothering, and touchy feely lately.

So instead, she told Jasmine there was some leftover lasagna in the fridge that she could have for dinner. She then slowly closed the door, not realizing it would be the last time she would ever see her sister alive.

2

Her work days rarely changed. Each day was a carbon copy of the one before. Specsavers main lab for the Devon area was huge – a vast, ugly warehouse. Sixty-two people worked along side her, all a blur of activity.

No one could talk because the machines were so loud. Even so, someone decided they needed the radio on in the background. All it accomplished was adding another irritating sound to mix in with the din.

Nicola was only meant to be on a nine-hour shift, but due to holidays and a busy spell, she was able, most days, to bump her hours up to fourteen. The managers didn't mind. She could sleep here for all they cared, so long as she poured out the work. No one battered an eyelid when they asked for her overtime each week.

Nicola worked in the surfacing department. The machines in front of her chugged and rattled, as they poured cold water and cream over the lenses. Next to her, others stood in front of identical setups. To the right were the cutting machines, where the blocked, thick lenses were cut down to the individual customer's specifications. The row of eight machines were very loud. To her left was where the lenses were taken off the wax blocks and washed, ready to be placed back in their trays and taken to another part of the building, somewhere warm. The glazing department didn't need to be kept so glacially cold. They cut down the large lenses even more to fit into the frames.

Nicola had to walk through their department to get into the cafeteria – it was so hot after her frigid section that sweat beaded across her forehead just walking through. Then, just as she became accustom to the warmth again, she had to return to the chiller.

The whole company stopped at the same time for lunch, 12:15 to 1 PM. She would prefer to work through lunch to get more overtime, but company policy stated that all the machines needed to stop, to give them a rest, to prevent overheating.

The canteen had a selection of meals available, but Nicola preferred to bring sandwiches; they were cheaper.

She sat on a table with three other females, who worked in the same section. One was only seventeen; her name was Loren, a loud, chavy girl who had no internal mechanism for regulating her speech; everything just poured out, regardless of how unimportant or rude. She had twin girls aged eighteen months that, according to her, were the bane of her life. The twins stayed at her mothers while she worked. The father was out of the picture.

In the background, Chris Rea's *Driving Home for Christmas* was playing on the radio.

Loren was explaining that she had a problem breastfeeding the twins, and that she's had an infection for months, which made a dark, blackish yellow pus seep out of her sore nipples.

Nicola lowered the ham and mustard sandwich she was about to take another bite from.

The two others around the table thought it was hilarious, and May, a forty-six-year-old, rake thin woman, who had lank greasy black hair, tossed her head back, giving a long hearty laugh, while showing all her cavity filled teeth.

Doreen, a thirty-eight-year-old, tubby mother of three gave Nicola a what-can-you-do look.

Nicola ate her chocolate bar, leaving the half eaten sandwich to one side.

"Darling, my nipples were so sore after breastfeeding my second that the third went straight on formula." Doreen nodded to state her words were true, while swiping a finger in the air as she flicked her head to one side. "My doctor said I should continue giving my third the best mother nature could offer. I told the stuck-up bitch, Doc, you wanna get your perky little tit's out be my guest, but the little bastards aren't mangling up mine no more!"

Even Nicola laughed along with the others at Doreen's indignant impression.

They were simply work mates; she never associated with them after work, and none of them ever commented on why she never spoke about personal matters – they were all too busy talking about themselves. If it were up to her, she would sit on a table by herself, but she didn't want to look like a loner.

May, spoke a little about her six dogs, which she talked about as if they were her children. At least once a week she would take out her mobile phone and show everyone some photos of them.

To Nicola, all six Great Danes looked the same. And she often wondered how May could afford to feed dogs the size of small ponies.

The rest of the afternoon labored on.

The machines continued to grind down lens after lens.

Nicola started to get a headache from the cold air, the rattling machines, and the irritating buzzing of the radio, which was not loud enough to pick out the words to the songs, just the bass.

At 4:30 PM the first shift ended.

There was a half hour between shifts where the workers milled around, preparing their work stations. Then by 5 PM everything continued as if nothing had changed.

Nicola didn't really know the second shift. She normally worked through to 10 PM without another break, so she never got to go and sit in the break room with the second shift.

By the time 10 PM arrived, she was exhausted physically and mentally.

She clocked out her work card and pushed through the door out into the freezing night air. She pulled her coat up tighter around her neck.

Nicola knew they needed more milk at home, and Jasmine didn't worry about such things, and Colin didn't even know what day of the week it was.

She walked through town every night; it was the quickest route home. She didn't like walking past all the pubs this late at night, not with all the drunks around. However, if she wanted to skirt around the main roads, and circle around, it would take twice as long to walk home.

Drunk people littered the streets, stumbling loudly, from one pub to the next. They walked in groups, crowded together, or arm in arm. People shouted, screamed, and laughed. They skipped from pavement to road, unconcerned by the traffic. Outside the pubs, the smokers gathered, relegated to the cold street if they felt the need to fulfill a habit. A cloud of hazy smoke surrounded every pub entrance.

Nicola kept crossing the road, from one side to the other, always staying clear of the pubs. The last thing she wanted was to be shouted at by a drunk, or rowdily grabbed.

Only last week a woman ran at her, shouting and crying at the same time. She didn't know what the woman was raving on about, and she was released from the woman's grip when the boyfriend dragged her away.

A group of about twenty scantly clad men ran across the street, all dressed as Spartans.

A group of eight mid-twenties females, all dressed in skirts the length of a thick belt, and tops with just enough material to make about two hankies, chased after them on wobbly high heels. Squeals of delight, followed by, "THIS IS SPARTA!" echoed up the street.

At one time, not too long ago that would have been me! She thought to herself. *A lifetime ago,* she reasoned. On so many levels, she wished it still was.

Nicola jumped to one side when a man appeared out of the dark doorway of Millets. He was zipping up his jeans. Nicola stepped over the yellow puddle.

"Al'ight loove? Looking fooor a little fun?" the man asked. He was so drunk he had to lean against the door frame to steady himself while he managed to get his zip sorted out.

Nicola didn't bother answering, rather she sped up her pace.

A burger van was parked next to the entrance to the market. The area around it was full of drunks trying to eat a hot, dripping meal with their hands. One lad was arguing with the woman behind the counter that she had short changed him.

Nicola crossed over to avoid two older men having a pushing match. She couldn't tell if they were fighting or playing.

Almost home, she reasoned. All she wanted was to have a bite to eat and have a hot shower then get to bed.

I wonder if Jasmine ate all the lasagna?

There was a small twenty-four-hour shop around the corner. She popped in for some milk, bread, margarine, and flour.

As she headed down Queen Street, she walked by a TV repair store. She glanced at a large plasma TV in the window; it was showing a birds eye view of a tropical rain forest. Across the bottom scrolled the word's Madagascar. Nicola gave it scant attention. She had enough problems closer to home without worrying about something happening on the other side of the world.

3

After leaving town, Nicola headed down a dark footpath next to Asda, which ran down along side Barham's Brook – which was, in fact, a fast-flowing river that ran through Baker's Park then through the town.

She left the overhanging tree-covered path and headed through an industrial estate, past a large kitchen warehouse. The large car park was empty. When she walked through it early in the morning, it was overflowing, with cars double-parked. There was always a Volkswagen Beetle parked next to some steps that looked old and battered and had old-fashioned boxes and luggage tied onto a rusty roof rack, as if the owner was forever about to head off on holiday.

She came out on to Bradley lane.

Large, old buildings crowded in on both sides of the narrow lane.

The wind whistled around the roofs and made the plastic grocery bag rustle.

Grit crunched under her trainers.

It was late, dark and cold.

She pulled her coat closer around her.

A cat screeched in the distance, sounding like a child in pain. It made Nicola jump.

"Shit!" she hissed. Steam billowed out her mouth.

Someone coughed behind her. There were loud footsteps.

The streetlights seemed too far apart.

Nicola sped up. Her right hand clutched a pepper spray in her jacket pocket. She hitched her backpack up higher on her shoulder.

She now turned the corner after walking up a slight incline. She came out on to Hunterswell Road, which joined onto Barton drive.

The person behind belched. Laughter soon followed.

Just a drunk, she thought. She relaxed a little.

The road widened as it joined onto Barton Drive. It was well lit and houses crowded all around.

Nicola relaxed a little more. She was almost home.

Jasmine would still be up, sat at her laptop, chatting with friends on Facebook – her curfew was 9 PM. She tried to get her to go out more, interact with them, rather than just on the web. She didn't seem too bothered though, stating why go out, when she could see everything online.

Nicola worried about her little sister. She should have a different kind of relationship, one where they were more like siblings rather than her taking on the motherly roll; trying to raise her while, Colin slowly sank deeper into depression.

She had nothing against Colin; he was just coping in his own way, but it was starting to grate on her. She had to buck up. She had to snap out of it and take control. It was her mother who died – she watched the woman she loved more than anything in the world slowly die in front of her eyes. She watched the pain rack her face. The tears, the hurt, the pleading to any god that this wasn't fair. Colin didn't have the monopoly on grieving.

Nicola crossed the road. In the distance, a car screeched around a corner.

She wondered where her real father was. *What is he doing? Did he ever think about us? Did he even know his ex-wife was dead?* These were questions that echoed through her mind on a daily basis.

Her father first met her mother in Africa, on an aid mission. They were both do-good hippies, wanting to change the world, one country at a time. Her father, Zachary Spencer Stone's latest conquest was digging a well in Cabo Delgade, Mozambique. The town had one small school which her mother; Abby Paige Shelly was teaching English for a six-month stint. They said it was destiny that they met.

He was her knight in shining armor – a man who thought enough about the planet to want to make a difference. The fact that he looked like a rugged Indiana Jones, with his strong jaw, piercing green eyes and muscular body, didn't help.

They became inseparable and spent another four years in and around Mozambique, Zambia, Angola, Botswana, and even crossing the Mozambique Channel to Madagascar. He went wherever he was needed, and Abby followed like a love drunk teenager.

They ended up in Madagascar, in the Antsalova region of Melaky on the northern coastline to help the Sakalva, whose name means, *People of the Long Valleys*. Large corporations were ripping apart the hills looking for minerals. Whole valleys full of native forest habitat was being slashed and burned, causing silting of the rivers. The area was turning into a dead zone.

Bizarrely, the Madagascan government in Antananarvio weren't interested in the indigenous people from the area, and the effect the mining was having on them, but when the destruction to the forest started to affect the breeding areas of the Ringtailed Lemur, the government had no choice but to step in.

That's when everything changed, while celebrating the news that eight valleys were saved from the corporation's machines, Abby announced that she was pregnant, and even though she loved Africa and Madagascar, it wasn't the place to raise a child.

At the end of the Second Trimester, at twenty-six weeks, they flew back to England, to Devon, to find a small flat to rent, to raise their family.

However, Zach wasn't happy being confined in one place, and having to buckle down and get married, and having to find a job to support them all. He went from living the dream, to suburban normality. Within months of Nicola being born, cracks started to appear in the relationship. By the time the second child, Jasmine came along; the marriage was all but over.

When Jasmine was three months old, Zach announced he was going off to Indonesia to save the Orangutans; apparently, as far as he was concerned, they were more important than his own children.

Abby did the best she could. She spent three years waiting on a man who never returned.

When Nicola was ten, her mother met Colin.

Colin seemed safe. A man with a steady, boring job as an electrician, and no aspirations in life. He was happy just to watch the world pass by. He didn't want to change it, or cared what happened outside his small section. He was just an average man, with an average life. He was a perfect candidate to raise someone else's family.

Nicola tripped on the pavement. She was tired and found it hard to pick up her feet properly.

She wiped a tear from her eye. Thinking about everything in her life made her sad. But thinking about her absent birth father made her mad.

Nicola remembered the time when she was fourteen, and she found a letter from her father in her mother's jewelry box, when she was rifling through, trying on earrings. It was hidden under the bottom tray.

Her father stated he couldn't return. He was doing something of the utmost importance – world changing. He stated he couldn't say more. It was an ambiguous letter that gave nothing away; just a man trying to clear his nagging conscience.

She wanted to rip the letter up. However, for whatever reason, her mother kept the letter safe and hidden. Nicola returned it to its place and never mentioned it.

Almost home, she thought. *A quick meal, a shower, and then bed. Then repeat. Working to support a household is so hard and monotonous*, she reasoned.

She gave Colin grudging respect for doing it for years, uncomplaining day after day, sometimes seven days a week.

Even though he's faltered over the last few months, I hope he pulls it together soon, before I have a breakdown!

They had both taken Colin's last name when he married their mother. Changing it from Stone to Breslan. He had even filled out the paperwork and adopted them as his own.

They never called him father or dad, only by his first name. They had always been aware that he was the stepfather not the father.

Nicola walked down the short drive that had Colin's van parked along one side. A van that hadn't moved in months.

However, she knew he left the house at some stage every few days, and walked the five minutes to Asda to get more beer. Partly, because she had shouted at him over a month ago because he complained there was no beer in the fridge. They hadn't talked since.

I hope he's crawled off to bed and not asleep in front of the TV again.

Her normal routine, when she got home – after saying hi to Jasmine and giving her a hug – was to turn the TV off, pick up all his empty cans, and then take out the rubbish.

She just hoped something changed, because she felt like she was losing her mind.

As she inserted the door key and pushed the front door open with her shoulder, she didn't realize just how much her world was about to change – and not in a good way.

4

The TV was on too loud. The news was blaring throughout the house.

Nicola was instantly on alert. Something wasn't right. Even if Colin, in a drunken stupor, had turned the TV louder, rather than off, by mistake, Jasmine would have wondered out and turned it off.

There were cans around his reclining chair, with an empty bottle of cheap whisky next to the TV remote.

Nicola went to reach for the remote to turn the TV down, when movement out of the corner of her eye made her spin around.

Colin was slowly walking down the hallway to the front room. He was naked, with his hands and swollen groin covered in blood.

Nicola dropped the plastic bag, and the backpack dropped from her back.

"What have you done?" she shouted, as she ran past him, knocking him over, as she ran to her sister's bedroom.

Nicola stopped by the open door. The room looked like it had been ransacked. Jasmine's laptop was on the floor with a broken screen, along with other items that had been tipped off her desk. The bedside lamp was broken, and the rug was rumpled up. One of the curtains was pulled off its rings. It looked like there had been a struggle.

Then Nicola's eyes zoned in on to the bed. All the sheets were rumpled up, with her sister's motionless body laid upon her back. Her nightie was pulled up over her shoulders, with a pillow over her face. Her lower body was so pale compared to all the blood around her inner legs and thighs.

She rushed to her side.

"No, no, no..." she muttered over and over, while knelt down next to the bed. She hadn't touched her sister yet, as if touching her would make it real.

Tears streaked her face, plastering her red hair to her cheeks.

Her hands hovered over Jasmine, unsure where to touch her. Her sister's body was all bruised, with one leg twisted at an unnatural angle, hanging off the bed.

Nicola tilted back her head and screamed, pouring in all her sadness and pain with every ounce of her soul – a scream full of primeval anger.

Her hand lowered onto her sister's chest, over her heart. Jasmine was still warm.

Nicola removed the pillow from off her sister's face.

Jasmine's eyes were wide open, and bloodshot – all the capillaries had hemorrhaged in her eyeballs when Colin choked her as he raped her.

Nicola brushed some hair off her sisters battered and bruised face.

Then she noticed the bite mark on Jasmine's small left, barely formed, breast.

"I'm so sorry Jasmine," Colin screamed over and over from the front room.

Something inside Nicola snapped.

She sprung to her feet, spun around and marched to her own room. Behind her bedroom door, hung from a hook, was her compound bow and arrows.

She hadn't touched them in months. She didn't have time to practice anymore. She used to be top in her archery class, and had won four regional, and even one national competition. She was told she had promise and if she continued the way she was going, she would be considered for trials for the British Archery Team.

Nicola pulled down the bow and grabbed a thirty-two-inch fiberglass arrow out of the quiver. Her sister's blood was on her hands, and as she notched the arrow, by clicking it into the knock, the blood covered the rubber feathers.

With the bow pointed to the carpet, Nicola marched to the front room.

Colin lay upon his back, with his hands over his eyes. He was still shouting at the top of his lungs, "I'm so sorry Jasmine; you look so much like her!"

He must have sensed someone was close. He removed his hands from his face and struggled to raise himself up onto his elbows.

Through drunk, bloodshot, tear streaked eyes, he said, "I'm so sorry."

Nicola stood over him, looking down at the man who had raped and killed her twelve-year-old sister. Without a word, she raised the bow. Her chest expanded as she pulled back the string with all her strength, then sighted down the peep-sight. Then, without so much as a facial twitch, she released the pressure.

The arrow slammed into Colin's face, punching straight through his right eye, jolting his head back with a thump, pinning him to the wooden TV cabinet.

As Colin lay twitching, Nicola calmly placed the bow on his chair.

On the TV, the BBC reported a serious outbreak of a virus in South Africa, which had closed down the airport and a three-mile area around the airport terminal.

Nicola ignored the news and grabbed the remote and switch the TV off. Then, like a robot on autopilot, she headed to the kitchen.

5

Nicola filled a bowl of warm soapy water and headed back to her sister's bedroom. With a flannel, she slowly cleaned the blood from her sisters cooling body as she quietly sung a nursery rhyme that their mother used to sing to them both to get them to fall asleep.

"The sun is not a-bed, when I at night upon my pillow lie; still around the earth his way he takes, and morning-after morning makes."

She then slowly lowered Jasmine onto the floor, and changed the bed sheets. After putting a clean nightie on her, she placed her back in bed.

"While here at home, in shining day, we round the sunny garden play; each little Indian sleepy-head is being kissed and put to bed."

Nicola leaned forward and kissed Jasmine on the forehead.

With her eyes closed, with clean sheets tucked up around her, her sister looked like she was simply sleeping.

"I love you Jasmine, and always will. Say hi to mum for me."

Nicola left the room and closed the door slowly behind her.

Back in her own room she grabbed a cloth bag from under her bed and tossed some clothes in from some drawers, and an old sleeping bag from the bottom of the wardrobe along with a small two-man tent she used only once to go camping with friends. She knelt and unplugged her phone charger, which she also tossed in along with her iPod.

In the kitchen, she grabbed some food from the cupboards and three large two-liter bottles of water.

Nicola rested the green cloth bag next to Colin's body while she slid the compound bow into a cloth carry case. She retrieved the arrows and put them in the side pocket.

Under the sink in the kitchen, there was a large metal torch. She placed it in the bag along with some spare batteries.

After taking her purse out of her workbag, and collecting the grocery money from a tin on the bookshelf, Nicola picked up the house phone and dialed nine-nine-nine.

"Which emergency service please?" a female voice asked.

Nicola ignored the operator and placed the receiver on the table. Once no one replied a police car would be dispatched to the residence, to see what the problem was.

Without a backward glance, she left the house, leaving her keys in the door, so the police could get in.

She was moving as if in a dream – everything felt like a nightmare. She couldn't face anyone. She couldn't face up to what she did to Colin – not yet. She needed time to grieve and sort her mind out.

Nicola headed back up the road toward a small lane that entered Baker's Park woods. She would hide in there for a few days until she gave herself in. She knew where there was an abandoned stone hut, that they both used to play in years ago.

6

Sunday 16th December 2012

Day 2

Nicola lay inside the tent that was erected inside the stone hut. The floor of the hut was soil, so she could still peg the tent down.

Even with the torch, the walk through the woods the night before was difficult. Darkness changes everything. The relaxing woods, with overhanging trees and a babbling river, becomes a creepy, alien world. And away from the streetlights and light pollution, without the torch she would be plunged into absolute darkness.

Putting the tent up was a bit of a challenge, but she found her mind was numb from shock, and she put it up without putting any thought into it. She then crawled into the sleeping bag in her clothes and lay looking at the inside of the tent's ceiling.

Nicola lay awake for hours. She turned the torch off to save the batteries. It was so dark it was almost as if her eyes were closed.

After her body relaxed into the sleeping bag, everything suddenly caught up with her – a barrage of emotions engulfed her stricken soul.

Then she started crying; her body shook with heavy sobs, as tears wet her face and hair, and soaked into her sleeping bag.

She didn't know what time she eventually fell asleep because she had turned her phone off, and she didn't have a watch on, and at that moment, time meant nothing to her – nothing did. All she could feel was a deep, gut churning emotional pain that engulfed her whole being.

All Sunday she spent curled up inside the tent. She only got out to go toilet just outside the hut. She drank a little water but couldn't stomach any food.

Thoughts kept churning around in her mind. It was worse than losing her mother, at least she still had Jasmine; now she had no one, and she was a murderer – even though the raping bastard deserved it. However, she didn't think the authorities would see it that way.

By nightfall her head was pounding. She had hardly sipped any water, and with the amount she was crying, she was severely dehydrated.

Before she fell into a fitful sleep, she downed as much water as her stomach could handle.

She woke several times feeling like there was someone else present. But there was just the sound of the wind rustling the trees, and small animals foraging in the undergrowth.

Each time she woke, she cried herself back to sleep.

Her dream was twisted and horrifying. She was walking around the house, naked, dripping in blood, and the floor was covered in congealing blood that she had to wade through. Large pulsating clots hung from the ceiling like stalactites, and it drenched the curtains and furniture. She could hear Jasmine screaming from other rooms, but as she tried to run her feet would slip on the blood, and she would land heavy, sliding along into furniture. And when she did manage to get to a room where the voice sounded like it was originating, the room was empty. However, what each room did have was a blood-soaked bed.

Nicola tossed and turned in the sleeping bag, kicking and punching in the nightmare. If anyone were around, so deep in the woods, so late at night, they would have heard the animalistic screams of pure anguish echo throughout the darkness.

7

Monday 17th December 2012

Day 3

The next morning, Nicola felt like she had run a marathon in her sleep. Her body ached, and her head was pounding.

She slowly crawled out of the damp sleeping bag. She sat with the tent door open, letting the cool morning air circulate, to take the smell of sweat out of the plastic.

Her throat was sore; her hair was knotted and her clothes rumpled and sweaty, but she didn't care. Her mind was blank – exhausted from crying and shouting in her sleep.

She looked down at her palms. They had bled in the night, where her nails dug into her pale flesh, from where she had clenched her fists. Also, on her sleeves was Jasmine's blood, all dried and dark – a reminder of her loss.

Nicola intended to get up and have something to drink and maybe nibble on some food. Instead, she sat hunched in the entrance to the tent, crying. Loud sobs pierced the morning air. She wanted to take the top off and toss it away from herself; instead, she rolled onto one side, on her back, pulled the sleeping bag up over herself and fell back into a fitful sleep.

She woke again around midday. It was cold and misty outside the hut.

The stone hut was situated deep in the woods, way off the beaten tracks used by dog walkers, joggers, and ramblers. She had found it along with Jasmine years ago, when they went exploring.

Jasmine liked to become famous people for the day, while reenacting what she was learning at school. On that warm summer's day, they were pretending to be Lewis and Clark, and the woods were the unexplored American wilderness. As they stumbled through the thick undergrowth, Jasmine explained that the woods around them were the uncharted land of the Continental Divide, and that they had to find a safe passage to the Pacific coast.

The hut they found was about fifteen feet by eight, with one empty window frame, where the wood and glass had long gone – even the door was missing. The roof bowed in the middle, and vines stopped two of the walls from collapsing. However, it gave protection from the elements, and the cold.

Nicola unsteadily got to her shaking feet.

When she looked over into the far corner, she could picture Jasmine crouched down, taking a soil sample, and putting it in one of mum's small Tupperware containers. Jasmine stated they would analyze the soil and determine who had lived in the hut.

She stood leaning on the warped door-frame, with her mind drifting back to the present.

Outside it was misty. The white shroud covered everything, as if hiding her from the world.

No birds sang. No dogs barked in the distance. It was eerily quiet. It was if the world was holding its breath.

Nicola went toilet again, and drank some more water. Her throat ached.

She took a bite out of a snicker's bar, and after a few chews she spat it out. She couldn't stomach food at the moment.

She had no idea what the time was. She didn't want to turn her phone on, because in the movies they could pinpoint a person's location from their mobile signal. She didn't know how accurate that was, but she didn't want to risk it.

The police would be searching for her by now. Her sister and stepfather were dead, and he had her arrow through his eye socket. It would only take them so long to piece it all together and realize she was missing and to start looking for her.

She was surprised a police helicopter, with its night-vision infrared camera, hadn't already been buzzing over the woods looking for her.

Nicola went and sat back in the entrance to the tent. Her belongings were spewed around the ground. Discarded while trying to pull out the sleeping bag.

Her head pounded, regardless of how much water she drank. Her eyes were swollen and tender. Every muscle ached as if she had been tense all night, like a coiled spring.

She hunched over, half in, half out of the tent.

Condensation dripped from the tent's ceiling onto her blue rumpled up sleeping bag.

Nicola couldn't get the image of her sister's body out of her mind's eye. It was almost as if it was burned into the back of her eyelids.

She kept playing things over in her mind.

If only I didn't work so much. If only I was at home more. If only I realized Colin was so bad. But a rapist – a fucking killer? Who could see that coming?

He raised her for almost ten years. He was quiet and half the time you didn't even know he was there. *"The perfect husband,"* her mother used to say. He worked hard and provided for the whole family – uncomplaining.

When he wasn't working he sat quietly at the kitchen table reading newspapers, or watching TV with the rest of the family. She had never heard him raise his voice or argue with her mother.

She spent years going to work with him on Saturdays, to get her out of the house and earn a few pounds for pocket money. She had watched him work, while explaining what he was doing. She used to sit and watch him repair things in the garage that was converted into his workspace. She got to the point where she could repair some of the electrical items for him.

Colin had been like a large, quiet lamb.

Nicola cried some more. She rubbed an arm up over her face, smearing snot and tears into her tangled red hair.

He couldn't have done it. I was tired. I heard him wrong. I killed the wrong man. I killed the man who stepped in to raise us.

She sat unmoving, with her arms placid at her sides. Her mind spinning, running everything over and over, and each time it all came out distorted.

Nicola was cold.

Looking up from her lap, she realized the night had drawn in. It was dark outside the stone hut, with silvery moonlight reflecting off overhanging branches. The mist that surrounded the hut glowed with an eerie, mystical light – making the ground and trees seem to glow. There was no wind; everything was perfectly still and silent, as if she had been transported into another world.

Nicola dropped back into the tent and rolled onto one side. She tried to fumble with the door zip, but gave up halfway. She was freezing during the night, but couldn't be bothered to do anything about it.

She cried throughout the frosty night. The tears cooled her face even more. She didn't even have the strength to wipe them a way.

The first stage of grief – Denial and Isolation – was almost over. The next stage – Anger, was about to consume her every thought.

8

Tuesday 18th December 2012

Day 4

Nicola climbed from the tent. She felt different – she felt angry.

Today she was mad. Mad at the world. Mad at everyone. She was left with a man who couldn't support them. She was only nineteen, and she had to feed the whole family. She had to work long hours to pay the mounting bills. The government did nothing to help; they simply bogged her down with mindless paperwork and promises. And all the doctor wanted to do was prescribe her medication to help her cope – drug her up, and shut her up.

Why me? She screamed over and over in her mind, as she kicked against the stone wall. Her trainers didn't even scuff the old stonework, she simply knocked moss away.

She noticed the dried blood on her jumper's sleeves. She yanked it over her head and tossed it into the corner.

She needed to shout at somebody, to dump the blame on someone's shoulders. Someone had to be responsible for everything.

God! She thought.

When her mother first became ill, she turned to God. Her mum had never even mentioned God before, as far as Nicola could remember. They never went to church. They never prayed before meals. God was as absent as their biological father.

Then as the illness progressed, and things seemed desperate, and in her delusional state, her mother would talk to God, having long conversations, as if filling in an old relative who had missed out years of a person's life.

Nicola would sit by her mother's bed and listen to the one sided mumbled conversation. They made her sad and angry at the same time.

As her mother got thinner and started to fade away, physically and mentally, Nicola became jealous that she was spending so much time talking to a God that obviously didn't care. A God who was allowing her pain to continue. A God who did nothing for her family.

After, when she stood in the funeral home with an arm supporting her little sister, as the priest talked about ashes to ashes, and spoke of other outdated glorified things that had no meaning in today's way of life, Nicola looked around at the statues and icons, draped in their gold and silver and rich materials.

Just stone and wood, she thought. *No more able to help than a book written by mere, earthly men.*

She had never believed in a God. She found it strange, later; when she gave it some thought that she could go from not caring, and not believing in religion, to hating it.

Now, as she stood facing the stonewall, she remembered her feelings and hatred, as she kicked as hard as she could – over and over, until her legs ached, and she fell onto the ground.

She lay in a pile of blown in leaves, looking up at the bowed ceiling. She cried some more as she flung her arms sideways, pounding on the compact soil. She rolled and kicked and twisted up her back, like a five-year-old having a tantrum. She screamed abuse at the gods and life, and how unfair it all was.

Nicola was cold. She only had on a long-sleeve shirt underneath her jumper, but she was too tired to move. She lay on her back and slept on the dirt and leaves, her tears creating wet patches in the soil. Then she would start again, kicking against the wall and thumping her shoulder against the ground.

By the time it was dark, and she crawled into the sleeping bag, she was covered in dirt and sweat, and ached all over. She fumbled in her bag and slowly pulled on a thick green woolen jumper.

She fell into a deep sleep, too tired to even cry.

9

Wednesday 19th December 2012

Day 5

Nicola's throat was raw; it hurt to sip the water.

She was dirty and smelly, and her stomach ached because she was so hungry.

She sat in the tent's entrance, rummaging through the bag, until she found the snickers bar that she had taken a bite from. She sat and slowly finished it off. Then she ate a tub of pineapple cottage cheese and some smooth peanut butter with her fingers.

In her heightened state, when she left the house, she had tossed in random food items. Luckily, because it was so cold, the cottage cheese was still edible.

She finished off the first bottle of water.

Nicola felt stupid for kicking the wall, and exerting so much energy thrashing and punching.

She looked at the patch of soil where she had tossed and turned. It looked like a mud snow angel among the leaves.

Then, without any conscious thought, she dropped upon her knees in the mud and started praying.

She churned up all the old recited prayers as a child, that she learnt in the assembly hall.

Please lord, help me. Make it all a dream. Let me wake up at home in bed and everything is normal. Let mum and Jasmine still be alive and happy. Let this all simply be a nightmare.

Forgive me for what I did to Colin, even though he deserved it. Forgive my unbelieving. Forgive my blasphemy. Give me the strength to continue. Give me the strength to believe.

After hours of kneeling, she crawled onto her belly, face down in the mud. She repeated her supplications over and over, like a mantra.

She ignored the woods outside and prayed with all her might.

She sung hymns that sounded out of place inside the stone hut.

"*All things bright and beautiful, all creatures great and small, all things wise and wonderful: the Lord God made them all...*"

She was amazed that after years of not hearing the songs, she could recall the words so effortlessly.

"*Morning has broken, like the first morning. Blackbird has spoken, like the first bird. Praise for the singing, praise for the morning. Praise for the springing fresh from the word...*"

She sung the hymns for hours, repeatedly, with fragmented prayers inserted between them.

Nicola dozed off facedown, with her forehead pressed against the dirt. When she jolted from her sleep, she continued singing and praying.

She ate some more peanut butter and a couple cereal bars, then gulped down some water.

She crawled into the sleeping bag. She lay staring toward the ceiling in the pitch dark. It was so dark it didn't matter if her eyes were open or closed. She sung herself to sleep after saying the Lords Prayer.

10

Thursday 20th December 2012

Day 6

When Nicola woke up, she felt stupid for singing and praying. She felt like she had wasted her effort. She felt no different. She was still in the same situation.

She realized that this was her fifth day in the woods, and no one had come looking for her. She had not heard one single helicopter.

She was tired and sore, and so sad her soul ached to its very core. She smelt like she had been living in a rubbish dump for a month.

She ran a hand through her tangled red hair, and sat in the entrance to the tent picking leaves off her jumper.

It was time to go home and face the music. She couldn't hide forever.

Slowly, she packed up the tent, and rolled up the dirty sleeping bag. She even tidied up the hut, picking up the rubbish and leaves. When she walked away carrying a large bag, with her bow and arrow case flung over her shoulder, the hut looked like no one had been there.

It took her twenty minutes of pushing through the undergrowth to make it to a public footpath – the case on her back caught on low hanging branches. Within another ten minutes, she was walking along Barton Drive towards her house.

She still didn't know what the time was, due to her phone still being switched off. But she knew it was mid morning. However, there seemed to be no one around, as if everyone was locked away inside. It didn't make sense.

Nicola loitered near a postbox a few houses away from her driveway. There were no police cars parked outside. There was no one watching the house.

She also knew; with her bright-red hair, she would be spotted within minutes of walking along her street. At present, her hair was tucked under an old beanie hat.

Looking as if she was about to walk past the bungalow, at the last second she jogged up the drive, disappearing down the side.

Nicola stood silently in the back garden, leaning her back against the wall, listening.

Nothing.

No one was about.

She pulled a plant pot to one side and removed the spare set of keys. Within seconds, she was under the yellow tape that said crime scene, and inside the kitchen.

She stood still.

The bungalow was eerily silent. It smelt strange, with a tangy metal smell dominating. She realized it was the smell of blood.

She wandered slowly through the kitchen into the living room. There was a patch of dried blood on the floor where the TV cabinet was.

She looked over to the Christmas tree next to the large front room window. She forgot all about Christmas. She noticed the box next to the tree. Jasmine must have put it there ready to finish off the decorations with her on Sunday.

Nicola noticed there was black dust on lots of surfaces. She realized it was fingerprinting dust.

There was a set of stairs going up to her mothers and Colin's bedroom. Jasmine's and her bedrooms were at the back of the bungalow.

Strange, she reasoned, *why I always call it a house, when technically it's a bungalow. She was stalling, avoiding what she knew she needed to do.*

Still carrying her bag, she walked and stood outside Jasmine's bedroom, looking in. The bed sheets had all been removed, along with the mattress. There was more black dusting powder everywhere. The broken laptop and other smashed items were gone.

Nicola slowly closed the door. She didn't want to go in. To her, it was a mausoleum, where she had put her sister to rest.

Her own room had black dust everywhere. Her bed was pulled apart, but nothing had been taken. Even her curtains were still pulled, where she had forgotten to pull them open when she left for work six days ago.

It seemed like a lifetime ago.

Nicola was confused that she could get into the house and walk around without anyone stopping her.

She dumped her bag and bow and arrows by her door and stripped off her dirty clothes, leaving them in a pile.

She walked naked down the hall. It felt refreshing not to have the dirty clothes clinging to her skin.

The bathroom had black dusting powder on the door handle; the taps, and cabinet handles. Apart from that, it was no different.

She knew it was a risk, but she stood in the shower for what felt like hours. She had never scrubbed herself so clean in her life. She washed her hair three times. She put conditioner in and sat in the corner out of the sprays reach, with her knees tucked up, letting the water wash over her feet.

She felt strange once she stepped out of the shower and dried herself off. Almost as if that was the last step – with the dirt and sweat poured the last ounce of her mourning.

As she walked back to her room, avoiding the windows, she noticed the clock in the kitchen read 1:46 PM.

She didn't want to turn anything on in case someone outside saw the lights, or glow from the TV and called the police.

She opened the fridge. It still had everything in it.

Nicola didn't know police procedure. It had been six days, but the power and water were still on. Maybe they needed a relative or someone to sort everything out. Maybe it was a lot of paperwork and took time. For all she knew, it could click off at any moment.

She returned to her room with a couple of cold hotdog sandwiches and a large glass of milk.

After consuming the food, and downing the refreshing drink, she hooked a blanket up over the curtains to make sure no one could see the light from outside. Luckily, her bedroom was at the back of the bungalow and there were tall leyladii trees around the back garden, screening off the neighbors to either side.

Nicola made her bed and curled up, warm and cozy for the first time in days. She didn't bother with any nightie or bed clothes. She had been constricted in her clothes in the sleeping bag; it felt refreshing to be so naked and free.

She lay looking up at her lampshade. She didn't cry. She thought being back at home would engulf her in emotions. However, the last six days had been such a rollercoaster ride, emotionally and physically, that her brain felt completely numb.

Nicola rolled over and fell into a deep, dreamless sleep.

11

Friday 21st December 2012

Day 7

For a few seconds, everything was normal.

Nicola woke up slowly, stretching while tossing back the thick duvet. She stretched and yawned.

It was a whole new day.

Then everything came crashing back down.

It was like a slow computer booting up, and as the memories flooded back, so came the weight and depression.

Nicola punched the pillow, rolled and screamed into it. Her muffled shout slowly died away.

She swung her feet to the thick beige carpet. Leisurely she wandered over to the wardrobe and grabbed some loose jogging pants and a black, baggy tee shirt.

Nicola was at a loss.

What do I do now? Wait until someone turns up at the house and finds me? Or do I phone up and give myself in? Or walk down to the police station?

Her laptop was where she left it. She wondered why the police didn't take it?

For all they knew I could have planned the murder over the Internet.

She decided that the police had something much more important to deal with, and she wasn't high on their priority list.

She grabbed the laptop and scuttled back into bed, pulling the sheets up and sitting up with the laptop on her lap.

If they can trace my Internet usage, maybe they will just come and get me.

She was surprised to notice that Virgin was still providing the house with broadband.

She clicked onto Google Chrome.

Her first, almost automatic reaction was to log into Facebook.

Old habits die hard; she decided.

Instead, she clicked on the BBC News, to see if there was anything about her.

Every single story was related to the same thing – a virus outbreak that was consuming the world.

Nicola sat in horrified silence as she read through the stories one after another.

So far, seventeen countries had cases. Tens of millions in America alone were in a comatose state. Hospitals were at breaking point. Even football stadiums were full of people lying on cots, thousands together, spaced out on the grass under protective covers.

She flicked through a couple more stories.

So far, England was uninfected.

She was shocked to notice the timeline – everything started on the day Jasmine died.

Nicola spent the rest of the day reading everything she could find, and watching YouTube videos about the virus.

12

Saturday 22nd December 2012

Day 8

Nicola realized the night before that the world was too preoccupied to be worried about her. The police had other things on their mind at the moment. So, for the first time in seven days she had a hot meal.

The remains of a fry-up smeared the large plate. She was absolutely stuffed full of sausages, bacon, tomatoes, eggs, mushrooms, hash browns, and baked beans, with bread fried in the oil residue from all the meat, all covered in tomato ketchup.

It was the best thing she had ever eaten in her whole life.

She sat at the table, looking down at the plate.

Only five feet away were the dried patch of blood where she had killed Colin.

She felt nothing.

Something changed in the woods – something had clicked. She had used up every spare ounce of emotions on what had happened and what she had done.

The world had changed while she hid in the woods.

Somehow, someway, she knew everything was going to be alright. She couldn't explain how she knew that, she just did.

It was almost as if the world had come into clarity. Everything now made sense. She was a survivor, and she would do whatever it took to survive, at whatever cost.

Nicola decided that she would stay in the house for a little while longer – it was the safest place to be. For now, no one would come looking for her.

She put the dirty dish in the sink and sat in Colin's chair. She settled down to a day of watching the news, instead of reading about it, and watching her small fourteen-inch laptop.

Everything she saw confirmed her theory. The world had changed along with her.

13

Sunday 23rd December 2012

The Day the Virus Reached England

Day 9

Nicola crawled out of bed at 11 AM. She sat in her nightie, eating corn flakes while watching the morning news.

While she was enjoying, a lie-in the virus had reached the shores of England.

The BBC News was reporting that The Royal London Hospital had announced a young woman, Jessica Redfern, who had just returned from a holiday in Cancun, Mexico, was showing all the signs of the symptoms.

Nicola watched the events unfold.

Within three hours, another case was registered in Manchester.

Over the next eight hours, Great Britain was locked down, completely quarantining itself from the outside world – no planes or boats would be allowed to enter or leave. Even the Euro Tunnel was closed.

A little bit late for that, Nicola mused. *The government should have locked the country down, stopping anyone from getting in. That's like locking the safe after all the money has been stolen. Idiots!*

She enjoyed seeing the queen give her speech, telling everyone to keep calm. The queen looked so small and dainty, like a plump dolly in her bright yellow dress and large hat.

Right, and I'm sure you're about to be whisked away somewhere safe.

It was announced that a parliament session had passed a bill bringing martial law into effect. The army would be released onto the streets of Britain.

A curfew was also in effect. No one would be allowed to move about over the next three days. So for Christmas Eve, Christmas Day, and Boxing Day, people would be confined within their homes, under house arrest.

It was announced that a window for collecting everything a household would need would be open on Tuesday the 27th, for ten hours, between 10 AM and 8 PM.

Nicola watched the TV for the nation's response to the news. It didn't take long. Within three hours, there was rioting in London, Glasgow, Bath, Plymouth, Leeds, Birmingham, and Sheffield.

It seems not everyone wanted to stay quietly indoors while the world ended around them.

At least no one will come to the door if no one's allowed out, she reasoned. It made her relax a little.

If only she realized that a lot of individuals would ignore their government's orders, and a couple of those people would break into her house while she slept.

14

Monday 24th December 2012

Christmas Eve

Day 10

Nicola snuggled down to another night in her warm, cozy double bed.

It's now Christmas Eve; she realized.

She lay in bed at 2:17 AM. There was no need to get to bed early. Plus, sitting around eating all day wasn't taxing. She wasn't really tired, just going through the motions.

The thought of Christmas, alone in the house, made her feel sad and depressed. She had repressed many bad memories over the last week, and she wanted to take her mind of the impending, lonely, Christmas.

She decided to pop in her earphones and listen to a few songs on her iPod, until she dozed off.

She reached track four of the new *Birdy* album: *Fire Within – Words as Weapons*, when some sixth sense made her jolt up in bed and tug the earphones out.

There was a silhouette stood in her doorframe, illuminated by a light, which someone had switched on in the front room.

Nicola froze, while holding her breath.

It looked like the muscular outline of a large man.

The world seemed to slow down. Fear changes everything.

Nicola stared, unmoving, for what seemed like hours.

The only sound was the tinny music echoing out of the white earphones on her rumpled duvet.

The man was motionless, staring in. Then his breath became faster, louder, more excited, as he realized what he had discovered. His head slowly lowered and his shoulders hunched up, like a predator reacting to easy prey.

Then, in an instant, everything changed – the man lunged.

Nicola instinctively rolled in the opposite direction, over the right side of the bed, away from him.

The man grunted as he landed on the double bed.

The room was dark, and Nicola's eyes were adjusted. Whereas the man had just walked in from a bright hallway.

The man tried to climb over the bed. He tangled himself in the duvet while racing to reach her – his excitement made him clumsy.

Nicola stood and turned. It was obvious what the man was after. Her fear turned to anger.

"Not again in this house! Not to me," she calmly muttered.

"Fucking sex-crazed men!"

She was mad – so mad; she had gone through anger and out the other side, with a strange calm that vibrated her whole body.

The man was struggling to climb over the bed, grunting from the effort, when the heavy bedside lamp slammed against the side of his face.

This wasn't meant to happen. He liked a little bit of a struggle, but not this. They're not meant to fight back. They are meant to cry and scream for help, while turning into a blubbering, wiggling mess. He liked it when they wiggled.

Nicola swung the lamp down again, as the white lead whipped around after it was ripped from the plug. This time the man was face down in the duvet. He was dazed and trying to raise himself up. The lamp base was made from a heavy metal; it caved in the back of his skull with a cracking, sucking sound.

The man twitched as the last few signals from his brain bounced around his nervous system.

Nicola spat on the man.

"Fucking animal! Go to hell where you belong!"

There was a creak of floorboards outside in the hallway.

"D-did ya say s-s-something Francis?" another man's voice asked. "And w-what's with all the ruckus?"

15

"Francis?" You know w-we are only m-meant to be stealing stuff, right?" The voice was moving up the corridor.

"There's b-bound to be loads in here. The police just shut the place up after that c-crazy bitch killed everyone."

The man stood in the doorframe, looking in.

"What the fuck! You t-taking a nap, Francis, or trying to h-hump the bloody bed?" The man rattled off a squeaky laugh.

The room was still dark.

"Francis?" The man switched on the light.

The situation became obvious.

"Jesus, holy f-fuck!" The man rushed into the room, oblivious to the danger. Ignoring the fact that someone must have killed Francis.

"Don't move a single muscle," Nicola said.

The door slowly swung shut, closing the three in the room.

She was hiding behind the door. She now stood staring down an arrow, pointed directly at the man's face.

"Whoa! Whoa! F-fuck! Fuck!" the man screamed as he fell back onto Francis.

Now the light was on; Nicola could see both men.

Francis' corpse was big, wearing faded, oily jeans and an old brown-waxed leather coat, with large Doctor Marten's boots on. He had broad shoulders, and plate sized hands. An image of a dockworker crossed Nicola's mind. She knew if she stepped closer, he would stink of cigarettes and stale sweat. It was hard to tell his age because he was facedown; and what was left of his head was caved in and saturated in blood and brain matter.

The stuttering man was small and runty looking. He had rat-like features – a thin face, with big ears and protruding teeth, and beady eyes that are too close together. His hair was long, black, and very greasy; looking almost wet. His face was covered in spots. One on his stubble covered chin was seeping yellow pus. He was wearing dirty white, cheap trainers, soiled jeans, and a black hoody with the yellow Batman symbol on the front, under a thin, tatty black leather jacket. He looked to be in his early thirties.

Nicola stood unwavering, with the arrow pointed at the small man.

"Wha-what's h-h-happening?" the scrawny man asked, his eyes wide with fright.

"You broke into my house; that's what's happening, dipshit!"

"Y-you-your house?" A bubble of spit popped in the corner of his mouth.

"I'm the so-called bitch that killed everyone!"

It seemed impossible that his eyes could stretch wider, but they did. Even his mouth was hanging open. Spittle dribbled down his chin, running over the big raw spot.

"And your friend there was about to try and rape me!"

"Whoa! W-whoa! He's n-n-no friend of m-mine! Just a d-drinking acquaintance." As he said that, he tried to move away from the corpse, as if distance would prove his words.

Nicola said nothing. She pulled back harder on the string.

"W-we drink in the s-same p-p-pub, The Swan. I just know him f-from there. He said he knew a-a-a place that was e-empty – e-easy p-pickings."

The smell of urine drifted over to Nicola. The man had either pissed himself, or the dead man's bladder had emptied over the bed.

"I didn't know h-he was a fucking rapist. Honest! Can't abide a-a-animals like that. Lowest of the l-low." He looked up with pleading eyes. His face was all screwed up, making him look even uglier.

"He kn-kn-knew the p-police would be busy. W-we were just gonna s-steal all the stuff we could sell on. N-nothing was mentioned about r-rape! We thought it was e-empty. There was police tape e-everywhere." The runty looking man kept filling the silence.

Nicola stepped a little closer, pointing the arrow down at him.

"W-w-what ya gonna do with me?" he said in a shaking voice, trying to lean back into the bed.

"This!" Nicola released the arrow.

16

It took considerable energy to roll the skinny man off the bed, and tie him up. After she released the arrow into the bed next to him, she was going to use the few second's distraction to rush forward and knee him in the face, to knock him out. However, as the arrow embedded into the mattress next to him, his eyes rolled back in his head, and he fainted.

Nicola collected some thin electrical wire from the garage and tied the man's hands up behind his back. She left his feet free. She then propped him up against the wall, next to her table.

Tucked into the man's waistband was a seven-inch hunting knife. She changed into jeans and slid it onto her belt.

She left the corpse on the bed. She was never going to sleep here again, so it mattered little to her what happened to the rapist's body. She decided cremation was probably too good for him.

She collected her stuff back together.

The sleeping bag could have done with a wash, but she couldn't use the loud washing machine or dryer.

She collected together some clean clothes.

After putting her bag and case with the bow and arrows next to the front door, she returned to the garage by the connecting inside door.

She collected Colin's spare petrol can, and proceeded to walk through the house, dousing everything in petrol.

Nicola washed her hands, and cleaned herself up in the bathroom. The smell of the fumes stung her eyes.

She then stood outside her sister's bedroom door. She rested her head on the cold wood.

I hope you're enjoying yourself catching up with mum? She gave a wane smile. She didn't enter the room. She simply caressed the door gently with her fingers.

We'll catch up soon Jas. Just not yet.

The slap echoed around her bedroom.

"W-what h-happened?" the little man asked, groggily. His eyed adjusted, and realization flooded back.

"What's your name?" Nicola questioned.

"W-what?"

"Your name. What is it?" She was knelt in front of him with the seven-inch knife wedged under his scrawny chin.

"Randall S-Saul Burke. My friend's c-call m-me Randy."

"His whole name." She nodded to the corpse.

"Francis s-something Bowen, I think. W-w-why?"

"When I'm stood in front of God on my Judgment Day, and He announces the names of the people I've killed, I want to be certain I know which ones He's talking about, so I can put a name to a face."

A thought hit Randy.

"What's that s-smell?"

"I've soaked the bungalow in petrol. I'm about to walk out, after lighting it."

His face contorted in fear.

"I don't wanna die! Please! I'm sorry for breaking in. I'm sorry Francis was a rapist bastard. I didn't know, honest. Please, I don't wanna burn to death." He burst into tears.

Nicola realized it was the first time he hadn't stuttered.

"I haven't tied your feet. After I leave, the fire will start in the front room. You can run out the back door, which I've left open." Then she added sarcastically, "Feel free to take anything you want with you."

She stood up.

"If you try to follow me, I will put an arrow through your eye. Understand?"

Randy was crying too hard to answer. He nodded hard.

Nicola stood in the front doorway, holding a box of matches from the kitchen draw. She swung the bags over her shoulders, then lit one match and pushed it into the box. She tossed it into the front room and slammed the door shut.

As she got down the short drive, the rush of air engulfed the fumes shattering the front room window in a billowing cloud of glass and splintered wood.

As her home burnt down to the ground, Nicola headed into town.

17

Tuesday 25th December 2012

Christmas Day

Day 11

It was almost 4 AM when Nicola stopped walking.

The town was completely deserted. No cars were on the roads. Normally there would be stragglers wandering around, people who went out drinking, celebrating Christmas. She did it last year with a couple of friends. She didn't enjoy waking up on Christmas day with a hangover.

She realized it was Christmas day.

"Merry Christmas everyone," she muttered into the cold night air.

She wondered what Christmas would be like all over the world, as the virus ravished country after country, with tens of millions in a strange type of coma.

It was cold, and her breath billowed out in front of her, as she walked along the pavement on Queen Street.

Most of the shops were dark, with no lights illuminating the windows, as they normally did at night. A lot had the metal shutters down tight.

The bags were digging into her shoulders. She was cold and tired. The adrenalin had worn off.

Nicola looked up the long road.

The Christmas lights were off apart from one; it was an image of a train made out of green bulbs; the train flashed on and off, while swinging in the cold breeze.

She looked back down and noticed a shop – Millets. She decided she could do with a new sleeping bag, and a few other items.

I'm a killer, what's a little thievery?

She backtracked a little and walked around the block of shops. Behind was a thin street. Large industrial blue and red bins filled one side of the road, pushed up against the back of the shops, near their back exits. The other side of the street was parking spaces and a low wall, which led to an ugly concrete path next to the fast-flowing River Lemon.

Nicola stood next to the back door to Millets. She didn't bother looking around; the place was deserted. No one would hear her.

She placed her bags on the ground, to free up her arms. She then pulled the seven-inch knife off her belt. The blade was strong and thick. She wedged it into the door, next to the lock. With a firm shove with her shoulder, the door clicked open.

The alarm started beeping; now the connection was severed. She had possibly a minute before the alarm started blaring.

She switched on the torch and surveyed the walls. The keypad would be within easy reach of the door. It was on the wall a meter away, next to a staff notice board.

Nicola strolled up to the flashing keypad, and inserted the knife behind the small plastic box. With a sharp, firm jolt, she wrenched the box from the wall. With the knife, she severed the wires.

She held her breath and waited.

Nothing happened.

She guessed right. It was a cheap alarm. Most people didn't realize, but some alarm pads had the dialer – which after the allocated time dialed either the alarm company, or direct to the local police station – built inside the same case as the keypad. Simply removing the power supply, by cutting all the wires stopped the telephone signal from dialing up, and killed the power to the alarm bell.

It was something she learned from Colin. It was a talk he gave to some customers if they asked him about what kind of alarm they should install.

Nicola retrieved her bags and pulled the door shut. She then wandered into the store via the small staff room.

She had never been in a shop in the dark. It was weird and eerie. Normally, the lights would be glaring, with people moving about and talking. There was no background white noise of conversation, just silence.

Items hung on racks and hooks. Objects made strange by the darkness. A shirt looked like it was floating in the air.

There were things in plastic sleeves, in boxes and cloth sacks.

Nicola wandered the rows and shelves, while picking up things she wanted. A sleeping bag. A two-man tent. A stove and a couple of tins of gas. Cutlery and pots that folded into themselves. She saw some snazzy rucksacks, but decided to keep her bag; it was a present from Jasmine.

After collecting armfuls of stuff, she wandered back to the small break room. She turned the light on. The door would stop people in the street (if there were any) from seeing the light.

She tossed her old tent and sleeping bag into the corner, and packed her new ones away, along with all her other new things.

Upstairs, she realized she hadn't been upstairs yet.

She left her things on a small round table and wandered back on to the shop floor.

Upstairs, there was a wall full of shelves holding shoes and boots. She ignored them.

The cash register was open, showing an empty tray.

There was a door leading to a short hallway with an office, a toilet, and a warehouse.

Inside the office, there was a large table, covered in paperwork and photos in frames. The walls were also full of family pictures.

Nicola stood staring at the photos. She didn't need her torch here; the streetlights illuminated the room.

Such a happy family. The mother, father, and three children. All happy and smiling. content with life. Happy to be together.

What do they know about happiness? she thought. *All stood there smiling. Stupid grins on your perfect faces. Idiots!*

She picked one frame off the wall. The three children looked to be between eight and fourteen years old. All happy, smiling into the camera.

Nicola stood staring at the photo for what felt like hours; her eyes burned from not blinking. Then slowly, a tear formed and flowed down her cheek.

Then something clicked. It was the anger and resentment against the happy family, when hers had been ripped away from her. All the pressure that had built up, which was pushed to one side, was released.

Nicola slammed the frame down hard on the corner of the desk. It shattered. She then turned and started ripping the photos off the wall – smashing and throwing them around the room. Then the ones on the desk. She screamed and punched the monitor, which crashed onto the floor, and thrashed the keyboard against the desk, sending keys flying in all directions.

The anger flowed through her, like a person possessed. She kicked at the furniture, overturning it. With all of her might, she pushed the heavy desk, hitting it against the wall – one corner went into the plaster.

She tossed the paperwork into the air, like you see people do in movies with piles of money. It fluttered down around her, covering the floor.

The release felt amazing.

Tears flowed as she cried loud and hard, mixed in with screams of exertion as she tossed objects around, smashing them up. She released the inner pent-up animal of rage.

She moved into the hallway, kicking over fire extinguishers, and ripping more picture frames off the walls.

Inside the toilet, she kicked the seat off, and used it to smash the mirror. After kicking the bin around, and pulling a few more pictures off the walls, and putting her foot through a door panel, she entered the warehouse.

Nicola ran along the narrow aisles, pushing items off the shelves. Then, at the far end of the aisle, she put her back against the shelving and braced her feet, and with all her strength, she managed to tip a whole section of shelving over, which was accompanied by a mighty crash.

On the main shop floor, she ran at the cash register, pushing it off the counter – it made a loud ringing sound. She flung her arms around, ripping things off hooks, tossing them to the floor as she trampled on them. She pushed display cases over – glass shattered, spilling out like a tossed bucket of diamonds. Objects hit the floor and rolled, or lay in a pile until it was booted across the room. She picked up the boots one at a time and tossed them as hard as she could – her arms swinging like a windmill.

Nicola's arms and legs ached, but she kept going, throwing things with all her might, while screaming at the top of her lungs. Tears soaked her face, and her throat was raw.

She almost fell down the steps in the hurry to start on a new, unaffected area.

The streetlights flooded in as she ran around like the Tasmanian devil from the cartoon, reaping destruction everywhere.

Nicola didn't know how long she spent smashing the place up – pulling things off the shelves and kicking things around. She lay in the corner, behind the counter, next to the sleeping bag section.

She pulled at the sleeping bags with the last of her strength, as she cried hard sobbing jolts, that wracked her body.

She had screamed her mothers and sister's names repeatedly, screaming she was sorry, screaming for forgiveness, and screaming just for the sake of screaming.

Nicola lay down on a pile of sleeping bags in the back corner of the store, and cried herself to sleep.

18

Wednesday 26th December 2012

Boxing Day

Day 12

Nicola woke up, aching all over. It hurt to move.

Something was covering her face. She tossed it to one side. It turned out to be a sleeping bag. She was nestled in a pile of them.

Realization dawned. Her actions during the night flooded back.

She felt no remorse. The release was helping her healing process.

She slowly got to her feet.

With the dull light of dawn streaming through the large windows, Nicola could see how much damaged she had caused.

The place was completely ransacked.

She had no idea how long she had spent trashing the place, but it must have been hours.

In the staff room, her things were where she left them. She pulled them on and left by the back door.

Her feet thudded on the pavement as she ambled along. She had no idea where to go, or which general direction to head off in.

She picked a random street and headed up King Street.

She was tired and needed a good long sleep. She realized she must have only slept a few hours all night, what with being attacked, then smashing up the shop; she had been busy.

She walked down next to the side of Wetherspoons. There was a Chinese restaurant on the other side of the road.

Nicola scanned side streets and buildings for somewhere safe to hide.

A few buildings along there was a large mortgage company three-story office. It was the tallest building on the road, and had no adjacent structures to either side. To the right was a walled in, private car park. To the left was another, larger car park, shared with the Paint Center.

Nicola wandered down the side through the large car park.

Around the back was a thin alley with a squat, one-story, high-pitched roofed building.

There was no alarm, and the flimsy door was easy to break into.

Inside was a large break room. A pool table with a pinball machine filled one end. A few chairs and a large couch filled the other. Halfway was a small kitchen counter with a sink, kettle, and microwave oven. There were two large snack vending machines against one wall, near a small TV on a bracket. There was one door leading into the large building.

Perfect, she thought.

19

Thursday 27th December 2012

Day 13

Nicola was wide awake at 5 AM.

After arriving yesterday she had fixed the door lock, securing the entrance, and quickly checked the three-story building. Everything was as she expected, dull and quiet. It was just what she was looking for.

She then made a bed down behind the couch, hiding her away from sight in case anyone barged in. She rested her knife next to her head, besides her bow and arrow that was resting ready to be snatched up. She then settled down to a day of sleep, snoozing, and snacking.

Her new sleeping bag was much more comfortable than the last.

In the first hour of getting up, she had rewired the large vending machines to dispense free food, after breaking the front lock, and disconnecting the lights, and then turning off the alarm.

Now she was sat on the couch munching on a Twix and a packet of sour cream Nik-Naks, while sipping on a can of orange Tango.

The TV was on. A boring government emergency advert popped on every thirty minutes. The man in military uniform announced, "*Do not leave your home. Do not try to leave the cities and towns. Stay put. Keep calm. The government is doing all it can to sort the situation out. Keep your families together and seal all windows and doors. Do not go outside! Do not approach anyone who looks infected!*"

After listening to it the first time, Nicola turned the volume down every time it flicked on. For some reason, the emergency announcement upset her.

By 10 AM, with the sound turned down on another announcement, she could hear people on the road outside. She remembered the other message, stating people had only so many hours to collect everything they needed.

That must be today? She mused.

She had an urge to wander the streets with other people. See someone normal, not someone trying to attack her.

She hid her things in a large cupboard. She just kept the large knife on her belt, underneath her coat.

By 10:30, she was walking along the road.

Her coat had a hood, which was pulled up over her flaming red hair, which was also tucked under a beanie.

She was shocked at the amount of people around. They jostled for space on the crowed streets. Some had obviously been out for a while, because they carried objects in their arms.

Nicola wondered why, at the end of the world; people would need a large flat-screen TV, or a microwave?

She realized they were all looting. Mobs smashed windows and rushed into shops. It was complete mayhem.

It reminded her of the riots on the news back in August 2011. They started in some London boroughs, then quickly spread to other cities and towns across the country.

She remembered having to do an essay on it in Social Media Studies.

It started after Mark Duggan was shot by police. Then a sixteen-year-old girl was violently restrained by officers. At first, people simply protested, then, via their mobile phones and social media sites – which ended up giving the riots the nickname The BlackBerry Riots – they became more organized. Soon, it turned from peaceful protests to rioting, looting, and arson.

In ten days, emergency 999 calls went up three hundred percent. Over three thousand people were arrested, with over a thousand charged. Five people died, and sixteen were hospitalized with serious injuries, with an estimated two hundred million in damages.

She stated in her closing chapter of her essay that people just needed an excuse to misbehave, act up against the authorities – Retaliate Against the Machine.

It doesn't take much to push the average person over the edge, to bring out their true nature; she thought, as she witnessed it firsthand all around her.

People were shouting and screaming at one another. They also pushed and shoved each other around. There were even a few punch-ups.

Everyone's gone crazy; she thought, as she was elbowed against the window of Superdrug.

So this is what people are like once they know no one is around to punish them. This is the true side of human nature.

And if this is now, what's it going to be like when things become much worse? Will we be openly killing each other in the streets?

There was not one single police officer anywhere too be seen.

Where was the army the government promised, who would walk our streets, protecting us? Or is that only in the main cities, where the real money is?

A man pushed another much older man to the ground, then kicked him once in the stomach, and then grabbed his iPhone out of his hand, before running off into the crowd.

Rape and pillage. I'm watching the devolution of the human race.

Nicola just wanted to get back to the solitude of the break room and leave everyone behind.

She didn't realize a couple of men were watching her, waiting to follow her back.

20

Nicola sensed she was being followed. With a quick glance, she noticed two older men tailing her. They weren't very subtle about it either.

Fucking men, is that all they wanna do, rape us? The world is ending and they just wanna stick their rancid dicks in any female who takes their fancy!

She remembered being disgusted at the news after hurricane Katrina devastated New Orleans, and reports started pouring in of hundreds of rapes being committed.

Men return to their most primeval instincts – to breed.

As people bustled around her, Nicola kept her hands in her pockets, with her head down, shoving people aside with her shoulders if she needed to.

She headed away from Kings Street, down Queen Street, around the corner and up Union Street.

Every now and then, she would catch a glimpse of her pursuers in the reflection of a shop, or parked car window.

They looked like they were in their mid-forties, and overweight.

She had a plan.

In Union Street, there was some kind of fight going on. A man was kicking someone on the ground. People moved away rather than help. Nicola crossed over and kept to the pavements. She had her own problems to contend with.

Soon she was on Torquay Road, a road that dissected a long section of Newton Abbot. Streets packed with houses on one side, and long roads leading down to the main shopping precincts on the other.

There were a few cars shooting down Torquay Road, but not many. The petrol stations were closed, and petrol was in short supply. There were cars abandoned on the sides of the roads already. A few were burnt-out shells.

There were a few people milling around; carrying their stolen goods home, but it was much quieter than the town center.

She reached the top end of King Street. The mortgage company building was at the other end of the road.

The two men were maybe forty feet behind her, casually keeping their distance. They only needed to see what house she entered – they didn't need to be too close.

As Nicola turned the corner, she would have possibly twenty seconds or so before the two men turned the corner and saw what she was doing.

As she disappeared from view, Nicola ran as fast as her legs would carry her, pumping them like pistons. She was relying on the fact that the two men were overweight and unhealthy. Hopefully, they wouldn't be able to run as fast, giving her a good head start.

On either side, the houses shot past at a blur. Her heart pounded, and she could hear the blood rushing in her ears.

She was a good hundred feet down the road when the men realized what she was doing. They gave chase.

Nicola was pouring everything she had into her legs. Her chest ached from the heavy breathing, and her head was going dizzy. But still she ran. Ran, as if her life depended on it. And in many ways, it did.

Some people carrying items up the road gave her scant attention. It wasn't their problem. It was now everyone for themselves.

She didn't want to risk looking behind. She could hear shouting and thudding of boots on the tarmac.

Then she reached the car park next to the break room. Without stopping, she rammed the door open, flying in. She rushed to the cupboard and removed her bow and arrows, and in a flash muscle memory movement; she notched the arrow.

With the bow held up, she walked out the door, along the small alley, and into the car park.

Nicola reached the road just as the men reached the car park. They were red-faced and breathing hard.

Without a second's hesitation, she released the arrow. It went straight through one mans leg. He tumbled over, crashing to the ground.

Nicola grabbed another arrow from off its resting place along the side of the bow, next to three other arrows, and renotched the bow.

She had slid on her leather wrist strap, with the little hook that gripped the string notch. She could hold the string back for much longer periods with the strap on. And with one simple push of a clip, the arrow would fly towards her intended target.

The other man was helping his screaming friend to his feet.

The injured man had a thirty-two-inch arrow sticking through his left calf muscle. Blood drenched his jeans.

"Carry him away now, or I will put an arrow through your heads next time."

"Crazy bitch!" the injured man shouted through clenched teeth.

The other man looked at her with pure contempt. Hatred radiated off him; it was almost palatable.

She considered killing him there and then. He looked the sort not to give in. He would be back.

He looked like he would make her look into his eyes while he raped her. He would enjoy her pain as much as the carnal satisfaction.

However, even with everything she had done over the last two weeks, killing someone in cold blood, while he walked away, was not something she wanted to add to the list.

“If I see you again, I promise I will kill you in a heartbeat,” she shouted as one man helped the other limp up the road with his arm around his shoulders. Neither looked back.

Nicola stood there until the men could no longer be seen.

A few passers by gave her a sideways glance and walked back the way they had come.

They didn’t see where I come from. Even if they come back they would have to find me, she reasoned. She decided it was safe to stay in the break room.

Back inside she was to pent up with adrenalin to sit still, so she kept busy.

Nicola walked through the whole three floors, checking each room, while unplugging every electronic device. Most of the computers were still turned on, with the screens glowing around the offices.

There were toilets on every floor. However, on the second floor, next to the toilet there was a shower.

Maybe some people worked late or early and didn't have time to shower at home? She reasoned.

Whatever the reason, she was glad to find it.

After securing the break room door, and hiding her belongings down behind the couch again, she went for a long, refreshing shower. She took the hunting knife with her.

Just as she stripped naked, and was about to jump into the shower, the power flicked off.

Shit!

Her first thought was the man was back. However, he wouldn't cut the power. He was the heavy-handed sort, not the thinking kind.

Naked, and gripping the knife in one hand, she stood looking out the window. It was hard to tell if the power was off everywhere, because it was only midday.

She was just contemplating grabbing her clothes, when the power flicked back on.

A power cut.

She waited for ten minutes. The power stayed on.

She rushed the shower, not wanting to be caught covered in soap and shampoo.

Refreshed, and in clean jeans and a black top, she sat on the couch, with the TV on and the sound off – just for company – she ate a Drifter and sipped a can of cherry coke.

The bow rested against the side of the couch, with the knife unsheathed on the cushion next to her.

Her new motto was, Always be Prepared.

She looked round the break room. It was comfortable enough. It had food, drink, and a safe place to sleep and sit. There was a pool table and a game, if she wasn't afraid to make a noise.

I could've done much worse; she reasoned.

She brought down a clock from off the wall in one of the offices. It rested on a chair to one side. It was 1:59 PM.

Nicola decided it was time to take a nap, due to the fact she knew she would be up as soon as it got dark. She had seen the look in the man's eyes that carried his friend away. She knew it wasn't over yet.

21

Friday 28th December 2012

Day 14

It was 4:18 AM and Nicola was on the second floor, looking down onto the street. She spotted him casually walking down the road.

The man came to stand in the exact spot where Nicola had shot his friend.

It was raining hard; the pouring rain bounced off his motionless body. He had something in his hand – a baseball bat.

Slowly, the man turned around in a full circle, staring at all the houses and buildings. He scanned the Paint Center and the Chinese Restaurant. He looked over the car park and the outbuildings. He stopped on the three-story mortgage company.

Nicola dropped down out of view. She could have shot him there and then, but she was hoping he wouldn't be able to find her. She was tired of killing – even though they deserved it.

I have already removed two evil people from the world. What is one more in the grand scheme of things?

As she hid down behind the wall, the power flicked back off again. She had no lights on inside the building, and she had unplugged everything. However, moments ago the street-lights shined in, illuminating the walls, providing enough light to navigate around the furniture, but they had flicked off with the power cut.

It was a full moon tonight, but the heavy clouds shrouded the satellite. The open office was plunged into darkness.

Shit!

Nicola had the torch on her, but turning it on would give her location away. There was still a chance the man would carry on straight past.

A crashing sound downstairs indicated he hadn't. The sound of glass hitting the floor reverberated through-out the building.

Surely he wouldn't walk around checking the whole building?

Shit! My stuff, it's still in the break room.

She knew most of it was down behind the couch. However, she had left chocolate bar wrappings on the cushions, and empty tins on the coffee table.

Crap!

Her bow and arrows were resting against the wall next to her. The knife was under her sleeping bag, ready for when she went to sleep.

Nicola strained her hearing.

Maybe he simply tossed a stone or something through a window, seeing if he could panic me, and flush me out, she reasoned. Her hands were starting to sweat.

She strained her hearing.

Nothing. Just darkness and silence.

Nicola then noticed a small red flashing light, from a plug, she must have missed unplugging.

So the powers still on, but for some reason, all the streetlights have switched off.

She heard a door creak downstairs. She wasn't sure if it was the floor below or the ground floor.

I can't just sit here. Then again, she thought, *why not. There is only the lift and the stairwell, and I can cover both from here. So when he walks through, I can simply shoot him before he knows what hit him.*

Nicola grabbed an office chair and quietly rolled it over to a spot where she could cover both entrances. She then slowly lowered herself on to it, and rested the bow across her lap, with the arrow notched, but with the string slack, ready to pull at a moment's notice.

Seconds turned into minutes. Minutes stretched into hours.

She had no watch on, and due to the darkness and shadows, she couldn't see a clock on any of the walls. However, she could hear one ticking, slicing away the seconds. It was starting to annoy her.

Nicola started to daze in and out of a sort of waking consciousness. Her eyes were open, but she would suddenly jolt, as if having spasmed from sleep.

She tried not to let her mind wander.

Maybe he's gone. He may have had a quick look around, and left.

Every now and then, the clouds would part and the moon's light would wash across the walls. From her location, she could hear the clock, but she still couldn't see it.

After what felt like hours, Nicola decided he had moved on. Or maybe he had never even entered the building.

Slowly, she made her way down the stairwell. At the bottom, she waited for a few minutes, listening carefully. Apart from the pouring rain beating against the windows, all was quiet.

She told herself she was being overly careful. No one was around apart from her.

Nicola slowly opened the door onto the ground floor. She stood by the wall listening.

Nothing apart from the sound of the rain.

She found a side window that had been smashed. A rock lay among the broken glass. There was no evidence that anyone had climbed in.

After checking the ground floor, she decided he was never inside. He had simply tossed the stone to see if she was inside and was going to react.

Next to the broken window was a freestanding bookcase. She removed a load of books, to make it lighter, then, using all her strength; she dragged the bookcase in front of the broken window. Glass crunched as the heavy wooden case ground over the top. She forced the books back in place. She then dragged a table over and wedged it against the shelving, to give it a little extra stability in the strong wind.

Nicola was drained. She also ached all over.

A good night's sleep is what I need. Or what's left of the night.

She casually carried the bow in one arm as she headed for the break room. Inside she rested the bow against the wall while she closed the adjoining door and wedged a chair up against it.

There was water on the door handle.

She then realized she could hear someone else breathing.

22

It took a fraction of a second to realize that he had been waiting here all along. He had possibly noticed her belongings, and while she waited patiently upstairs, he was waiting for her to return.

In the dull dawn morning light, that was trying to illuminate the room; she could see him sitting in a chair, with the baseball bat across his lap.

He stood and rushed at her.

Nicola knew she would never grab the bow, raise and notch an arrow in the fraction of a second it took for him to reach her.

She ducked and jumped to one side. She could feel the breeze of the bat as it swung over her head.

She dived into the shadows.

The man grunted in anger at missing his prey.

"Bitch!" he spat. "I'm gonna kill you for what you did to my brother." His voice lowered, becoming a threatening whisper. "That is, after I've had some fun."

"What's with you, men and your limp dicks?" Nicola said.

The man spun around. He had lost her in the gloom.

"You fucking cunt! Shut your whoring mouth!" He laughed. "Then again, I've got something I can use to shut it for you."

Now the surprise was over, there was no need for darkness. The man slammed his hand against the light switch. The room appeared, awash in the glaring light.

The man blinked against the brightness, after he had been sitting in the dark for hours.

He swung around.

Where is she?

The room was empty.

At least her bow is where she left it.

He kicked it to the floor. The arrows came off the front and scattered over the carpet.

"Come out, come out wherever you are."

He slowly walked the long room.

She hadn't left; he reasoned, *because the doors and windows are closed.*

He crouched and looked under the pool table. Nothing. There was no room behind the pinball machine. The vending machines were pushed up against the wall, with no gap to one side.

The couch!

"I know you're behind the couch, bitch! Come out now and after I finish with you, I will let you live!"

There was a couple heartbeats of silence.

"You promise to let me live?" Nicola's shaking voice replied. It was almost a whisper.

"Sure. I'm a generous guy." He sniffed loudly. "You may even enjoy it."

He wandered closer to the couch, pulling at his crotch with one hand, to make room for his growth, while resting the bat down against the coffee table.

"Come out!" he muttered. "I have a present for you." The sound of his flies opening echoed around the room.

Nicola got up slowly. She was hugging herself, with her head down. Her flaming red hair cascaded around her face.

"That's right. Come to Phil."

His jeans were around his ankles now. He pulled down his underwear.

"You promise to be gentle and not hurt me mister?" she muttered all submissive in a whisper. Her voice broke, and she started crying.

Nicola walked around the couch and stood an arm's length away.

"Get on your knees," he said in a threatening, low voice.

Nicola still had her arms crossed, protecting herself. She slowly dropped to her knees.

The overweight man grabbed her head, massaging her red hair.

She was so close she could smell the musty, sweatiness of him.

"Oh yeah. That's right, you know what to do, don't you?" he muttered as he pulled her face towards his swollen crotch.

"Yes I do," Nicola murmured as she uncrossed her arms.

The man stretched back his neck, relaxing, and opened his legs, to stand more comfortably.

"Am I your first?" he asked gruffly.

She gripped him in one hand.

"No!" Nicola shouted, "You will be the third rapist I've killed!"

"What?"

The man was confused by her sudden raised voice and words. He looked down just as the strip-lighting flashed off something.

Nicola slashed sideways with the razor-sharp seven-inch hunting knife that she had collected from under her sleeping bag and hid with her crossed arms. She just needed to get close enough to use it.

He screamed and stumbled backwards, gripping at his bleeding crotch. Blood was spurting from between his fingers as he fell onto the floor, reeling in pain.

Nicola stood up. Her head and shoulders were saturated with his blood.

"I believe this is yours," she said as she tossed the flaccid lump on meat at him.

She looked down at him as he screamed and thrashed about on the floor. She walked over to the door and picked up her bow, then retrieved an arrow off the floor.

She stood over him with the raised weapon. His blood dripped from her hair, running down her pale skin.

"It would seem that I'm the one who fucked you in the end?" She stretched back the string to its full capacity.

"All you had to do is stay away."

"Please," he screamed in a high-pitched voice, "Show mercy." He raised a trembling, blood covered hand.

"You have a sickness inside you. I am showing you mercy, by putting you down."

She took aim at his squirming body and let go. The arrow punched through his raised palm, slamming his hand back as it carried on through into his face.

23

Thursday 4th January 2013

Day 20

He had collapsed on a carpet, so it wasn't too difficult to roll him up and drag him outside and leave him down behind a car, in the darkest corner of the car park.

He had left a large stain on the floor, but luckily, it was the industrial type of small square carpets that lay separately. She found a box of them in the janitor's closet next to the break room.

She didn't leave the building again.

Nicola spent the last six days living on food from the vending machines, and some sandwiches, and a Tupperware bowl of Shepard's pie, and an old thin plastic Chinese food container containing some kind of tomato pasta, that some of the employees left behind in the fridge.

She heard singing in the morning on New Years Eve. When she climbed the stairs and looked out the windows, she saw a long row of naked people, covered in ash and carrying large wooden crosses walking down the main street.

She watched until they disappeared around the corner, then shrugged her shoulders and returned to what she was doing.

She was woken up at midnight one night, with loud explosions going off in the distance. She realized it was fireworks. She then realized it was a whole new year – 2013.

What idiot would want to advertise their location, she thought. She rolled back over and ignored the rest of the banging, and went back to sleep.

She watched TV, when it worked, and read Alden Bell's *The Reapers are the Angels* that she found in a desk draw.

The power was intermittent.

The days became long and boring.

It was perfect.

Several times, she was sure she heard someone outside. However, they sounded like they were running past.

Once, when she was checking drawers on the top floor, she looked out a window and saw a naked man running down the street, covered in blood. He looked strange, but because of the distance, and speed he was running, she couldn't say why.

Several times, she heard loud bangs, like explosions. She had no idea what they were. She presumed it was some arsonist playing with matches. When she looked out the topmost windows, she could see many plumes of dark smoke rising heavenward.

Three days ago, she turned on her phone. She decided it was safe to try. The service provider wasn't working – the 02 mobile network was down.

Then yesterday, as she was washing out a tee-shirt in the sink, using some Fairy liquid for soap, she noticed the shirts label. It was an old top she had had for many years. Her mother had scribbled Nic on it, so Jasmine wouldn't wear her clothes.

Nicola stared at the label.

I am no longer called Nicola; she decided. *Nicola died along with my sister. Nicola couldn't do the things I've had to do.*

Her full name was Nicola Arusha Breslan. Her mother, after seeing her for the first time uttered Arusha.

Her mother had traveled extensively before meeting her father, and one of her favorite places was India.

Later, when she was older, her mother explained that Arusha was a word used prominently in Hindu mythology, referring to the red of the rising sun.

She said she gave her the middle name because of her flaming red hair, a sign, she said that she was touched by the gods.

Red will be my new name, signifying the colour of my hair and the blood I have spilt.

She then grabbed the nametag and ripped it from the top.

It's time for me to leave here and start my new journey in life. Tomorrow will be a whole new start.

BETTY AND LENNIE'S STORY

Betty Roselyn Temple

Eighty-six year old female
Park View (Old People's Nursing Home)
Forde Park
Newton Abbot
South Devon
England

Abel Jr Lawrence Temple

Thirty-four year old male (Betty's Grandson)
Redwood House (Home for Adults with Special-Needs and Developmental Disabilities)
181 Vansittart Road
Torquay
South Devon
England

1

Betty Roselyn Temple
Park View (Old People's Nursing Home)
Forde Park
Newton Abbot
South Devon
England

Saturday 15th December 2012

The Day of the Outbreak

Day 1

The alarm bell was a muted ringing that was supposed to wake up the residences softly, to prepare them for another long boring day, until they left this mortal plane behind.

"Ah, I see you're up Mrs. Temple," said the blonde haired, early twenties, heavyset female, who was dressed in a dull pink, tight uniform that turned her stomach into a collection of chubby rolls. Stuck to her upside-down watch that was pinned on her chest, was a clump of green tinsel. She also wore snowman earrings.

"Aren't I always?" Betty gruffly answered.

The young woman said the same line every morning when she entered after lightly knocking, even though Betty was always up and waiting.

"A little tetchy this morning, aren't we?"

Betty grunted, as she sat fully dressed on a tall wingback green chair by the window, which overlooked the manicured garden. She would prefer to be on the other side of the building, so she could look out across the park, but she was waiting for Mr. Grant to die so she could have his room. The old codger just kept going like a Duracell battery.

Betty was tetchy, because she didn't like the way they were made to get up at a certain time.

We're all old, why do we need to be up at seven? We have nowhere we need to be. Dress, eat, then wander into the large lounge and sit, comatose in front of the telly all day, watching endless daytime programs – all time filling crap.

"I will just tuck those in for you."

"It's just fine the way it is," Betty mumbled, as the young spotty carer went around retucking the bedding in. Betty did her best, but her arthritis made it impossible to do it properly.

"You know, Mrs. Temple; you wanna get some nice ornaments, and some more pictures. It looks a little stark in here."

"Mind your own beeswax. I'm happy the way things are."

I don't understand why people collect such trinkets. Why they surrounded themselves with small china objects that collect dust and look gaudy?

Mrs. Simons in the room opposite had every inch of her room covered in china teddy bears – small figurines no more than a few inches high, all doing something different. One was reading a book, another making a cake, another dressed as father Christmas – hundreds depicting human actions and personalities.

Why? She has spent possibly thousands of pounds on inanimate objects, when she was coherent. It's simply mind-boggling.

Betty sometimes pops in to see Mrs. Simons. She rarely leaves her bed; they simply prop her up like an old manikin doll – it's too much trouble to dress and move her everyday, when she doesn't even know what's happening around her. Once they have fed and wiped her mouth and chin clean, and turned on the TV next to her bed, they would hand her one of her china teddy bears, and she would spend the rest of the day stroking it, and rolling it gently around in her frail hands while staring at the wall away from the loud television.

"Well at least let us put up a few decorations."

Betty ignored her comment.

The rest of the nursing home was saturated with Christmas decorations; tinsel hung from every possible surface where it could be attached. Large weird, possible representations of snowflakes, which were the size of footballs and made from reflective who knows what, hung from the ceilings like alien pods. And in the main lounge there was a Christmas tree that would make the attempt in Trafalgar Square look measly. It was so tall it touched the seventeen-foot ceiling and the angel on top looked like it was having a bit of a lie-down.

Betty kept her room clear, so she had somewhere where her eyes didn't hurt from all the glinting reflections.

"It's Saturday! You know what that means? It's full English breakfast today," the carer said all chirpy, to change the subject. She refluffed one of the pillows by whacking it unnecessarily hard, as if it had in someway offended her.

Sounds drifted in from the hallway, as other carers prepared the old people for another day.

Betty did, in fact, like Saturdays, but not because of the food, but because her grandson would be here around 11 AM so she could spend the day with him.

Betty rolled her eyes.

"Full English! More like cold food sliding around a plate of congealing grease."

"Oh, behave," she said while chuckling. "You know you love Eddy's gastronomic delights!"

Betty was surprised the young woman knew such a long word.

Eddy was the nursing homes full time cook. In other words, he's the guy who has been let loose in the kitchen. If he had been given training, he was hiding it well. Eddy was a bold, short, obese man in his forties. His complexion was greasy and ill-looking, and he was always short of breath and looked like he was about to have a heart attack and keel over. Even the carers joked that most of the food he touched ended up on his wide apron. He cooked vast amounts of tasteless food for the sixty-two residents each day. The carers brought their own; they knew better than to try to digest Eddy's muck.

"You know you love Eddy's black pudding."

"Tsk. Black pudding?"

Betty was twelve years old when the second world war started. She survived six years of eating rations and what her father could get his hands on, and for many years after while the country recovered, and in all those years of scraping by she had never experienced anything like Eddy's black pudding – they could use his thick slices for clay pigeon shooting.

"I've seen road-kill that looks more appetizing than Eddy's fry-ups," Betty said as she repositioned her skinny body in the seat.

"That's a lovely dress suit you have on. Is it new?" the carer asked, deciding to change the topic as she readjusted the curtains.

"No! You have seen me wear this a hundred times; you daft young bugger!" Betty smoothed down her pale green dress.

"Now you know you've been told not to call us names Mrs. Temple." The carer drew herself up to her full five-foot one-inch height. She placed her plump hands on her waist.

"Well, stop being such a douchebag for five minutes."

"Oh my god you did not just call me that!" Her eyes were wide with disbelief. "You wait until Mrs. Fredrick hears about this! I'm surprised she hasn't spoken to you yet after you asked me if I've had a sex change."

"You did get your knickers in a twist about that one. It's just; you have such large masculine hands, is all."

The moment was interrupted by the carers phone chiming, to announce she had a message.

The woman ignored Betty as she pulled her iPhone from a pocket and started tapping away as if she was speed dialing.

Jesus, look at her go. That's today's youth, attached to their phones as if by an umbilical cord.

The carer giggled like a school girl.

Her phone chimed again.

Her hands swiftly moved over the touch screen to reply, even if they were large and hairy.

Betty stared at the carer with a deadpan expression.

Within a heartbeat the phone was secreted into a pocket, and the carer came back to the moment at hand.

"Right, let's get you some breakfast, shall we, hmm?"

"Only if you're not too busy."

"Hmm, what was that Mrs. Temple?"

"Nothing. Lead the way, oh great care giver." Betty stood, ready for the woman to open the door.

"What?" Confusion clouded the carers face.

Betty didn't bother answering; she just stood placid while waiting for the carer to open the door, so she could move past her.

The carer opened the door, and was about to walk out when Betty sped through.

"You are meant to follow me down to the dining room." The chubby woman stood stock still, with her arms crossed.

"I know my way around; I've been in this prison for nine years. I don't need you leading me like a dog on a lead."

Before the carer could reply, Betty was already down the hall.

"Hmm. Okay, I will go and feed Mrs. Simons then."

"Whatever Mrs. Doubtfire."

2

Betty sat around a table with three others. They all had their assigned seating, like school children.

To her right was the impeccably dressed ninety-three-year-old Mr. Perkins, who had an outstanding collection of antique style suits. He is a jolly little portly man who had a perpetual smile on his round face, that had the largest mustache she had ever seen on anything apart from a walrus. Mr. Perkins used to own a saw mill, and he walked through the nursing home tapping on wooden doorframes and tables, tut-tut ting at the inferior wood. Because of his Alzheimer's, he still believes he owns the company, and he walks around handing out business cards. This week he has been telling people he can get them a good deal on bulk mahogany. The staff collects all the cards back up and places them on his sideboard in his room, so he can do it all over again the next day.

To her left is Mrs. Todd, a skeletal, sickly thin eighty-nine year old, who has alopecia areata, which makes her head as shiny as a cue ball. However, it also made her eyebrows fall out, which gives her a menacing appearance.

Mrs. Todd never talks. She sits forking food into her mouth, whereupon she would slowly chew it as it dribbled back out down her front, collecting in a plastic bib around her neck.

Directly opposite sits Mrs. Comb, a completely normal looking seventy-one year old, who has a severe nervous twitch that makes it look like she is forever being surged through with electricity. She also dresses like the queen and wears a hat even while indoors. Today she was sporting a bright blue dress and matching tall hat with a large blue colored rose to one side, with delicate blue netting that hung down over her eyes. She looks like she was about to head off to Ascot.

Betty looked down at her plate of congealing animal body parts, and puddle of baked beans. She didn't bother picking up her cutlery; she simply removed a cereal bar from her pocket and ate it instead – dipping it into her cup of tea to soften it a little.

She picked out a fleck of tinsel that had floated down from the long strands of it that draped the light fittings above.

In the centre of the table was a collection of tinsel, baubles and a branch from a pine tree, which was made into a decorative pile. She had to concede it looked pretty and festive. The only problem was; it took up the room where the condiments normally rested, so everyone had a little less space.

Mr. Perkins had already commented on what kind of tree the twig was taken from, also where it grows, the height it reaches before being felled, and how many planks could be made from one standard tree.

She looked around at the other collection of tables, where the occupants chatted softy among themselves. She knew she had been placed at the loony table because of the way she talked to the carers, but she didn't mind. At least she didn't have to pretend to like anyone or converse in awkward conversation.

A ruckus broke out on the next table.

Mrs. Moreau and Mrs. Ederstark were at it again.

Mrs. Moreau is a ninety-four-year-old French woman who moved to England after marrying a British army captain after the second world war. Mrs. Ederstark is a ninety-year-old German, who ended up marrying one of the nine British soldiers whom she hid away at her farm.

One believes the other is a Nazi sympathizer, who passed secrets back to their country. The other believes they have found a French underground resistance fighter that was responsible for an act of sabotage, which killed her daughter when the power station next to the school was destroyed, which also burnt the school to the ground.

At present, the wheelchair-bound Mrs. Moreau was trying to toss a slice of black pudding at Mrs. Ederstark, who was attempting to return fire by flicking a spoonful of hot baked beans.

"Va te faire foutre! Enfoiré!" Another slice landed about two feet away from the throwers weak toss.

Mr. Keller, who was sat next to Mrs. Moreau, covered his ears with his hands and shut his eyes, while making a loud hissing sound; he sounded like a kettle was boiling.

"Küss mein arsch! Schlampe!" The spray of baked beans splattered across two feet of the tablecloth and dribbled down the side of Mr. Keller's glass of orange juice, and wilted the tinsel on the centre display.

I'm living in a madhouse.

Five carers rushed in to break the tectonically slow fight up. You would think with the amount of people and fuss that it was a gang fight at a maximum-security prison.

Betty left her food and wandered back to her room. She had just over three hours to kill before her grandson turned up.

3

```
Abel (Junior) Lawrence Temple
Redwood House (Home for Adults with
Special-Needs and Developmental
Disabilities)
181 Vansittart Road
Torquay
South Devon
England
```

Abel sits on the edge of his bed dressed in his blue denim dungarees, with his checkered yellow and orange flannel shirt, topped off with a yellow baseball cap – it was his favorite set of clothes. He fiddled with the edge of his Bob the Builder bed sheets.

Today was Saturday, the day he went by train to see his grandmother.

Abel liked trains. He enjoyed sitting with his head against the large window, feeling the vibrations through his forehead.

He loved his gran; she was all the family he had left. He couldn't remember his mother. But he knew he must have had one, because he was told everyone does.

Abel looked up at the posters that plastered his small room's walls. As well as Bob the Builder there was Fireman Sam, Pingu, Thomas the Tank Engine, and Barney. However, Bob was his favorite. He wanted to be a builder and drive around on Scrambler the blue quad bike.

There was a knock at his door.

"Have you had breakfast yet, Abel?" John, the adult social care worker asked as he walked in.

Abel nodded and pointed at a splotch of yellow on his dungarees. He had just returned from breakfast.

"Soldiers? I do love eggs in the morning," John said. John was twenty-three and looked like he was from the band Munford & Sons due to his farmyard style clothes and scruffy hair with the bitty start of a beard.

"That's an awesome Christmas tree you have there."

In the window was a small plastic foot high tree, which had flashing lights built into the branches. Across the ceiling hung paper coloured loops that Abel had cut and glued together in the art room. On the wall, next to the poster of Pingu, was a large painting of a snowman in watercolours that Abel painted yesterday. He also had one rolled up ready to give to his gran.

"Let's get your coat on, and we shall head over to visit your grandmother."

John was almost six feet tall, and even he had difficulty getting the scarf wrapped around

Abel's broad neck. He then helped him put his thick yellow down coat on. The puffy coat made Abel look even bigger. At seven feet, two inches tall, with thick broad shoulders, he was a giant thirty-four-year-old man who needed to have his clothes ordered from a specialist store in America.

Abel stood still as his garments were put on and adjusted.

"Take a seat." John said. He then proceeded to push Abel's large size twenty-two boots on, that were also made to order by an American company.

"All ready." John looked around the room, and on the bed. "Where's Bob?"

Abel pulled a stuffed toy out of his coat pocket.

"We don't wanna forget him now do we."

Abel smiled.

"Come on then, grab your bucket and spade, and let's go see your gran."

4

Betty sat in her room, on her tall wingback chair and stared out the window. On her lap lay a paperback book: Mary Shelley's Frankenstein.

She wasn't enjoying it, there were too many oldie words and expressions, which made it feel disjointed because she had to keep stopping and try to work out what was being said.

Last week she'd tried to read Moby Dick, but she gave up after page twenty-six.

Her favorite authors were John Grisham, Mo Hayder, Michael Connelly, and James Patterson – books you could get into. However, she felt she should give the older classics a chance – see what all the fuss was about. *They were called classics for a reason;* she mused. She wanted to try to read something meaningful, something supposedly worthwhile, not just cheap paperbacks before she Kicked the Bucket.

In Newton Abbot, there were a few places she could get inexpensive books. There was an Oxfam book shop, and a secondhand store in the indoor market. She would buy a couple of books a week, and take them back when she went down for more, getting half her money back. It worked out at two pounds for two books a week.

The classics though were not the sort of book's people so readily tossed away. They were the kinds of books people put on shelves to let other's know how intelligent they are for owning such a marvelous intellectual collection.

For books by ancient writers like Thucydides, Plutarch, and Plato, and classics like Dante's The Inferno and Anthony Burgess' A Clockwork Orange; she had to go to the public library.

Newton Abbot's large multilevel library, was named The Passmore Edwards Public Library – after the benefactor who paid for it to be built in 1904 in memory of his mother. It had just had an expensive two-year makeover. In her opinion, it was a beautiful building, with its yellow terracotta mouldings over the doors and windows. And now, after the refurbishment, it was so light and airy.

It made her sad to walk around the tens of thousands of books on multiple levels and find it so deserted. She knew people these days didn't have time to sit down and read a book, what with spending so much time vegetating in front of the TV watching things like X-Factor or reality shows. And all these new fangled electronic e-book devices that were much thinner and lighter than a real book, but could hold thousands – a complete library in the palm of your hand.

Children nowadays wouldn't be able to make memories such as hers. She would take a book and wander into a field and lay on the grass for hours, just getting absorbed into the story and enter a fantasy world from the mind's creation. There were no distractions – no mobile telephones and the Internet. She survived without them. However, kids these days couldn't go five minutes without checking Facebook, or Twitter, or checking to see if they had a text.

It reminded her of what Albert Einstein said, *"I fear the day that technology will surpass our human interaction. The world will have a generation of idiots!"*

She knew that all she had to do is watch a group of people, and most wouldn't be talking to each other; they will be on their phones, checking the digital world.

The other day she sat in a cafe in town sipping tea, while waiting for the rain to stop, and watched a family on the table opposite. The father spent the whole time talking to someone via a Bluetooth headset, as the mother sat texting on her phone, and the daughter who looked about six was glued, unblinking at a handheld computer game, while ignoring her food, and the teenage son sat listening to his iPod while swiping a finger over a computer tablet. They didn't talk to one another; they were all in their own electronic worlds.

Welcome to the future, she remembered thinking at the time.

It also made her sad that kids hardly played outside anymore; they all sat in front of flat-screen TV's playing on computer games.

A brave new world, some say. A world of technological marvels. A world where mankind ruled from a chair, tapping a small screen.

Betty closed Frankenstein and placed it on the windowsill. She would skip that one. She picked up John Steinbeck's Of Mice and Men. She would give it a try. She absentmindedly placed it on her lap.

It will become a world enslaved by technology; she continued to ponder. *A world where everything is done for us. We will become like those tubby people on the animated movie* WALL.E; *all sat staring at screens and not interacting with real flesh and blood humans. We would rather chat with them on a touch screen keyboard in an electronic chat room.*

Betty sighed and stretched her back.

Not that it matters for me. I'm old; my time is almost numbered. But something needs to happen for people to sit up and take notice. The world needs a wake-up call.

There was a knock at the door.

"It's open! It hasn't got a lock!"

It was the young Mrs. Doubtfire. She ignored Betty's sarcasm.

"Mrs. Temple, your grandson is downstairs waiting for you."

"Would you like to carry me, or am I allowed to walk?"

5

Betty stood and walked over next to the door. She slipped off her slippers and slid her feet into a pair of green comfy, flat-bottomed shoes. She removed her dark-green jacket off the hook on the back of the door.

"Let me help you with that Mrs. Temple," Mrs. Doubtfire said, as she stepped forward.

"I'm fine, leave me be." She shrugged the coat on. She then dropped Of Mice and Men into her black-and-white leather, long handled handbag, and picked up her cream with green stripped umbrella.

"Are they waiting in the drawing room, or the second parlor?" Betty asked in a posh voice.

"Huh, you what?"

"Lead on sweet child."

The carer squinted at Betty, while trying to figure her out. Then without a word she turned and headed downstairs.

Abel was sat watching the telly along with a splattering of old people in a collection of different style seating – some wide and comfy, others tall and narrow. It looked like a blind person had walked into a furniture store and bought whatever they had bumped into.

On the TV, there are a group of people wearing ridiculous large red and blue scarves, while checking out antiques.

Abel was glued to the screen.

"Hi Mrs. Temple, I hope you are well?" John asked as he stood and walked over to greet Betty.

"I'm super thank you John." Betty liked John; he was respectful and knew how to look after Abel. John would stay with them both all day, trailing along behind like the tail of a comet, but he never spoke until spoken to, he simply faded into the background until needed.

Abel's last care worker used to fuss and jump around like he was on a pogo stick. All it accomplished was to upset Abel and distract from their time together.

"Hi Abel, I see you have your bucket," Betty said.

Abel's head slowly turned from the huge Christmas tree, and his eyes refocused on his grandmother. Without a word he stood, lumbered over and embraced her in a gentle hug that made Betty almost vanish behind his thick arms.

"That's enough of that you great lummox," Betty said, rubbing his arm gently as he pulled away.

Abel stood back and lifted his small plastic bucket that had a faded image of dancing crabs around it. Inside was a small plastic spade that looked like a spoon in his large hands.

"Ready for the beach?" Betty asked.

Abel's smile almost split his face in two. He handed her the picture he had painted the day before.

Mrs. Doubtfire was stood to one side chatting with John, while checking him out. She always hung around, trying to catch his attention when he arrived with Abel.

"Once you prize Jezebel off, we will be outside," Betty said to John as she walked by holding Abel's hand. She passed the rolled-up painting to the wide-eyed carer.

"And make sure that is left in my quarters."

Around the corner, in the hallway, it sounded like Mrs. Moreau had been waiting to ambush Mrs. Ederstark.

As the carers ran past to break up the second fight of the day, Betty shouted back into the room as she was walking out, "Don't wait up, we might hit a few clubs after!"

6

Betty stood on an expanse of concrete that dropped down into the ocean below via a collection of steps. There she stood, bag in one hand, umbrella in the other, just gazing out upon the water.

They always came to Torquay, and she could've met them down here, since Abel lived just up the road, but he liked the train trip, and going to pick his grandma up was the highlight of his week.

Abel was off to the right, down a small incline. There he would stay until either Betty or John told him it was time to move on. Regardless of the weather Abel would sit on the sand making a long row of sandcastles. Luckily, the sand was dry. It was cold, and if Abel dug down too far it started to get wet, but if wasn't too uncomfy for him.

John sat on a step twenty feet behind him, allowing him space to enjoy himself without feeling he was being shadowed.

All along Torquay seafront was a collection of towering steps that dropped down from a concrete walkway that ran the length of the long seashore. The steps led to a sandy beach. Depending on the time of day, and month, the water might be right over the beach and halfway up the steps. Today there was a vast stretch of dark sand with strips of green seaweed, which had been washed ashore. There was a splattering of people, some walking their dogs, others strolling along with their children. There were even two old ladies out in the frigid water, swimming back and forth while keeping close to the shoreline.

John sat reading a book on his kindle HD. Every now and then he would look up to check on Abel.

Abel was now wandering the waterfront, looking for shells and pebbles to decorate his castles with. He noticed one of the old ladies bobbing up and down with a bright yellow swimming cap on. He watched her doing breaststroke for a few minutes before losing interest.

Betty stood looking out over the water. In the distance a large cargo ship was surrounded by smaller vessels. It looked so strange – so much metal floating out on the water, like a vast metallic island. There was a slight mist between the ship and the water, which made it seem like it was floating just above the waves, like a giant alien mother ship had come down and settled.

She liked to just stand and watch the large cargo ships pass. Her late husband, Abel senior, was a captain for a Singapore shipping company. Almost thirty years ago he went missing while captaining a large vessel categorized as a Handymax – a ship that could carry up to fifty thousand tonnes deadweight.

He, along with all the crew, vanished while transporting dry goods through the Malacca Straits, a narrow channel between Indonesia and Singapore, which was well known for its pirate activity.

It still felt unreal to hear he may have been killed by pirates. The image it invoked was an old-fashioned wooden ship with large billowing sails full of swashbuckling men with beards in tights and shiny cutlasses. The reality was dangerous, lawless men in speedboats hefting AK47s and rocket launchers.

The vast vessel was found drifting forty-eight nautical miles off course. No one was onboard, just lots of blood and gore and spent bullet casings. Around the ship there were smears, to indicate where the bodies had been tossed over to feed the sharks.

Betty liked to think Abel senior, (Abel junior was named after his grandfather) somehow escaped and was living on a deserted island somewhere surround by scantly clad young ladies who ministered to his every whim.

There was a grave, with a beautiful headstone for him, but it felt empty and wrong when she went to visit it once a year to tidy the grave and put fresh flowers down. She felt closer to him here, with the large vessels off in the distance. Here she could feel his spirit on the salty sea breeze.

She thought about all the lost years they could have had together. How his disappearance tipped the balance for their daughter Sophie, and how she ran away, leaving Abel Jr with his grandmother. That was only a year after her father went missing, and she hadn't seen her daughter since. So she had two losses to contend with while trying to raise a child with learning disabilities.

Luckily, she received a pension from the shipping company. It was tight juggling everything, but Abel never went without.

Betty prized her eyes away from the long shadow on the distant horizon and looked down at her grandson.

Abel was knelt in front of a scattering of sandcastles, while delicately pushing shells into the sides with his plate sized hands, then draping seaweed around them, as if making green moats.

I am blessed to have such a gentle grandson, who wouldn't hurt a fly.

She felt sad that she could no longer live with him. She was deemed too old and incapable of looking after someone with

Profound and Multiple Learning Disabilities – as they labeled it. They came up with new categories each year. In a few years, he would be labeled as having something different, or worse.

"Poppycock, you interfering bastards!" she had shouted when they arrived to cart Abel away.

A woman in an ill-fitting dress suit announced he needed to be somewhere where they could give him the level of support that he needed to maintain a quality of life for someone with his needs. She remembered thinking the woman didn't have children of her own. All her so-called knowledge came from books, not experience.

So they took him away from the only relative he had and stuck him in a large, impersonal care home, surrounded by strangers that simply looked at him as part of their job.

Imbeciles all of them! Bloody paper pushing idiots who tallied up numbers and percentages. Putting people in different columns and then writing them off.

Betty flicked a glance back out to the cargo ship, saying a quiet good-bye to her husband for another week. She then slowly walked down the steps to stand next to John.

John looked up from his tablet.

"He's building Windsor castle by the looks of it," John stated, while sliding his kindle into his leather satchel.

"Coffee?" Betty asked.

"Please."

"Be right back." Betty headed off to one of the kiosks that dotted the seafront.

Within minutes she was back with two coffees and a coke for Abel. When she walked out to hand it to him, he mumbled thanks, then took the opened can, gulped it down in one swig and handed it back, before returning to his sandy domain.

It was close to 1 PM.

After half an hour of watching Abel they told him it was time to grab something to eat, and the three of them headed down the seafront to their favorite fish and chip shop.

"Hi Abe," Lucy, the young waitress said. The skinny, pretty blonde girl looked about eighteen, and she had been serving them every Saturday for almost two years. She stood next to their table that was nestled up to the window looking out over the beach, ready to take their order.

Abel blushed and lowered his head. He fiddled with Bob the Builder who sat on the table, leaning against the tomato sauce bottle.

"Same as always?" she asked, directing the question in Betty and John's direction. They were both sat opposite Abel, due to Abel taking up one whole side to the table.

"Please midear," Betty answered.

When the food arrived, Lucy told Abel that she made the cook put more chips on his plate and the biggest battered sausage they had. She said this every week, and every week the big man gave her a million-watt smile in return. Lucy even cut up his sausage for him.

After lunch they walked along the shoreline up to the train station.

Abel hugged his grandmother good-bye.

Betty climbed aboard the train heading back to Newton Abbot, leaving the other two to walk back to the care home.

Betty waved out of the window as John led Abel to the side of the platform.

Bless him, she thought. *If only we lived together. I guess that will never happen now.*

She was too old and, according to others that apparently knew better, too fragile to look after her own grandson.

We will be back together soon; she mused as the train started to pull away from the station, while Abel stood waving both arms like a windmill.

She couldn't explain it, but she just knew that soon they would be taking care of each other.

Bah, I'm a daft old bugger if I think anyone's gonna let us live together again.

She wiped a tear away as Abel disappeared from view.

7

Betty didn't go straight home. She walked up a steep hill to Courtenay Road. The view from the top was spectacular. Then again, that was why she picked the bungalow to be their home.

Abel senior was away a lot with work, sailing the high seas, and she would spend months at a time alone with their daughter Sophie.

She looked down on the property from the road. She could see the roof and garden, but most of the bungalow was hidden by tall trees and overhanging bushes.

She remembers long afternoons during the summer sat on the porch enjoying the view, while little Sophie played with her toys on the grass.

From the front of the bungalow, a person could look right across Newton Abbot and the village of Kingsteignton. They could also see part of Bovey Tracy in the distance, and Bishopsteignton and some of Teignmouth. Dartmoor stood high and beautiful to one side, with Hay-Tor rock jutting up like a sentinel looking down across the deep, long valley.

In the distance, the River Teign snaked around a hill, heading off toward the ocean.

The sound of the traffic on the motorway in the distance, and tens of thousands of people living their lives floated up as a wash of white noise.

Betty settled down on a bench, placing her bag and umbrella down next to her.

She liked to sit and take in the view every now and then. It was hectic at the nursing home, and sometimes she just needed a few more hours away from the noise, the smells, and the hustle and bustle of all the people squeezed into one building.

Dark heavy clouds were piling in, filling the valley. The wind picked up a little, tossing her hair to one side.

It was 2:32 PM, and the sky was starting to darken already. Within an hour or so it would be almost pitch black. It got dark early this time of the year.

Betty removed another cereal bar from her handbag and sat sucking on it.

Two pigeons, from a nearby tree, glided down and started circling the bench while bobbing heads at each other.

The song, *Walk Like an Egyptian* ran through Betty's head. She tossed some crumbs onto the ground.

She could have done with a cigarette right about now. She hadn't smoked since she became pregnant with Sophie, but even decades later the want was still there, when the mind wandered and the solitude dragged up old memories and cravings.

Betty routed around in her bag. Right at the bottom was a packet of Players Navy Cut Medium Cigarettes. It was the last packet she ever received, decades ago. She had smoked half the packet until a trip to the doctor announced she was pregnant. After that, her husband stopped bringing them home. At the time he was in the navy.

The cigarettes had long disintegrated to dust, but if she held the faded packet up to her nose, she could still smell the musty rank of them.

She wasn't sure why she had carried the packet with her for over fifty years, but for some reason it brought her comfort. And that feeling of comfort helped her over the last week, especially after the bad news she had received from the doctors.

8

Betty arrived back just after 4 PM. It was like the middle of the night outside, and Mrs. Fredrick muttered something about how she was going to get mugged one of these days while walking around by herself in the dark, as she ambled past.

Mrs. Fredrick, the manageress, was a smallish woman in her late fifties. She was almost as round as she was tall, and had a beehive haircut straight out of the fifties, and wore bright dresses of eye watering, psychedelic colours with huge circular earrings that a buggieregard could perch on, and glasses that took up most of her flushed face.

Mrs. Fredrick wandered off to shout at one of the carers that was two minutes late returning from their break.

The main lounge was almost full.

The lights from the huge Christmas tree were so bright; it was as if a helicopter's search light was being shone into the room.

Some residents were watching the TV, zoned out, hardly blinking at whatever was on. A few were asleep, bent over awkwardly, looking uncomfortable. A couple of others were at tables near the back of the room, playing chess or draughts or some other board game. Three were sat at a couple of tables pushed together, where they were completing a huge thousand piece jigsaw of a group of dogs dressed up as people playing a game of cards.

Three carers were stood by the entrance to the lounge watching the TV.

The news was on, and the reporter was rambling on about some kind of outbreak in Madagascar. So far two airports were closed off, one in Madagascar and one in South Africa, where nine loggers, who carried the virus, had been airlifted to.

Bah, Betty thought, *there's always some major catastrophe happening somewhere in the world. If it's not one thing, it's another. That's the problem with the news today, there were so many networks fighting to grab the latest breaking news, that they would jump on absolutely anything.*

She couldn't see how nine sick people on the other side of the world warranted coverage on British TV.

It must be a slow news day, she thought as she climbed the stairs to her room.

Someone had thought it was a good idea to wrap tinsel around all the bedroom door handles. Betty pulled hers off and dropped it onto a tall table that rested against the hallway wall, which was already bursting with baubles, wilting branches, and plastic snowmen.

Her curtains were already pulled, and her bed turned down. There was absolutely no concept of privacy whatsoever. Sometimes she woke in the morning and the door to her room was wide open, giving anyone walking past the chance to stare in. A carer had obviously checked in during the night, to see if she had croaked it, and had wandered off, leaving the door ajar.

It was like being a teenager again, and adults couldn't trust you being in a sealed room, in case you got up to some kind of mischief.

And all the carers wondered why she was so grumpy towards them.

Betty shut the door and hung her coat over the hook on the back. She kicked off her shoes and slid her feet into her slippers.

She didn't have a television in her room. She didn't want to get into the habit of just turning a television on and watching whatever was available.

She pulled Of Mice and Men from her bag and settled down for a few hours reading until it was time to go down for the evening meal.

Because they had a large cooked breakfast, and those that stayed in, which was almost everyone, had sandwiches for lunch, supper was a bowl of vegetable soup and freshly baked chunky bread, followed by cheese and crackers.

Most of the residents plodded off to the lounge for some Saturday night TV. They all settled into their seat, getting comfy, ready for X-Factor.

Betty took Of Mice and Men and went and sat in the large conservatory. It was warm and cozy, and she had it all to herself, due to it not having a TV anywhere in sight. Also, because of the plastic frame, and there being nowhere to push a pin into, it was relatively free of decorations.

Unlike some of the other classic books she had tried to work her way through; she was really enjoying John Steinbeck's masterpiece. One character really hit a cord – Lennie, the large slow witted man. She could just imagine Abel in his place.

Half an hour later a carer strode in. The dour woman was wearing a Father Christmas hat.

"I've been looking for you everywhere," she announced.

"Why, am I the woman of your dreams?"

She ignored the comment and handed Betty a small plastic medicine cup, which had two large pills in it, and a plastic cup of tepid water.

"This is your new medicine the doctor prescribed."

"Great," Betty said while taking the cup and looking inside. "Just what I need, more pills."

"Suit yourself, don't take them, I can't make you. It's no skin off my nose. If you want your kidneys to pack up, that's up to you."

9

Saturday 22nd December 2012

Day 8

Betty stood looking down at the long, dull stainless steel worktop.

She was upset because Abel wasn't able to come and visit this weekend, due to the virus that was ravishing the world. Well, she presumed he wouldn't arrive, because she had phoned the home where he lived, but she couldn't get through – the line was dead.

It worried her. She just hoped it was because there was a problem with the phone lines, and not something more menacing.

The outbreak that started in Madagascar didn't just fade away, and end up a small column on page thirty of the newspapers. It turned into a pandemic that was sweeping the globe, country by country.

One week on and America was already quarantined, with tens of millions of people infected. Hospitals were at breaking point and football stadiums, concert halls, shopping malls, and any venue capable of holding thousands were converted to hold the comatose victims.

Betty followed the news carefully. She had acquired an old fourteen-inch TV that now rested on her dressing table.

She remembered the bird and swine flu, from years previous, had just faded out. However, this was different. This time the new outbreak was deadly. No one had yet died from it, but it had reached what some specialists called the second stage, after the rapid eye blinking, and confusion, came the comatose stage. What was next? Stage three – death?

Seventeen countries had confirmed cases, with more countries joining the list each day.

The virus hadn't reached England yet, but it would; in time, it was inevitable – there was no invisible bubble surrounding the small island; it was in just as much danger as everywhere else.

The news, when it wasn't showing stadiums full of people on cots covered in plastic hoods, was showing two things. Firstly, people were panic buying.

The shops were being picked clean, everyone hoarding as much food and water as they could get their hands on. Supermarket shelves were bare, and they were having trouble keeping up with demands.

Secondly, the streets were full of riots.

London, Glasgow, Bath, Plymouth, Leeds, Birmingham, and Sheffield looked like war zones on the TV. Mobs were fighting the police in the streets and destroying property.

The clashes were so bad that the government was in session deciding on whether to release the army onto the streets.

To try to control the damage the government had announced every citizen was under house arrest. No one was to leave their home for any reason.

A window for gathering provisions was set for Thursday the 27th from 10 AM to 8 PM. If you were seen walking the streets between now and then, you would be arrested on sight.

Half the staff from the nursing home stayed home. The few that did risk arrest were stretched beyond their limit. As the day's progressed, and the virus spread, even less staff arrived each day. Now only four members were trying to dress, feed, clean, and look after fifty-nine old people. Sadly, due to the staff being stretched so thin, three people had died in the last week. It was believed that in all the confusion and stress, tablets had been mixed up, and wrong doses given.

Mrs. Fredrick lived on the premises, and she spent hours on the phone each day trying to find someone who could authorize her staff to leave their homes, so they could go to work. She couldn't believe that the government had overlooked such an obvious flaw in their plans.

She kept phoning the local police station, but no one picked up. The national nine-nine-nine number was constantly busy.

Betty, and a few other able-bodied residents were helping out. Betty's job was to cook for everyone, ever since Eddy stopped coming. It was a choice between feeding them, or wiping their asses. She went with the top end.

She stood in the kitchen trying to get meals out of what was left in the large walk-in freezer and storeroom. There was plenty of provisions left, but it was a new experience, having to cook for so many on such a large scale.

Yesterday she cooked beef casserole in a pot big enough for her to climb into and have a bath. It had been nine years since she last cooked a meal. Even so, going from cooking normally and adding a pinch of salt, to having to add a cup full, felt strange.

It took Betty two hours to sort out breakfast today, which was simply breakfast cereals. However, it was just her in the kitchen and she had to prepare the dining room, and clean up after.

Normally, a sullen male teenager that went by the nickname Spider, for some bizarre reason, used to do the dishes. He would stand at the sink listening to oversized headphones.

What she wouldn't do for an assistant right about now.

After she finished breakfast she had to start preparing for lunch. She had no idea what she was going to do for tea.

Today's lunch was sausage casserole. She tried to work the amount out. With fifty-nine residents, plus four workers, plus extra, what with a minimum of two sausages each, still amounted to about a hundred and twenty-eight sausages. Eight chunky sausages weighed roughly a pound, so altogether it was about sixteen pounds just of meat.

I'm eighty-six; I should be sat with my feet up, watching people bitch and complain on Jeremy Kyle.

For tea, it was what was left of the cheese and biscuits.

Sadly, after tea, when the few who could help were getting everyone ready for bed, Mrs. Moreau was found dead in her wheelchair in the garden by the stumps of the rosebushes.

She must have known she was about to die, due to the crumpled letter found in her clenched hand. It said she had lived a good life, and she was looking forward to seeing her husband and three children she had outlived. It ended by saying she hoped Mrs. Ederstark caught the virus, and that she died slowly and painfully.

After twelve hours of cooking and cleaning, Betty stumbled into bed. She hoped the government had some answers, or a cure, because she couldn't handle another day like today.

10

Monday 24th December 2012

The Day the Virus Reached England

Day 9

Betty was having a day off from cooking. She had cooked four days straight, and after Sundays tea, she fell back into a chair while collecting the dirty plates. She was found by Mrs. Fredrick an hour later. She had fainted from exhaustion.

Mrs. Fredrick was taking a turn in the kitchen to give Betty a rest.

Only one carer had arrived to help today. The others had given up, or were hiding indoors with the rest of the country, protecting their families.

Those that needed help dressing were left, sat up in bed. Their food was delivered to them. It still took a lot to help them to the toilet and wash them, and what with the tablets to be dispensed, another two residents were found dead on Monday morning.

Betty was angry that only four different families had arrived over the last week to check on their aged relatives. They took them away with them, to care for them at home and to keep them safe.

But mostly the old people's home was simply a dumping ground for those no longer useful to their family or society.

Out of sight, out of mind.

Who wanted grandma sitting in the front room, zoned out, hogging the telly, taking up space, farting and dribbling, and eating their food? Who was going to watch her? What if she fell over and needed taking to the hospital? What about having to sort out all her pills each day? What about all the extra clothes and sheets for washing? Having to sort out her doctor's appointments. Having to chop up her food and feed her. Who had time for all that? They forget that they did it all for them when they were young. What comes around, obviously doesn't go around.

However, Betty understood. This virus was scary. Unpredictable. Everyone was hiding at home, trying to save their own skins and those closest to them. They presumed that the government would be doing all they could to keep their care homes running at normal standards. They obviously didn't know the government had simply abandoned them to fend for themselves.

While sat in bed, having an extra hour, to regain her strength, before getting up to help wash and feed those incapable of doing it themselves, the news was announced. The deadly virus had reached the shores of Great Britain.

Apparently, a young woman returning from holiday in Mexico was the first to be registered with it in the country. The Royal London Hospital broke the bad news. Within hours more cases started to pop up.

Within eight hours, England was quarantined. Nothing in or out. All airplanes were grounded, and all boats docked.

It was only a matter of time; Betty reasoned. *And being such a small island, and packed in like sardines, it will not take long to spread.*

Her thoughts drifted to her grandson. She hoped he was getting the care he needed.

The power went off.

It had been doing it a few times a day over the last week. Sometimes it would be for a couple of minutes, sometimes an hour or so. Each time she was afraid it wouldn't flick back on.

It's something's you take for granted. You don't realize just how large a part of your life it is, until it's gone. Without electricity, everything is just lumps of plastic and metal.

Betty feared what it would be like, trying to look after everyone if there was no power. No warm water. No heating, due to the large boiler-room in the basement needing electricity to run the complicated computer panel that regulated all the rooms. No lights. It would be chaos.

After the power flicked off for the third time, at the beginning of the week, Betty had collected every bowl, dish, and container that could hold water, and filled them all up. If the power could go off, so could the water. They could manage without electricity, but from watching TV she knew a human could only last about three or so days without the life-sustaining liquid.

Betty wandered to the phone in Mrs. Fredrick's office. She still couldn't reach Abel's home.

She would pray that he was okay, but she had given up on God when her husband failed to return home safely, and when her daughter also went missing.

God, as far as she was concerned, was for people who didn't face facts. People who needed something larger than life. People who needed someone to dump all their problems on. *God will sort it out. God knows best. God willing. It's in God's hands now.* All sayings used to justify their consciences.

Where was God now, when millions screamed his many names, in hundreds of languages the world over, asking to be spared? she reasoned. *Where was God as millions lie unconscious, possibly dying?*

Where was God as his so-called creation was slowly being wiped from the surface of the planet? Where indeed.

With all the work and stress of the last week, she just realized it was Christmas Eve.

Blah humbug!

Betty was tired of hearing the busy signal; she placed the phone back in the cradle and wandered out to help Mrs. Stamp go to the toilet.

Betty rolled her eyes when she saw Mrs. Stamps walking frame – it was covered in so much tinsel and hanging plastic decorations; it must have doubled its weight.

11

Christmas Day

Day 10

It was the worst Christmas ever. There was no happiness, apart from a few residents who were happy regardless, but that was mainly due to giving them too much, or the wrong medication.

Betty was really worried about Abel, but there was nothing she could do apart from wait. Waiting was something everyone was getting used to.

Mr. Grant had died in his sleep.

A good way to go, I suppose; she reasoned. She hoped when her time came it would be just as peaceful.

The other problem was the bodies. The ambulance didn't come to take them away after the doctor had arrived to announce them deceased. They were wrapped in their bed sheets and taken to the bottom of the garden. Seven stark white bundles lay in a neat row, under clear plastic, next to the muted colours of the winter-dead flowers, and sprinkled with a splattering of frost.

After the first night they had to wrap a thick plastic sheet over the top, holding it down with rocks from the adjoining rock garden. It didn't occur to anyone that the foxes – or any type of animal – would rip open the flimsy sheets and chew on the meat beneath. By the time the second body was carried down the garden, most of Mrs. Moreau's face and all of her fingers were missing.

When Betty went to help, she was grossed out at finding a hedgehog – when they pulled back the sheet – chewing on one of Mrs. Moreau's big toes. She would never look at the little creatures the same way again.

Cute? My arse, she thought, when she saw the blood and strips of flesh around the animal's mouth. *Aren't they supposed to hibernate?*

When she approached it, the little thing made a hissing, growling sound. She booted the little spiky bundle down the garden.

All washed and cleaned up; she had to start the main chore of the day. Even with everything going on, people still needed to eat. After only one day Mrs. Fredrick was eager to hand the responsibility back to Betty.

In the freezer was five large turkeys, all bought ready for Christmas.

Betty decided to cook a large Christmas roast. She had nothing better to do, and it would take her mind off worrying about Abel. Besides, they all had to eat, she needed to cook something regardless, and if the power went off for good, the meat would be ruined.

After mixing twelve boxes of stuffing together she rammed it inside the poultry along with some skinned whole onions. She found it therapeutic, forcing her hand up a turkeys butt. She wondered what Sigmund Freud would make of that?

The three large industrial cookers worked overtime with the five large turkeys wedged inside. She wrapped the sausages that were left in smoked bacon and placed them around the birds. After the potatoes were peeled by the large, noisy peeler, which simply tumbled them around inside until it scraped all the skin off, she boiled them and added them to the spitting trays, with some salt and pepper and mixed herbs.

There weren't any fresh vegetables left, so she had to make do with a bucket sized tin of mixed veg.

Betty popped the lid off a large cranberry sauce jar, and filled little pots and placed one on each table. She then pulled a load of Christmas crackers off the massive tree and put them by the plate settings.

Once the turkeys were carved and served, and everything was dished up, with lashings of bread sauce, all the residents pitched in, feeding those who couldn't quite manage it.

It might be the worse circumstances ever, but for an hour, while they all sat down for Christmas dinner, and then popped their crackers after, the world outside was forgotten.

12

Thursday 27th December 2012

Day 12

The day had arrived. People were allowed to travel the roads and collect what they needed between 10 AM and 8 PM.

It was 9:56 AM.

Betty made a plan with Mrs. Fredrick. They needed food and provisions, not to mention medicine. The nursing home's sixteen seater minibus would be used to collect everything they needed. Four would go, so there were enough able-bodied people left behind to look after those in need.

Mrs. Fredrick would drive. She stated she was the only one presently at work who was insured for the vehicle.

Today Mrs. Fredrick had swapped her signature bright dress for a luminous yellow tracksuit, that Betty was sure circling satellites would be able to see.

Betty had on a loose-fitting tracksuit as well, but hers was in a light teal with two white stripes down the side, as well as her comfy walking trainers. Her sleeves were rolled up with blue sweatbands on her wrists and one around her forehead, keeping her hair out of her eyes.

There was also Mrs. Armstrong, which regardless of her name, which conjured up an image of a thickset, muscular person, was, in fact, a tall, stick thin, seventy-year-old who had chronic asthma and was blind in one eye, and had difficulty seeing out the other.

The fourth member was Mr. Warren, a sixty-eight-year-old who looked like a pot-bellied accountant, and was partially deaf and hadn't spoken a single word in four years.

However, these were the fittest people available.

Both Mrs. Armstrong and Mr. Warren were also in tracksuits, as if a memo had been sent out, or it was common knowledge that away missions required comfy, loose-fitting clothes.

The four looked like a geriatric bowling team.

They climbed in behind Mrs. Fredrick.

The streets were busy. Cars rushed around ignoring the traffic lights. There were also a lot of abandoned cars along the side of the roads. Petrol was scarce; the petrol stations ran out within days.

The closest supermarket was Sainsburys, down next to Penn Inn roundabout, literally down around the corner.

They made the mistake of heading the back way. A low bridge led to the supermarket. There was a lorry wedged in it. What was left of the lorry had been set alight. The road was impassable.

They had to backtrack, going back around Forde Park and down onto the main road.

There were people everywhere.

It seemed strange to Betty to see so many different people after only a week of being stuck in the same building, staring at the same faces.

To go from everyone hiding inside, to seeing everyone pouring out onto the streets was unsettling.

People were heading to the supermarket. A few were heading home, pushing shopping trolleys loaded with provisions. Obviously, they ignored the curfew and left early.

The supermarket parking lot was complete chaos. Vehicles were parked every which way, with everyone trying to get as close to the main entrance as possible, while ignoring the car parking spaces.

Mrs. Fredrick parked back next to McDonald's, which was inside the supermarket's large expanse of concrete.

The burger joint was ransacked. The windows were smashed, with tables and chairs littering the drive-through, along with scattered, wet burger buns. There was a small, bright-red and black Smart car smashed into the ordering booth.

The four of them had to navigate around haphazardly parked vehicles and dropped electrical objects.

Betty stepped around a toaster.

Mr. Warren almost face-planted the concrete when his foot got caught in a coat hanger.

There were a couple of men who looked like they were fighting over next to the pharmacy's late night, twenty-four-hour dispensing window. One was holding a baseball bat. She then realized they were trying to batter their way into the chemist.

Inside there was pushing and shoving. People screamed at each other, and fought one another. It was complete pandemonium. The noise and constant movement was an assault on the senses.

It was too dangerous for them to try to collect anything. And if they did manage to find anything on the shelves, someone younger, and stronger, would simply take it off them.

It was no place for four old people whose bones could snap like twigs at the first push.

They safely retreated back outside.

"Get in the minibus, I have an idea," Betty stated. It was something she noticed when they first drove in.

Mrs. Fredrick didn't have chance to climb into the driver's seat; Betty beat her to it.

"Give me the keys!"

"I'm the only one insured"

"Look around you Joan, I don't think that matters anymore. The world has turned to shit!"

Mrs. Fredrick handed over the keys.

"Everyone sit right at the back, and belt up."

Betty waited for them to click the seatbelts into place.

"Now hold on, and get ready to do as I say. Oh, and prepare for impact!"

"Impact?!" Mrs. Fredrick mumbled. "This bus is only three months old."

Betty ignored her as she gunned the engine, revving the needle into the red. She then released the handbrake and the minibus shot forward.

Everyone's heads snapped back.

As she sped through the car park, dodging parked cars, and people, she put her foot to the floor, while slamming her hand on the horn to warn people to move or become a wet smudge on the tarmac.

"Hold on," she shouted as the minibus hit the large gates to the loading dock area. The minibus lurched as it punched through – the grating sound was deafening. The front windscreen cracked into a thousand spider webs. One side of the gate was caught on the minibuses' nearside rearview mirror. It rattled and sparked as it was dragged across the ground.

I've always wanted to do that, she thought as she struggled to keep her grasp on the juddering steering wheel.

It was just like in the movies!

With a wide smile on her face, Betty gripped the handbrake, and as she pulled it, she stomped on the breaks. The minibus wheel skidded and spun in an arc as it screeched to a stop. The gate fell off, ripping the rearview mirror away with it. It clattered onto the ground.

Betty clicked the button to open the back doors, then she rammed it into gear and jerked the vehicle forward – the back doors flew open. She then put it into reverse and drove it into the loading dock, bumping over the gate, and wedging the bus up against the concrete. She unbuckled and ran down the aisle.

"Let's move people," she screamed.

With a grunt, Betty stepped up onto the large expanse of the loading dock.

It was just as she expected. People were sticking to what they knew. To most, it wouldn't occur to them to look for food in other parts of the supermarket, not until the food ran out on the shop floor.

There were a couple of people over near the back of the loading dock, piling food into a trolley, but that was it.

For now, they will soon come pouring through.

"Here, this one. Make a line and hand them to each other and fill the minibus up."

Right next to the open back door, possibly the last load to be delivered, and hadn't had chance to be moved before the virus outbreak, was a group of pallets.

"I don't like Pot Noodles!" Mrs. Armstrong said, as she read the label as she passed another box along the line.

The pallet was stacked high with boxes. Each box contained forty-eight pots.

"It's food! So shut up, and keep moving!" Betty shouted, rallying the small group of thieves.

They had every intention of paying for their food when they left the nursing home. In fact, they had to wait while Mrs. Fredrick returned inside, because she forgot the checkbook. However, upon seeing the state of society, and their actions, this was the only option left to them.

Secretly, as her arms started to ache from lifting the boxes, she was thinking of how much time it would save if everyone was eating only meals that needed hot water to prepare them.

Within five minutes the front half of the minibus was full of Beef & Tomato, and Chicken & Mushroom noodles. They ignored the Sweet & Spicy and Bombay Bad Boy because none of them relished having to clean up after those flavours went through an old person's digestive system.

To one side was a delivery of Sainsburys own brand lemonade.

As good as water, at a push. With added sugar and carbohydrates, she reasoned.

The large two liter bottles were slower going. Luckily, the adrenaline of punching through the gate, and looting provisions was keeping them all going.

Boy are we gonna be aching in the morning.

There was a ruckus behind – people were pouring into the docking area.

"Let's go!" Betty didn't want to have to fight someone off who reasoned that pinching a minibus full of food and drink was easier than getting their own.

By the time Betty was in the driver's seat, and the others squeezed into whatever space was free, they were all knackered.

Mr. Warren didn't bother sitting down; he lay on his back in the aisle.

Betty drove slowly, while trying to see through the smashed windscreen. She would've liked to have kicked the screen out, like she'd seen at the movies. However, there were three problems stopping that scenario. Firstly, she hasn't got her leg up that high in thirty years. Secondly, she didn't have the strength to kick the screen away from the rubber binding, even if she could reach it. And thirdly, and most importantly, if she could do the first two, rather than succeeding in making the screen shatter onto the road; she was more than likely to dislocate her hip.

They headed into town. They needed to collect their prescription drugs.

As she drove down next to the train station, they could all see how bad the town was. Shop windows were smashed, with objects littering the streets. People were everywhere, and everyone was carrying something.

There was smoke billowing from a couple of buildings.

There was no hope of driving up the main street to the chemist the nursing home used, not with all the people and discarded objects. Besides, with what she had seen so far, there was no way the pharmacists would be untouched; they would've been one of the first places looted. And she didn't relish driving past, advertising a bus load of provisions to the obviously desperate people who was looting the town.

There was only one option Betty could think of, and that meant returning to the supermarket.

13

First Betty dropped the food off. If everything went pair-shaped, and they lost the minibus, she didn't want to lose the food and drink as well. Besides, she needed to collect a few things for the plan to work.

At the nursing home, everyone who was physically able to lift anything came out to help. Within ten minutes the food and drink was stacked in a messy pile in the driveway.

Mr. Warren had to be carried inside. His back went while lifting the lemonade bottles.

While the bus was emptied Betty went to search the rear garden for what she needed. It was in the gardeners small shed. She grabbed the hefty pickaxe and a length of musty smelling rope. It was so heavy, after lifting all the boxes, so for most of the way back up the garden she dragged it along by the handle.

After a few miss attempts, and with Mrs. Fredrick's, and Mr. Tomkin's help, she smashed one of the back door windows. She then managed to slide the wooden handle down through the gap in-between the metal door handle and the back door, and rest the base of the pickaxe onto the back footplate. One spike pointed into the minibus, through the smashed window, and the other pointed out by just over a foot. She used the rope to make sure it stayed in place.

Perfect! I hope.

With a handful of black bin liners from the kitchen, and a collection of thick coats off the hooks by the front door, she left the others carrying the food inside, and with only Mrs. Fredrick she headed back to the supermarket.

Betty explained her plan to the short, round manageress.

Mrs. Fredrick just stared, then she mumbled, “Shit!” Then, while staring at Betty with hard, squinting eyes, and pushing her glasses back up her nose, she shouted, “Fuck it, let’s do it!” She punched the air, which made her elbow crack.

It was the first time in nine years she had ever heard the manageress swear.

She may be dressed all in yellow, but she’s no chicken-shit!

They took the same route to the supermarket, with Mrs. Fredrick sat behind Betty.

Once there they weaved through the parked cars, and Betty reversed the minibus into position.

“Ready?” Betty asked.

“No!” Mrs. Fredrick said, while sweating profusely. “But let’s do this!”

Betty slammed the minibus into gear and floored the accelerator. The small bus wheel spun then shot back. Luckily, the section where they needed to be was relatively free of cars. But one car, which was parked in the way was hit on the rear, spinning it around and out of the way.

Betty corrected for the hit and kept her foot down. Her neck was hurting from leaning sideways, looking backwards.

"Stay on target," Mrs. Fredrick shouted. Just at the last second, before impact, Betty spun around and wedged her head against the headrest.

The sound of the minibus hitting the gates was nothing compared with the sound of what they had just achieved. It sounded like a tonne of bricks had just fallen off the back of a lorry.

Betty changed gear, jolting the bus forward while flicking the switch to open the back doors. The impact wedged them shut.

"I'm on it!" Mrs. Fredrick shouted. She unclipped the seatbelt and jumped up and ran the length of the bus and slammed the full weight of her shoulder against the doors. They flew open. She had to grab the handrail above to stop herself flying out the back.

Betty reversed back, forcing the doors against the wall, with a jarring metal screech, creating a barrier no one could get through. She then pulled the handbrake on as hard as she could and double-checked the front door was locked.

She grabbed the coats and black bags.

In the wall, square in the middle of the opened back of the bus was the smashed thick window of the supermarket's pharmacy.

The spike of the attached pickaxe, along with the weight and force of the bus had done what others couldn't – they had breeched the thick shockproof window.

Betty lay the thick coats over the sill of the frame, then slowly she climbed through, lowering herself down carefully.

Someone was banging against the security door that led out onto the shop floor with a heavy object. It rattled on its hinges, but it was made to take a battering.

Come on door, hold them off for just five more minutes.

Betty ran around tipping all the small glass bottles and plastic containers from the shelves into the black bags. As she filled them up, she passed them back through the window to Mrs. Fredrick.

She emptied everything out of all the drawers and cabinets. It wasn't a very big pharmacy, so it didn't take long to grab it all.

"Incoming!" Mrs. Fredrick shouted.

Betty passed another bag through the window. She was sweating profusely, and every part of her ached, but she was buzzing with adrenaline.

Well doc, you said I needed more exercise.

Some men had seen what they were up to, and were now outside slamming their hands on the windows, and trying to pull open the minibuses' front door. Their muffled shouts and insults resounded throughout the shell of the bus.

"Last one," Betty announced as she moved a chair over so she could climb out.

She hoped there were some tablets she could use. She was told her kidneys were packing up. There was a full pot of her new drugs at home, but they would only last so long.

Sod's law, she reasoned. She was never a heavy drinker, or an excessive eater. As far as she was concerned, she lived a healthy lifestyle. She was told because of her age a transplant was out of the question. With the right medication, and regular sessions on the dialysis machine, she was told she would live another two or three years.

With the way the world is going, I will be lucky to last a month anyway.

Betty gave a quick glance around. There were computers and other expensive apparatus inside, but she wasn't interested in stealing in that sense, but they did need the drugs, else residents were going to die.

One of the men had found a pipe or something metal on the ground, and was now whacking it against the door window. Cracks snaked out. He then noticed the front windscreen was already damaged, so he started on that instead.

Betty jogged down the bus as fast as her old legs would carry her. She dropped onto the seat.

"Hold onto something."

Betty revved the engine until it sounded like it was going to explode, then, while ignoring the man smashing away at the windshield, she wedged it in gear. The minibus lurched forward, sending the man flying to one side.

Another tried to grab one of the swinging back doors, and was rewarded by being hit on the shoulder with the point of the pickaxe.

The bus screeched off through the car park, hitting the corners of a few cars in the haste to escape, with the sound of the man screaming in pain behind.

Betty was still buzzing with adrenaline, as they screeched out onto the main road. So much so that she was shaking all over. She hasn't felt so alive in years.

When they returned, they found someone was at the nursing home waiting for her.

14

Betty helped carry the black bags inside. She then noticed Abel sat quietly in a chair, staring at the flashing lights on the Christmas tree.

He was wearing one of the boiler suits the home got him for helping around the home's gardens. He proudly showed Betty when he first got them. They weren't orange and yellow, his favorite colours, but they were real working mans clothes. That made him a worker, he had stated.

"Abel?" Betty shouted, as relief flooded through her body. She didn't realize just how worried she was until she saw he was okay.

Abel slowly climbed from the seat, which creaked when his weight left it, and ambled over, and embraced his grandmother in a hug. He didn't say a word, he just held her for what felt like hours.

Within the next hour, she was going to tell Mrs. Fredrick that she was going to use the minibus to go get her grandson. It occurred to her last night, that if the old people were left to fend for themselves, why would it be any different for the adults in Abel's home?

"How the hell did you get here?" she finally asked as he pulled away, while her small hands gripped his huge plate sized ones.

"Train!" he mumbled. His dull eyes locked onto her lips.

She knew all public transportation was halted, to stop people mingling and the virus spreading. It dawned on her what he meant.

"You walked along the train track?"

Abel came with John every Saturday for years. He remembered the route, and walked it. The normal nineteen minutes, eight miles train journey had taken him three days to slowly walk.

Betty was gobsmacked. She hugged him again.

"Hungry," he muttered into her hair.

Betty took a step back and looked him over. He was dehydrated and starving, and covered in mud and grime.

Betty sat him in the dining room and got a plate of leftover Christmas dinner. It was two days old, but Abel gulped it down, along with half a bottle of lemonade. He was still dirty, but she needed to get some nourishment inside him.

She sat opposite, watching her grandson eat.

If only we had you a few hours ago, we could have cleaned the docking bay out. No one would have tried to mess with us if you were there.

Abel sat eating, making content sounds.

You're just like Lennie, from Of Mice and Men. Hmm, it's a good nickname; she reasoned.

She got him to carry a mattress into her room, and place it on the floor. It would be the first time they had slept in the same building together for over nine years.

Betty then made him strip, and while he slowly wiped himself down in the shower, she took his clothes to the laundry room and washed them. Hanging his huge overall up took some doing; it was so big, and heavy when wet, it was difficult for her to get it over the washing line in the boiler room, which was so warm; clothes dried in no time.

She removed another overall from the bag he was carrying. Inside was a few tee shirts, jeans, a jumper, and underwear, all neatly folded, as well as a collection of stuffed Bob the Builder toys, and the one framed photo of Betty and Abel that rested next to his bed.

When she returned forty minutes later, he was still stood under the spray from the shower. She forgot he did exactly what you said.

He would probably stand in there all night if I didn't tell him to dry himself off.

Abel sat in front of the television. Most of the channels were showing just a static screen, but a few were running reruns of old movies and TV seasons. Every half an hour a government announcement interrupted whatever was on. The man was dressed in military uniform.

"Do not leave your home. Do not try to leave the cities and towns. Stay put. Keep calm. The government is doing all it can to sort the situation out. Keep your families together and seal all windows and doors. Do not go outside! Do not approach anyone who looks infected!"

Bugger it. It sounds like it's getting worse.

And what's this about doing all they can! Don't they mean, ignoring everyone?

There wasn't enough tape to seal all the windows and doors. The larger gaps were stuffed with rolled-up rags and clothes, with the curtains bunched up and forced behind the radiators.

She left Abel in the lounge while she went to boil a huge vat of water, ready for a round of Pot Noodles for tea.

Throughout the remainder of the evening, she found herself calling him Lennie without even realizing it. He didn't mind. He kind of liked the name, it rolled off the tongue.

15

Tuesday 1st January 2013
New Years Day

Day 18

Betty didn't think things could get any worse.

They did.

She was woken up by being shaken in her sleep.

"What is it Lennie? You know where the toilet is, go on your own." She had been calling him Lennie for five days now. She reasoned it was because it was a new start for them, being together again. Also, while stood in the kitchen preparing the food each day, she had lots of time to think. Her husband, Abel senior, was on her mind a lot, and deep down, it hurt every time she thought of, or heard his name. Besides, it seemed so natural, and he seemed to like it, and responded to it.

"Smell!" he mumbled while starting to cough, while rubbing his eyes with his large hands.

She realized; in her sub consciousness, that she had heard banging, like small explosions for the last hour or so. However, she was so tired from feeding everyone, and helping to clean them, then sort through the piles of medication, which she had stolen, and try to work out from the long list of what the residents were on, and what they needed, and did they have it in one of the piles in front of her, that her mind simply ignored it, and she refused to wake up.

It dawned on her that some idiot somewhere was letting of fireworks. It sounded close.

She then noticed smoke drifting under their door.

Betty sprung from the bed like a trapeze artist. She rushed to the door and placed a palm on the wooden surface. It was cold. She gingerly tapped the metal door handle. Also cold.

"Good that means there's no fire directly outside this door." She looked at Lennie.

"Grab the bag, and put your overall on!"

Lennie slowly dressed and pulled the bag over his thick shoulders. It was an emergency bug out bag she had prepared.

She saw a TV program about it years ago; Bear Grylls described it and what to put in it. The bag had everything they needed to survive for twenty-four hours, in case they had to get out fast. There was food, water, and some clothes. Betty couldn't find any sleeping bags in the building. She guessed eighty year olds seldom went camping.

She didn't like wasting time, but if there was a fire raging throughout the building, she wanted to be prepared once the door opened.

Betty felt awful when a little voice at the back of her mind said, *That's right, take your time. The longer you take, the less people there will be to cook for, to clean for, and wipe the ass of.*

She pulled on an old brown dress, a green polo neck jumper, and pushed her feet into some trainers. She then grabbed two blankets off the bed.

"Put this over your head," she said. She knew it would help with the smoke.

She couldn't understand why the fire alarm wasn't ringing. It then dawned on her, there was no power.

She hadn't thought to turn the light on as she rushed around due to the bright light of the full moon pouring in the open curtains – Lennie didn't like to have the curtains closed; he didn't like the feeling of being closed in.

She flicked the switch up and down – nothing.

Betty slowly turned the handle. The door felt stiff. As she pulled she understood why; the fire had consumed a lot of the oxygen in the building, and due to most of the gaps in the doors and windows being sealed, her room was now like a vacuum. The door handle was sucked from her hand and slammed closed.

Ah, crap!

Think, think, think!

Betty rushed towards the window. There was a long nightgown forced into the gap at the bottom of the creaky window. She gripped the frame and pulled it up.

Lennie stood behind, like a statue, waiting for instructions.

More smoke started to pour under the door.

Betty grabbed the duvet off her bed and tossed it at the base of the door, and kicked it into place.

There was shouting in the hallway outside, followed by a loud, pain filled scream, and a rushing sound.

Someone had ignored the pulling weight of the vacuum that the fire had caused and obviously swung their door open.

The rushing sound turned into a roar; light bulbs could be heard popping like dull gunshots.

"The window is our only hope!"

Betty looked down at the roof eight feet below. The roof of the lounge was flat and covered in a splattering of dirty, plastic bubble windows. One of the windows was melting; thick black smoke poured out, with orange flames licking up over the rim.

"We need to hurry, before the roof collapses!" She looked across the roof. It was the kind covered in roofing tar, and sprinkled with gravel. In places it looked like the tar was starting to melt.

"You climb out first, and then help me down."

There was a shattering sound of glass and a high-pitched scream. Betty looked to the right just in time to see Mrs. Lee flying through the air engulfed in flames. Her body hit the roof with a wet smack; it lay twitching, with the body fat spitting.

"Let's go!" She shouted over the roaring sound originating from the other side of their bedroom door.

Lennie grabbed the window frame and shoved upwards. The old window had been sticking lately. Lennie just cured that. The frame shot up, wedging wide open, while cracking half the panes – one fell out, tumbling to the roof top.

Their bedroom door creaked and buckled. The paint on it started to bubble and run over the duvet and pool on the carpet.

Slowly, Lennie put one foot through, followed by his shoulder. It was a very tight fit. The bag got caught.

Betty pushed with all her might. The bag squeezed through.

It was eight feet to the roof. Lennie was seven feet two inches. As his feet touched down, he stepped back, allowing his grandmother room to maneuver. As she was halfway out, he plucked her off the sill and lowered her to the roof.

"Over there!" Betty shouted to be heard over the sound of the roaring flames that billowed out of the windows to their right. Another window shattered with the smoke pouring out, followed by curling flames.

As they carefully moved over the roof, as fast as they could, the tar below their feet was melting. The sound of the sticky, hot tar sucked at their shoes.

They made it to the edge of the roof. A garden arbour, with a pitched roof, and latticed sides, which had two seats inside, was up against one wall.

Carefully, they climbed onto the roof and used the side lattice as a ladder to climb down.

They quickly moved away from the windows. As they did the power flicked back on. The fire alarm started blaring. Lights flashed on in rooms where they hadn't popped.

They jogged around to the front of the property. The large front doors were locked.

So far, no one, apart from them, had made it outside.

"Where is everyone?"

Another window two stories up exploded in a shower of glass. A burning curtain floated down onto the grass.

"Lennie, open this door!" Betty said, as she stepped back from trying the handle.

Lennie lumbered forward, and with one kick the door reeled open, hanging off one hinge.

The large reception hall's ceiling was rolling in thick smoke.

Betty shouted at Lennie to stay where he was, as she pulled the polo neck jumper up over her mouth and nose, then pulled the blanket on her shoulders over her head, and ran into the burning building.

16

Betty ran straight through the reception hall, straight into the large lounge.

The first thing she noticed was the towering Christmas tree, it was burning like a Roman candle. The tree hissed and spat, as the sap boiled. The baubles exploded, and the tinsel went up in flames as if it had been doused in petrol. The curtains were whipping about as they burned, as if they were reeling in pain. Most of the chairs were burning, and so was sections of the carpet, where the superheated smoke had set the decorations alight, and they had dropped – burning – to the floor.

The stairs to the upper levels was over next to the flaming tree. There was no possible way of reaching them.

The stairs were acting like a chimney for the superheated air, forcing it upstairs. It was so hot, even the plaster was dropping off the walls.

The roar of the fire was deafening. Wood cracked like gunshots. Objects hissed and popped.

Betty could see a charred body at the foot of the stairs.

Just then, the upper floor creaked, and a large section collapsed onto the stairs. Burning embers billowed throughout the room.

All this took mere seconds to register.

The wide-open front door now gave the fire new oxygen to feed on.

Just as Betty ran in, registering the destruction, the fresh air poured around her, billowing in, filling the void.

A mighty roar filled the lounge as the fresh oxygen filled the room. In a fraction of a second the flames doubled in size.

Dear god!

Betty could feel her hair frizzling under the intense heat.

Just then a huge arm grabbed Betty, hefting her off her feet and carrying her outside.

Lennie may be slow, but he knew danger when he saw it. He learned at an early age never to play with fire – it hurt.

He put her down outside, on the driveway.

Betty stared in silent fascination, wrapped in the blanket as the building burned.

Slowly, like she was in a nightmare, Betty walked around the whole building. She was checking they weren't the only ones to get out.

Lennie ambled behind her.

After walking around the nursing home twice, she realized it was useless. No one could have survived.

A few neighbours stood in their gardens, or on the road. They didn't come over to offer help; they were simply checking the fire wasn't going to spread to their property.

No fire engines, or ambulances, or police appeared. It was if the death of all those inside meant nothing.

Betty stood shivering, as their faces flashed through her mind.

It was a long list.

Tears ran clear lines in Betty's soot covered face.

Dawn was slowly arriving, with the sky growing brighter by the minute.

Surely, we cannot be the only ones to get out alive? Then again, if it wasn't for Lennie, I would have probably slept until it was too late. And I would've probably broken a leg climbing out of the window.

Without the power, and the fire alarm, they really didn't stand a chance. Most of them probably didn't even know what was happening. Hopefully, the smoke got most of them before the flames reached them.

A week ago, they found out that someone had broken into the outbuilding, next to the kitchen, and stolen parts off the nursing homes backup generator.

Because of the power cut, and no backup, the sprinkler system hadn't kicked in.

They stood for in the predawn light watching the building burn. After an hour, the roof gave way and collapsed into the main structure.

To Betty, it reminded her of when a large bonfire falls in on itself; when the wood gives way, and a towering shower of ember's dance high into the air.

17

Day 19

They stayed till the afternoon.

The worst of the fire was over.

The place looked like a war zone. The roof was gone, and all the windows were blown out. Debris littered the garden and driveway and out onto the road. The once colourful lively house was now just a dirty, smoke stained, blackened shell.

Smells filled the air – burnt paint, melted nylon carpets, and the sickly sweet smelly of overcooked meat.

Betty gripped Lennie's hand, and they started walking. She didn't know where. Just anywhere away from the fire. They needed to find somewhere to stay, somewhere to sleep.

All they had was the clothes on their backs and what was in the bag.

Walking through the quiet, winter park, was a shock to the senses after watching a building burn to the ground, killing everyone inside. Leaves scuttled across the grass. Branches swayed in the wind.

Betty decided the town was their best option. The supermarkets were picked clean.

There was a better chance of finding food where there were more shops.

They slowly walked down through Devon Square. She thought about checking inside the large church, but decided against it when she noticed a huge red cross painted on the large front wooden door. She hoped it was paint. The last thing they needed was to bump into a group of fanatics – bible wielding happy clappers looking for a victim to sacrifice. These sort of circumstances brought the weirdos out of the woodwork.

Queen Street was deserted, as if the population were hiding after they had ransacked everything, thinking a reprisal was on the way.

There was rubbish littered all over the pavements and roads. Vehicles were abandoned everywhere – some were just burnt-out shells.

Lennie walked beside her; his feet pushed through the rubbish rather than lifting them over it.

Betty couldn't understand why people would do this to their own town?

Shop windows were smashed. Large metal shutters hung all twisted and battered. Objects were dragged out onto the street and then abandoned.

Thick, slate-grey clouds loomed above, promising a heavy downpour.

They needed to get inside. The last thing they needed was to get soaking wet. Plus they hadn't eaten all day, and Betty's throat was parched.

They walked past hair salons, a video repair store, a butchers shop, and a chemist – all looted and ransacked.

In the distance a door slammed shut.

On the right-hand side was a primary school. The building looked pretty much unaffected by the looting.

Betty led the way.

The front door was kicked in.

Inside a hallway went straight down the middle, with classrooms on either side. There were coat hooks down both sides of the hallway. Many small coats and bags hung from the hooks, as if everyone had disappeared; running off and leaving them behind. There were a few books, pencils, and scraps of paper scattered around on the floor.

The classrooms were unaffected. Betty expected the tables and chairs to be smashed up and thrown around.

Maybe people felt bad looting a children's school? she reasoned.

The cafeteria was empty; all the food had been taken. Pots and pans were strewn about, along with the cutlery.

The nurse's office had been ransacked, obviously people were looking for any kind of drugs. However, the cot was there, where sick children could have a lie down if they were feeling unwell.

Betty told Lennie to take a nap. She left him on the cot, with his legs hanging over the end, and the bed creaking in protest, as she headed back up the main hallway. She had an idea.

18

Day 20

They took turns sleeping on the cot.

Betty's hunch had worked; she found food.

The children's hanging school bags still had their pack lunches inside. The sandwiches were moldy, but the crisps, packet food, and sweets were edible. And they had a pile of drink cartons to add to the bottle of water they had in their bag.

Betty collected a stack of bright, colourful children's books from the classrooms, and Lennie sat looking through the pictures.

It wasn't an ideal place to stay, but they had enough food for a few days and something to sleep on, and it was out of the cold and rain.

The children's toilets were useless, as they looked like they were built for midgets – which, in a way, they had. Luckily, there were the teachers full-sized toilets next-door to the nurse's office.

The day passed quietly.

Lennie sat flicking through the books, and playing with his stuffed Bob the Builder toy, while Betty searched the school for anything she may have missed.

As they were settling down for the night, a loud noise made them stop what they were doing.

There was someone out in the hallway.

There was boisterous, angry shouting, as a heavy object was tossed against a window. The sound of the glass shattering echoed throughout the empty corridors.

Betty moved over to the door. She used a finger to move the plastic blind aside that was covering the door's window.

She could see four people in the hallway.

"There it is, grab it!" a youngish lad said who was wearing a red hoody, with a white base ball cap underneath. He was swinging what looked like some kind of sword around.

Then the bark from a dog echoed throughout the school.

Lennie jumped to his feet; the books fell across the floor. He stood behind his grandmother and gripped the blind and ripped it off the door, as his body maneuvered his grandmother out of the way.

"Shhhh, no Lennie," she whispered, hoping they hadn't noticed the movement.

"Doggy!" Lennie muttered as he leaned down and pressed his face right up against the glass, while trying to search the corridor through the small window.

There was a loud banging as the three others joined in by swinging weapons.

The dog howled in pain.

Lennie became upset – someone was hurting an innocent animal. He gripped the door handle and almost pulled it off the hinges while swinging it open.

Lennie ducked under the doorframe and stepped out into the hallway.

A chav, about twelve years or so old, noticed movement. He wore a black bomber jacket with a red Manchester United F. C. shirt underneath, and dirty grey tracksuit trousers. He was gripping a baseball bat.

"Fucking hell! It's Goliath!" the kid shouted.

The others didn't hear, because one lad, who looked about twenty, dressed in a grey tracksuit, swinging a cricket bat had caught the dog, and was proceeding to beat it to death.

Lennie witnessed the carnage. He became enraged.

An earsplitting roar poured from him as he started charging down the hall towards the yob with the bloodied cricket bat.

"No Lennie!" Betty screamed as she stepped into the corridor and saw what was happening.

The other three turned to see what the new noise was. They were shocked to see a huge, angry man, who almost filled the hallway with his bulk, running at them like a steam train.

Survival instinct kicked in – the cowards, who could beat on a helpless dog, but not defend themselves against an enraged giant, turned and fled.

The one with the cricket bat slipped on the blood, falling face down. He scrambled to his feet and ran after the others.

As he ran, Lennie grabbed a small wooden chair that lay on its side, and tossed it at the oldest looking yob that was retreating.

The older, overweight man, who looked anything from between thirty and forty, was wearing a long army poncho. The guy was already injured. He used a curtain pole as a walking stick. There was blood on the bottom of his jeans on his left leg.

The chair just missed his head.

Lennie reached the dog. It lay panting heavily. It's golden fur was matted in blood.

Lennie leaned down and made a gentle shushing sound, as he stroked the Labradors head.

By the time Betty reached Lennie the dog was dead.

19

Friday 5th January 2013

Day 21

Betty decided they would be okay to stay for the remainder of the night. The chavs would be too shaken up to return so soon. But she knew their type. After a few calming beers and bravado talk, they would be back, looking for revenge.

First thing in the morning Lennie carried the dog out to the back of the school. There was a small patch of grass, next to the large playground. Betty watched as Lennie used his hands to dig a grave.

"Don't you worry; he's in doggy heaven now," Betty said. "And as soon as we can, I will find you a doggy to look after."

Lennie looked up as he wiped his forehead, smearing mud over his brow. He gave a weak lopsided smile.

They needed to get moving. It was coming up to 10:30 AM and if the lads were going to come back, it would be soon.

They had eaten all the food she had found, and they were down to their last couple of drink cartons. They needed to find food and drink.

Such a simple thing, eating and drinking, something I used to take for granted. Food was always available. Water was just a tap turn away. When you have to physically search for it, everything changes. Something so simple, becomes life-changing – a matter of life and death.

Lennie put on the bag and turned, waiting for instructions.

"Don't worry, we will find somewhere safe soon. Somewhere where we are wanted and needed."

Her grandson will follow her anywhere, regardless of the destination. Her words were mainly to booster herself.

They left the primary school and continued down the main street.

As they got to Wetherspoons, for some reason, she decided to turn up King Street. There were houses up there, long rows of them. She reasoned there could be an empty one, a house that still contained food.

They checked inside a Chinese restaurant. It was looted and wrecked. They didn't linger; someone had used one of the corners as a toilet.

Just up the road a little was a tall building. Betty looked up at the three-story building. It was a mortgage company of some kind.

Then there was a strange sound – more of a vibration. It started in the pit of Betty's stomach and then rose in tempo. Suddenly, it assaulted her ears as a helicopter flew over. It was flying erratically, trailing black smoke.

Betty was just deciding on whether to follow the helicopter, which looked like it was about to crash in Courtney Park, when an ear piercing scream made her spin around.

Running down the road was a handful of naked people. Even from their distance she could tell something was wrong. They were covered in blood, and their faces and throats were deformed. Like a flock of birds they turned as one, and smashed through the door to the large Paint Centre.

There was probably a side entrance into the mortgage company building, but Betty did not want to give those things time to change their minds and head towards them.

"Lennie, quick, kick the door down!"

DOCTOR LAZARO'S STORY

Doctor Melanie Ann Lazaro BSc PhD

419 Pinhoe Road
Exeter
South Devon
England

Works at Exeter University in the Microbes and Disease section of the Biosciences Department.

1

Doctor Melanie Ann Lazaro BSc PhD

419 Pinhoe Road
Exeter
South Devon
England

Saturday 15th December 2012

The Day of the Outbreak

Day 1

Melanie rolled over and stared at the alarm clock. It had green tinsel on it.

6:15 AM, the glaring red light announced.

She had to be up in fifteen minutes, but she always woke up before the alarm went off.

The twenty-inch fan next to her bed hummed. She always slept with it on. The humming and vibrations stopped the sound of the traffic on the busy road next to the house from keeping her awake.

Melanie stared at the ceiling. Christmas decorations crisscrossed it. She followed the same crack that had been there for over ten years. Her father always promised he would sort it out. However, he was always too busy in the basement, working on his project. Now he was retired, he had more time to spend in the windowless room. Besides, he was too old and unwell to go climbing around on a ladder.

I need to get a life! It's Saturday, and I'm still getting up at 6:30 to head into work. I need a...

She was almost going to say boyfriend, but she stopped herself just in time. It was because of her ex that she was living at home again. Well, that and because she made any excuse to run home to mummy and daddy.

She had now given up on men and concentrated on her job. She hadn't had a boyfriend in over six years. She had also had ample opportunity to move out, but living at home was cheap and easy, and she did enjoy living with her parents.

Due to being a child prodigy – with an IQ of 157 – she spent from the age of ten at a school for the gifted in Manchester. She returned home only one weekend a month. At the age of thirteen, she was one of only four people ever to be accepted into Cambridge University at such a young age. She took her BSc degree in Biomedical Science, and then her PhD, passing at the age of nineteen. And even with her busy schedule she still managed to write extra papers on DNA sequencing, which were published by science journals the world over.

Parenting Issues, her ex used to shout, when they fought. He said she never had time to grow up properly.

She thought about it a lot after they argued, and she agreed with him; she was damaged goods when it came to the emotional department. *It should be called the Michael Jackson Syndrome;* she decided.

Her ex was called Jack Jenkins, or JJ as his friends called him, or Junkie Jack her parents nicknamed him towards the end of the relationship.

Her mother used to berate her, "*You have a brain the size of a country, and yet when it comes to picking boyfriends you act as if you're a stupid, rebellious love struck teenager, looking for a bad boy.*" She would then go to walk away, mumbling, "*Even Stephen Hawkin's IQ is only three points away at 160, for Christ's sake!*"

Of course, her mother was right. What woman didn't like the bad-boy element? The dangerous side? However, the boyfriends she ended up with weren't so much the bad boy, more a dim-witted lowlife.

She didn't want to say, and hurt her feelings, but it was because of the way her parents treated her as a child, pushing her harder and harder that she ended up the way she has. She never had her parents around to support her; she was pushed into a routine where strict rules had to be followed.

JJ looked tough, and was tough; that is, when it came to hitting females. He talked the talk, but never walked the walk. And when the drugs started flowing, she'd best be as far away from him as possible.

Then she turned up back at home, having to leave wherever she was renting, losing the deposit her parents had given her because she left her ex behind, and they always stayed until they were forcibly kicked out – after trashing the place.

At the time she was away in university, and instead of living on campus she rented out, and it wasn't long before the *insects* started to gather around her light.

Melanie was already blacklisted and severely in debt, all before she even turned eighteenth, all thanks to her list of deadbeat boyfriends.

It was such a regular occurrence that her room was always ready for her to return to at a moment's notice, until her parents could get her back into some sort of campus dwelling, or sort out another flat or bed-sit. The commute up to Cambridge was just too far from Exeter.

Her mother was good at reading the signs. Her mood swings. Ignoring their phone calls. The bruises.

When Melanie did turn up, standing on the doorstep with her bags in her hands, with her mascara running, she would find her bed turned down, with the lights on, and a towel ready for a shower.

It was a regular occurrence at one stage. From the age of sixteen, she could legally move out without her parent's permission, and even though she continued with her schooling, she refused to follow their rules.

There was Michael Hodge, or Mickey as he liked to be called, who lasted three months. He trashed the flat they were living in at the time, and stole her laptop with all her research and syllabus work, and swapped it for an ounce of weed.

Then there was Jason Clack, nicknamed Snappy, who lasted only two months. He broke into her parent's house and stole their flat screen telly, so he could buy an eight-ball of cocaine.

Next came Gerald McSteel, who lasted only one month, nicknamed Glass due to his taste in drugs – crystal methamphetamine. Technically, she didn't dump him; he died from an overdose. She woke up in the morning to find him on his back next to her, having drowned on his own vomit.

Then came Jack Jenkins, who it turned out, was Gerald's dealer, who she met at the funeral. It's a small world.

At least the lease on the flat wasn't in her name the last time, because she moved in with JJ.

He lasted only two weeks.

She lay on her back, reminiscing as to why she was single.

Melanie had returned from the university due to a free period, and she caught JJ in bed with Dolly, the fifty-one-year-old washed-out junkie that lived in the flat downstairs.

JJ didn't see the problem, as he pointed out Dolly was short this month, and she was paying for her drugs in flesh.

Melanie had packed up her things and caught a bus straight to the clinic to get tested. She then caught a train home back to Devon.

Why can't I find Mr. Right? A nice guy. A man with a job and responsibilities. A man who treats me like a lady? Every woman who has ever lived has probably wished for the same thing, she reasoned.

When you see a couple arguing in the supermarket, or walking down the street, with three kids in tow, shouting at each other, as the children act as if it's an everyday occurrence. No one would start a relationship if they thought it would end up like that, surely? Would they?

Melanie flicked back the duvet.

At what point do people give up and accept that their lives will never change? When fighting in public doesn't even bother them?

Her string of deadbeat boyfriends was her way of rebelling against her parents who forced her into a life of studying. Her rebellion only lasted a year, and she returned to the university's campus just after her seventeenth birthday.

Amazingly, all the upheaval and trouble didn't effect her studies, and because her studies weren't interrupted, and she passed with flying colours, the incidents were never mentioned again.

"She will put it down to experience," she heard her father telling her mother after she passed her PhD. "At least she got it out of her system. And hopefully she has learned a valuable lesson?"

Her parents had her late in life – her mother was forty-six, and her father was fifty-two when their only child turned up on the scene.

They were both retired now.

Her mother was a botanist. She had worked at the same university for twenty-eight years. Her father was a dentist, owning and running his own clinic for thirty-six years.

Melanie slowly walked over and pulled back the curtains. It was still dark outside.

She stood looking down across the back garden towards the large infant and nursery school that was situated behind the detached house. There was a set of swings and a slide, with hopscotch painted on the playground's tarmac. Circling the large playground was squat wooden buildings painted in pastel colours.

When she was young, and she returned for the school holidays from The Academy for Gifted Children, she would look across at the normal school, from her bedroom window, and feel envious. Her holidays were slightly out of sync with normal schools.

They had a childhood – they played and ran around, fighting and playing football, or kiss chase, or whatever it was they did at such a young age. All the while Melanie sat behind her desk in her room looking out at the children playing while she did her vast piles of homework.

She could still hear their laughter, their screams of joy, the hollow thud of the football. The only sound she made was her pen scratching over the paper. She had no friends around where she lived.

Besides, her mother always used to say, *"You have no time for childish games; you have a higher calling. God gave you this gift for a reason."*

One game she used to love watching was the girls playing with the skipping rope. Two would swing the rope in a large loop, while others would try to jump in and last as long as they could. She could still remember the words they used to sing, that drifted up to her open window.

Robin Hood, Robin Hood dressed so good, got as many kisses as he could. How many kisses did he get? One... Two... Three...

She would sometimes count along with the other children, pretending she was playing with them.

Her bedroom used to be at the front of the property, but she soon started to have nightmares, and she was moved to the back of the house. Across the road was a large church, surrounded by crumbling gravestones.

Death at the front. Life at the back.

The nightmares started when she became old enough to understand what the graveyard was. There were dead bodies buried just across the road!

After weeks of sleepless nights, and having Melanie screaming that they were coming to get her, her parents swapped her room with the spare room at the back of the house.

When she thinks back, she found it strange that a child could be placated so easily, not realizing that the bodies were still there, simply a little further around the building.

Out of sight, out of mind.

Melanie wandered to the bathroom and commenced her morning ritual. Toilet. Shower. Straighten hair. Clothes. Makeup.

Her parents couldn't understand why she would want to straighten her long curly black hair. Her mother pointed out that if it was straight, she would probably sit and curl it every morning.

Melanie conceded she had a point. People always want what they don't have – they are never happy with what they've got. It is human nature.

She dressed in smart long black trousers with a cream coloured blouse and open V neck jumper. She liked her clothes clean lined and simple. Muted, earthly colours, accentuated with black shoes or skirt or trousers. She reasoned she was a professional; she needed to dress like one.

She slipped on her black, flat bottomed, comfy, Hush Puppies. They wouldn't turn heads, but she was on her feet most of the day and comfort won every time. If she did need to go to a meeting or pop out, she had a pair of smarter shoes in her locker.

Melanie grabbed her worn brown leather work bag off the chest of drawers and slid in the file off her bedside cabinet, that she was reading late into the night, and headed down for breakfast.

She stopped at the full-length mirror – which also had green tinsel around the top. Her mother had decorated her room while she was at work.

She looked elegant and professional. She was average height with a slim athletic build.

She mimicked a chavy teenagers voice, while pretending to chew gum, while placing a hand on one hip and tilted to one side. “Hi, I’m Melanie; I’m twenty-three, single, and I’m a workaholic.” She smiled to herself and headed down for breakfast.

2

Her mother was already up, stood over the sink washing dishes.

Margery was a woman who was forever busy. To show for it, she didn't have an ounce of fat to spare. She had never smoked, and her face, even though old, was fresh and vibrant, with rosy red cheeks. Since retiring she always wore an apron around the house over the top of a long simple dress.

Melanie hopes that when she reached sixty-nine that she would look as good.

"Morning dear. Good night I hope?" Margery asked, while still leaning over the sink with her back to her. Her mother could hear a cat sneaking across a carpet on the other side of the house.

"Morning. It was great, thanks." Melanie put her bag on the floor and settled into an old style, thick chunky, farmhouse wooden seat.

Her mother asked her about her sleep every morning, ever since the nightmares, over thirteen years ago.

Her parent's kitchen dated back to when the house was built in the 1950s. It was neat and clean, just old fashioned, with thick chunky pine wooden doors and shelves.

Why change it if it works? her father always stated. His motto.

Her mother wouldn't dream of letting her prepare her own breakfast. It was a different story before she retired. Her mother spent every waking hour at the university. She was trying to make up for it now.

After finishing the dishes, she dried her hands and wandered over to the cooker.

"Omelett?"

"Please."

There was already a glass of orange juice ready for her. Melanie grabbed the Daily Mail that was resting on the other side of the table.

"He's already downstairs I take it?"

"He's an eager beaver, you know him. Why sleep when he could be tinkering down in his dungeon."

His project was ongoing. So far, Edward had spent every free minute, over the last ten years, since he retired down in the basement.

Melanie couldn't remember ever spending more than a few hours a month with her father, and that was only because her mother would sometimes make him come upstairs for his meals. As well as a dentist he considered himself a bit of a chemist.

Margery cracked two eggs into a bowl and started whisking with a fork. She added a pinch of salt, pepper, and a sprinkle of fresh herbs she had just cut up, then dropped a knob of butter into the hot frying pan.

In the background, an old radio played Elvis Presley's *Blue Christmas*.

"Is that new?" Melanie asked, nodding to a flower in the windowsill that was surrounded by loose baubles.

"Yes dear, it's a Medinilla Magnifica from the Philippines," her mother replied as she poured the eggs into the spitting pan.

The plant had large waxy green leaves, and pink flower heads that drooped, which had hundreds of small pods dangling out of them, like bright pink chandeliers.

"It's very difficult to grow. It takes a whole year just to cultivate from a cutting."

The whole house was inundated with flowers. They filled the corners, shelves, sideboards, and hung from hooks, and rested on the work surfaces – and on every space that was big enough to hold a plant.

There was also the conservatory, which unlike normal people's homes that had seats inside, theirs was filled to capacity with tropical plants. It was even rigged to spray mist twice a day. As a child, Melanie would sit on the small patch of stone tiled floor with an umbrella and pretend she was in a tropical rain forest.

Also, because it was Christmas, the whole house looked even busier, because there was green tinsel everywhere, as if the flowers had started to secrete weird shiny creeping vines.

The front and back gardens were bursting with plants, trees, and bushes. Since her retirement, her mother had won five garden in bloom competitions for the area of Exeter five years in a row, and had even won the national prize once.

The back garden also had two long polythene tunnels where she grew all the organic vegetables they needed. Any spare was sold to a local green grocer who sold them on his stall down in the market.

Her mother didn't just have green fingers, as the saying goes, her whole body was green.

As she flicked the omelett with one hand, the other held a small water spray bottle, which she was using to spray the Marjoram, Tarragon, Garlic and Sage, that were in pots in a line on the fridge.

Even the kitchen had light green tiles and wallpaper covered in large green leaf motifs.

Her mother plated the omelett and placed it in front of Melanie, onto the white and green squared tablecloth.

"Thank you." She tucked in.

Margery poured Melanie some coffee from the percolator pot, and returned to the sink to dry the dishes. She never sat down and ate breakfast with her daughter; she was just too busy.

The omelett was perfect, light and fluffy and was just right to start the day.

"What are you working on at the moment?" her mother asked while drying a plate.

Exeter University is one of the leading research facilities in England. The research department had an annual budget of almost fifty million pounds. The funds came from the government and large international companies.

The research was broken down into different groups: Behaviour, Ecology and Conservation, Evolution, Cellular and Chemical Biology, Environmental Biology, Microbes and Disease, Biodiversity and Renewable Energy, Earth System Science Group, and Wildlife Research Co-Operative.

The Microbes and Disease research focused mainly on infectious diseases and their interactions between microbes and their hosts. They studied bacteria, fungi and fungi-like organisms, and algae. Including pathogens that infect humans and diseases that infect crop plants and livestock. They also specialize in abiotic stresses in plants, focusing on the responses to infections and host-pathogen interactions. This is broken down into four groups, plant pathogens, genomics, molecular signalling, and vaccine development. They were also using next generation sequencing to understand the dynamics of the pathogens, and creating mathematical models of antibiotic utilisation.

This was Melanie's specialties, and because of her ground-breaking sequencing theories, she was quickly snapped up by the university.

She was also an expert in cellular and chemical biology, which overlapped with her microbe and disease research. She looked into how the properties of living cells emerged from interactions of their constituent molecules. She utilised microscopy, biochemistry, crystallography, molecular genetics, and mathematical modelling to investigate key cellular processes, including cell-cycle, organelle motility, and metabolism.

So far, Melanie made fundamental breakthroughs with live-cell imaging and the discovery of new enzymes for biotechnology and molecular diagnostics.

Because of her the funding was pouring in.

"At the moment I'm helping out the Evolution Department from our Cornwall Campus; they need a hand sequencing a host-parasite coevolution, and how this parasite's genes enable it to mimic its host genetic patterns," she said as she lifted another piece of omelett to her mouth.

Her mother nodded. She was probably one of the only people she knew outside of work that understood what she was talking about.

Margery didn't bother questioning why she was going in on Saturday. When she worked in the university, it wasn't unusual for her to work seven days a week.

"I'm not sure what time I will be home; I have some Petri dishes I have to monitor real time. I need to check in hourly on the culture cells."

Melanie finished up her omelett and downed the last of the orange and coffee.

"Have a good day darling."

"Say hi to dad for me."

"I will."

3

Melanie left the house just after 7 AM. She climbed into her Smart car and headed down Pinhoe Road onto Blackbay Road, towards the roundabout.

There were several routes she could take to work, but she preferred the one heading along the B3183. It was a little longer, but fewer chances of congestion.

She drove down Longbrook Street, past all the tall red-brick houses on either side.

Christmas decorations hung from buildings and people's homes, and across streets. You had a few crazy people who made a competition out of it, where almost every conceivable surface of their house and garden was covered in gaudy plastic, and flashing lights.

It was Saturday, so there were no parents dropping their kids off at school. And due to it being so early, it wasn't too busy.

There were a few shop assistants carrying signs out to place on the pavement. Some joggers wearing earphones. A cyclist on an expensive looking bike, who was wearing tight-fitting Lycra clothes, and a funny pointy helmet.

Melanie parked outside *The Upper-Crust* cake shop and darted inside. It was her turn to bring the doughnuts in today.

Two sisters owned and run the shop. They were a little quirky, but Melanie liked their happy, contagious demeanor.

After a five-minute talk, and taking way too long to put twelve assorted doughnuts into a box, she returned to her Smart car and placed the box in the small boot.

The traffic was still light as she pulled out onto the Prince of Wales Road. The sprawling university came into view.

There are three different sites to the University, there was the Tremough campus, in Cornwall, that Melanie was liaisoning with for her latest assignment, which covered seventy acres of land. Also St Luke's, which was just over a mile away from the main campus, which covered sixteen acres. She worked at Streatham, the main three hundred and fifty acres campus.

There were just over thirteen hundred academic staff, two thousand admin staff, and eighteen thousand students.

Her science department was one of seventy research centres inside the university grounds.

Melanie drove through the main entrance.

To one side was the universities emblem on a large sign, with the motto *Lucem Sequimur* written beneath – *We Follow the Light*.

She drove slowly through the university grounds, past a wide range of different looking structures. Some squat, others towering high above. There were old-fashioned red-brick towers, with walls full of arched windows, others with modern squared windows set in a lighter red brick. Some looked straight out of a Harry Potter movie; others looked like normal office blocks. All of it was set in acres of manicured lawns, with pruned bushes and towering trees, and sweeping winter flower gardens. Intertwined among it all was miles of footpaths and pavements, car parks and hundreds of signs.

Even on a Saturday morning the campus was already bustling with activity.

Melanie drove into her departments car park. Opposite was the sports facilities, and the Great Hall, which was used as a gym.

She removed the box of doughnuts from the boot, and grabbed her bag.

The entrance to her department was through a large glass set of doors. Inside was four lifts, each one went to a different level of the five-story building. She never understood why each level required its own lift?

Contamination protocol possibly? she reasoned. Each level dealt in all kinds of viruses and pathogens.

Melanie stepped into the lift to the Microbes and Disease Department on level three. She needed to punch a code into a keypad before the lift activated. It only went to level three, so there was no button to push. The lift ascended.

4

The lift door swished open.

"Do you want me to take that?" Jeffery Grant asked, as he was walking past.

Jeffery was a tall lanky nineteen year old, who wore clothes that would suit an old man. Today he was sporting a pair of brown corduroy trousers with a button-down dark-green shirt, with a brown stripy cardigan under his open lab coat. His shoes were old-fashioned brown leather country brogues lace ups.

The top two percent of the university's students were given the opportunity to work in the different research departments for extra credit, and help with their fees.

Jeff was Melanie's lab assistant. He was on his second year of undergraduate studies in Biological and Medicinal Chemistry. Jeff had been working with her for five months.

"Thanks Jeff." Melanie gave him the box.

"I sanitized and prepared the Petri dishes last night by placing them in an autoclave at one hundred and sixty degrees celsius for one hour. I then prepared the dishes with batch C of the nutrient solution. It's now solidified and ready for inoculation."

They walked down the stark white corridor towards Melanie's laboratory.

"Thank you Jeff. I don't know what I would do without you." They pushed through into the lab. "I think the first plating will be with samples eleven through to thirty-one."

"No problem. I will get right on it." He dropped the file he was carrying onto a long work surface.

"I will just drop these over to the canteen." He vanished back out the door.

Melanie walked into her small office and dropped her bag on her Spartan table. There were a few yellow post-it notes stuck around her monitor. Jeff was also her unofficial receptionist when she wasn't around.

She scanned through them. There was a call from Doctor Barineau from the French Ecole Normale Supérieure University, wanting to know if she could critique his latest sequencing model paper? Also one from Professor Kamp from Yale University in America, asking if she would be available for a four hour lecture in February? She would call them both back later after she checked her schedule.

None were urgent.

The only concession to the fact it was Christmas in her whole department was a small, cheap and tacky foot high Christmas tree on the corner of her desk, which Jeff had brought in.

As her computer was booting up, she wandered over and removed her long lab coat off the freestanding old-fashioned coat stand by the door.

She sat down as she was popping the last few buttons closed.

There were a few emails from her colleagues from around the world. A couple from other doctors from the university, and one from Professor Tang who was wondering if she could spare forty minutes to give a lecture next week for his students. The rest was junk mail. She highlighted the ones she wanted to respond to later, and put her computer on standby.

Jeff had returned and was stood next to the centrifuge machine, removing small vials; each glass tube had a number on top. He wore blue powder free rubber gloves and a cone mask with an eye shield in case of viral or bacterial contamination.

Melanie pulled some gloves on from a box, and removed her mask from a hook next to the equipment.

"Right then," she said, which came out slightly muffled, "let's see if we can pinpoint those particular parasitic genes, shall we?"

5

The first Melanie heard about the outbreak was from Doctor Sandoval, who sent her an email about it.

Melanie sat down at 11:18 PM to close her computer down for the night and head home.

She decided to double-check that Doctor Wies, from the Tremough campus, had received her email with attached files on today's discoveries.

Doctor Sandoval was head of the Microbes and Disease department, and he was forever sending her links to outbreaks and viruses that were happening in third-world countries or little-known regions around the world. He would contact research groups or local scientist in those areas to try to get a sample sent to his department. In some rare cases, he even sent someone over to collect samples.

Melanie read the report twice to check she read it right, due to being so tired. She then clicked on a link to watch a CNN news report.

"A group of nine loggers were airlifted out of a work site next to the Nosivolo River in Marolambo, Madagascar, and taken to Cape Town, South Africa, after apparently suffering from some unknown malady.

"Reports are sketchy at the moment, but what is known is within eight hours of the helicopter leaving for the Mananjary Airport, eighty-one miles away, the Madagascan government declared Marolambo, in the Atsinanana Region, in the Province of Tamatave, a quarantined area. All twenty-six thousand residents are said to be under house arrest.

"Also, the city of Mananjary, Fianarantsoa, where the plane took off from, has also been quarantined, with an estimated twenty-eight thousand civilians under house arrest.

"As the news comes in, we will update you."

She knew all about viruses and their Basic Reproductive Rate. This one was spreading fast.

Melanie decided to keep an eye on the outbreak and check back in with Google first thing in the morning.

She shut down her computer and turned the lights off to her office. The building was quiet, with just the sound of large refrigeration units humming in the background.

As she was driving home, she received a phone call from Doctor Sandoval

6

"Hi Doctor Lazaro, I'm sorry if I woke you?"

Melanie pulled over to the side of the road.

"I have just left the university. I'm on my way home," she said confused. The head of the department had never rung her private number before, whenever he needed her, he sent an email or wandered down the corridor to chat.

"I need your help with something. It's a little unusual and requires complete secrecy on your part." He let his words sink in.

"I'm listening." She was intrigued.

"As you know, a lot of our budget comes from the government. What most don't realize is that it comes from the MOD." The words hung in the air. "That's the Ministry of Defense," he clarified, in case she didn't know what the acronym stood for.

No surprise there, she thought. *Everyone knew it, just no one talked about it.*

"I have just received a phone call from a Brigadier General William Hay. He told me he would send some representatives to the department tomorrow, and he wants you to liaise with them."

Melanie just held onto the phone.

Why me? she was thinking.

"Doctor Lazaro... Melanie?"

"I'm here, sorry Doctor Sandoval; I'm just a little shocked." She was confused as to why they would ask for her personally. She knew she was the university's *golden child*, but there were other doctors and professors from the university with decades more experience than her.

"Do you know what it's about?" The inside of the car was steaming up. She was breathing hard.

"Apparently it something to do with the new outbreak in Madagascar. The General is sending two of his top scientists to speak with you about it." The line went silent for a minute.

"Are you still there Doctor Lazaro?"

"Yes, yes of course. Sorry, it's been a long day." She hit a button to wind down the window to help demist the windscreen.

Flashing Christmas lights, in the distance, were just a blur.

"What time will they arrive?"

"I was told they had left and will be there waiting for you first thing in the morning."

Melanie was worried. The government didn't just send a team in to check things out. They worked with a purpose in mind.

For years, she heard rumors about scientist's research being swallowed up by the Ministry of Defense. Whole sections in other universities being shut down, or relocated somewhere a little less public. However, she presumed it was all just urban legends among the academic communities – he said, she said, kind of thing. She had never known anyone personally who has been visited by MOD representatives.

If a team from the army was arriving to liaise with her, it was because they knew exactly what they wanted, and they were going to get it from her one way or another.

7

Day 2

Melanie didn't sleep very well.

It was 5:57 AM.

When she went down for breakfast, she looked like a zombie. In her heightened stress, she had even put two odd shoes on before she caught it in the mirror.

"Problem? Did you have a good night's sleep?" her mother asked while putting a plate down in front of her husband.

Margery gave Melanie a long stare. Her daughter had never gone into work on a Sunday before.

Melanie was so early she had actually caught her dad before he disappeared down into the cellar.

"I'm fine. Just a lot on at work at the moment." She looked across towards her father. He had a note book open in front of his fry-up, perched up against the mayonnaise bottle, and he was using his soiled knife to turn the pages, while mumbling softly under his breath. Every few minutes he would remove the stub of a pencil from behind his ear and make a correction.

"Morning dad." It was the first time she had seen him in three weeks. He looked thinner and paler than normal – he spent too much time underground with no natural light. He also hadn't shaved in a while. His brown beard was streaked through with grey and white, and a little yellow around the mustache due to his habit of smoking a pipe, every once in a while. At seventy-five, he was still one of the most active people she knew.

"Hmm? What?" He looked up for the first time since Melanie walked in. His small round glasses were perched right on the end of his nose. "Hi Pumpkin. How's it going kiddo?" He looked back down to his scribbles on the page. His notes looked like a drunk centipede had fallen into an ink pot and then tap-danced across the page.

"Super dad, just hunky-dory."

"That's the spirit, keep on plugging away."

Her mother placed scrambled eggs with strips of crispy bacon in front of her.

"Thanks."

"You got home late last night. Did you manage to find what you're looking for?" Margery leaned over and wiped a blotch of baked beans off the table that had fallen over the side of Edward's plate.

"Melanie?" Her mother turned to look at her.

"Sorry, a little tired, that's all." She took a small mouthful of eggs, and washed it down with coffee.

Her mother fussed around at the sink. Her father ate, scribbled and mumbled. Melanie slowly pushed her breakfast around the plate.

"May I have another coffee, please?"

Her mother raised her eyebrows, then lifted the glasses that were on a string around her neck up to her eyes and studied her daughter.

Two coffees was rare.

The last time she needed two coffees in the morning was when she finished a five-week stint working on a new sequencing theory for locating genetic anomalies inside the genotype of a host viruses DNA strand.

"You're not about to appear on the cover of Science Monthly again are you? Because if you are, I would wear a different top."

Today she wore loose-fitting black trousers, with what was called a Peter Pan collar mock layered jumper in red and black. It looked more like casual wear rather than work. However, it was Sunday, so she was rebelling a little. Also, she hadn't straightened her hair. Today it was tied up in a ponytail and then clipped to the back of her head. Some strands had already made a run for it, and hung down her face. She pushed them behind her ears.

Melanie had given up with the eggs and was eating a strip of bacon with her fingers. She looked at her fingernails. Her red nail varnish could do with a retouch. She picked it because she liked it being described as *Barn* Red.

Her father was still engrossed in his notebook.

Melanie decided to change the conversation's direction.

"Cracked it yet dad?"

Her father scooped another mouthful of eggs.

"Your daughters talking to you Edward."

At hearing his name her father looked up from his pad.

"Hmm?"

"How's the project going?"

"Almost got it. Another day or so, for sure." With that he jumped up, grabbed his note pad and after giving his wife a kiss on the back of the head, and leaning over and doing the same to Melanie, without a word, he unbolted the padlock then vanished through the door, down into the cellar. They could hear a bolt sliding closed.

"Has he brought any new equipment lately?" Melanie asked.

"There is stuff turning up every week. I don't know where he keeps it all. It must be like the Tardis down there."

Melanie dropped the bacon back onto her plate as her mother placed another cup of coffee on the table.

"Thanks."

Her mother started clearing away Edward's soiled plate.

"Have you got much on today?" Melanie asked as she pushed the plate away.

"I've heard that the garden centre, the new one on the Sowton Industrial Estate, has a rare orchid called a Paph Venustum, of the Paphiopedilum family in stock. Thought I might check it out."

"That's nice," she muttered, wondering if the people were already at the university, waiting for her.

Melanie pulled her BlackBerry out of her bag. No messages or missed calls.

She stood and took the plate over to the bin and scraped the food off.

"I will do that."

She ignored her mother and placed the plate into the washing-up bowl and started cleaning it.

"Are you happy mum?" she asked over her shoulder.

"What?" Her mother flustered around the table, wiping it down, while rearranging the salt and pepper.

"What a silly question dear, of course I'm happy."

Melanie wiped her hands on a tea towel and then, as her mother stood up and turned around, she grabbed her and gave her a hug.

She hadn't hugged her mother in years. She felt too thin, as if a strong wind would blow her away.

Her mother was all tense. But she slowly relaxed into it. She lifted a hand and started stroking Melanie's long neck.

Without a word Melanie pulled away, kissed her mother on the cheek, then turned and picked up her bag and left the house without saying a word.

8

Melanie drove as if in a daze with Belinda Carlisle's *Runaway Horses* playing on the radio.

It was still dark, and the roads had patches of black ice on them.

She drove slowly.

The roads were quiet so early on a Sunday morning. There was only an odd jogger here and there, and some early-morning delivery vans.

She had never been in on a Sunday before. No matter how busy she got, she always allowed herself one day off. She reasoned that she didn't want to end up like her mother.

Melanie made good time getting to the university. She got a shock when she reached the main turn in – there was an army truck parked across the entrance.

She didn't know what type of truck it was, but it was obviously military because of the colouring, and the two men dressed in combat camouflaged clothing who was stood next to it.

One man approached as she pulled up. She pressed a button to lower the window.

"I'm sorry miss, but the university is closed today." He didn't have a gun on show. However, he had a commanding presence, and he could have all kinds of weapons concealed beneath his clothing.

"I was told to come. I'm Doctor Lazaro." Her voice was a little shaky.

Closed? What does he mean closed? But she said nothing.

The man straightened and waved a hand. The large trucked started to roll back, giving Melanie room to squeeze her small green car through. The man then stepped back, allowing her passage. She could see him raise his hand and talk into a device on his sleeve.

She presumed she was to drive through. The man didn't return to her window.

As she drove onto the campus, she noticed other army vehicles. They were dotted about everywhere. Military personnel were also walking around. Every one of them was carrying something.

Melanie was confused. She was told two representatives from the Ministry of Defense were coming to chat with her, not the whole army?

When she reached her building she noticed the car park over by the large Main Hall was full of bulky military transportation sixteen wheeler lorries. Seven of them were in a row, and surrounded by dozens of army personnel who were in the process of emptying the lorries and taking large metal containers into the hall through the fire escape with forklift trucks.

In her departments car park were smaller army vehicles; they looked like Humvees, like she had seen rich celebrities driving on the TV, but these looked slightly different; they weren't brightly coloured with large alloy wheels – these looked deadly.

She parked up and grabbed her bag.

Outside the main glass doors to her building was another soldier.

As he watched her approach he took a step forward.

"Doctor Lazaro?"

"Yes."

"They are expecting you." He grabbed the door and opened it for her. He said nothing else.

Melanie walked through and headed for the lift. Inside, when the door slid shut, she almost sagged.

What on earth is going on?

She had never heard of anything like this before. She tried to think through all the work she had been doing over the last year or so. Nothing jumped out. Nothing that would attract this sort of attention.

The lift stopped and the door silently glided open. Two men were stood waiting for her.

9

"ID please," the tall man on the right asked, with an outstretch arm.

"What?" Melanie was flustered. She presumed the hand reaching out was going for a handshake. She withdrew her hand and fumbled through her bag. No one had ever asked her to show her ID on the campus before.

"Um, here." She passed across her university identification badge.

The tall man took it from her and scrutinized it, looking back and forth.

"It's worse than my passport photo," she joked, trying to ease the tension.

Neither laughed.

They weren't dressed in army fatigues. Both men wore black trousers with black polo necks under a black lab coat. They had an insignia on the chest pocket; it looked like a black egg shaped object on a red background. She had never seen the emblem before.

The tall man was in his late fifties and had a long thin, horsey face, with a high forehead and greased back black hair. His eyes were ice blue and piercing. He also looked like he had smoked sixty cigarettes a day for most of his life. His skin was waxy and pale.

The shorter man was pudgy, with a balding head and wobbly jowls. His dull brown eyes looked like two poached eggs, all watery and running. He was possibly in his late forties.

"I am Doctor Sementem," said the tall man. "And my associate is Doctor Zeru."

"Pleased to meet you," the shorter man announced.

Sementem is the Latin word for seed. Zeru is also the word for seed in Sumerian. So they don't want to give me their real names. Why?

Melanie had a gift for languages; she used to study ancient cultures as a way to relax.

"Good to meet you both." She paused, not sure whether to ask the next question.

What the hell, she thought.

"That's a coincidence, what with you both having the word seed as a last name."

Dr. Zeru's eyes opened wide in surprise.

Dr. Sementem showed no emotions.

Stalemate, she thought.

"We were told of your superior intellect, I think they underestimated you."

No one moved.

They were starting to annoy her.

Who the hell do they think they are?

"Are you going to tell me why I have been brought in, and what's with all the secrecy and mystery and silly names? And, while we're at it, what's the army doing all over the campus?"

"Shall we go into your office?" The tall one said.

"Lead on Seedy."

The shorter man actually smiled.

Melanie sat down at her desk. The two men used the two seats facing her.

When they were all comfy, the taller man pointed at the computer monitor.

"You have read the news?"

Melanie didn't notice it straight away, but her computer was on; her password had been cracked, and the story about the virus in Madagascar was up on the screen.

"Yes, Dr. Sandoval sent me a link to it yesterday. I perused through it."

"Forget the swine and bird flu. Forget the Mayan prophecy. Forget super volcanoes and solar flares, because this one is the original doomsday scenario."

"I'm not following you. Are you saying this one is going to become a pandemic?"

It was the short mans turn to talk. "This is the big one. The final straw. What is coming is going to be on a biblical scale."

"How do you know this virus is that contagious? It's only been running for two days! The World Health Organization hasn't even got involved yet!"

"It's been around a lot longer than that. Trust us when we say nothing is going to escape unless we can find a cure." The little man sat back.

Before Melanie had chance to reply, the taller man continued.

"We are setting up centres all over the United Kingdom to start running samples. We have seventeen locations in the process of being organized." He looked at the short doctor.

"Exeter University will be our facility in South Devon. There are three doctors in your department. Altogether, there are twenty-nine of you capable of understanding and helping out with our research. Another twenty-five will be brought in from outside to help in other sections of the university."

Melanie thought of the seven lorries full of equipment that was being taken into the large gym. She leaned forward, lacing her fingers together.

The taller one continued. "You will be in charge of the scientific part of the facility."

Melanie went to speak, to point out there were others more qualified.

"Trust us, you are the best for the job." He repositioned himself in the seat.

"As of now, you run Exeter's laboratories in conjunction with the other seventeen locations."

"Do I get a choice?"

"I'm afraid we are way passed choices now. This is much bigger than you could ever comprehend. It is now do or die!"

10

Sunday 23rd December 2012

Day 8

One week on and it was complete chaos at the university.

All nonessential staff and students were made to leave. Only the scientists in the different departments were allowed on site, along with their assistants.

The army now ran the facility. One combined army's brigade made up of infantry and armoured, as well as support staff. They started turning up on Sunday afternoon. There were now hundreds of them.

The whole three hundred and fifty-acre university was too big to surround and protect. The five-story science building, with adjoining Great Hall, which served as the main gym, as well as a collection of smaller structures next to it, including the Botanist building, was surrounded by a high wired, barricaded fence. There were soldiers stationed at points all the way around the perimeter with high-caliber weapons.

As the week progressed, the virus had spread. Now seventeen countries were infected, with more being added to the list each day.

America, China, France, and Africa were asking for international aid. Across the world hundreds of millions of people were in a comatosed state, filling every building capable of holding them, or in some cases, just left lying on the ground. However, every country was in the same boat, or was preparing for it. They didn't have the resources to help other countries as well.

As of yet, Great Britain was virus free.

As the news got worse people changed. At first it was peaceful protests. By the end of the week there were rioting and looting going on across the country.

In England, the police were at breaking point. The government ordered the army out onto the streets of its own country.

The violence was so prolific that a curfew was implemented, that would take effect from midnight – no one would be allowed outside for any reason.

A date was arranged so people could leave their homes, so they could collect provisions. Thursday the 27th from 10 AM until 8 PM. They also had what was left of today to collect what they needed to last them five days.

So far, each night the scientists could return to their families. However, that was about to change.

Melanie was told, via a message passed on from Brigadier General William Hay, whom she had yet to meet, that tomorrow morning she would be picked up at home at 7 AM. She was to pack everything she would need to last two weeks. She, as well as all the other scientists, would now be living in the university. Instead of a normal working day, the scientists would work in shifts, so there would always be someone working on the vaccine.

They weren't given a choice.

They were also told to leave their mobile phones at home. They would be searched when they returned.

Melanie was inundated by the other scientists when they found out they would be kept at the facility, and that they wouldn't be allowed to contact their family for any reason. She pointed out she had no control over the situation, that she was just a figurehead and that the General really ran the show. Her job was to just gather up any important information and pass it on.

On the work front Melanie was working her way through hundreds of Petri dishes, and microscope glass slides, supposedly of the two stages of the virus so far. She wasn't told of their origin, but it disturbed her to note that they were all human tissue samples that they had to prepare the smears from.

Also the dishes were sealed, and she was only allowed to open them inside one of the ten containment boxes stationed around the different laboratories.

The slides were prepared inside the sealed boxes, with their HEPA filters, to stop the virus from being absorbed through the scientists skin. The slides were double sided, sealed glass, which was then placed onto an automated; computer operated system, so there was no need for human contact.

In one laboratory, three rooms over, they were using the biocontainment isolator unit to transfer the human DNA samples into the Petri dishes, before being sealed ready for the containment boxes.

So far, she has used every option available to her – with the universities Illumina high-throughput HiSeq 2500 and Illumina MiSeq systems. She tried Genome and Denovo resequencing, RNA-sequencing, small RNA, ChIP-sequencing, Meth-sequencing, and Bioinformatics analysis. She was running hundreds of test each day, with hundreds of samples per run. The data she was producing was mind boggling.

There were eighty-seven of the scientist's research assistants filling the rooms on the floor below, all scanning through reams of printed results and on laptops. Some of the more complicated runs could churn out six hundred gigabits of data in one session.

Before everyone from the university was sent home, there was more staff to choose from, but as Melanie pointed out to the two black-clad doctors, they needed people who could understand what they were reading, else something important could be missed. She personally went through all two hundred and eleven lab assistants to hand pick the final eighty-seven.

She was running out of options. Even with all their technology and facilities within the university, they were completely unprepared to handle such large quantities of data.

And this was also happening in another seventeen facilities all over Great Britain, and the rest of the world. There were hourly updates from hundreds of other research groups. There were eleven scientists in a room just sifting through all the data in case someone somewhere was closer to cracking it.

Every facility the world over could pinpoint the virus, and separate it from the host's DNA to analyze it, but it was like nothing they had ever seen before. Every disease and virus had certain characteristics; that's what placed them in their categories, but this was unlike anything anyone had ever experienced before.

Exeter alone had thousands of virus samples sent to them every year, from around the world, and each one was different in its own way, but they all had traits – similar factors, all having mutated from another known virus. However, this one was in its own league – completely unfamiliar.

She was told by Dr. Sementem and Dr. Zeru that she needed to map the different stages and alterations, and try to create an effective vaccine to stop the virus from spreading. But how could she create a vaccine when they didn't even know what they were dealing with?

11

Monday 24th December 2012

The Day the Virus Reached England

Day 9

Melanie kept her parents in the loop. Even her father started staying later at the breakfast table, so he could hear what Melanie had to say.

They knew today would be the last time they saw her for a few weeks, or until the virus was stopped. They were hopeful, so far England was unaffected.

Melanie's three bags were ready by the front door. For the first time in years her mother was also sat at the table, rather than fussing over the sink, or cooker.

There was no food on the table, just coffee.

Her mother held her father's hand. It was the first sign of affection she had seen between them in years. Yes, her father pecked her mother on the head everyday before going down into the basement, but that was from force of habit, not love.

Her mother put her cup down and gripped Melanie's hand.

"We are so worried for you," her mother stated, while using her thumb to rub the back of Melanie's hand.

"Surely they can't make you go?" her father added. "It's not right to force people to do things. This isn't Korea; you should have a choice!"

"It's okay," she said, trying to keep a positive attitude for their sake. She told them bits and pieces, but not the full extent of the problem. She knew they were both intelligent in their own right, and they knew she was holding back from them. But they didn't press the point.

"The news stated last night that Germany, Italy, and Frankfurt had confirmed cases," her mother said.

Melanie took another sip from her lukewarm coffee.

"We're close to breaking it now," she lied. She tried to give them hope; it was better than telling them the virus was alien to them.

Her father was looking straight at her, almost as if he was expecting this to be the last time he ever sees her. He reached across and grabbed her spare hand, creating a circle.

Melanie couldn't remember the last time she held both their hands at the same time.

Why do we always put things off? We are always afraid to show our emotions. To hold one another. To tell one another we love each other. Just human nature, she decided. *We don't appreciate what we have until it is about to be taken away.*

"I will be home before you know it, and this pandemic will be a thing of the past, just like the swine and bird flu." She gave a weak smile.

All anyone had to do is watch the news, and they would see how desperate the situation was. That's if they could find a channel that was working. The government was regulating the news feeds. Half the channels were just static. The ones that were working were showing reruns. And whatever station you watched, a figure dressed in military uniform, interrupted the program giving a governmental public warning every thirty minutes.

The lights flickered and went out.

They sat in the gloom. There were storm clouds outside, making it dark in the kitchen.

The power flicked back on. The fridge gurgled and rattled.

The power cuts were becoming more frequent. Luckily, at the university, they had their own generator big enough to run the whole facility.

"I don't see why we can't contact you? Why you can't keep your mobile phone close at hand?" her father asked.

Strange? For someone who doesn't talk to me for weeks, even months at a time, even though I live in the same house, and now he can't; it's affecting him!

She pushed the thought to one side. Now wasn't the time to dredge up family issues. Besides, things were different now, after his illness manifested.

"They have their reasons." Even though for the life of her she didn't know what they were.

The old saying, *a happy worker is a productive worker*, flashed through her mind. It was a proven fact. A good work environment made for better workers. Telling them they had to live in the university, and they weren't allowed to contact family members was going to cause some real problems. It was almost as if they were trying to sabotage the workforce.

"I rung the Chancellor last night. We talked for an hour. But I'm afraid she has no say in what is happening at her university anymore. In fact, I was shocked to learn she isn't even allowed on campus!" Having worked in the Botany department for almost three decades, her mother still had connections.

Melanie hadn't told her family that she is in charge of the scientific side of the facility at the moment. Mainly, because in her mind, she was simply a figurehead with no real power. She was merely there to make the other scientist's feel like the army wasn't in complete control – which they were.

Even after a whole week, the army officer in charge hadn't even come and introduced himself. She would have gone to see General Hay, but none of the non military scientist's were allowed in, or anywhere near, the large gym. As well as armed soldiers walking the perimeter, they also guarded the entrances to the Great Hall.

Melanie appreciated her mother phoning the Chancellor; she knew her mother would try everything in her power to help out. Sadly though, there was nothing she could do.

Her father squeezed her hand. She looked up into his sad eyes. He was looking all his seventy-five years today.

"You will miss my unveiling day," he muttered.

"Unveiling?" Melanie questioned.

"I'm almost finished. A day or two at most!"

"I will see it as soon as I get home. I know it's going to be amazing... World changing!" She gripped her father's hand tighter.

He smiled back at her.

Her mother was thankful that her daughter hadn't broken her fathers dream.

They both knew that there wasn't any real project. Edward had been suffering from dementia for over a decade. He had to retire early because he couldn't manage the clinic anymore – reality was slipping away.

He had a rare form of dementia – frontotemporal dementia. Unlike normal symptoms, which affect the understanding and production of language, the cell damage in his frontal and temporal lobes effected his behaviour.

A few weeks after he was diagnosed, he started heading down into the basement. Within a month laboratory equipment started turning up – test tubes, evaporating flasks, erlenmeyer flasks, volumetric flasks, funnels, extension clamps, beakers, bunsen burners, crucible tongs, and much more besides.

His doctor told them it was good news; apart from his slightly odd behaviour he was perfectly normal for his age, and it was a slow process; he could stay the same for up to fifteen years before it became worse.

Every couple of days Margery would pop down into the cellar when Edward wondered up for his midday siesta, just to check everything was okay.

The basement looked like Frankenstein's laboratory. Or more accurately, it looked like a glassblower had a really bad case of the hiccups. Three walls had benches against them, and those benches were covered in a network of connecting flasks and tubes. The fourth wall was covered in scraps of paper and handwritten notes. It looked like the wall of a serial killer's lair. However, the topic was much different, the Philosophers Stone.

Edward's fixation was discovering the mystical elixir of life.

However, after he first started going down into the cellar, Margery asked Melanie to check out what her father was boiling in the flasks. It turned out that the bubbling and simmering flasks and beakers were filled with only coloured water, coffee, and household substances watered down.

But to Edward, it was real. He truly believed he was on the verge of a discovery that would change the world.

"We will all need something to take our minds of what's happening throughout the world. Your discovery will do that. It will be a balm," Melanie announced.

Her father nodded.

"Yes, a balm. I like that word." He went to reach for the pencil behind his ear. It wasn't there.

Her mother squeezed her hand, thanking her.

The moment was interrupted by the doorbell. The army was here to take her to the university, against her will.

She gave her parents the biggest hugs of her life. Then, as she was about to leave, after a soldier had taken her bags off her and put them in the small transportation vehicle, Melanie turned and grabbed them both at the same time.

"I love you both so much. Take care, and I will see you both very soon."

The soldiers didn't say a word as she climbed aboard.

She felt like she was being transported to prison.

With tears in her eyes, she had a feeling deep in her gut, as the vehicle pulled away, that she would never see her parents again.

12

Christmas Day

Day 10

It didn't feel like Christmas day.

The mood among the scientists was depression mixed with simmering anger. It was Christmas Day, and even though a virus was ravishing the world, they were still upset due to being separated from their families.

There were reports of heavy-handedness when the soldiers went to pick everyone up. Dr. Stevens had two black eyes and a plaster across the bridge of his nose. Apparently, he had had an argument with the butt of a rifle, and lost.

It was a bad situation made worse. Everyone knew they were fighting a bigger problem, a problem that was spreading rapidly. Overnight it was reported the virus was confirmed in another nine countries.

Time was running out.

Everything was turned up a notch.

New shifts were arranged. Everyone would work twelve hours on, six off. The machines were to stay on constantly, and the data would be scanned through continuously.

Melanie spent hours looking into an electron microscope. They were using all three types of microscopy. Others were using standard optical devices and advanced scanning probe machines.

When she needed a break from staring into the microscopic world, she went into her office.

All the data thought to be important was sent to Melanie. Her room was emptied of all furniture. The walls were then stripped of pictures and charts and her diplomas, and she had used a sharpie pen to write her theories and ideas on the magnolia walls, along with post-it notes and sheets of paper, looking like they were randomly stuck to the walls. Her whole room was now a whiteboard.

The walls was starting to look like the basement at home.

They just couldn't crack it; no one could anywhere in the world.

Tens of thousands of scientists, the best in their fields was working on this. What makes me think I can suss it out?

Melanie was exhausted; she had been going all day, for fifteen hours straight. She sat on the floor in the middle of her room, just staring at the walls, hoping something would click.

There has to be an answer. Every problem has a solution.

She ran a hand through her hair. It was tangled and greasy.

On the floor next to her was a cold half eaten shepherd's pie on a plastic tray, and a crumpled can of diet Pepsi.

She looked at the clock – the only object still hanging on the walls.

11:14 PM.

She wanted to scream. To tear at the walls until an answer presented itself.

Her body sagged. She closed her eyes for a minute. Her head snapped up – she had nodded off to sleep for a few minutes while sat up.

It was a light tapping sound on her door that had woken her up.

"Sorry to disturb you Melanie, but there's more paperwork for you." Jeff stood holding a foot-high pile of folders.

He looked even worse than she did. He hadn't shaved for a week, and his clothes looked like he had slept in them. His casual unique retro style was now replaced with a casual homeless person look.

"You need to get some sleep, Melanie." Formality had gone out the window; everyone was using first names now. They were all prisoners, unable to leave.

Jeff left the pile by the door.

"My shifts over, but I gonna head downstairs and paw over some of the data for an hour or so." He sounded so tired.

Jeff was working hard to save his four sisters and mother. His father had left when he was young. He was the man of the house now.

Melanie simply nodded. She gave him a wane smile.

Jeff smiled back and wandered off through the laboratory.

Melanie was too tired physically and mentally to move.

Just five minutes more and I will head off to bed.

Because only a small section of the university was cordoned off and barricaded, they had to sleep wherever there was space. Melanie's bed was a military cot set up at the end of the corridor, in a windowless supply cupboard next to the toilets and shower room.

She lay on her back, with her head to one side, just staring at all her handwriting filling the walls. The words blurred together as she fell into a deep sleep.

13

Thursday 27th December 2012

Day 12

The day had arrived when the population could once again wander the streets to collect supplies. It didn't effect the scientists at the university; they weren't allowed to leave. Everything they needed was supplied by the military.

Melanie had heard rumours about civilians who had approached the barricades, asking the soldiers what was happening, and what were they hiding or trying to protect?

They were all turned away.

She became mad when she heard this. She remembered thinking, *weren't they supposed to protect everyone, not just a chosen few?*

Last night she had even heard gunfire, which jolted her from her sleep on the office floor.

However, regardless of what happened outside she had a job to do.

Melanie spent the first part of the morning scanning reports that the different departments had accumulated for her.

It was coming up to 2:30 PM.

She stood looking out of the window in her office. She rarely took a moment just to stand still and soak up her surroundings. She realized she hadn't looked out of a window in days.

In the distance, Exeter city had towering plumes of dense smoke curling up to heaven.

She opened the window and stepped closer.

Without the double glazing, the sound from the city washed over her. Alarms blared in the distance. She could hear shouting and fighting.

What is happening out there?

Below, to the right was the large gym. Soldiers stood guard. The army's own scientists worked inside. They didn't mingle with the university's academic staff.

She then realized the muted screams, and clattering sounds wasn't echoing across from over the city; they were originating from the gym.

As she watched a man dressed in a type II hazmat suit walked out of the door. He wasn't wearing the mask; it hung down the back of the suit. He chatted with the guards on duty while he smoked.

She knew all the samples were coming from the gym. Obviously, the remains of the infected were being stored inside, and their scientists were preparing the samples to be sent over for analysis.

However, the tissue samples were degrading – they had come from dead subjects. But the news was stating no one had yet died from the virus. So far, hundreds of millions the world over were in a comatosed state, but not one mortality had yet been officially confirmed.

She didn't want to think too hard about it. She closed the window and wandered back to the lab.

Ignorance is bliss.

A long stretch of work bench, that ran around the room, had nine scientists sat at different machines. The microscopy department was the busiest room on the campus. People sat at the containment boxes feeding the prepared slides onto an automated belt which fed the machines. Printers to one side churned out endless reams of paper. An assistant sat behind a computer compiling the masses of data into desktop folders, ready to be emailed.

Melanie left the room and walked next door.

The aptly named Computer Room was manned by seven assistants. Information was pouring in from around the world. They scanned it to see what needed deleting or passing on. One sat sending the data they had accumulated off to other laboratories all over the world. So far, there was a mailing list of four thousand six hundred and seventy-one recipients. The list was growing daily.

A dull boom echoed throughout the room, bouncing off the buildings; it originated from somewhere in the city.

A few technicians looked up from their monitors. After a few shrugs they returned to their work. Another person walked in carrying a tray of coffee. He distributed the caffeinated drinks.

Melanie left the room and wandered up the corridor.

There were people in the corridors. They carried files, or boxes of data, or they walked while reading reports.

Melanie looked into the boardroom, which had been turned into a brainstorming room, to see if between them they might stumble upon a theory that worked. Three doctors were stood pointing at graphs on a large whiteboard.

Something has got to give. There are thousands of us all over the planet working on this one problem – probably the largest single project ever undertaken by humanity in history. There has to be a breakthrough soon.

She walked past the canteen. At one end, a few people sat eating dinner. Their heads were lowered, and none were talking. They needed to eat in peace, to switch their brains off for a few minutes.

Today it was spaghetti bolognese. The food was the only thing the army had got right so far. There was plenty of it, and it was cooked well. There were also tables along one side full of packaged snacks and refreshments, so people could take the food and continue working in their departments.

At the back of the canteen was rows of cots, with personal belongings piled on or next to them. Nineteen people called this home.

Melanie was glad she had snagged the supply cupboard. The benefit of being in charge – supposedly.

She popped into the toilet.

As she was washing her hands, she could hear someone crying softly in one of the cubicles. She dried her hands and left the person in peace.

We all cope in our own way; she decided. *If that person needed to cry in the toilet, then so be it.*

Melanie closed the door to her cupboard. She was officially off for six hours. She would catch a quick nap and return to work. She was no good if she was exhausted – the last thing she needed was to add sleep deprivation to the list.

She lay on the cot and rolled onto one side. She flicked on her fan, which she had brought from home. The noise and vibration made the sounds in the corridor outside fade away.

14

New Years Eve 2012

The days were blending together. Even her hours became erratic, working and sleeping was now her life. She would look at the clock and realize it could be 4 AM or PM; it was all the same now. Windows just became dark or light splotches against the walls.

The specialized air filtration system, which moderated the air flow throughout the floor, similar to an air-conditioned system, but it also siphoned out microbial dust that may be floating around the laboratories, was having difficulty laboring against so many people being in such a confined space. Over the last day, the department was starting to smell like sweaty onions.

Scientists and lab assistants were getting cabin fever. She was ordering people to go for walks around the building, getting them to change their environment, even for ten minutes. They were not permitted to just wander the grounds. The army had sectioned an area off where they could walk around, like sheep.

Fights were becoming everyday occurrences. Tempers were frayed.

Gunfire from the army on the perimeter fence was becoming a daily occurrence. She hated to think about who they were firing at.

Yesterday the body of Nadene Gethard, a nineteen-year-old undergraduate student from South Africa, was found dead from an overdose in the toilet.

Melanie just hoped it wasn't Nadene she had heard crying in the toilet a couple of days before.

She asked the soldiers guarding the building to pass messages to the General in command asking if she could talk with him. So far, her requests have gone unanswered.

It was 1:17 PM, and Melanie was sat in the canteen surrounded by nine other, silent, scientists and a couple of assistants while picking at a bowl of beef stew.

At the back of the room a couple of people snored as they slept during their breaks.

Melanie wondered how sanitary it was for her to be eating where nineteen people slept? She mentally shrugged and lifted the spoon to her mouth.

Then the gunfire started.

Normally, there were one or two pops, then it died away. Today it just kept going.

After a minute of continuous firing, some of the people started to gather around the windows, trying to see what was going on. The room didn't have a good view of the barriers.

As Melanie looked down a group of soldiers ran out of the gym, heading to the main entrance. They were all carrying automatic weapons. More gunfire erupted, joining in with the first.

"Jim and I are going to check out what's happening. You coming?" Doctor Peter Frank announced. Peter looked like he had lost weight. His third child was due four days ago, and it was eating him up not knowing what was happening to his family.

What the hell. Why not? It's about time I got some answers. They supposedly put me in charge. About time I asserted that authority.

"Let's go!"

Most stayed by the windows. Five of them headed for the lift.

When the lift reached the foyer, and the doors slid open, there were two soldiers stood directly outside the lift with their automatic SA80 rifles raised.

"Return to your work," the youngest announced looking down the rifles sights. He was so young his face was still covered in acne. She would be surprised if he was older than eighteen.

"Please come with us, Doctor Lazaro," the older of the two stated.

Peter went to stand in front of her.

"It's okay Peter." She gripped his arm and walked around him. "It will be fine." She smiled as she looked into his sad eyes. "Maybe I will finally get some answers."

"If you hurt one hair on her head, so help me God," Peter mumbled through clenched teeth.

God has abandoned this world, Melanie randomly thought.

As Melanie stepped out, the youngest soldier stepped forward, reached around and hit the button to return them to their floor.

She watched the lift close.

In the distance, the gunfire continued, with shouting and screaming mixed in. A loud concussion explosion sounded like it was just on the other side of the tall building.

"Please follow us Doctor Lazaro. Someone wishes to speak with you."

The oldest led the way, with the youngest at the back.

15

Melanie was led around the side of the building and into the section her mother used to work in – the Botany Department.

Even though she only worked next door, it had been years since she had stepped inside the building dedicated to fauna.

The inside looked like a garden centre with plants and flowers in rows against the walls, and hanging from the high ceiling, and planted in a large circular display in the middle of the foyer. The air was warm and swampy, thick with the aroma of wet earth and vegetation, and due to the sustained artificial environment, a lot of the plants were in bloom.

Sadly, the smells and greenery reminded her of home. She hoped her parents were coping well.

She was led through the main lobby to a connecting door, then in past the laboratories and into the offices.

There were soldiers everywhere. One walked past with just his boxer shorts on and a towel around his neck. His hair was wet.

It must be where they sleep.

She wondered what her mother would say if she knew a soldier was using her old office as a bedroom?

On the right, through large windows, was the botany departments pride and joy, the arboretum. The huge arboretum is the third largest collection of cultivated tropical trees in Europe. Over two hundred were inside the large dome. The misting system was obviously switched off, because military cots were scattered between all the trees.

Now that is something mother would have a few things to say about.

The two soldiers stopped and stood to either side of a standard looking office door.

Melanie presumed they had reached their destination. She didn't bother knocking; she simply walked straight in.

A man was sat behind a large mahogany desk. He was just a regular looking man – nothing about him stood out. He was an average height, with bland brown hair in a basic centre parted style, with plain features and dull grey eyes. He wore black trousers and a polo neck shirt with the red and black emblem, similar to the two doctors who first set the facility up. You would walk past him in the street and not give him a second glance – he would fade into the shadows and from your memory.

"General Hay?"

He looked up from the paperwork that he was scribbling a signature on.

Didn't he hear the door open? Unless he's just rude?

"I'm afraid I'm not General Hay. He is indisposed at the moment. You will have to deal with me instead." He stood up and walked over to a shelf that was covered in exotic plants. The rest of the room was full of academic books.

"I love this building, with all the greenery and the smells." He snapped the stem off a rare orchid and started twisting it around in his fingers.

"And how about that arboretum, huh? I find it amazing that mankind can build and create fake environments to grow hundreds of full-sized trees; and all inside!" He shook his head. "Truly astonishing!"

He returned to his seat.

He then changed the subject. "Your scientists are not making any progress," he simply stated.

Melanie was still standing. The man had offered no seat or handshake. She decided to remain on her feet. He was getting on her nerves, and she had only just met him. There are some people you meet and you just instinctively dislike them instantly. He was one of those kind of people.

"What's your point? There are tens of thousands of scientists working all around the world, what makes you think we are any better than any of them?" She gripped the back of the chair she was stood behind. Her knuckles turned white.

"But none of them have the great Doctor Melanie Ann Lazaro." He lifted the stem to his face and sniffed the delicate blue flower.

"Who are you?"

He exhaled noisily and just stared at her. He then came to a conclusion.

"You can call me Mr. Shepherd." He smiled.

"What no mysterious last name derived from an ancient language?"

"Sadly no. Mine is much more fitting for my position within the society."

"What society? The Illuminati? The Free-masons? The Priory of Sion?" Sarcasm was heavy in her voice.

"Let us not drift off topic."

"Who are you, and I don't mean your name, tell me more about this society you represent?"

"I represent everyone's interests." He said no more.

"Whatever! This is going nowhere. Why bring me here if you're just going to play silly buggers?"

"This is a very serious situation that we are all in," he announced.

"No shit Sherlock! I hope you haven't been sat in here for two weeks working that out? I could have told you that ages ago."

He actually smiled.

"What I mean to say is, yes, the outbreak is disastrous, but I don't think you understand just how catastrophic it is going to get?"

"There are hundreds of millions of people incapacitated – comatosed, all over the world. You think that's not bad enough?"

"You misunderstand me. I'm telling you, what's happening at the moment is just the tip of the iceberg. Things are going to become worse, much worse."

He dropped the stem onto the desk. The blue flower looked out of place on the mahogany surface.

"Stop looking at this as a virus. Yes, it follows similar parameters, but as you have already found out, you can't continue treating it like a bog-standard non-bacterial pathogen." He leaned forward in the chair and rested his elbows on the table and placed his hands together as if praying.

"Since 1898, over five thousand viruses have been discovered since the Russian botanist, Dmitri Ivanovsky described the first in his famous article – which incidentally was discovered by someone else and attributed to Ivanovsky."

He paused to give Melanie a chance to ask who originally discovered the first virus.

She didn't.

He continued.

"There is believed to be millions of different types. Viruses are found in every ecosystem on this planet and are the most abundant type of biological entity known to man. As you are well aware the study of viruses is virology, a sub-specialty of microbiology – your doctorate of choice." He knitted his fingers together.

"Virus particles consist of two or three parts: the genetic material, long molecules, and a protein coat. Some even consider viruses as a form of life, because they carry genetic material and can reproduce and evolve. As you are also aware, there are many different ways a virus can spread; from plant to plant and animal to animal, even cross contamination between flora and fauna."

It was Melanie's turn to sigh. She knew all this. Even a first-year student knew these facts.

"Please be patient, I and building up to my point." He sat back in the chair.

"The range of host cells a virus can infect is called its *host range*. This can be narrow or it can be capable of infecting many species, as you are well aware. The host immune response normally destroys the infecting virus, or in cases where the host cannot fight the virus, a vaccine can be produced to artificially boost the immunity. But as the world is aware, there are viruses such as AIDS and viral hepatitis that can chronically infect the host. Antibiotics and antiviral drugs have no effect."

He's got to be building up to something?

"As you are well aware–"

It was annoying Melanie how he kept repeating that word.

"–viruses attach themselves to the hosts genetic material. That is how evolution created them." He leaned forward again. "What if, say, there is a new virus, one so old it hasn't mutated along with the others over the millions of years of this planet's evolution. One which has laid dormant since before the dawn of man. A strain which doesn't just hitch a ride, it actually genetically changes the host to its desired plan?"

Melanie just stared.

Her synapses fired up.

"Shit!" Melanie mumbled. "If that were true, or even possible, that would mean we have all been looking in the completely wrong place. If the virus is a new strain, one so old it predates everything we know, we would have no way of genetically tracking its development and pin-pointing it within the host's DNA!"

She lowered her head while thinking.

"We have pinpointed it on the human DNA strand, but we can't isolate it." Her head snapped up.

"Fuck-a-duck!" Her eyes stretched wide.

"It's not hitching a ride; like a normal virus, it's actually genetically changing the host! That's why we can't map it, because we're not looking for all of it. Some of it has mutated, mixing with the human DNA, creating a new strain!"

"Bingo!" Mr. Shepherd said.

"But nothing like that exists!" She creased her forehead. "It would have been discovered by now, surely?"

He gave a chuckle.

"We know more about the surface of the moon, or Mars than we do about our own jungles or ocean floors. There's lots we don't know about our world. Trust me on this."

She wanted to ask why she wasn't told about this sooner. Why they have been allowed to wander in the dark for weeks? Instead, she turned and headed back to the lab.

The youngest soldier followed in her wake.

She moved as if in a daze. Everything was starting to make sense. Before she did anything else, she had to recalibrate the machines to look for something different, that is, after she worked out what to tell the machines to look for.

Mr. Shepherd stood as the remaining soldier walked in.

“Prepare my transport,” he announced. “I am heading back to The Ark.”

16

New Years Day 2013

Day 16

Melanie didn't hear the fireworks go off in the night, or the gunfire out on the parameter barricade; she was too engrossed in her work.

She had been sleeping as little as possible. Every minute counted now they knew what they were looking for. But even so, it was tough going.

The machines were recalibrated to the new parameters they needed to look for. It took eighteen hours before they got their first look at the complete virus.

The virus strain – now they could see it in its entirety – completely absorbed the host's DNA. Unlike every other known virus, rather than simply piggybacking on the DNA, it absorbed the hosts genotype, changing the DNA double helix down on a subtonic level – the virus actually added a new addition of nucleotides to the existing DNA chain, creating a new, unknown genetic species.

If the situation was different, and the host wasn't the human race, then the find would have changed the science community in a good way, leading to all kinds of new theories and branch fields of research.

The new information was packaged and sent to every research facility on their extensive email list.

There was access to the Internet, so they could see what was happening to the world outside. Luckily, their Internet server was government run, so even when civilian servers started going down, one by one, theirs continued working regardless.

In the rare moments when she had a spare few minutes, she would check to see what was happening outside their barricades.

There was all out fighting in the streets of all major cities. Supermarkets and shops were empty, so mobs were attacking food preparation factories, anywhere where there could be food.

Cows and sheep were being slaughtered in the farmer's fields by people who used to squirm if their burger was undercooked.

Hunger changed people.

Petrol stations were empty. Abandoned vehicles blocked roads.

The smaller towns and villages looked deserted in the news feeds. Litter filled the streets, blowing around in the January winds, and turned to mush by freezing rain. Shops were destroyed, many burnt to the ground.

It was complete chaos.

She was amazed that so much could change in such a short period of time.

What would happen if this continued for a year, or two, because no cure could be found? What would the population resort to, to find food and water?

It was shocking to think that people she chatted with only weeks before – neighbours and friends – would now be fighting each other over scraps of food.

Melanie hoped her parents were okay? She had no way of getting in contact with them.

The university servers now only worked on certain, approved sites. Every email went via the military before it was sent. There was a list of websites that their computers could join with, but no web browser. They were being completely regulated.

There were a few computer geniuses within the assistant student ranks, but even their tweaking, and skills couldn't crack the military firewalls.

It was like being in a concentration camp, except they were getting fed. Some of the scientists even met in quiet areas, discussing possible breakout strategies. They were desperate to get home to check on their families.

A group even tried to get over to the gym, to speak with the general in command. They were herded back to their building by armed soldiers. Since then, they have been banned from even leaving the building. All lifts were switched off, and the stairwells guarded.

Yesterday, thirty-two-year-old Doctor Lim killed himself by jumping from a top-floor window.

The other scientists needed someone to blame. Because she was the supposed liaison between them and the army, she got the brunt of the backlash.

Whenever she went to check on results, everyone in the room stopped talking. People started ignoring her. If she stopped to chat with someone, or ask a question, they would simply walk away. She heard them whispering and calling her childish names. *Bitch* was the most popular.

It was all completely irrational, but for some reason, it all seemed to make sense to them.

Melanie now sat working in a small room on her own.

She had become an outcast in a building where everyone was locked in together.

In a time when she needed her friends the most, they had all turned their backs on her.

17

Wednesday 3rd January 2013

Day 19

Last night, at about 3 AM, while finishing up his night shift, Doctor Lewandowski went berserk. Without any warning he started attacking the other five scientists who were in the same room.

He killed three of them with his bare hands. Another one was so badly injured the military doctor doesn't think she will last the day. The only one who escaped alive was the scientist closest to the door, who escaped with only a broken arm and contusion to his face.

Doctor Russo, who escaped, ran screaming down the corridor, cradling his broken arm.

Everyone poured out into the hallways, wondering what the noise was all about.

Lewandowski then ran out into the hallway and attacked a group of assistants who had just exited the Computer Room. He was covered in his victim's blood, and his face was a mask of madness. He snapped the neck of a young woman who didn't flee in time.

A group of five men tried to subdue him, because even though he was insane, he carried no weapon.

He broke the jaw of one, fractured the eye socket of another, and bit another's bottom lip clean off his face.

In the screaming and confusion, Doctor Lewandowski forced open the lift door and jumped to his death down the shaft.

The army swarmed into the building and removed the bodies, leaving the scientists to mop up the blood and gore.

The events unsettled everyone. They all started becoming paranoid that whoever was sat next to them might go the same way as Lewandowski.

It made a bad situation even worse.

It didn't help that some of the blood stained the floor and walls, and was a constant reminder of what happened.

Today, the building was eerily quiet. No one chatted unnecessarily. People ambled about, doing their jobs in a sullen, tense mood.

Some people were letting themselves go physically; they didn't wash or change. Some refused to even work, they simply lay on their cots, moping.

The whole place was becoming a powder keg.

Melanie collected everything she needed to lock herself away in her small research room. She had bottled water and packaged food from the canteen. She only left the room to go to the toilet or to catch a few hours sleep. She spent every waking minute staring into an electron microscope and adjusting her results on her laptop.

She needed to sort this all out and map the virus. The sooner she completed the task, the sooner everyone could go home. Because at the rate the situation was deteriorating, give it another week, there wouldn't be anyone left alive in the building.

18

Thursday 4th January 2013

Day 20

The breakthrough came at 9 AM. Melanie sat staring at the eyepiece. She sat for most of the day double checking the data and her notes.

She felt like something was going right for the first time in almost three weeks.

She didn't run up and down the corridors screaming that she had done it. She sat silently in her room, alone, and went back over the data, to double and triple check.

Melanie didn't feel bad that she was keeping the information from the others. After the way they had shunned her, she didn't care if they never talked to her again. She had known some of them for years, and within days they just cut her off as if she was a leper.

After she had finished all the checking, she rewrote her report. She then left the room to go and collect another two samples. Upon returning, she copied her results down to the last detail, to check it wasn't just a fluke or a mistake. Both new batches gave identical results, even though they were from two different host samples.

She had done it!

She sat and stared while she softy cried with relief. She would be able to go home soon.

She was so hyped on adrenaline, she didn't realise it was so late. Checking and rechecking, and rewriting took all day and the best part of the night. It was now 2:18 AM.

She prepared a message to give to a soldier, so they could inform the General that he had no choice, he had to speak with her personally, because she had cracked the virus.

There was, however, one problem. A vaccine couldn't be created to cure someone infected. So all the hundreds of millions, all over the world who had already contracted the virus couldn't be saved.

The virus was unlike anything she had ever seen. It didn't piggyback; it completely took over, readjusting and altering the host, creating a hybrid species.

Also, her results showed four main stages to the virus. They had seen the first-stage – rapid eye blinking and confusion. The second stage was gripping the world at the moment.

However, this was just a drop in the bucket, if her results were correct. The third stage was unlike anything she had ever seen before, and she needed to warn the General, so he could pass the information along. And the fourth stage was even worse.

The way things were looking; it was going to be the most devastating outbreak to ever effect the human race since the Spanish influenza of 1918, which infected five hundred million worldwide, and killed over a hundred million of them – which was five percent of the world's population at the time.

As devastating as the Spanish Influenza was, it would pale into comparison compared to what she had just discovered – there would be a hundred percent mortality rate – no one would survive.

However, there was hope for those not infected. With the right equipment, and time, a blocker could be created to stop others from being infected.

Even though it was late, she went and found a soldier so they could pass the note to the General.

She returned to her room and spent the time waiting going over her results.

She was too hyped to sleep, so she went and packed her things.

Surely, I will be able to go home and see my family now?

At 4:38 AM, a soldier found her. He informed her that the General would meet her in the morning at 8 AM.

Brilliant, she thought. *I will explain everything, and my report will be distributed around the world, and by lunchtime I will be back home with my parents.*

The Sixth Extinction continues...

THE SIXTH EXTINCTION

The First Three Weeks

The Squad

A new four book series will soon be released, following the military squad through the first three weeks of the outbreak.

Echo's Story

The Captain's Story

Bull's Story

and

Coco's Story

THE SIXTH EXTINCTION

One Year On

Noah, Red, and Doctor Lazaro's story continues.

We take a look down inside The Ark one year after three survivors of a global pandemic managed to escape a virus that was decimating the human race.

We follow each of them as they come to turns with the new situation, and the challenges their unfamiliar surrounds bring, and as they discover the underground city is much bigger than they first realized.

However, they're not the only survivors. In all the chaos others managed to descend into the top-secret military bunker, which was created to hold thousand. Individuals who upset the balance and want more than their fair share. People who know there is no longer any law – they are the law.

Instead of living in harmony, and being thankful for what they have – and what they have survived – they split into two separate groups. Fighting breaks out, which is soon followed by murder.

THE SIXTH EXTINCTION

The Seven Seeds of the Gods

(A collection of seven short stories)

The oldest secret known to man. Four ancient stories. Three recent discoveries.

Four stories cover the original discoveries of four of the seven pods by the ancient civilizations in Egypt, Mexico, Cambodia, and Canada, and how our ancestors dealt with these Seeds of the Gods. Empires were changed forever – worship, fear, wonder, love, upheaval, and mighty wars ripped continents apart, steering the course of human history for thousands of years.

Three stories cover the recent discoveries of the remaining three pods. A British Museums field collector called Clarkson's discovers one in 1898 in a hidden valley in Tibet. A well digger stumbled on one in 1947 at Groom Lake, Nevada. The last was found in December 2012 by nine loggers in a remote section of tropical rainforest in Madagascar.

The final discovery released the spores that our ancestors kept hidden and safe for thousands of years, creating a pandemic that will cause the next mass Extinction.

About the Author

Glen Johnson was born in Devon, England in 1973. He lives in Teignmouth, just a stones throw away from the English Riviera, in a large converted nunnery, while he plans on running away to travel the globe. (He will be releasing a collection of books about his traveling adventures as they unfold). He loves to travel and has already visited twenty-nine different countries, and lived in Mexico City, Mexico for far too long for a pale skinned European. He has also been married twice – and still refuses to say where he buried them.

Why not add Glen Johnson as a friend on Facebook. From his author's page, you can keep up to date with all his new releases, and when his kindle books are free on Amazon. He checks it daily, so pop on and say hello! Don't be shy he's a friendly chap.
`www.facebook.com/GlenJohnsonAuthor`

Alternatively, click 'Like' and you can follow Glen Johnson on Sinuous Mind Books official Facebook Page.
`www.facebook.com/SinuousMindBooks`

Or on `www.sinuousmindbooks.com`

Why not check out Glen Johnson's other books.

LAMB CHOPS AND CHAINSAWS

LOBSTERS AND LANDMINES

THE DEVILS HARVEST

THE GATEWAY

PARKINGDOM

THE SPELL OF BINDING: PART ONE

WAR OF THE GODS
PART ONE: THE DEVILS TAROTS

Also available from Sinuous Mind Books

For the latest news and updates about Glen Johnson, visit
www.sinuousmindbooks.com

LAMB CHOPS AND CHAINSAWS

NINE DISTURBING SHORT STORIES ABOUT THE DARKER SIDE OF HUMAN NATURE

What are your neighbours really like once their front door slams shut? Are your children's teachers' sound-of-mind? Has your partner got an evil, sinister side? Is a member of your family a murderer? These questions, and more, are examined in a collection of nine disturbing short stories; tales about the darker side of human nature.

Read about a wannabe serial killer who starts his reign of terror on the wrong footing. A Kindergarten teacher who has deep psychological problems that jeopardizes the safety of the children. How a child of nine turns to violence in retaliation for drug smugglers slaughtering her parents. A fanatical mother who believes her thirteen-year-old son is possessed by the Devil. How one killer spirals out of control and in his haste for victims makes a fatal mistake. A government trained killer who was set up as a scapegoat. Or a serial killer who has captured the attention of the world, and has setup one final, sickening display. What does it take to push someone that little bit too far and turn them into a killer? Find out when a savage murder is committed over a packet of lamb chops.

Strangers will never seem the same again.

LOBSTERS AND LANDMINES

ANOTHER NINE DISTURBING SHORT STORIES ABOUT THE DARKER SIDE OF HUMAN NATURE

Lobsters and Landmines is the second book in the Human Nature Series, following in Lamb Chops and Chainsaws footsteps, by continuing to look at the darker side of human nature, by delving into the dark twisted world of the sick minded, the perverse, the psychos and sociopaths; people who take pleasure from hurting others. Individuals, who could be your next door neighbour or your lover, even a close family member.

Read about a Captain who discovers the perfect lobster bait after a violent outburst. A HIV infected man who injects women with his tainted blood. A disfigured ex-army bomb disposal expert who has carved out a piece of paradise for himself in Vietnam, who keeps females as slaves and children as objects to sell. Or the sad story about two friends who are forever parted on September 11th 2001. And the airhostess Jenny who finds the perfect job on a Brazilian airline, but it seems they want more from her than most employers. What about the sweet little old lady who wins awards for her cakes, but what are her secret ingredients? Or the doomsday prepper that spends every waking minute of everyday prepping for the end of the world, until one critical mistake changes everything. Or a computer firm that sells its algorithmic computations to cosmetic firms, cutting out the need to test on animals, but below ground, the vast computer server hosts a disturbing secret. Finally, a businessman who realizes a little too late, what is truly important in life?

THE DEVILS HARVEST

A SHOCKING SECRET

Jacob Cain's life changes forever when he starts to receive a series of reanimated corpses, each impart a fragment of a message. An ancient tale unfolds as old as time itself relating humanities darkest untold secret – the biblical story from the Devil's point of view.

A DESPERATE QUEST

As the chain of events unfolds, Cain repeatedly finds himself confused and covered in blood. Suddenly he becomes a fugitive from the authorities, wanted in connection to multiple murders, his garden now a mass grave.

A HORRIFYING TWIST

Guided by one catastrophic event after another, Cain finds whole villages eerily silent with corpses littering the streets as a new plague from an unimaginable source starts to sweep the country. At an old farmhouse, he comes face-to-face with mankind's worst nightmare. And buried in a field is the answer to all the riddles that climax in a terrifying, unearthly twist.

As Cain fights for his life, he must unravel the shocking truth, before billions die. He is all that stands in the way of a global pandemic on an apocalyptical scale.

THE GATEWAY

(With Gary Johnson)

WORLD ONE OF THE SEVEN WORLDS

THE SEVEN WORLDS

Eons ago entities with god-like powers brought together seven worlds, joined them by means of conduits—Gateways—each supplying the next with what it lacked, from a surplus of what that world produced, making life on all seven worlds possible. Then they disappeared. Each world became an individual.

THE BROTHERS

Two brothers stumble on the Gateway passing from our world to the next, and are endowed with powers beyond comprehension, vital for survival in this hostile and intelligent world where nightmarish creatures feed on the weak.

THE WAR

Titanic battles rage; good against evil, magic against machinery, mortal against immortal. A civil war rages between spirit creatures and a powerful self-proclaimed God. Why is the American government sending an army of mass destruction with the latest military technology through? Time is short, the armies are amassing.

And what is the prophecy about scratched on a wall of a prison cell by dying hands?

PARKINGDOM

YOU CAN BE SMALL AND STILL MAKE A BIG DIFFERENCE

A SECRET WORLD

Parkingdom is home to a hidden society of tiny gnomes whose whole world resides inside the tall walls of a vast inner-city park; watched over by their Watcher from a large billboard. Then, without warning she disappears along with all the noisy humans.

A MISSION

Fisher and Bel have been sent away by the city elders to the Great Green Gates, to the Wardens Office, to find out why? It is a perilous journey through the deserted human section of the park and across the uncharted Wild Lands. Soon they find themselves travel companions with a witch's ferret and a scrawny long toothed rat, and befriended by a strange little green snotling that knows a startling secret.

HOPE

Upon returning, they discover their city under the control of a hostile neighbouring city's army. Has their Watcher deserted them in their time of greatest need? Will the elders understand their Watcher's cryptic message? Moreover, will they – along with their rebellious Elders – be able to do anything to save their family and friends?

Join Fisher and Bel as they embark upon an adventure that will change their small world forever.

THE SPELL OF BINDING
PART ONE
THE MAGIC

The World was almost destroyed by science – billions died. The survivors gave up looking for God and looked within themselves. They could hear a new song emanating from the ruins of the past. An ancient song, older than religion and time itself – they heard the magic.

THE DEMON ARMY

But the holocaust caused a spell uttered eons ago – when the magic was strong – to weaken. A spell that now released unmentionable creatures back into the world; creatures their ancestors had banished. Science failed to destroy humanity, now it's the powerful Demon Kings turn to try – back with vengeance and a vast army.

HOPE

Powerful sorcerers could stand in his way, but they have grown old and tired with time, leaving the hope of all New Mankind on the shoulders of a female magus, a slaphappy, lovesick human, a drunken whimsical elf, an ambitious dwarf and a grumpy angel, all looking for a Spell that has been hidden for a thousand generations.

PART ONE

Simeon, the head of the Council of Magi, has spent decades deciphering an ancient leather bound book. He sends word to Minika, a sorceress close to where he believes the Spell is hidden – a female magus who is not quite what she seems – and with the aid of a human, an elf and a dwarf, she heads out into the barren wasteland to try and reach the Spell before the demon king Vorr, and his vast army. But the demons are the least of Minika's worries; someone else seems hell bent on stopping them – someone powerful. Someone who is using magic that hasn't been seen for thousands of years. And the Great Prophetess has just announced the prophecy that Vorr has been waiting to hear for over two thousand years: "In a time of great sorrow seven will heal the world."

WAR OF THE GODS

PART ONE: THE DEVILS TAROTS

A WAR

A war is raging that most don't even realize exists – a war of the Gods. An age-old story, good against evil and hatred against love.

THE FALLEN ANGEL

Satan was bound and thrown from heaven, and his angels – now demons – were tossed down with him. He resides on earth, imprisoned in an ancient holy building. So his soldiers fight his side of the battle, misleading mankind, confusing and destroying spirituality, replacing it with greed, pleasures and lust.

THE ORIGINAL TAROTS

Created by the Devil himself, the tarots now fall into the hands of a mere human. Catastrophic events unfold, reaping death and destruction to millions. But the tarots are a key, a key to an ancient forgotten bloodline that will turn the tide of the battle.

THE MAN

Unbeknown, the future of mankind's very existence rests with Caleb Black. Forced from his home in London he ends up fighting for his life at every turn. Caleb and an old ex-girlfriend – who harbours an ancient secret – are all that stands between Satan's New World Order and the return of the Grand Creator. Time is almost up. Both sides position their pieces for the final conflict.

PART ONE: THE DEVILS TAROTS

Caleb Black's world is falling apart, he's on the run after a body is found in his apartment building – and he's the main suspect. And to make matters worse the dead are talking to him, and he's being chased by strange men with tattooed foreheads with powers beyond explanation. The key to all his problems is a set of tarots that a vagabond old man gave him. All he needs to do is find a fortuneteller named Mamma so she can guide him through the madness. An ex-girlfriend is also on the scene, but she just brings more questions than answers.